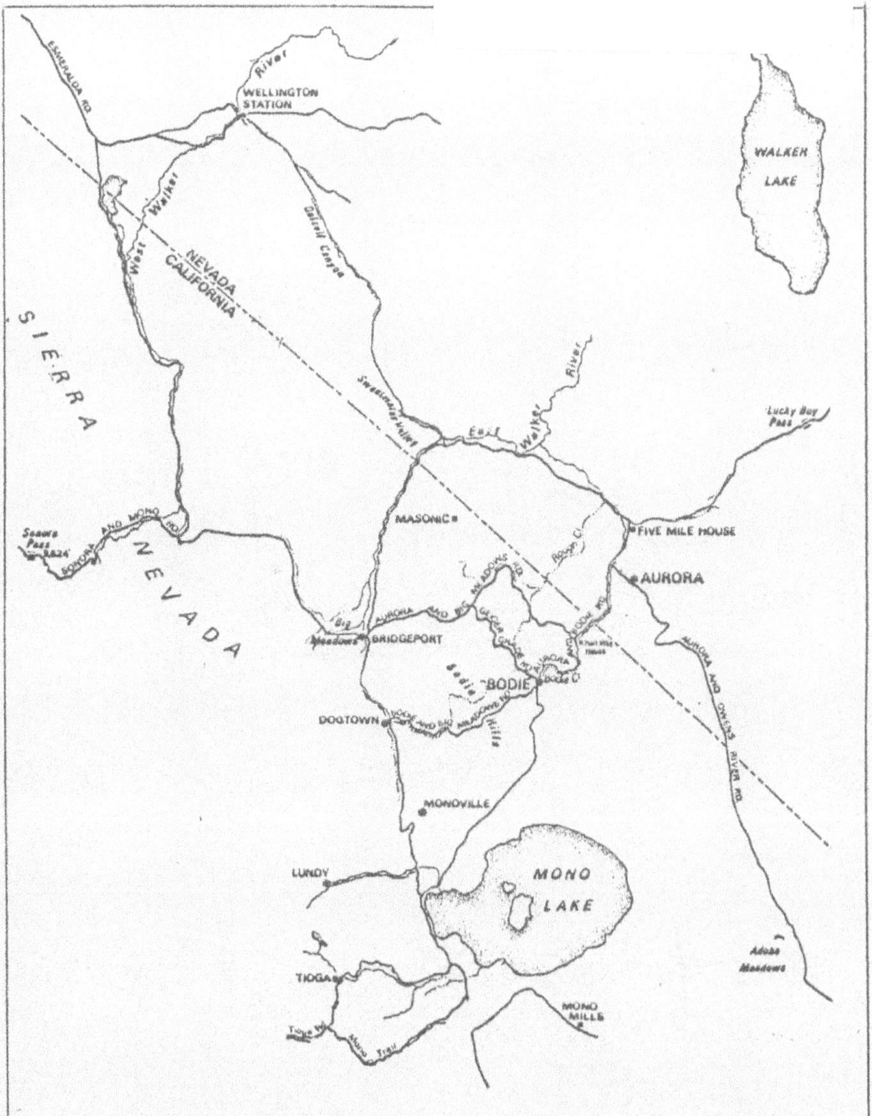

STAGE ROUTES & WAGON ROADS
Circa 1880

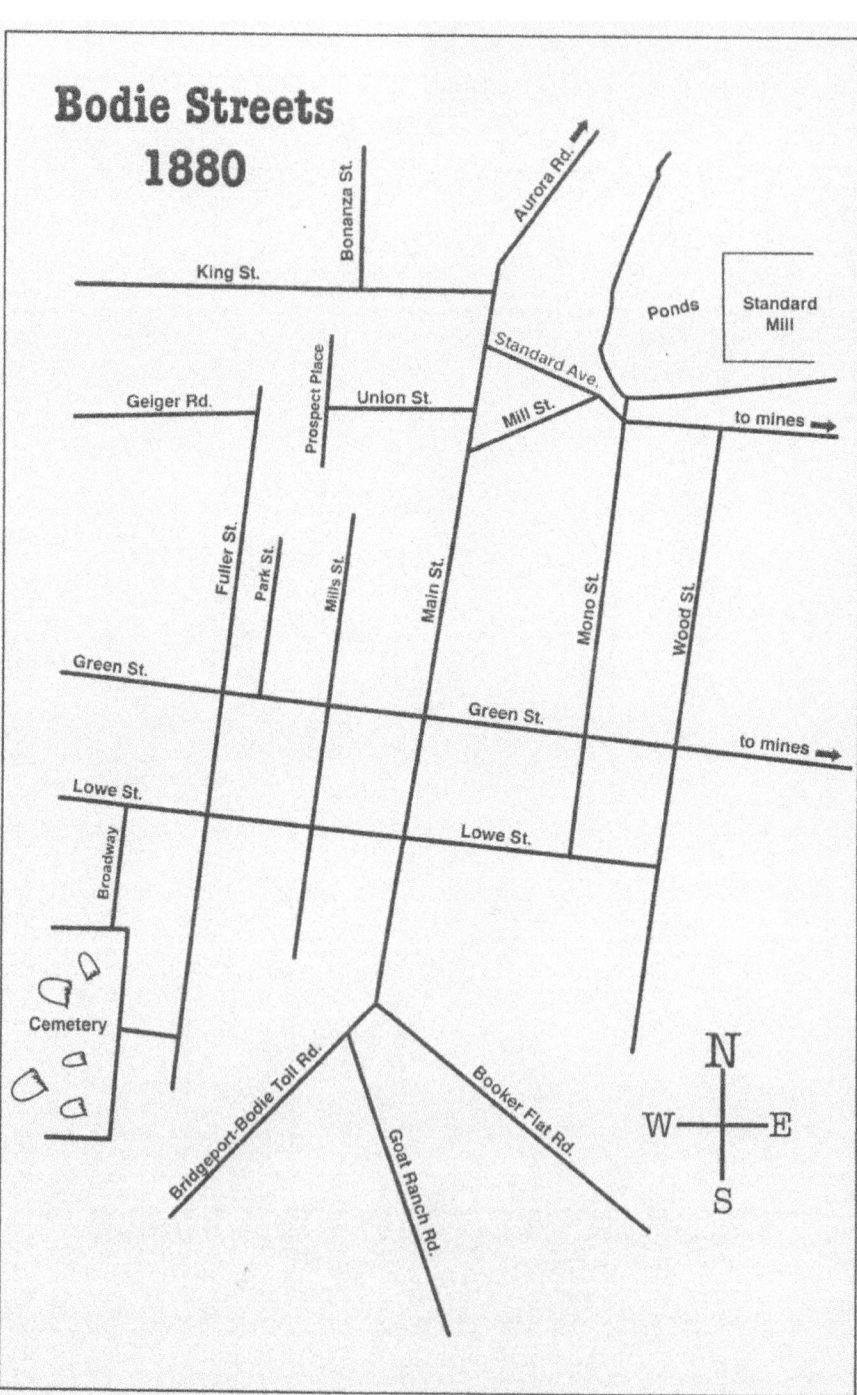

NO TREES FOR SHADE

BODIE, CALIFORNIA 1880

A Novel by

Kathleen Haun

Aventine Press

Copyright © 2013 by Kathleen Haun

Without limiting the rights under copyright reserved above, no part of this publication may be reproduced, stored in or introduced into a retrieval system, or transmitted, in any form or by any means (electronic, mechanical, photocopying, recording, or otherwise), without the prior written permission of both the copyright owner and the publisher of this book.

Published by Aventine Press
55 East Emerson St.
Chula Vista CA 91911
www.aventinepress.com

ISBN: 978-1-59330-817-9

Printed in the United States of America
ALL RIGHTS RESERVED

TREES...

Where branches reach out in welcome
And weary bodies find succor and rest;
Where roots are nourished by cool earth
And birds find sustenance to carry on;
Where emboldened animals find shelter
And dispirited souls find uplift and peace;
Where the trail ends and hope prevails.

Kathleen Haun

A Brief Time Line of Events Leading up to 1880

1857: North of the Mono Lake region is an area that has seen placer activity since 1852. In 1857, men find enough gold on the East Walker River to make the organization of a mining district worthwhile. The settlement where they congregate is called Dogtown, located at the west end of what is later the Bodie and Big Meadows Toll Road.

June, 1859: Eighty miles to the north thousands of men head to Washoe, Nevada to seek the fabulous wealth of the Ophir vein of the Comstock Lode.

Those from Dogtown who don't migrate north, go further south to the rocky ravines and dusty gulches above Mono Lake. They call their camp Monoville. Among those working the area are W. S. Bodey and his friends Terrence Brodigan from Ireland, the half Cherokee E. S. "Black" Taylor, Patrick Garrity and William Doyle. Mr. Bodey is a slouchy individual of medium build, about 45 and with a dark complexion and an accent some say is Scottish, and who several times has referred to a wife and children in an unidentified location.

They head northeast, testing for gold as they travel. As they approach Mormon County in what is then Utah Territory, Indians force them to turn back to Monoville. After crossing a barren ridge over 8,000 feet in elevation, they descend into a shallow valley Brodigan feels is a likely place for gold and they begin digging.

Bodey's shovel finds pay dirt. The men build a ramshackle cabin at the site, and sensing a harsh winter approaching, Bodey and Taylor return to Monoville. Brodigan, Garrity and Doyle go to Sonora by way of the Placerville Road.

Bodey and Black Taylor then decide to spend the winter at the cabin and set out on foot with a pack mule back to where they had discovered the gold. On November 22 snow begins to fall and a week later it reaches a depth of five to six feet.

When Bodey collapses, Taylor wraps him in a blanket and fights his way through deep snow to the rude cabin. Storms rage one after the other and it isn't until May that Taylor locates Bodey's bones less than a mile from the cabin and buries them on the spot. The area where they had discovered the gold becomes known as "Bodey's Diggings". As miners file claims in the area, they do so under various spellings, e.g., Bodey, Body, Bodie.

1860: Terrence Brodigan works the summer in Virginia City; Pat Garrity in Aurora; and Black Taylor, who is haunted by the death of his friend, ends up in Hot Springs later known as Benton.

July 10, 1860: Miners organize the Bodey Mining District.

August 25, 1860: Gold is found twelve miles northeast of the few buildings composing Bodey's Diggings. It is organized as the Esmeralda Mining District and the town is called Aurora. Men come there from Virginia City, Bodey's Diggings, Dogtown and Monoville.

Fall, 1860: Brothers John and Ben Hasslet, at their hay ranch and stable on the road west out of Aurora, hire sign maker Bob Howland from Aurora to paint their sign. He decides to spell the name "Bodie Stables". The spelling sticks.

April, 1861: California creates Mono County with Aurora as its county seat.

July 1, 1861: The *Bunker Hill Mine* is located on the slope of High Peak Hill in the town of *Bodey* by L. H. Dearborn, O. G. Leach, and E. Donahue. However, the claim had already been recorded on June 17, 1861, by J. Kerlew, J. Tucker and S. Lamb.

November, 1861: Nevada Territory is cut from the western portion of Utah Territory and Esmeralda County is formed, with no one knowing for sure if Aurora is in Nevada or California. The Territorial Governor, however, thinks it is in Nevada so he establishes it as Esmeralda County's county seat, although Mono County also claims it as its county seat.

1862: Piutes surround Black Taylor's cabin. His bullet-riddled body with severed head is found by men from Aurora on their way south to fight in the Owens Valley Piute Indian War.

September, 1863: Aurora is declared to be three miles within Nevada. Bridgeport becomes the county seat of Mono County, California.

1863: After the *Bunker Hill Mine* changes hands several times in what is now being called *Bodie*, the Bodie Bluff Consolidation Mining Company owns the Bunker Hill and all the paying ledges on High Peak Hill and Bodie Bluff.

April, 1864: The *Bunker Hill* is sold to New York investors known as the Empire Gold and Silver Mining Company. Men begin to arrive to work the mine.

October, 1864: The Empire Company drives three tunnels into Bodie Bluff and High Peak Hill to find the mother lode. It is not found.

1865: The Empire Company builds a huge Gothic style stamp mill to go along with its boarding house for employees. Bodie now has 16 stamps, 8 amalgamating pans, 3 settlers and 4 shaking tables, and is in the business of processing ore.

April, 1867: Failing to make a profit, operations are suspended. Bodie is abandoned by all but a few stubbornly optimistic people. Aurora is also declining.

Remaining in Bodie is Peter Eshington, Louis Lockberg, and William O'Hara, a large black man who is known as a friend to everyone. Mr. O'Hara is kept on the payroll of the Empire Company to watch over the company's abandoned properties. As repayment of a small loan from him, he is given the Bunker Hill Mine. Later, Eshington and Lockberg agree to work the claim and pay him $8,000 for the mine out of whatever they make. This they do.

June 11, 1875: The name of the mine is changed from Bunker Hill to *Bullion Lode*.

Fall, 1875: The mine caves in and exposes a rich seam of gold-bearing quartz. Few in the area believe the find significant. Using arastras located on Rough Creek, they manage to produce $37,000 over the following year. Fear of the mine "pinching out" convinces Eshington and Lockberg to sell.

October, 1875: San Francisco speculators organize as the Syndicate Mining Company and buy the 16 stamp mill and a few of the Bodie Bluff properties of the Empire Company.

June 9, 1876: Eshington and Lockberg receive $67,500 for their claim, equipment, tools and two horses.

September 16, 1876: The Engineering and Mining Journal reports that the Syndicate Gold and Silver Mining Company made $5,587.94, and that the vein is about eight feet wide and gold bearing. They say it is worth only $8.67 an ounce because there is a considerable amount of silver in the ore. "The company has in operation a fine mill, and their prospects are excellent, as they have only attained a depth of 200 feet."

1877: The Bullion Mine's shaft is at the 400 foot level. So much is being taken out that a 20 stamp mill at the foot of High Peak Hill begins construction.

April 11, 1877: The Bullion Mine owners organize as the *Standard Gold Mining Company* with capitalization of $5,000,000 presented by 50,000 shares of stock. They begin buying up the surrounding properties including what they call the Bulwer.

July 20, 1877: *The Standard Mill* is completed and the mine's shaft is at 600 feet. Men flock to the area.

March 17, 1877, the Inyo Independent from Bodie: "We also have quite a town started here. We have already two stores, and considerable preparations for numerous whisky mills and hash houses. ... Jumping of town lots and watching mining claims that might be jumped, has commenced. ...six-shooters are kept in order in case they might be needed."

September 15, 1877, Inyo Independent: "There is about one hundred and ten houses, and two quartz mills running 36 stamps night and day. We have a population of about 600—and lots of Piutes. Two stores, one kept by Bryant of Bridgeport and the other by S. B. Smith of Aurora; 7 saloons, 5 eating houses; 2 lodging houses; 2 meat markets; 3 lumber yards (and not able to supply the demand); from 3 to 6 houses are started every day, besides quite a number of tents and mud cabins."

September 28, 1877, Gold Hill Daily News: "A trip to Bodie involves a deal of personal discomfort, annoying dust, heat, and extreme cold, especially while passing through the Sweetwater country. The stage line is abominable, consisting of rackety old coaches, mud wagons, and half-starved stock, and prices high enough to bankrupt a man of ordinary means. ... If my trip is an average specimen, their fastest time does not exceed 6 miles an hour."

January, 1878: John Kirgan, a lean man in his middle 40's, comes to Bodie in 1877. By 1878, he is well known as the architect of the jail and is building a saloon. He is a man who is willing to back up his sense of right with the Colt Peacemaker that he carries on his hip, rather than hidden away in a pocket as most men in Bodie. A hero of the Mexican War, he was the sergeant at arms during California's first constitutional convention and also during the first meeting of the state legislature at Vallejo--California's first state capital.

February, 1878: A newspaper declares that "there are 6 or 7 good mines and about 700 locations for mines. The average number of arrivals each day is ten."

February 26, 1878, Reno Gazette: "Many persons in Bodie are elated over the prospects of the camp, while others speaking of it use language wholly unbecoming a Christian."

March 30, 1878: After a short stint as a saloon owner, John Kirgan is appointed by the Mono County Board of Supervisors as the first Constable of Bodie—and is referred to by locals as "the boss lawman".

July, 1878: A newspaper notes that, "There are 27 saloons in Bodie and it is estimated that there are over 1,700 drinks taken every day over the bars."
August, 1878: "Bodie is honored with no less than 13 law firms."

December, 1878, Grass Valley Union: "Bodie has a population of 5,000, including the suburb around the Bodie and the Standard Mines. Main

Street is nearly one mile long and lots are staked off in all directions on the hillsides. Average arrivals are about 30 and all departees intend to return. ... There are 47 saloons and ten faro tables. This is not a disparagement of the district, but evidence of its prosperity."

"The bullion product is only limited by the milling facilities. There are at present in Bodie only 4 mills: the Standard, 20 stamps; the Syndicate, 20 stamps, running on Bodie ores; the Bodie, 10 stamps, running on Bodie tailings; the Miners, a custom mill, 5 stamps. Early in the spring the Bulwer will erect a 20 stamp mill and the Standard will increase its facilities. It is safe to predict the bullion product for 1879 will average $1,000,000 per month for ten months of the year."

June, 1879, Reno Weekly Gazette: "The streets of Bodie are crowded with men. A fight or a fiddle will draw hundreds of heads together and render the passage of teams slow and difficult. Every stage coming in is loaded. Men are flocking in on the Sonora Road on foot, on horseback and in wagon. They are nearly all looking for work, and not one in five has money enough to live on for a week. The population of Bodie is now between four and five thousand, and there is work for about 800."

June, 1879, Reno Weekly Gazette: "The climate of Bodie seems to be very unhealthy especially for men. Yet there are over 300 children here and they seem to enjoy the best of health. Ladies also are seldom sick. In 15 months only 4 women and 1 child have been buried, while for many weeks there has been a funeral every day. The enemy is pneumonia which attacks the strongest men in preference to the sickly or the weak. The air is light and cold, the men who become overheated are chilled almost instantly, unless extraordinary precautions are taken and their lungs have to bear the whole shock."

> What is not mentioned in this article is the fact that only the strongest of men work in the mines, and are daily exposed to mercury fumes and the fine dust that is always floating in the air of the tunnels.

January, 1880: Leo Scowden makes a survey of Bodie as a first step toward forming a town site in the hope of someday incorporating Bodie. This gives town leaders the authority to create solutions for water, fire and sanitation problems—pressing issues the rapidly expanding town faces.

CHAPTER 1
JUNE, 1880

The southbound stagecoach traveling through Nevada's Sweetwater Valley careened suddenly to the right. Only by grabbing the loop of leather hanging from the side wall did nineteen year old Amanda avoid falling sideways onto the lap of a large man with a long drooping mustache who wore a rumpled suit that smelled of smoke and sweat. The pretty young woman smiled at him with relief and apology as she righted herself, while the man barely managed to hide his disappointment.

The coach then swung abruptly back in the other direction and Amanda swallowed a wave of rising nausea. When the wheels thumped over yet another rain-worn rut cutting across the hard dusty road, she clenched her teeth and closed her eyes. She was finding long distance travel by stagecoach challenging.

It was the second day of June, 1880, and the long and severe winter just passed had pushed spring into the beginning of summer. Lavender wild flowers sprouted along the edges of the road and white fields of low-growing blooms spread up the side hills. An occasional splash of red or yellow caught the eye and gave refreshing variety to the otherwise monotonous hours.

A fine film of gray dust had settled on her small fashionable blue hat, while tendrils of dark auburn hair curled from beneath it. With the stage line having run out of linen dusters for the passengers, everyone's clothes showed a light sheen of gray grime. She brushed somewhat effectively at her long blue skirt, but had no doubt that her black high-buttoned shoes were especially filthy, considering everything she had walked through at the many stage stations; mud, horse droppings, cow patties, and urine-soaked straw. The filth, however, she could accept more philosophically than the incongruous mixture of hunger and motion sickness she had been contending with for the last half hour.

Amanda sighed and asked herself, not for the first time, if this journey would ever end? Although she had started out in Placerville, California on the western side of the Sierra Nevada, the journey now was taking her south through Nevada. With more than half the trip behind her, to take her mind off her discomfort she looked across the gray miles of desert sagebrush to the eastern slope of the Sierra.

A moment of sadness welled up as she realized that only a far view would now be her closest association with this majestic mountain range, after having been her home all the years of her life. She smiled as she thought of how many people called it the *Sierras*, plural. Maybe they could not accept that a mountain range hundreds of miles long, and in several places over 14,000 feet high, could be a single chain of uplifted granite. She hugged to herself this bit of educated trivia that she had read in a book, knowing that although still theory, it made sense to her.

Even now in June a thick blanket of snow draped the mountain's crest, so deep that much of it would remain throughout the summer. Amanda fought the clutching tightness in her throat as her thoughts wandered once again back to her beloved Placerville with its cool forests and rushing creeks.

Visions of her mother filled her mind as she cast aside her recently acquired emotional discipline and let her thoughts wander. Surprised to find that the urge to shed a tear was upon her, and determined to avoid such an embarrassment, Amanda turned her thoughts instead to the father who had deserted the family two years before when he had joined the rush to the Bodie mines. The anger that always accompanied the thought of him immediately dried her tears.

She remembered standing at the edge of the road while watching him ride out of town on his big mule. Even now the memory brought to her the same confused sense of sadness and relief that she had felt back then. It was this father, John Blake, who was the reason she was on the stage. He had asked her to join him in Bodie--a mining town reported to be producing more bullion than Virginia City ever had. But it also had a reputation for violence that was reported in newspapers throughout the region, it being reported that the town had a dead man for breakfast almost every morning. Even allowing for the exaggeration of such statements, she figured at least some of what was reported must be true.

That was why it was so surprising to her that her father had remained in Bodie all this time. John Blake was a man in his late thirties, of medium height, dull brown hair, short mustache, and limpid brown eyes. His bland temperate nature matched his appearance and served well to define him as non-threatening, much as a desert lizard melds into the background and is therefore unnoticed by predators.

Amanda nevertheless remembered him as an energetic man with dreams larger than his income. In the early 1860's he had peddled mining equipment from a small Placerville storefront on Main, had tried his hand at blacksmithing, and occasionally had tended bar at various saloons. There had been other jobs, but they had changed so often that Amanda could no longer recall them. But she did remember that John had never taken employment that would keep him from rambling around in the hills trying to find color—the elusive gold nuggets, or at least dust, that he had been convinced was his due. Unfortunately, the success he sought had each time eluded him and was declared to be in the next creek into which he planned to dip his pan.

It was this restlessness and dissatisfaction, expressed every day of his life, which had worn down his wife Mary. Amanda pictured her mother, a fragile prematurely aged woman who had spent much of her life in bed with one minor ailment after another. Each had been just debilitating enough to keep her from cooking meals and cleaning the house. For that, she had turned to Amanda. After her father had left them, sending them money most months but not all, the illnesses had become serious. Finally Mary had died after a short bout with pneumonia during the previous year's unusually severe winter.

John Blake had not been close to his daughter. He had always made it clear to anyone who he thought might show him some degree of sympathy that when his wife had been expecting he had hoped for a boy. When Amanda was very young, there had been the added comment that he yet hoped for that boy. When it became evident that Mary would never again conceive, he changed his oft spoken lament to, "But this is all I'm going to get."

Upon receiving Amanda's letter informing him of his wife's death, John had sent her a curt response inviting her to join him in Bodie, but saying nothing about how she would pay for the trip. Being that he was all the family she had, and assuming that her father's years as a hard rock miner had given him an appreciation of home ties, Amanda had sold the rented home's furnishings to pay the stage fare.

The stage gave a hard lurch and with a start Amanda brought her thoughts back to the present. It surprised her how different this portion of the trip was from its beginning. The ride over the Sierra on the Placerville Road, and then through Hope Valley south of Lake Tahoe, had been dangerously steep, narrow, and winding, but incredibly exciting and with beautiful views at every turn.

She had loved the huge rock outcroppings amid dense forests of tall red-barked pines, the road edge dropping off into deep canyons lined with trees showing new leaves of green, and the rugged gorges where the American River at the bottom roared over smooth boulders. Because the Placerville Road was a major route across the mountain for freight wagons and stagecoaches, it was routinely dragged by road crews and toll keepers to keep it fairly smooth. Its main drawback was the amount of traffic on it; wagons, pack trains, stagecoaches, herders, riders and even foot traffic.

The Nevada portion of the trip from Minden to Wellington had been uneventful to the point of weary monotony, with only increasing thirst to focus upon after her canteen was empty. On the road south from Wellington, where the stage station had been housed in a large two-story white house, the road had alternated between powdery dust and thick mud. Now they passed through miles of small scrubby pinion pines and gray sagebrush in Dalzell Canyon on the approach to the Sweetwater Valley.

Her companions had been a changing mix throughout the journey. Out of Placerville several had been men in suits with brushed hats and silk vests beneath their coats, including the muscular young man across from her near her own age. They had smelled of good cigars and had shown her the utmost courtesy, although she caught two of them casting surreptitious glances at the snug bodice of her traveling suit.

The men who had joined them in Nevada had been dressed in worn denim pants, scuffed boots, and dirty felt hats. These men had smelled of horse and steer, as well as dried sweat and cheap tobacco. They too had tipped their hats to Amanda, but had not bothered to hide their bold appreciative leers. Two of them were still on the coach, but had dozed most of the time.

As for women passengers, from Hope Valley to Wellington they had been joined by a woman all in black hiding herself behind a veil of lace and who had uttered not one word. An elderly nun had ridden with them for part of that way, but had disembarked in Minden just in time to catch a stage north to Genoa.

In Wellington three men in scruffy clothes had taken up space on the roof, and after catching a whiff of their sour smell, Amanda had rolled her eyes to the heavens in gratitude. The friendliest and most talkative of her fellow passengers was the tall, muscular but lithe young man with light hair and a thick mustache who sat across from her. He had the slight soft burr of an accent that was of Scotland, and a warm smile that reminded her of an eager young puppy. She had stolen more than one glance at his bulging biceps that no amount of coat fabric could obscure. He had introduced himself as Duncan McMillan, and the closer they came to Bodie, the more excited he seemed to become. He informed her that he had been away from the town for some time and was eager to return.

Eighteen miles past Wellington, they approached the Sulphur Springs stage station where the stage came to such an abrupt halt that the passengers were thrown into one another. They hurried to right themselves and then exchanged looks of fear as a deep muffled voice hollered for the driver to throw down his strong box. At the same time, on each side of the coach men with handkerchiefs tied over the lower portion of their faces and with hats pulled low on their heads, pointed guns in at the passengers. Being next to the window furthest from the door, Amanda found herself looking down at a gun only a few inches from her nose. Consequently, when they were ordered to get out, she pushed at her slower moving neighbor so she wouldn't be perceived as not following instructions. Those riding on top of the stage had already climbed down by the time the inside passengers began lining up.

Without being told, the men from the stage stood next to the coach with their hands raised. Seeing this, Amanda followed their example while the large young man that had been seated across from her moved partly in front of her in a show of protection. Amanda immediately ceased resenting the amount of room his large legs had been taking up in the coach.

The hold-up artists, after a brief glance at her youth, ignored Amanda. One of them, possibly a little more intelligent than the others, eyed her fashionable dress and wondered if she might not have a good deal of money on her. But their leader had cautioned them to never interfere with the passengers, who were after all mostly simple, hardworking people like themselves. Besides, whatever was in the strong boxes was all they wanted as they assumed it could not be traced.

The bandits were soon intent on the Wells Fargo box which they had dragged a few yards to the side of the road. Once the contents were stuffed into saddle bags, they ordered everyone back onto the stage. There was no need to command them a second time.

Amanda huddled against the side wall of the coach beside the small window, afraid to look out in case the bandits might be displeased. Her heart thumped so hard she could barely breathe and her throat was so dry that she thought it might seize up if she tried to talk. Only when the coach lurched forward and the horses began to lope down the road, did Amanda slowly exhale her repressed tension.

All the men with her began to talk at once, no one wanting to listen but only to have his say. It occurred to Amanda that maybe the men also needed to release the tension of fear, but without admitting to it. The muscular young man across from her gave her a wobbly smile that was less than reassuring.

When they later met the northbound stage at the Elbow Ranch Station on the east fork of the Walker River, the driver called out, "Hey, Billy, watch out ahead. We were robbed just the other side of Sulphur Springs. There're three of 'em."

"Thanks, Bob. I've got Mike Tobey and Woodruff with me, and they've got lots of ammo. We'll be fine."

Amanda's stage bumped its way through repetitious miles of gray desert scrub with only a brief stop at Nine Mile Ranch station, its neglected out buildings made of scrap wood and rock. Everyone on board breathed a sigh of relief when early in the afternoon they finally arrived at the substantial town of Aurora, Nevada, which as one passenger noted, was "within spitting distance of the California border." At least here there were a few scrubby trees scattered over the low rolling hills surrounding the town's surprising number of brick buildings.

The passengers were told to eat quickly, an announcement heard at each station. It was something Amanda had found easy to do after being presented with the greasy victuals at the stage stations. Evidently, as long as there was coffee in the pot, with the addition of a little water it could be boiled and served again, each time becoming blacker and thicker.

She hurried to the privy behind the Aurora station, fearful of being left behind by an impatient driver. Her things were being transferred to Mr. Fairfield's stage that would continue on to Bodie over a 14 mile sandy and rocky trail. When she returned to the coach, a small crowd of excited men were standing around the driver. As she stood nearby listening to the men talking, her stomach clenched as graphic details were brought out for the benefit of the passengers.

"It was earlier this week?" the driver asked. "I was still in Sacramento and didn't hear."

A tall man with a long beard told him, "Yeah, it was last Tuesday. Henry Martin killed an Injun at the Bodie Ranch. Blew him full of holes with his shotgun." The stage would pass this ranch three miles from Bodie.

"Why did he kill him?"

A young, clean-shaven Aurora man spoke up with evident excitement. "A small group of Piutes approached Martin and accused him of having killed one of their horses. He took out his shotgun and waved it around, trying to get 'em to back off. It went off and one of the Piutes was killed."

"Accident or on purpose?"

"Not sure," the bearded man put in.

"I don't guess the Piute's family cares," the younger man added soberly.

The driver shrugged. "I know Henry and I don't think he'd steal a horse. But who knows, huh? I wonder what will happen now."

"It already did," the young man told him, jumping in quickly before the story was taken from him. "They brought him up before the Justice of the Peace and the jury said it was self-defense. He's out and around again."

The bearded man commented in a low voice, "The Injuns aren't much pleased."

"I can't say I blame 'em," the driver nodded. "I hope they don't cause trouble over this."

As they climbed into the coach, Amanda asked the young man across from her, "What kind of trouble might the Indians cause?"

"Oh, probably none," he smiled reassuringly. "'Course they could set the evil eye on the men who were on the jury."

Amanda gave him a suspicious look, pretty sure he was having her on. She turned and looked out the window, not willing to let him see her disgust with his cavalier attitude about what could be a serious situation that after all included the death of a man with a grieving family. On the other hand, since the dead man was Piute, she knew most people would not think of the man's family as having such emotions.

Thinking of the young man with the charitable character in Aurora, she felt it a shame that she wouldn't be able to get to know him better. Although she didn't consider herself as looking for a husband, she was not far off from being considered a spinster, and her friends were wondering why she was not yet married. These friends were her age or even younger, some with children, and she knew they thought her too particular.

Leaving the Half Way House stage stop on the long winding Bodie and Aurora Road, Amanda experienced relief to be so near the end of her journey. Even though her nervousness over once again seeing her father was somewhat getting in the way, she was surprised to realize that she was hungry again. The food at the stations had varied less than the passengers, covering the narrow range of beans and coffee to beans with unidentifiable meat and coffee. The only exception had been the Wellington stage stop, where not only had they enjoyed fresh bread and stew, but also had feasted on apple pie. A few stops had only offered them water, but that had been a welcome opportunity to fill canteens. The trip had been a lesson in gratitude for the smallest of blessings.

The stage picked up speed as the horses loped down the northern approach to Bodie, eager for what they knew would soon be a good feed. They passed heavily loaded freight wagons heading into Bodie piled with hay, which was followed by a long pack train of burros each carrying a load of wood in specially constructed packs.

At the rise of a hill, Amanda glimpsed in the distance what at first appeared to be a single sprawling white wooden house with a floor of mud and a ceiling of bright blue. A moment later her reason clarified that it was actually a town of mainly two story buildings shoved together and only occasionally leaving a narrow alley between. Some of the whitewashed buildings had a raised false front over the door, some bore a large sign reaching above the roofline, some had a railed balcony off the upstairs rooms, and some were small unpainted square boxes with only a tiny sign on the solid door. They all faced a wooden plank sidewalk a foot above the wide and long mud puddle called Main Street, with the whole length of the sidewalks roofed over so that in winter they could more easily be kept clear of deep snow. Now there were straw and canvas sun shades hanging from the leading edges of many of them. Beyond Main were half a dozen short streets branching east to the mines or west to low hills dotted with a few ramshackle Piute camps.

Duncan explained to her that on the other side of town the Bodie and Big Meadows Road headed west to Virginia Creek and Dogtown, where it turned north toward Bridgeport, also known as Big Meadows. The Big Meadows Road was tree-lined through meadows and rocky hills and was a favorite of freighters, as the stations along its length were good ones and there was plenty of water for their teams. The new Geiger Grade Road, after passing a large slaughterhouse, headed northwest out of town along the curve of a low hill and joined with the Aurora and Big Meadows Road. It wound around several wide gullies where small camps were located, and eventually ended up near Bridgeport.

One of the men next to her wearing denim pants topped by a rumpled suit jacket and a stained felt hat that had been stomped on a few times, commented that at least the last snow fall had melted. Another man broke out with a sharp laugh and said, "Wait a week."

When the others in the coach also laughed, Amanda realized that what she had heard about Bodie's infamously quixotic weather was possibly not exaggeration after all. In fact, only a few days before, icicles had been hanging from some of the buildings, and a layer of ice had been removed from the water troughs in the morning to allow the horses to drink.

Amanda returned her attention to the hills, ridges and bluffs bordering the town to the east. Here were the famous hard rock mines that were the talk of the whole country. The hills and canyons through which they had just passed had been covered with small pocket dumps next to *coyote holes* with latticed hoisting works over the small digs made to test for the presence of paying ore. But the hills east of the town were a much different prospect.

Seeing her interest, Duncan told her, "The hills you see from left to right are Bodie Bluff, High Peak Hill, Silver Hill and Queen Bee Hill. The openings at the bottom of the hills are tunnels that go straight into them. But most of the wealth is at the top, where they have to go down for it. The big fancy brick building nearest us is the Syndicate Mill. It used to be the Empire Mill, the first one here."

These large hills and the lesser ones between were covered in a network of narrow dirt roads between the mills with their multiple black smoke stacks protruding from the roofs. These huge buildings covered hoisting works that pumped out water from the lower regions, and others that lifted up tons of rock. In between were office buildings with men crowding around the front, aerial tramways with iron carts rolling along the tracks, and boarding houses for the miners crammed with rows of bunk beds.

Not far from each mill was a huge pile of neatly stacked cordwood fifty feet long and ten feet high. It was used to fuel the steam engines that ran the hoisting works and the stamps in the mills. Lower on the hills were acres of corrals attached to huge barns over a hundred feet long and kept heated during the winter; the homes of the mules that pulled the loaded ore carts out of the tunnels, as well as the horses that pulled the wagons.

However, to Amanda who had spent her entire life amid the forests of the Sierra, the greatest shock was that as far as the eye could see in every direction there was not one tree of any size. All vegetation was sage brush, rabbitbrush and greasewood; it mattered not its name as it was gray, gray-blue, or dull green, and none of it leant shade.

The stage's horses splashed through the muddy street and the coach slewed to the side of the road where it stopped in front of the stage station. While the larger mines had created ponds for their run-off, some of it still overflowed into the streets and the smaller mines were now pumping out waste water at the 450 foot level. The sloppy state of the roads was an on-going contentious issue for the citizens who had to deal with them on a daily basis. Recently an underground piping system had been approved that would carry the water away from the roads, but its completion was still a couple of years off.

The passengers had for miles been hearing a constant dull thud that had reached them as a hollow echo. Now that they were in town, the source of the noise became clear. This echoing clang was created by a battery of five 700 pound iron stamps rising and falling together on rock in order to pulverize it small enough that gold could be extracted. The wealth of a mining camp was measured by the number of these noisy stamps in its mills. In Bodie this noise was not from one or even two dozen of these, but closer to two-hundred.

The air was rent with this pulverizing ritual twenty-four hours a day, and those walking on the east side of town could even feel the vibrations of it beneath their feet. On the rare occasions when the stamp mills ceased, babies born in Bodie began to fret in the strange silence, while adults awoke with a start and then sighed with pleasure even while finding it difficult to get back to sleep.

The piercing scream of a steam whistle from one of the mills suddenly shattered the air, quickly followed by another. It was time for a shift change. The stage horses barely flinched, so accustomed were they to this violent blast of sound peculiar to large mining camps. Amanda on the other hand felt every organ in her torso react with a constriction tighter than the lacings of her corset.

The stage had stopped in front of a long covered porch across the front of a large freshly whitewashed building. It was the Grand Central Hotel and at the north end of the porch was a sign that read *U.S. Stage Line* with a private entrance into its office.

Eager to finally be released from the confines of the coach, as soon as the door was opened by the driver Amanda slid forward on the seat. Immediately a large crowd of men swarmed around the coach amid raucous cheers and whistles. Amanda quickly shrank back against the leather seat.

Muscular young Mr. Duncan, however, stepped out wearing a big grin and waving his hand. Several men slapped him on the back and hustled him off to Wagner's Saloon only a few doors south of the hotel. The only man still in the coach, an old man with a long gray beard grinning at the excitement, explained. "He's a member of Bodie's Caledonian Club. He's returning from the annual Scottish games in Oakland where he won four first places."

"In what events?"

"The heavy and light hammer throw, and putting the heavy and light stones."

A few moments later, Amanda and her fellow passengers retrieved their luggage from the sagging leather boot at the rear of the coach and made purposeful movements in various directions. Amanda stood alone on the hotel's porch with her large suitcase and small satchel at her feet, accompanied by a nervous roiling in her stomach as she tried to get her bearings and decide what to do next.

Several women walked past, each one eyeing this new arrival and trying to determine which class of Bodie society might apply to her. She wore what was considered a simple suit of the day in a more modern city, but of a fashion yet to be seen in Bodie outside of a magazine. The form-fitting light blue cashmere and silk suit jacket, worn over a simple white waist, had a standup collar bordered by a banding of white grosgrain ribbon that was repeated at the cuffs. The snug jacket fell to just below her hips over a skirt of the same fabric.

Amanda shifted with unease as the women walked by and looked over their shoulders to see the back of her outfit, where a small flounce of fabric was gathered. The era of the large protruding bustle had passed and was not yet ready to reappear in a smaller version. Day costumes in the West were designed with the dirt of the streets in mind, so the skirt had no train, but was decorated with knife pleats beneath a swag of fabric across the front and gathered into a flounce at the back. Her Langtry bonnet was of the small close-fitting variety and topped with one simple curled ostrich plume. She was glad that her scuffed calfskin boots, buttoned several inches above trim ankles, were hidden beneath her skirt. They were the only shoes she owned.

The outfit may have impressed those who passed her as belonging to a lady of considerable means, but it was the best of what she owned. The clothing stuffed into her luggage could most tactfully be called serviceable, and she was thankful the other women could not see her two plain black wool skirts, the gray unadorned cotton waist and the black silk. In her satchel was her only other set of basic under things, a white knitted shawl, and a well-worn flannel nightgown and robe.

While others may have been interested in *her*, it was the town before her that held Amanda's interest. People in Placerville had of course heard of Bodie, so she knew about the incredible wealth of the Standard Mine at the top of High Peak Hill with its mill below and almost level with the town. The Bodie and the Mono mines were on the ridge below the Standard, while the Bulwer was to the north. Smaller mines filled the hills between these, while the Noonday and North Noonday were at the extreme south end of the hills.

While she had expected the far-reaching views of mines and mills, she had not expected the over-stimulated energy that radiated from the very wood of the buildings and the people on the streets. The Queen Anne style of architecture was just coming into vogue and this created windows with diverse shapes, some with tops arched and others flat. Many of the steeply pitched roofs were plain while others were edged in elaborate cut-out latticework and carved corbels under the eaves. Many windows were outlined in decorative latticework, as were doors with the addition of heavy iron knobs and latches. Among these sturdy and decorative constructions were small plain houses little more than cabins, only some of which were painted.

The mix of people was as diverse as it had been in Placerville, which had supplied towns on either side of the Sierra. Bodie, however, was an end destination that greedily consumed all that it received of wood, food, mining equipment, and people. It produced only gold mixed with silver, and wild rumors.

To do the mining of this valuable product there were almost 400 miners working in the two dozen mines dotting the hills. Most of the remaining 7,000 townspeople were there to support the mine owners and their workers, providing food, clothing, alcohol, entertainment, and private moments in Bonanza Street brothels. Among the thousands of *decent* people could also be found several thousand gamblers, criminals in hiding, an eclectic mix of society's outcasts, the Chinese district, prostitutes, and the chronically unemployed. These last had quickly discovered that jobs were few outside the mines, and the mines had all their jobs filled. Openings occurred only after an accident or illness took someone out.

The north end of town where Amanda now stood was the oldest section and the location of the saloons, dance halls, brothels, opium dens, and the jail. One street over to the west was facetiously referred to as "virgin alley", but on the maps it was shown as Bonanza Street. It was the location of the *fair but frail* sisterhood who worked from a line of small cribs which were rough eight foot square cabins, or a more fortunate woman might be on offer in a large two-story brothel. Women "in the business" did *not* work in or frequent the saloons unless escorted by a man.

The southern end of town was considered the abode of the *proper* citizens, and any smart crook or drunk stayed away unless they wanted the wrath of the citizens and the constabulary to fall upon them. Newcomers quickly learned that what happened at the north end might be accepted as part of its rhythm of wild abandon and drunken release after a hard day in a mine, but the area where the shopkeepers and proper women lived with their children was strictly out of bounds.

Amanda was interested to see so many of the colorful Piutes from the hills present in the town. Most of them watched the townspeople walking past them with a frown and in many instances met any effort of friendliness with a glare. Amanda remembered the story told to the stage passengers in Aurora. The Indians were not unacquainted with Anglos being set free due to the justification of self-defense, but it didn't make it any easier for them to accept.

A stage with a full complement of passengers inside rumbled past heading south toward the road to Bridgeport. Recently some of the outgoing stages carried more people than those coming into town, and *For Sale* and *For Rent* signs were being seen more often than made for a comfortable state of mind.

Rather than recognize that a change was taking place in the town, people repeated to one another that the "frantic growth of the town over the last three years to 8,000 people had been unrealistic anyway," considering that the town could only realistically support 4,000. There were about 6,000 people present now, and since some men slept in alleys, on pool tables, in stables, among the logs at the wood lots, and on the back porches of any household willing to tolerate them, people convinced each other that it was only the unemployed that filled the stages leaving town.

But for Amanda, the town presented an overwhelming first impression—the sound of shrieking whistles; barking dogs roaming everywhere, most with tags on their leather or rope collars but many without; the press of wagons pulled by a dozen mules passing down the muddy main street and driven by loudly swearing freighters; and the press of people around her yelling to be heard above it all.

Then there was the pungent *smells* from the open trenches, piles of used straw hauled out of the stables, and rotting produce behind the markets. One local wit said he could also smell the fetid breath of desperation as some of the smaller mines began playing out.

Beyond the confusion that surrounded her in the town there ranged low hills dotted with brush huts. For a woman alone with little money, all of this brought home the crushing realization of being stuck in the midst of something she could not escape. Amanda reminded herself that she had chosen to come to Bodie in order to be with her father, and therefore decided to accept that this was her new life. However, she was not so sure she could accept the unrelenting thud of the iron stamps that reminded her of the throb of a bad headache.

A huge wooden freight wagon filled with crates of goods under a large tarp rumbled past, its wheels as tall as Amanda. It was pulled by two horses and ten mules with the muleskinner shouting and whistling as he rode the left of the two large horses hitched immediately in front of the wagon. The animals were bathed in mud up to their chests as they slogged down Main. Another similar wagon followed it loaded with hay, and behind that was one piled with lumber, followed by yet another moving slowly beneath the burden of huge logs. Smaller wagons loaded with lighter goods for the markets, spring wagons, light black rigs and men on horseback filled the spaces between. Amanda blinked at the spectacle and went into the hotel, the entrance to a bar and gambling tables to her right.

Walking to the desk to the left of the lobby, past a small arrangement of a velvet settee and several chairs arranged around a parlor stove, Amanda introduced herself to the woman at the counter. Mrs. Emee Chestnut, the hotel's new manager, had been in charge of several smaller hotels and for a short time her own boardinghouse. The woman, somewhere between thirty and forty, looked up at Amanda and smiled in a proper business-like manner. Her hair was parted in the middle and pulled severely over her ears into a knot at the back of her neck, emphasizing high cheek bones, a prominent chin, a wide forehead and deep-set dark eyes set in a pleasantly full face. Her crisp brown calico dress hugged her neck, gripped her wrists and fell gracefully to just above the floor. Only the kindness in her wary eyes softened her vaguely exotic appearance. And of course she wore no makeup.

Amanda explained her situation. "May I leave my luggage here while I look for my father?"

"Of course, dear," Mrs. Chestnut answered. She looked at this pretty young woman and wondered how such refinement would fare in the rough town. "And who would you be?"

"I'm Amanda Blake. My father John works in one of the mines."

"Oh? Which one?"

"I…I don't know. He didn't mention the name in his last letter." She avoided saying that it was only the second letter she had received from him since he had deserted the family. "I don't even know how to begin my search for him."

"Well, no matter," Mrs. Chestnut told her with a nonchalant shrug. She felt a wave of compassion as she saw the young woman blush at having to admit the long absence of her father. To Mrs. Chestnut, it was a familiar story. More than half the men in mining towns had family somewhere else, tucked away safely while awaiting word from the breadwinner about his fortune made, or lost. She smiled kindly and told Amanda, "The gentlemen at the Miners' Union Hall will be able to help you. It's one long and one short block south of here on the same side of the street and just beyond Green."

Amanda walked outside the hotel onto the crowded wooden planks of the sidewalk, aware again of the pounding stamps in the distance. What was there about this place that made her father think it would be her preference over Placerville? There she had been surrounded by ordered streets and modern accommodations, not to mention dear friends of long acquaintance. When she had written to him after her mother had died, Amanda had mentioned that she had moved in with a friend and her parents so that he wouldn't worry about her welfare. That he probably would *not* have worried about her was a reality she preferred to ignore.

And yet she could see that the area was not without its own type of singular beauty. There was a bright blue sky washed over with windswept white clouds above the town's gleaming whitewashed buildings, most with lace curtains hanging at the windows and surrounded by neat white picket fences. And there was permeating everything the almost mystical feeling that the mineral gods of the ancient earth were, at this very moment in time, finally willing to release their treasure.

A steam whistle blasted through Amanda's contemplation, causing her to jump and startling a horse that whinnied shrilly nearby. She chuckled to herself, thinking that it too must be new to the town. Beginning her walk south along the street, she made her way around shop goods that were piled outside on the sidewalk. Amanda admired the bins, barrels and crates filled with vegetables, fruits and dry goods and looked forward to having the time for leisurely shopping.

But her mouth twisted into a distasteful grimace when she realized that crossing this muddy street was going to be a daily trial. The solution, however, was presented by a young boy shouting to a man who was hesitating on the opposite sidewalk.

"Hey mister, here, here!" The boy was a solid brown wash of mud from the waist down and up to his elbows. He stood just off the sidewalk holding two long wooden planks, muddy on one side. The man approached the boy and handed the filthy urchin a coin that the boy slid into a mud-crusted shirt pocket. The boy laid down the first of his two long boards just as a southbound wagon and a northbound pack train left a break in the traffic. As the man approached the end of this plank, the boy laid down the other board and hurriedly waded through the deep mud to retrieve his first board now behind the man so he could put it in front again. It was all done so quickly that the man crossed in only slightly less time than it would have taken if the street had been dry.

Amanda would later learn that these *board boys* earned a good subsistence living and were greatly appreciated. When summer arrived and dust replaced the mud, they would join other boys in the mills, some as young as eight. There they would crawl along the rafters over the machinery, hanging by their legs if necessary to lubricate the machines that never ceased, and gaining for themselves the term *grease monkey*. It was arguably the most dangerous job in town, and more than one boy ended up horribly injured or even dead. Child labor laws were a thing of the next century, but women still objected to this practice. The men, however, ran the mines and they thought it a good practice. It therefore continued.

Amanda sighed and wished she could return to the lovely hotel with its velvet chairs, dark wood floors, crystal chandeliers and white lace curtains. The town's hotels had always sought to illustrate their refinement, proclaiming their superiority in handbills that vaunted such things as "handsomely furnished rooms", "many years' experience in hotel keeping in the mountain towns of California", "spacious bar and reading room", "leading papers of the day", and "best wines, liquors and cigars furnished". Regardless of these claims and the lace curtains adorning windows at the front, the small windows on the long plain sides usually had only roll shades. The interior walls were often simply wooden studs covered in cloth and heavy decorative wallpaper. It was lovely, but it was a lucky light sleeper that was not housed next to a room with a heavy throat breather.

As she looked down the street, Amanda quickly realized that no matter the number of restaurants, markets, newspaper offices, laundries, hotels and other civilized businesses, there was a far greater quantity of saloons. Most blocks housed half a dozen, with a name that made clear it was in a mining town: Comstock, Occidental, Oriental, Gold Brick, Dividend, Bank Exchange, Mammoth, and Rosedale, to name only a very few. They ranged from modest single-door drinking parlors to two-story establishments with double glass doors and verandas. What the interiors might look like, Amanda could only imagine. She had, of course, surreptitiously glanced inside while passing saloons as she grew up. What girl had not?

A short man with a pungent smell bumped into her from behind as he passed, and Amanda watched him continue on without acknowledging her. He walked in a lurching manner while his head swiveled from side to side as he scanned the area, and she wondered if he was looking for a place to collapse, maybe where he wouldn't be stepped on while sleeping off the effects of too many bends of the elbow. She would never know, as he passed around the corner and up King Street, disappearing into the Chinese district.

Only a few steps down the street from the hotel she looked up and saw that she was in front of Wagner's Saloon, the largest of its kind in town. Two overly refreshed businessmen left the saloon and stumbled onto the sidewalk before heading north. Their exit brought to the street the peppy serenade of a tinkling piano, the clinking of glasses, and the raucous laughter and bluster of loud men.

Amanda took advantage of the moment and quickly looked through the double doors of frosted glass that had been propped open. Beyond was a small vestibule with short batwing wooden doors that opened directly into the saloon. It was well lit by large ornate coal oil chandeliers and wall sconces and she could see to the left a long, heavily carved bar of some dark wood with a brass rail running across the length of it near the floor. White towels hung from the edge every few feet, and half a dozen polished brass spittoons sat on the floor within easy spitting distance. The towels were for the convenience of the more fastidious of the patrons who desired to wipe their chins or beards.

The highly polished dark wood of the looming back bar gleamed the length of the matching bar in front of it and reached almost to the ceiling, framing a mirror in the center. It was elaborately carved on the corners and across the top, and had cost John Wagner $500. It was a source of great pride for the bartenders and the regular customers, who enjoyed the welcoming and friendly atmosphere. The walls of the saloon displayed a collection of large paintings, some of reclining female nudes, but others of lakes, mountain views, or proud racing horses.

Here men could spend a *bit*, or twelve and a half cents, to buy a drink or a pint of lager. If a man only had a two-bit piece, which was usual, the drink was fifteen cents with change in the form of a *trade bit* that bore the name of the establishment and was good for one drink; however, it was generally expected that a man would purchase two drinks for his quarter, even if one of them was for someone else.

There was also a bar along the right hand wall although not quite as long as the other one, and with a row of tall stools in front of it. This was the Capital Chop Stand managed by Messrs. Radovich and Gillespie. Here quick meals, mainly steaks and chops, were sold for as little as 25 cents and as much as $2.50. John Wagner lived with his physician wife back of the saloon.

Forgetting herself, Amanda moved past the glass double doors braced open and neared the short wooden batwing doors. From there she took in at a glance the rich interior and the two bars, with dozens of faro tables at the back of the room near the poker tables and a billiard table. It was in this back area that the majority of the patrons congregated. While men lost and won, and lost again, they did so to the tune of an upright piano not far from the closed doors of private rooms.

To Amanda the saloon was a single male beast that moved its parts while roaring, swearing, spitting, and laughing. The beast's smell of tobacco smoke mixed with stale ale and spilled whiskey, over-full spittoons and the acrid sweat of miners fresh from work, hit her in the face like a physical thing.

A tall, immaculately groomed man in a tailored gray suit separated himself from the near end of the bar and strode purposefully toward her. Recalled to the bold inappropriateness of what she was doing, Amanda turned around and fled to the sidewalk. She looked over her shoulder to find the man in the doorway looking at her face, which was now aflame with embarrassment, as though he had never seen a woman before. But there was humor shining from his dark blue eyes, and no hint of condemnation or scorn as she had expected. Nevertheless, she hurried around the large barrels at the end of the sidewalk and crossed King Street.

The man chuckled to himself and stepped out further to observe this young woman who had more curiosity than propriety. Roger Murphy was a popular and highly regarded sport, a gambler who ran his own faro table at Wagner's Saloon, and who was known to keep a *square* bank. Not much was known about him except that he had a sharp wit, spent most of his time at work, kept his dealings with women private, was moderate in his drinking, and was a regular at the monthly Mason's meeting. To the men of Bodie this made him a respected acquaintance if not exactly a friend. Considering that he had to occasionally take their money, this was fine with Roger.

He had of course admired many young women during his twenty-five years, and had known a few of them very well indeed. But this girl wore her innocent curiosity and naivety as obviously as her creamy complexion and her naturally dark lashes that made her eyes look as though they were smudged with charcoal. He liked that she wore no large bonnet topped by masses of silk flowers and bird parts, but had instead opted for a simpler one with a single feather. It highlighted better the mass of dark auburn hair twisted up beneath it, and showed to best advantage high cheekbones and amber eyes that slanted up at the corners in a natural flirtation, of which he was sure she was unaware. With a sigh that only his deepest yearnings could understand, he went back inside where men who favored his table waited for his break to end.

After crossing King Street, Amanda stopped before the windows of the Gilson & Barber Store to collect herself. Never had a man looked at her so boldly, and never had she felt such a rush of heat course through her body. Every detail of the man, obviously a gambler, was imprinted on her mind—the insolent blue eyes, the high forehead overhung with locks of thick black hair, the thin neat moustache, the strong chin, and the broad shoulders beneath his fine wool coat open to show a silver vest over a starched white shirt. This mental picture of him, along with the aromatic memory of his clean Bay Rum scent, was so real he might have been standing next to her.

Loud cheering suddenly erupted to her right from a crowd of people gathered several yards up the slope of King Street. Amanda walked slowly toward the noisy crowd and edged to the front. She peered over the shoulders of men crouched down on one knee and saw in the middle of a circle a small bobcat and a bull terrier staring at one another with barred teeth and frizzed fur. The dog had several bleeding scratches on the side of its face, and the bobcat's fur at the neck was chewed and a chunk was missing.

When Amanda saw money changing hands, she realized that this was a sporting event. She swallowed her ire and pushed blindly back through the crowd, chastising herself for her over-sensitivity as she picked up her skirts and stepped up onto the planked sidewalk. It wasn't that she had never encountered such a thing before, as it was a popular sport in many towns, but she knew what barbarous fate lay in store for the animals involved.

Working her way through the crush of men and women on the sidewalk, several of the men tipped their hats to her with courteous respect and what few older women she passed smiled at her with motherly kindness. After these encounters, she relaxed and felt like laughing at her earlier timidity and near panic.

Although she still found the thought of the animals battling one another repugnant, she realized that what she had seen was probably a good representation of the forces at play around her in Bodie. Amanda reminded herself, not without a sense of a finger shaking itself in her face, not to forget that she was to be living in a town known for its rough way of life. She sternly told herself, "Just take a deep breath and stand the gaff, girl."

Before crossing in front of Kingsley's City Livery Stables, she hesitated. The sidewalk was interrupted by a ramp of wood that sloped up from the street so that wagons and rigs could pass through the wide opening into the dark cool stable. Joseph Kingsley stood in the opening smoking a small cigar, and upon noting Amanda, he tipped his old white hat and smiled.

Joe was a transplant first from his birth place of Massachusetts, and then more recently Bridgeport. His father, known in the early 1860's as *the old man at the bridge*, had run the first Bridgeport hotel that had also been used as the town's courthouse. His son Joe was somewhere in his thirties, tall and broad-shouldered with a long aquiline nose, deep set eyes, large ears, silky hair cut short, and a strong jaw hidden beneath a short square-cut dark beard. Some said he liked well-bred horses because he had in common so many of their finer attributes of appearance, and was just as handsome.

Amanda asked him, "Am I near the Miners' Union Hall?"

"Yes, ma'am. Just keep on going after you cross Green."

"Thank you." Stepping gingerly around several piles of steaming horse droppings on the ramp as Mr. Kingsley retreated inside, she reached the continuation of the sidewalk several inches higher than the ramp.

Looking down at her feet to be sure she didn't lift her skirts too high above her ankles, she heard a woman say, "Be careful, dear. The second board from the edge is loose."

Amanda looked up ready to offer thanks, but was brought up short when she saw the speaker. The woman was a good ten years her senior and yet wore a dress of lemon yellow silk with drapes and flounces across the front, and a neckline that showed mounds of white flesh. A red and yellow paisley shawl hung loosely around her shoulders, and there was more paint on her face than on some of the buildings.

Amanda tried not to pass judgment, but she was nevertheless shocked at being addressed by such a person. She then noted that the woman's eyes were gentle even if they were looking her up and down in a forthright manner. But Amanda was busy with her own evaluation, and her imagination being more highly developed than girls raised in a more cloistered home, she could see how this woman would be popular with men of a certain predisposition.

"You alone, honey?" the woman asked in a raspy voice.

"Yes, ma'am."

The woman laughed lightly, but it didn't match the sudden hard glint in her eyes. At the same time, her mouth showed a willingness to be kind; at least until shown that the recipient was unworthy. It was Amanda's opinion that this woman lived a harsh existence, but even so had not lost her good natured approach to life. The woman asked, "Got kin here?"

"Yes." She felt like she was being questioned by an inappropriately dressed school mistress giving her some kind of strange oral examination.

"Well," the woman drawled, "if you ever need a job, you come look for Lou at the Spanish Dance House on North Main."

"Thank you." She didn't know what else to say, considering that the work involved had not been mentioned. Although truth be told, Amanda thought she had a pretty good idea that it would involve more than dancing. However, she would have been wrong. Some of the girls at the dance houses did nothing more than dance, drink and talk with dozens of lonely miners each night to earn their ticket money. Of course, some of the girls *did* do more—much more.

At the corner of Main and Green she gave a longing glance at the Boone and Wright Mercantile and the large warehouse behind it. Harvey Boone had been a popular man in Bodie ever since he had arrived in the spring of 1878. His father William was a cousin of Daniel Boone, and his mother Sarah Lincoln was the grandaunt of the still much lamented Abraham Lincoln. Mr. Boone's substantial house was on west Green on the south side of the street.

Promising herself time in the Boone and Wright Store's packed interior, she hurried across Green to the front porch of the Bodie House and stopped to catch her breath. To the west behind the hotel was a large red barn with a network of corrals out the back filled with horses and mules, and also belonging to the prosperous Mr. Boone.

Finally reaching the Miners' Union, organized in December of 1877, she stepped through the door onto the bare expanse of a pine springboard floor installed to give bounce to those using the place for dances. But right then she only wanted to get off her aching feet and sighed as she lowered herself into one of the pine chairs lined up along the wall.

The room was long and narrow enough that twenty-five chairs were lined up along each of the side walls, and twelve more with their backs to the raised stage at the far end. Nearby was a table overflowing with newspapers and other periodicals, but Amanda ignored them to observe her surroundings.

Light flooded the room from three windows on either side of the room, their shades rolled to the top. The sheer curtains over the closed but not air-tight windows moved slightly as a rising breeze pushed against the south side of the building. Between the windows on both walls was a large painting darkened by the dusty air and hundreds of cigars, pipes and cigarettes shared daily in the room. The ceiling was narrow bead-board running front to back, while the walls were made of horizontal boards above the dark panels of wainscoting.

The central focus of the room was the small stage that filled the far end. On each side, five narrow steps led up to an angled door between the stage and the back wall where a tiny dressing room was set aside for performers. Against the back of the stage several rolled backgrounds painted on canvas hung from the ceiling so the scene could be changed for a musical, a political speech, or a play. The stage was also used as the pulpit for Sunday morning Catholic services, followed in the afternoon by the Methodist congregation. It was reported that construction crews had been too busy building saloons to have time to build a "gospel mill" as well.

Men with thick mustaches and wearing old suits with watch chains looped across the bottom of their vests congregated around a large desk next to the front door. They watched Amanda with curiosity while smoking big cigars and talking in an undertone. As soon as she could feel the blood returning to her pinched toes, she approached the desk. The man seated behind it, not much older than she was, showed his surprise when she announced that she was John Blake's daughter.

"I didn't know ole John had kin, much less a daughter," he mumbled indistinctly. Looking a bit sheepish, he turned his head and spit out a brown wad into a brass spittoon next to the desk before announcing more clearly, "I'm Hank Webb."

"How do you do? I'm Amanda Blake."

She glanced at a blond young man standing next to Hank and noted his weak chin, thin tubercular physique, and pale eyes focused on the bodice of her suit. She decided not to smile at him, not wanting him to think her forward, or interested.

Instead, she turned to Hank with his fluffy black mustache and black bowler, which he didn't bother to remove, and explained her errand. He handed her a piece of paper upon which he had written "Noonday Mill" along with a small sketched map indicating that she should turn east onto Green.

"Wait for the wagon at the rise of the first hill. John will be coming off his shift that ends at four." The man referred to his pocket watch and added, "That's fifteen minutes from now."

At a little over 8,300 feet above the level of the sea, most people found it took some little time to adjust to Bodie's elevation. Amanda thanked him and followed his instructions, panting for air after the long and hurried walk up Green.

At half past four, an open hay wagon approached pulled by four large draft horses. But instead of hay, the wagon was filled with exhausted men fresh from a long day at the mines. Her father was sitting on the edge of it with his legs dangling almost to the ground, as were a dozen other men. The youngest of these miners were clean-shaven, while the older of the men had mustaches of varying lengths and thicknesses. Only a very few of the men sported beards, and these were the oldest. Amanda wondered if degree of facial hair was a symbol of earned status.

Almost like a uniform, or possibly evidence of what was carried in the local shops, the men were dressed in worn denim or canvas pants without a belt but sometimes suspenders. Their limp shirts were dark in color and their dusty jackets of a dark denim or canvas. Upon each head was a billed cap or narrow-brimmed slouch hat, and all wore boots that looked ready to be replaced but which would be worn until they could no longer be repaired. Every one of the men was covered in a layer of gray dust that they tried to shake off after jumping from the wagon.

The owners of the Noonday would not be with these men. The big mine owners had riding horses or black roll-top rigs pulled by matching teams. They wore wool trousers with white shirts under dark vests and pressed jackets, and their hats were most often Stetsons, with their feet shod in Frye boots that were freshly polished each day.

John Blake was a mere laborer in one of the mines belonging to such men and he doubted that he would ever be anything more. He was not quite forty but looked to be in his fifties, so lined was the skin on his ashen face and so pronounced the stoop to his shoulders. Amanda was surprised at the bags of skin beneath his red-rimmed eyes, the tired droop to his long dark mustache, and what she suspected had become a perpetual look of dejection.

Although this had not been his attitude until of late, it was definitely now his main state of mind. There never seemed to be enough time away from work to fully recover his energy, or to clear his lungs of the dust and chemicals always in the air at the mill where he worked. It was his main job to feed ore beneath the feet of the stamps, and although he wore wax ear plugs the noise was starting to affect his hearing. He was beginning to feel that life was very hard, and not at all what he had hoped it would offer him by moving to Bodie. But the four dollars a day he earned was good pay, and he didn't know what better work he could do elsewhere.

The wagon stopped so John and several of his friends could jump off and continue their journey into town on foot. Thinking he would stop more readily at his name than his paternal title, Amanda called out, "John?"

He didn't bother to look up as he continued to walk down the hill, but after realizing that it was a young woman who had called to him, told her, "Sorry lady. I'm too tired."

She drew herself up and asked, "Father, don't you recognize me?"

John came to a halt and moved his eyes over Amanda's sleek traveling suit before staring into her face with evident surprise. When he still said nothing, and feeling as though pleading her case, Amanda asked, "Weren't you expecting me?"

He swallowed and found his voice. "Well, yes, but not quite so soon. I mean, you're so grown up." He took a step forward and placed a tentative hand on her shoulder. "It's good to see you, girl. Come on home. You can fix us some supper."

Amanda fell into step beside him, telling herself that she refused to be hurt by his less than enthusiastic greeting. They walked down Green Street under the glare of a sky rapidly filling with white fluffy clouds and a breeze that was working itself up into a steady wind.

The surprised stares of men followed them closely as they wondered who this young woman, dressed so smartly, might be. Those who didn't know John, smirked as their imaginations traveled in wanton directions. Those who claimed John as a friend were surprised and flustered, for the woman with him was not only young but obviously of quality. This last the men knew because they were only too familiar with the other kind.

The house to which John brought his daughter, who was suddenly feeling shy and nervous, was on the southwest corner of Mono and Green streets. Amanda realized that she must have passed this narrow street on the way to meet her father, but it was such an unassuming area that she was not surprised that she hadn't noticed it. The street was sandwiched between Wood to the east and Bodie Creek to the west, with room for only a few houses along the west side of its narrow length that ended to the south at Lowe.

There were no architectural details on the house, but merely a tall window on either side of a single slab door beneath the peak of a sharply pitched roof. The house appeared extraordinarily small to Amanda, but once inside she realized that it was longer and wider than it appeared from the front. Two bedrooms were to the left off the small parlor filled by an over-stuffed sofa and two bulky upholstered chairs arranged around a small low table cluttered with newspapers and dirty coffee mugs.

Behind the right half of the parlor was the kitchen furnished with a painted blue dry sink in the middle of a built-in counter along the right wall, and next to an oak four-compartment upright ice box. A floor to ceiling cupboard was built into the far corner and a pierced tin-fronted pie safe was centered on the back wall next to a small window that gave a view of Bodie Creek and the back of the buildings facing Main. A rectangular pine table with four cane-seat chairs sat in front of the wall to the right of the door, and was covered with the evidence of dirty dishes from more than one recent meal.

On the left wall stood a relatively new two-eyed stove that had not been cleaned and blacked for some time. Beyond the stove a narrow door led to a storage room off of which another door led out into the back yard. A shed near the back door was filled with large pieces of wood.

Walking with his daughter back into the kitchen after the short tour, John told her, "You'll probably have to go to the market tomorrow, but for now there's some food in the pie safe and the cupboard. I'm going to take a nap. Call me when supper's ready."

With this said, he started toward the smaller of the two bedrooms. Amanda called out to him that her luggage was still at the Grand Central Hotel. John sighed, nodded his head, and left the house to walk down to Boone's stable where he could borrow a rig.

Amanda stood in the kitchen, somewhat surprised at her father's cool greeting and lack of eagerness to visit with her. Then, rationalizing that he was probably just tired and hungry, she told herself that there was plenty of time for their relationship to develop.

Amanda removed her jacket and rolled up the sleeves of her white waist. It took her well over an hour to bring in wood from the back porch, what little there was that was cut small enough to fit into the stove, and get the fire started. While wondering what was taking her father so long, she soon had combined a mix of limp vegetables and the last of the rice into a soup. There was only half a loaf of stale bread in the pie safe, but since she also found a small chunk of hard cheese and a few eggs along with butter in the ice box and adequate spices in the cupboard, she decided to make cheesy crackers.

After rubbing the dry bread into fine crumbs and grating the cheese, she poured in some melted butter and two beaten eggs, added a pinch of ground mustard and black pepper, and a dash of cayenne. After it had settled for half an hour, she kneaded the mass into a paste, rolled it out very thin, and cut it into small pieces with a sharp knife. She then set them in a hot oven to bake for a quarter of an hour.

Realizing that every dish in the house was in the sink unwashed, she began her next task. Thankful that the water barrel by the back door had recently been filled, she drew out enough to heat on the stove in a large pan so she could wash two bowls and two plates.

John returned just as she had the food ready, the smell of recently consumed lager now added to his already pungent aroma. After dumping his daughter's bags on the far side of the sofa under the front windows, John sniffed the air and headed to the kitchen. At this point the front door burst open and two men dressed in dirty overalls walked in. It was a contest as to who was the most surprised, but Amanda's reaction was tempered with fear and confusion.

John greeted them casually. "Hi, guys. This here is my daughter Amanda. She's come to take care of us."

Amanda looked at her father with raised brows and a sense of alarm. "You expect me to do for these men as well?"

He was obviously puzzled. "Of course. You have to earn your keep, don't ya? And they live here too. Didn't I mention that in my letter?"

"No." She kept her voice level, not wanting him to see her disappointment. She had assumed her life was to be companion to what she had thought of as her poor lonely father, and of course doing the cooking and cleaning. However, instead of objecting to his assumption of her servant status, Amanda simply announced, "Supper is ready. I'll wash two more bowls."

With that said, she went back into the kitchen followed by the men. They sat at the table without talking as they watched this lovely new addition to their lives prepare food for them, fascinated by her dainty yet efficient efforts on their behalf. They could hardly believe their good fortune. Amanda placed a bowl of soup in front of each man and watched with satisfaction as they eagerly spooned it down their throats while reaching out for the crackers.

After several minutes of not one word spoken, Amanda turned to the two strange men and said, "It might be nice to know your names."

The older of the two had a shaggy red beard that matched his hair and large green eyes that lit up when he smiled, which he did often and easily. He smiled now and said, "I'm Matt Wheeler. Nice to meet you."

The other man had no beard or it had not had time to grow, as it was doubtful that its owner had reached his twenty first year. He was tall, with slim long legs, light hair shaggy over his ears, and dark eyes that fixed on Amanda with a hunger that held hope for the fulfillment of thoughts he dared not verbalize. His lips turned up in what was more a smirk than a smile as he announced, "I'm Mike." He made it sound like a revelation that should impress, but in fact made Amanda feel an awkward discomfort.

She divided the rest of the soup between the men, reserving for herself a handful of crackers and a small cup of broth that she sipped as she worked at the sink. She made slow but steady headway on the stack of dishes to the tune of the men's slurps and burps. After finishing their meal, they adjourned without comment to the parlor where they lit pipes and cigars before picking up one of four newspapers. Matt and Mike collapsed into the two chairs, while her father sprawled on the small sofa.

Amanda pursed her lips, curbed her temper and turned away from them. After she dried the dishes and stacked them in the corner cupboard, she swept the linoleum-covered floor. When she walked into the parlor, no one seemed to notice so she asked loudly, "Where am I to sleep?"

Her father looked up at her, clearly not having thought through this communal problem. "Well, I have the small room and they share the other one, so I guess you can sleep on the sofa here."

Amanda said nothing. She pulled her two suitcases into the kitchen unaided and took out the shawl to wrap around her shoulders. The sun had gone down an hour before and it was quite chilly, even with the lingering heat from the stove. After sitting at the kitchen table for half an hour reading a newspaper, she heard the men moving around and went in to find that they had all retired to their rooms. Her father had placed three blankets on the sofa for her.

She looked at the closed door of his room and tried to mask hurt feelings with sarcasm by murmuring, "Good night to you, too."

In front of the stove she removed her white waist, suit skirt, underskirts, the boned summer corset, and lastly her leggings. Leaving on the muslin drawers and camisole, she slipped over her head her flannel nightgown with its high neck and pleated bodice. Donning her robe, she wrapped herself in two blankets and rolled the other one into a pillow. It wasn't the most comfortable she had ever been, but she was tolerably warm and her exhaustion propelled her into a deep sleep that ended only when she heard her father leaving at three o'clock in the morning. He had to be at work at four o'clock for his twelve hour shift, but as he left he put a small stack of coins on the table next to her.

Finding it difficult to return to sleep, her thoughts wandered through impressions of her first day on the eastern side of the Sierra. First, there had been the long and arduous stagecoach trip that had included a robbery, but which she remembered more from the bite of grit whenever she had been so forgetful as to lick her lips. And of course, there had been the filthy and evil smelling privies at the stage stations.

She thought of her arrival in town and Main Street more liquid than solid, the jeers and hoots of enjoyment as people watched two beautiful animals tear each other apart, the unreadable smirk of the handsome blue-eyed gambler, and the less than enthusiastic greeting of her father. It was with this last in her mind that she fell into a tense and restless sleep. She awoke fully when a loud rooster crowed repeatedly nearby at five in the morning.

Since there was nothing in the kitchen that she could use to prepare a breakfast for herself and the two men, Matt and Mike said they would stop at a cafe on their way to work. No one mentioned what she might do for food, but at least before leaving each man gave her two dollars in coin to purchase food for the house.

She fingered the old silver dollars struck back in 1850, the year California had become a state. On one side was a flying eagle and on the other was the figure of Lady Liberty. She thought them almost too pretty to spend. With a derisive laugh she cancelled that thought and looked through the cupboards to see what supplies she did *not* need to purchase. It was a short list.

Amanda then heated water on the stove and washed herself, something she had noticed that the men had not done the night before or that morning. Maybe they had visited a bath house earlier that week on their day off, but remembering their pungent scent, she hoped they would do it again soon. After dressing in a plain black skirt and the gray waist, she ate some crackers and washed them down with the last of the previous evening's cold coffee.

Topping her simple outfit with the white knitted shawl, she sighed and murmured aloud, "Well, if I'm to be a servant, it's time I get started with the job."

Leaving the house, she found there was no lock on the door and wondered at the faith this illustrated. She would soon learn that violence between men did not necessarily equate to petty criminal activity such as housebreaking, which indeed in Bodie was a rare occurrence. It would not be the only strange anomaly to which she would have to adjust.

CHAPTER 2
JUNE, 1880

Shopping for food being the first essential, Amanda remembered seeing the Union Market just south of the Miners' Union Hall and the brick post office. Carrying a straw shopping basket she had found on the service porch, she turned right onto Lowe Street at the end of Mono. She passed the spring that trickled into Bodie Creek, stepped off the narrow footbridge over the creek, and a moment later was on Main.

Seeing the Union Meat Market across the street, she gave a quick look at the window display of dressed fowl and a large pig with an apple in its mouth. As she opened the door and stepped onto the sawdust-covered floor, the cool of the room was a welcome greeting. Looking around, Amanda was amazed at the many halves and quarters of beef hanging from hooks at the back of the store. There were also sausages and chops in glass cases nestled between blocks of ice that had been cut the previous winter and buried in sawdust in the ice house out back.

To her right two large chunks of tree trunk stood on wooden legs and served as carving blocks. Behind the carving blocks, rows of finely honed knives hung from racks, each sharp blade waiting for a strong hand to give it purpose. To her left a long counter held a large cash register, its ornate brass housing kept highly polished and gleaming in the sunlight each time the door opened.

A tall thin man in a white apron with a thick black mustache stood behind the counter near the front of the store. He was laughing at something a man in a rumpled suit was telling him, the lines radiating from the outside corners of his eyes deepening with mirth. The man to whom he was talking had a long beard, a broad chest and thick arms.

"Thanks for bringing me the livers, Charley," the aproned man said.

"No problem. I was coming down to the post office anyway. You coming to the slaughter house later?"

"Yeah. See you then." *Big* Charley (as differentiated from *Little* Charley who also worked at the slaughterhouse) pushed open the door with a force that gave the impression he was doing it a favor by leaving it on its hinges.

The butcher smiled and shook his head as he approached Amanda, a practiced but warm smile on his face. "Good morning. Can I help you, ma'am?"

Amanda returned his smile. "I'm new to the town and I need a couple of days' worth of meat for my father and the two men living with us."

"And you'd be?"

"My father's name is John Blake. He's a miner at the Noonday. I'm his daughter, Amanda."

"Well, I'll be." The smile broadened and his mustache fairly quivered. "I know John. We're both Knights of Pythias. I'm William Mercer, one of the butchers here at Mr. Kilgore's market."

"You have a very clean shop."

"You sound surprised," he chuckled. "Miners eat a lot of meat, but we sell to the restaurants too."

"I imagine with all the people here that that amounts to a large quantity indeed."

"We figure last year 200 beef cattle and 900 sheep were processed at our slaughter house, which is one of two here. And of course we processed hundreds of hogs and chickens. The man that was here is Charley Cohl who works at the slaughter house. You can find the corrals, pens and cauldrons north of town." Then, possibly realizing that he was talking to a young lady who might not find bovine and hog slaughter as fascinating a subject as he did, he cleared his throat and asked, "What did you have in mind to purchase? I've got dressed beef at ten cents a pound and I have fresh mountain trout from Lake Lundy at $1.50 a dozen or two bits a pound if you only want a couple."

Because the shops were two blocks from the house and she would have to carry whatever she purchased, Amanda only obtained two pounds of stew meat, some pork sausages, and a half pound slab of bacon. Having thus spent a dollar of the money the men had given her, and needing many other things, she carried her wrapped meat purchases two doors south to Ben Eggleston's market.

Ben was a clean-shaven man near her father's age, but unlike John, he was a walking advertisement for a healthy lifestyle full of hard work and only a minimum of time spent in a saloon. The market was narrow but deep, long shelves lining the walls fronted by dark wood counters, beneath which were built-in glass-fronted bins of dry goods such as beans and dried pasta, and even some candy. Down the middle of the room were barrels of flour, corn meal and buckwheat flour, crackers and other goods, as well as crates of turnips, melons, bags of potatoes, and pumpkins.

Behind the cash register a shelf was filled with small jars and boxes of spices, along with cream of tartar which was used as a leavening agent.

She looked at the colorful labels on the cans stacked on long shelves. Canned vegetables only recently had become available in the variety before her, and were pricey. As long as fresh was available, most cooks preferred the fresh.

Since 1850, canning had become known to the general population, but it was the availability of condensed milk during the Civil War that had brought it into popular use. With the advent of the Mason jar in 1859, with its porcelain-lined lid, housewives in Bodie had taken advantage of the abundance of fruits and vegetables in the markets. Those few who could afford a pressure cooker, available since 1874, and were skilled at sealing jars safely, got together with their friends to help them fill their shelves before winter set in.

Amanda soon had the counter stacked with corn meal, oatmeal, potatoes, cheese, beans, a cabbage, dried pears, crushed sugar, green coffee beans, canned milk, and tea. At the last moment she grabbed up a piece of honey comb shipped in from the Big Meadows area of Bridgeport, and a dozen eggs fresh from Bodie chickens brought in by their owners in trade for needed items. She eyed a gallon of coal oil for the lamps, but decided that would be much too heavy.

Supplies for the town arrived from two main directions. One was via Carson City after arriving there by train from San Francisco and Reno, and then on by wagon south through Aurora. The other was by wagon from Sacramento over the Placerville Road and south to Bridgeport before heading to Bodie. Occasionally the ranchers around Mono Lake to the south brought in gull eggs and produce, but such delicacies couldn't be counted on.

Mr. Eggleston told her, "I had strawberries for 24 cents a box in April, but I'm out now. Check back often, as I get different fruit in all the time and it gets bought up quick. I'll have apricots and pears soon."

When Amanda's items were added up, she realized that she was $1.69 over the $6.00 the men had given her. "Oh, dear, I'll have to put some of it back," she told Mr. Eggleston, looking at her items. "Father and the other two men only gave me $6.00 and I spent a dollar of that at the meat market. I guess one of the men can come and pick this all up. Then they can get the coal oil at the same time." Looking up at Mr. Eggleston, she asked, "Can you hold everything for them?"

"Oh, don't worry about that or needing to put anything aside," he reassured her with a smile. "You just bring me the rest of the money tomorrow or the next day. I can box up all of this, along with your meat purchases, and have my boy drop it off at your house early this afternoon. You'll have it in time to make supper. Will that be okay?"

"Oh, you're so good," she gushed gratefully, once again impressed at the kindness of the men in Bodie. "Uh, can I add the coal oil now and a firkin of butter?" Nearby were several containers of fresh "dashed" sweet butter made locally, but it was much more expensive than the firkins of butter shipped by rail. Consequently, Amanda picked up a small crock of the good butter to serve with hot bread, while the other, a little bitter and very salty, would be used for cooking.

"You get whatever you need."

"Thank you so much. I'm afraid my father has allowed supplies to get very low at the house."

"Think nothing of it, miss." He tried not to put too much of a questioning emphasis on the *miss*, but when she didn't correct him, he knew that he had been correct in his assumption. "And if you return the firkin, I'll give you two bits off your purchase of the next one."

While she was walking down the length of the room toward the door, thinking Mr. Eggleston a clever businessman, that gentleman was watching the slight sway of her hips. He smiled as he recalled the arch of her fine brows over sparkling amber eyes that had looked into his with such warm appreciation. It made generosity worth the cost. Then the all too familiar picture of Mrs. Eggleston's pursed lips came to mind and he quickly turned to the task of stacking cans onto his shelves.

It was well that he did, as his lady love came in from the back where she had been tidying the cellar. Its thick walls and floor of rock was dug down into the ground and allowed them to keep cool the more fragile and therefore valuable merchandise. She immediately noted the large number of items on the counter awaiting delivery and looked at her husband with approval. Seeing this, Mr. Eggleston smiled back at her, the picture of an innocent man interested only in commerce.

Amanda stopped at the post office to mail a quick note to a friend in Placerville. The building was two square stories of red brick, with a single tall window on either side of the door that was arched over with a fan of vertical bricks and three smaller arched windows above that. Inside there was a grilled window set aside just for ladies, and Amanda took her place behind the short line of women who wore a mix of calico, muslin, light wool, and silk. Their bonnets were simple, with some of the poorest of the ladies sporting only ribbons in their hair, as no woman would have thought of going into town without something added to her hair. Short capes or shawls were loosely thrown over shoulders, more a nod to propriety than for warmth.

Finally it was Amanda's turn. She waited for postmaster George Putnam, standing in while his clerk ran errands for him, to turn from a large oak sorting rack and greet her with a smile. After introducing herself, she handed him her letter and coinage. As she turned to leave, he told her to let him know if there was anything he could do to help her settle into the town. Somewhat overcome by the generosity of spirit she had experienced so far that morning, she hesitantly thanked him and walked out into the glaring sunshine. She thus missed seeing the astute looks of the women still in line who watched the postmaster's eyes follow her through the door.

Feeling her stomach rumble, Amanda eyed the Excelsior Restaurant across the street, but saw that it was crowded with miners and no women. As she continued north along Main, the heels of her boots resounded with tiny hollow raps on the wooden planks that when added to the steady flow of humanity walking with her, created a staccato of dull thunder. But the rattle of passing wagons, and the shouts of the teamsters as they encouraged their teams in colorful language, easily drowned out any such subtle sound.

Whispered conversations were seldom possible in town and most greetings were exchanged loudly and briefly before passing on or moving indoors. With the dozens of saloons in town, men had no problem finding a retreat nearby; women found a shop, a restaurant or a bakery.

Amanda enjoyed looking through the shop windows while feeling the sun on her back, at least when the window was clean enough to see through. Boone and Wright's General Merchandise on the corner of Main and Green displayed interesting things on the counters and tall shelves. One could purchase miner's tools, women's dress forms and fabric (as only men's outer clothing could be purchased ready to wear), boots and shoes, buckets and brushes, heavy crocks, fancy stationery, digestive pills, and more that she could not see from the sidewalk.

On she walked; past the Champion Hotel, Mr. Stewart's drug store, Kingsley's Stables, several saloons and chop houses, Mr. Weiler's cigar shop, and a newspaper office. Looking at the town with a new appreciation, she tried to imagine the kind of men who came to such a desolate place, and thought they must be at the end of their rope. What she was too inexperienced of the world to realize was that Bodie was a place for men with dreams yet to be fulfilled, of hopes not yet squelched, and undying anticipation of better times to come.

Down these streets every day passed men who had been witness to the brutality of the Civil War, ranchers who had wrestled their herds from the wild, farmers who had busted sod with the reins of the plow horse around their neck in hundred degree heat, Indian fighters from the plains, border ruffians, and old men who had been young and strong during the gold rush. All these men had already tested their spirit, their muscle and their nerve; and therefore they had no doubt that they could conquer a mere mining camp. Bodie would not intimidate them. It gave them excitement and a final chance to show the world what they were made of.

A burst of deep laughter drew her attention to the corner of Union Street and Main where a small group of Piutes on the edge of the sidewalk were playing games with stones, flat sticks painted red on one side, and pieces of animal bone worn smooth with years of handling. She was surprised and curious about the number of Piutes in the town, and noticed that some townsmen greeted the Indians by name as they passed and were greeted in return by name. Other townsmen received an abruptly turned back.

The relationship between the Indians and the Anglos (a classification used to mean anyone not Indian or Hispanic, and sometimes even including the latter), was complicated in the extreme. Few men ever knew what they had done so that one week they seemed to be in favor with a particular tribal member, and the next week would find themselves shunned.

Several blocks further north, and with the help of two plank boys, Amanda crossed to the east side of the street to the Delmonico Restaurant, advertised as a French Rotisserie, where she enjoyed a nice dinner for only fifty cents. She was loathe to leave the refined interior of the restaurant and extended her meal to the extreme of what she thought polite. As she walked slowly back to the cramped house that was now to be her home, without being in the least homey, she began to list in her mind the number of chores that lay before her.

Soon after she arrived home, Mr. Eggleston's delivery wagon pulled up. It was driven by a boy not much older than twelve, and after he carried her basket and the wooden boxes to the kitchen table, she handed him a nickel.

After taking an inventory to be sure nothing had been left out, she put the food into the cupboard and the ice box lined with tin. Opening the small door beneath the ice compartment, she emptied the catch pan of water from the melting ice block. With the candles and coal oil stored on the service porch shelves, Amanda turned her thoughts to the need for wood. If she was going to cook supper that night, she needed a good sized pile of wood next to the stove.

Approaching the small shed that showed an inch of light between the planked sides, she carefully opened the squeaky door on its loose hinges. A frustrated sigh escaped her. The logs were not split, but were still in large chunks. She slipped a dark blue pinafore apron around her neck and maneuvered one of the large pieces of tree out onto the ground. Picking up the heavy axe from just inside the shed, she ineffectually hacked away at the log.

Aware of several men walking past who must have seen her, she gritted her teeth when none of them offered to help. A frustrated voice at the back of her mind urged her to call out to them something sharp and sarcastic. That she did not actually do this she attributed to the fact that she could think of nothing so clever that it would overcome her deeply instilled sense of proper feminine decorum.

Venting her irritation by mumbling words better suited to the freighters on Main, Amanda once again hefted the axe and chipped off a few more splinters of wood. When she came down too hard and the axe became stuck in a cut, she decided to give her aching back and sore wrists a break. Leaning against the house, she rolled up the sleeves of her white waist and dabbed at the sweat on her forehead with the edge of her apron.

"Pardon, mademoiselle? Can I be of service?"

Startled by the gently spoken words uttered in an accent reminiscent of France, Amanda looked up to see a man in denim pants, red shirt, fine leather jacket and broad-brimmed felt hat standing nearby. Her eyes swept over him in a quick assessment. He was of medium height, but with a stance that proclaimed he felt taller, with clean shaven skin darkened by the sun, dark eyes flashing bold insolence, and thick curly brown hair.

"I'm sorry if I frightened you." He smiled in a most charming manner while keeping a respectable distance from her. Amanda realized she must have been deep in thought, for he had ridden up and tied his horse to the iron ring hanging from a low post at the corner of the house without her even hearing him.

"I was just startled." She smiled and told him, "I'll recover."

He chuckled in response and asked, "Do you need assistance?"

"Are you offering to help me chop wood? Because I would be very happy to pay you. Say about two bits?"

"Ah, the price of two drinks." He stepped forward and removed his jacket, placing it carefully on the step of the shed with his hat on top. As he placed his hand on the axe handle, he told her, "Instead of money, possibly you can get me a large glass of water."

"Of course." She rushed into the kitchen and as she added a slice of lemon to cover the slightly off taste of the water, she heard the crash of the axe.

By the time she returned, the man had divided three of the largest logs into short split pieces that she could easily get into the stove. As she handed him the water, she took a moment to note his carefully groomed appearance even after this warm work. The long brown hair was still neatly combed and the line of his jaw was not even flushed.

He was not what one would call handsome, but he definitely had an appeal that was difficult to define. There was about his bearing an assumption of his charms that might have been nettlesome. But he applied these charms with such a light touch that it made naïve young women feel flattered and older women remember fondly their halcyon days of courtship. Young men seemed impressed with his manner and were disposed to disregard their suspicions of him, which allowed them to throw their money into his various schemes. The older men could not overcome their undefined suspicions of such a "smooth talker" and mostly steered clear of him.

Looking at him square in the face as he handed her the empty glass, she realized it was not so much the piercing eyes that caught her attention and made her pulses race, but rather the sparkle in those eyes that spoke of an acceptance of his control over the world around him, and maybe a rakish disregard for consequences. To Amanda, his smile hinted at things she didn't yet understand but that challenged her to discover.

There had been boys in Placerville who had presented themselves as men, but their immaturity had always showed in their actions. She wondered if this was what it was like to be the focus of *a man of the world*, although she wasn't sure exactly what that phrase meant. But she knew instinctively that this man had tasted sensual mysteries about which she could barely imagine. She found it somewhat disconcerting, but not at all unpleasant.

"I can't tell you how much I appreciate this," she told him after he had piled up a large stack of cut wood.

"My pleasure, Miss...?"

"Amanda Blake."

"You are related to John?"

"I'm his daughter. I've come to stay with him."

She watched his brows rise. "You are living with three men and you are the one chopping wood?"

She smiled. "No, sir. You are chopping the wood."

He laughed at her quick response, showing white teeth that had obviously not bitten regularly into tobacco. "You must insist that the men chop the wood from now on. If you do not insist, they will take advantage of you."

She nodded, acknowledging the wisdom of his words. "I feel fortunate that they gave me money for groceries when I asked them for it."

"But do you not see? That is the point. You asked them for it. You must stand up to them and demand they do this, for it is a man's work after all."

"You're right, of course, Mr..."

"I am Joseph DeRoche. I own the Booker Flat Brickyard south of town. You have perhaps seen my large brick house on the west side of Fuller Street?"

"I haven't had much time to explore the town yet. I've only been here two days."

"In time I hope to be able to show it to you." He reached for his jacket. "But for now, I must return to my own work."

He mounted a well-groomed brown horse, tipped his hat to Amanda, and rode south down Mono Street toward Lowe. She watched him for a moment before returning to the house with an armload of wood.

Soon she had a fire flaming in the stove and was at the sink peeling carrots. While she did this, she thought about the living arrangements there at the house and the discomfort of another night on the old lumpy sofa. With a sudden resolve, and remembering what Mr. DeRoche had just said, she went into her father's room.

At the end of an hour, she had moved his things into the room with the other two men and had changed the linens on his bed. She then put her luggage in what she now considered her room, hanging her robe, coat and suit jacket on the hooks nailed to the wall. To accommodate her father, she arranged the sofa cushions on the floor of the men's room in a corner and stacked three blankets on them for his use, muttering to herself, "See how you like it."

That afternoon when her father came home he immediately noted the change. "Hey! What have you done?"

Relieved that he was more puzzled than angry, she told him, "I've made this house a decent place for three men to share with an unmarried woman."

Somewhat taken aback, John thought a moment before saying, "Oh. I guess I should have realized that. Sorry."

"I'm afraid you'll have to get another bed. Is there some place in town I can visit tomorrow and have one delivered here?"

"I'll do that tonight myself when I go into town. There's a Knights of Pythias meeting at the Union Hall. Is dinner almost ready? I'm starved."

"Almost. Why don't you sit at the table and visit with me until then?"

"Okay, I can do that." It didn't seem to be his preference, but Amanda didn't care. He took out a large handkerchief and blew his nose, ran his fingers through his hair and pulled out a chair on the far side of the table. When Amanda took a bottle of beer from the ice box and put it in front of him, John smiled up at her and suddenly relaxed. He reminded himself to have Mike bring another block of ice home from the ice house in town, as the block in the ice box was going to be melted in a couple of days.

John watched his daughter as she worked in the kitchen, glad that she wasn't an annoying chatty type like her mother had been. Amanda walked to the stove and put a small scoop of lard into a hot skillet and when it sizzled she laid in two thick chops. As the sound and smell of the frying meat filled the kitchen, she sprinkled them with salt and pepper before opening the oven and removing the bread. John watched her mash the potatoes with a wire masher in a heavy crockery bowl, add a generous scoop of butter and a slosh of cream from a glass bottle, and whip it fluffy.

He smiled to himself, suddenly aware that he had not spoken for some minutes while he enjoyed the comfortingly domestic scene before him. Feeling that she probably expected something more than his stony silence, he sought a conversational gambit. "It's getting hotter in the mines. It's the worst part of summer."

Amanda asked, "How long have you worked at the Noonday?"

"About a year. Before that I worked at the Standard and lived in a boarding house near the mill. The Noonday was developed in '78 and follows a rich ledge. Not as rich as the Standard, but close. We used other mills until Christmas Day of last year when the Noonday and North Noonday Mill opened. It's the fifth and largest stamp mill in the district. Thirty stamps!" His smile broadened. "Now that was a real shindig, the day it opened. The stamps were so loud that we couldn't hear each other, so we just drank." He laughed heartedly at the memory.

Wondering how she could compete with shindigs and drinking, she asked, "How large is a stamp?"

"Very big and very heavy," he said with dramatic emphasis. "About seven hundred pounds each, and five together to form a battery that falls down to crush the ore. Then we have 24 circular amalgamating pans and 12 settlers to extract the gold and silver."

"Do you like working at the Noonday?"

He shrugged. "I like eating regular and having a roof over my head." He said it without intentional humor, although it made Amanda laugh. John noticed and thought that maybe having someone around who found him interesting wasn't so bad. He was surprised to realize that he had been lonelier these past years than he had thought. The Bonanza Street gals helped, but it wasn't the same as having family around. And Amanda could cook.

"Of course," he continued, "it's dangerous work in the mines. I've lost a few friends to accidents. Another friend who worked at the Blackhawk Mine, John Peters, got drunk one night and on his way home he fell down a 110-foot shaft. He didn't have one broken bone, probably because he had been so drunk." John shook his head in wonder. "Of course, the place is nothing now like it was back in the boom years. When I got here in late '77 the Standard Company had just got its twenty-stamp mill up and running and there were just about a hundred people here. Then William Lent of the Standard bought the Bodie mine, adding it to the Standard Consolidated Company and when word of its wealth got around, people flocked here. Then we got our first newspaper. The Bodie Standard News came out weekly and we felt like a real town then. It proclaimed that our Standard was the richest gold mine in the world and of course that meant even more people began to arrive."

"With all those people arriving, building must have been at an incredible rate."

"Oh, Christ, yes." John grinned and nodded. "But in the middle of February of '78 we had our first fire at Sam Chung's lodging house on King Street. A defective stovepipe. The only way the fire was contained was by tearing down two or three buildings between the fire and Gilson and Barber's store on Main. There were about fifteen-hundred people here by then and more arriving every day, so the buildings were rebuilt. By that time we also had seventeen saloons, several stores, half a dozen restaurants, four lodging houses and all the rest of what a town needs. We even had doctors and lawyers who set up for business. After that the town began to grow so fast that by the end of last year the population had increased to around eight thousand."

"I noticed when in town that there's also a telegraph office."

"Yeah." He picked up his knife and fork and did some damage to the chop Amanda had put in front of him. Swallowing happily, he said, "The first telegram was sent to Genoa in Nevada back in early May of '78. But if you want evidence of civilization, we have our own baseball club. The Bodie team and the Red Cloud team. The diamond is out by the race track below the willow grove southeast of town."

After a few minutes of silence, she said, "This is a nice house." Actually, she was thinking that it could be with a few more lamps, better curtains and some newer rugs on the floor.

"I haven't been here long," John told her. "I used to live at Josiah Brown's near the Noonday south of town."

"At his home?"

He laughed. "No. At Brown's Hotel and Restaurant. When Matt agreed to go in half with me I decided I could just afford the house. When Mike said he'd rent from us if we bought it, that settled it."

"Can I ask how much it cost?"

"Sure. It was $300. We got the furniture free." He smiled somewhat sheepishly.

"Really? How's that?"

He took a moment to fill his mouth with potato and then swallowed before explaining, "The day before we moved in a neighbor took himself off unexpectedly. His wife decided to move away then, and the man who owns the brick yard brought their furniture over here." He looked her in the eyes and declared somewhat defiantly, "It wasn't doing anyone any good in an empty house. And the new owners could buy better stuff."

Ignoring the scruples of what he was justifying, Amanda started to tell him that she had met this brick yard owner, but changed her mind without knowing why. She carried the empty plates to the sink as she asked, "Why would he do that?"

John smirked. "He wanted something from me, of course."

She turned back to him, a frown between her eyes. "What was that?"

"My vote at an up-coming Miners' Union meeting."

Amanda frowned. "You said the neighbor left and *then* his wife moved. That sounds odd."

"Well, actually I said he *left unexpectedly*. That means he was killed."

"Oh. An accident?"

"No. He got into an argument in a saloon while drunk. The other guy was drunk too, only not as far gone as ole Jim. The other guy also had better aim."

"Does that happen often here?"

"More often than makes most of us comfortable. But you needn't worry. That kind of thing only happens at the north end of town. There's even been talk of a 601 Committee being formed if the law doesn't step up."

"What's a 601 Committee?"

"It's the code name for a vigilance committee."

"What does 601 stand for?"

"Six feet down, no trial, and one rope."

She stared at him in surprise. "You mean mob rule? Hanging people?"

"Hanging indicates a judge's ruling. A lynching means the people decide." When he saw her look of surprise, he added, "It's not really as lawless as it sounds. The men involved stand for law and order when the local law isn't doing its job. And there's usually a warning given. The one targeted either stops what he's doing if it's something not too serious, or gets out of town. The alternative if they get caught again is getting whipped, branded on the face, or hanged." He showed his impatience. "It's not like you've never heard about this kind of thing before. It wasn't that long ago that Placerville was called Hangtown for a reason."

"Yes, of course, but I always think of such things as before my time."

"Hell, no." John stood up and stretched. "There'll probably be some form of it around way after we're gone too. But it's only idle talk here."

He took up his beer bottle, drained it in a single swallow, and put it down with a thud. He then announced that he was going into town to have a drink with friends before his meeting.

Not long after John left, the other two men returned home. When Matt went into the bedroom, he immediately noted that the usually dry water pitcher was filled with water and sitting in its matching bowl. There was also a bar of soap and two towels on the small table next to it. Matt took the hint and availed himself of the water, then called to Mike. Both men showed up at the table cleaner than previously and even with their hair combed. Amanda said nothing, not wanting to embarrass them, but she found it difficult to hide a smile.

After they had consumed the chops, all but one slice of the bread from the loaf, and almost all of the coffee, Mike asked, "What are we having for breakfast?"

Amanda, tired from the efforts of the day and having just cooked a large meal, turned and glared at him. Summoning her courage, she said, "The wood is out back and the axe by the door. If you want a cooked breakfast you need to cut the wood small enough that I can get it in the stove."

Mike puffed up and started to object, but changed his mind when Matt nudged him and jerked his head toward the back door. Amanda had seen Matt act this senior role before and was once again surprised how easily Mike gave in to him.

The next day, June 4, she got up at two-thirty in the morning to make her father a cold breakfast of bread, butter, and cheese. Before heading to the mine, he would take his lunch bucket to the nearby Bodie House that offered miners the service of packing them a two-bit lunch. The cost of this was supplemented by the mine owners in an effort to get more work and fewer accidents out of well-nourished laborers.

With dawn only a vague glow beyond Bodie Bluff, and with Mike and Matt still sleeping, Amanda went back to bed and dozed fitfully until she heard the neighbor's rooster crow.

Dressing quickly, she decided to fix a nice breakfast for Matt and Mike in an effort to get to know them better. By the time they arrived at the table, she had ready for them fried bacon and thick slices of bread dipped in egg, fried and slathered in jam. They pulled out a chair, swung a leg over the back and plopped onto them at the same time they reached for their forks. They immediately began eating with a gusto that should have been gratifying to Amanda, but instead only served to irritate her.

After pouring their coffee, she stood before them with hands on hips. "Two things," she announced. "One, when you come to the table it would be nice to hear 'good morning'. Two, if you want to continue eating as well as you did last night and this morning, you'll have to give me more money for groceries."

They blinked at her for a moment before Matt cleared his throat. "Sorry. Good morning."

Mike ducked his head, swallowed, and said, "Good grub."

Amanda nodded and began cleaning the kitchen. The men didn't say anything else, but before leaving each left a stack of coins next to his plate. Paper money had stabilized somewhat since the war, but it was still easily counterfeited so it was not much trusted, especially in the West. Although its use was becoming more common in eastern cities, in Bodie the use of coin was still the standard.

The first thing Amanda did that Friday morning after dressing was to go out to the privy, not simply to use it but to clean it. She dumped in a considerable amount of lye from a bag in the corner of the wood shed, swept the floor, and put a clean stack of torn newspapers next to the hole in the wooden bench. Sheets of what was called *therapeutic paper* had been invented the year before in the east, and the Scott brothers had recently improved on the idea by putting tissue paper on a roll that they called Scott Tissue, but its sale had not yet found its way to Bodie.

With that odious chore completed, she took a mop, a coarse brush and a bucket from the back porch and scrubbed the floors throughout the house. While they dried, she sat at the table rubbing her sore knees while sipping a cup of tea and reading the previous day's newspapers.

One of the papers she had kept out to read was the May 29 *Bridgeport Union*. In it was an article regarding the Chinese tradition of binding the feet of women in order that they might have the enviable status of tiny feet, regardless of the intense pain it caused them. Amanda had noticed that some of the women she had seen on King Street had these tiny bound feet, while others did not.

The article explained this as those from provinces with a more nomadic habit not binding the feet of their women. However, the article said "of the women attending the missionary schools in Swatow about 60 per cent have their feet bound. The binding does not take place until the child has learned to walk. ...the desire to have small feet is so intense that girls will slyly tighten their own bandages in spite of the pain."

Amanda shuddered and shook her head, passed harsh judgment on a little understood culture, and moved on to other articles in the paper. This perusal of the paper was cut short by the raucous clanging of fire bells coming from the north end of town. Grabbing her light shawl, she rushed outside and looked down Green to Main where hoards of people were hurrying north. But she smelled no smoke and saw none rising into the air.

Wanting to avoid the bulk of the rushing crowd, Amanda hurried north down Mono toward the big wooden bulk of the Standard Mill. She stopped to look at a handsome but narrow two-story house across from her. It was the most closed up, yet occupied, house in town and although attractive, it also gave her an odd sense of foreboding. Amanda would soon learn that it belonged to the Wilsons, a childless couple in their early forties. He was a miner, and she took in mending and light sewing.

Cherry Wilson was a kind but somewhat forthright lady who never hesitated to state how much she wished they could move back to San Francisco. She hated the dirt of Bodie more than anything else, whether the dust of the short hot summers or the mud of all other months. That she had ended up in such a place as Bodie was more a bewilderment to her than something she resented. She dusted her tiny parlor and kitchen downstairs and two bedrooms upstairs twice a day, and was every day unsatisfied with the results.

On this morning, Amanda's attention was drawn to the Wilson home's narrow attic window just under the sharp peak of the roof. The curtains over the window were being held back by a small person who upon closer inspection Amanda realized was a child. Her long white nightgown merged with the white curtains, leaving only a pale face framed by long black hair hanging down over her chest to her waist. Hearing the crowd growing louder, Amanda glanced down the street toward the noise. When she returned her gaze to the window it showed only the curtains now closed over the glass. Puzzling over this, and wondering if she had actually seen a child at all, she hurried on her way.

When she reached the end of the street, the sun was glinting off the Standard's tailing ponds with a brilliant sparkle that hurt her eyes. This waste water, mixed with finely crushed ore and mercury, had been pumped out of the mill and had joined the other runoff pumped from the shafts. Later on it would be further processed and would garner small additional profits. Leaving Mono, Amanda turned left onto Mill Street, which created a small triangle of buildings with Main and Standard Avenue, and at Main she turned right and merged with the flow of the crowd.

Someone in the distance yelled, "The son of a bitch has gone too far this time!" There was a roar of agreement from the gathering crowd.

As Amanda drew closer to Standard Avenue, she could see that there was now a fence across the width of the short County road that had been open for public use for the last fifteen years. The fence might have garnered only laughter and a few jeers, but there was also a small building newly erected right in the middle of the street.

The crowd that had gathered was a mix of those laughing and those swearing, but all were in a state of indignation. Everyone soon realized that the perpetrator of this fiasco was Dr. Blackwood, a strange and unpredictable man that few of the good women would allow to touch them. Harvey Boone quickly gathered together those men whom he deemed key decision makers in the town, along with those few others who usually went along with the leaders. They all retired to the Boone store.

There they discussed this latest outrage by the doctor, a man of dubious moral turpitude and frequent outrageous behavior. The group nominated T. A. Stevens chairman of their committee, because of course every committee to be legitimate had to have someone in charge. Then J. W. Wright, Mr. Boone's business partner, was appointed as secretary because his handwriting was easy to read and every meeting, of which there were many every week, had to have notes taken of the proceedings.

Harvey Boone, posing as the voice of reason, declared, "Of course, we don't know when or if the law is going to step in and make the bastard remove the obstruction, but it could be any time."

"We don't want to wait as long as that might take," Chairman Stevens stated. Everyone made noises of agreement.

Harvey nodded. "But we should at least give him a chance to desist before taking more drastic measures."

So they appointed James McVarish to return to the site of the problem and give the doctor ten minutes to begin his removal of the building. When Dr. Blackwood simply stared at McVarish without saying a word, much less promising to do as he was directed, McVarish returned to the committee to report.

The group, patience gone and anger now their prevalent mood, passed a motion that the building in question should be removed immediately. The sound of the "yea" vote was barely uttered before the men rushed to the site and began tearing down the building with the help of other appointed men from the crowd. While they did this, the fence was brought down by a jubilant crowd of people who wanted to show their opinion of the doctor's presumptuousness. They underscored this by taking away the fence posts for their own use. Dr. Blackwood stood by waving his arms while demanding that everyone stop, but the cheers and jeers of the crowd drowned him out.

After the lumber had been thrown into a cart provided by the Hook and Ladder Company, it was hauled off to the tune of three cheers given by the whole of the crowd. Dr. Blackwood stomped all the way to his office in the nearby Mono House while various rude comments were yelled at his retreating back.

As the crowd dispersed, Amanda was jostled backward and almost fell into the man behind her. Turning around to offer an apology, she recognized the Frenchman who had chopped her wood, his hat pulled low on his forehead to avoid the glare of the sun.

He smiled and said, "No need to apologize, mademoiselle. I enjoyed it." Amanda smiled and felt her face grow hot. An insouciant mirth twinkled in Joseph's eyes as he told her, "I am happy to see you once again."

She looked around at the scene while charging herself to say something intelligent. "It looks like the excitement is concluded here. I have to get some shopping done and return home to do laundry."

"Oh, no," he exclaimed. He boldly took her hands in his and said, "Hands as lovely as yours should never do laundry, especially here where there are so many Chinamen to do it for you. The celestials are very good at it and very cheap."

Thinking of the money in her pocket left her by the men that morning, she decided that maybe she could indeed use some of it for laundry and just purchase fewer groceries.

"May I have the honor of escorting you to luncheon?" he asked.

Thinking of the bite of cold bread she had eaten that morning, she accepted eagerly. He led her to the Can-Can Restaurant, a popular gathering place run by George Callahan at number 69 Main Street and therefore only a block north of where they stood. It flitted through her mind that the restaurant was only a few doors past Wagner's Saloon, but she shook off that unexpected thought and hurried to keep up with Joseph.

The Can-Can not only had a large dining hall, but also ten private rooms where men could transact business, or men and their fancy women could meet away from prying eyes while dining. For families with children there were two rooms to accommodate them. One reason for the café's popularity among men was that the rear yard, which held crates and pens of future entrées, extended into the alley separating Main from Bonanza Street.

As they entered, Amanda looked around at the large restaurant's main dining room. Wooden chairs encircled a dozen tables covered in white cloths near a large round heating stove with a black pipe stretching up through the roof. Although it was unlit now, it had been cleaned and was full of wood.

Gesturing toward it, Amanda commented, "It's summer. Why does it look so ready for use?"

"It's not that uncommon for us to have snow in June. In fact, we can have snow any month of the year."

"Even in July and August?"

"Oh, yes." He smiled and leaned back in his chair. "That writer who used to work at the Virginia City *Enterprise* once said a Bodie summer is just the ending of one winter and the beginning of another, or something like that." He frowned a moment. "What was his name now? Oh, yes, Samuel Clemens. He calls himself Mark Twain now."

As they moved through the room to a table by one of the large front windows, Joseph introduced Amanda to several men. Two of them were well-dressed enterprising looking gentlemen in their early twenties, Iver Boysen and Frank Struckman.

"They own a photographic studio," Joseph informed her. "It's just north of the Delmonico Restaurant across the street."

The two men murmured a greeting, one of them smiling in a stilted but benign manner, but the other glaring at him before briefly nodding at Amanda.

Joseph commented, less for Amanda's benefit than for that of the men, "They're in competition with J. C. Kemp, a friend of mine. He just turned twenty-seven and his photographic studio on the upper floor of the Occidental Hotel is flourishing. Unfortunately, not all can be so successful."

When the two men said nothing, simply glaring at Joseph, he took Amanda by the arm and led her to a table. A waitress in a black dress, white apron, and white starched cap approached them to take their order. When she left them, Amanda looked Joseph in the eyes and said, "I'm not stupid or unobservant. Was there a reason you brought up Mr. Kemp in front of those men?"

He responded with a chuckle; a low throaty sound that harbored little mirth. "Oh, that. They too have a photographic studio, and I've had business run-ins with one of them. But Kemp is right now more successful in bringing in business because of his placement at the Occidental Hotel."

"So you were making a mockery of them?"

"Yes, but subtly. I didn't want to anger them."

Thinking to herself that he hadn't been very successful at that, she asked, "Is your business doing well? I've heard talk about some businesses having to close because of the mines slowing down. Some business owners are even leaving town."

"Mostly only the Chinese are leaving." He leaned forward and looked into her eyes with a slight smile as he prepared to add something more.

Whatever he had been about to say, however, was interrupted by the shadow of a tall man blocking the light from the near window. Amanda looked up to see the handsome gambler she had talked to her first day in town.

Pointedly ignoring Joseph, the man addressed Amanda. "Good morning. Allow me to introduce myself. I'm Roger Murphy." Being a gentleman, he of course did not hold out his hand, but when Amanda offered her hand to him, he took it eagerly if briefly. As she told him her name, out of the corner of her eye she saw Joseph frowning.

She turned to Joseph to explain, rushing her words and too flustered to slow them. "I met Mr. Murphy after I got off the stage in the middle of the confusion surrounding Duncan McMillan who was my traveling companion. I had just left the Grand Hotel where I'd left my luggage and was in a hurry to get to the Miners' Union Hall so they could direct me to my father."

Joseph looked up at Roger and leaned back in his chair, a sardonic smile doing little to hide his contempt for the gambler. "Hello, Murphy. Lost any cards up your sleeve lately?"

Roger's jaw tightened as he glanced at Joseph with clear disdain. He turned back to Amanda with a strained smile. "Mr. DeRoche and I are acquainted." Shifting his weight so more of his back was to Joseph, he asked Amanda, "So, Miss Blake, how do you like Bodie?"

"It's a rather overwhelming place," she admitted courteously while trying to avoid Joseph's obvious irritation. "There always seems to be something happening noteworthy for the papers."

"Yes, that's very true." With a quick sideways glance at Joseph, he said, "It's always a good idea to be careful what you do in this town." With the words "or who you do it with" hanging in the air unspoken, Mr. Murphy tipped his hat to Amanda and immediately left the restaurant.

Amanda turned to Joseph. "Do I sense tension between yourself and Mr. Murphy?"

Joseph shrugged, but what was usually a slight accent was suddenly more pronounced. "Mr. Murphy tends to be judgmental about things he does not fully understand. Let us not dwell on that." He flashed a quick smile at her. "Did you settle the matter of who will chop the wood for you?"

"Yes," she laughed. "It was as easy as asking, just as you said." She looked out the window and commented, "It certainly is a nice day."

"Hard to believe that earlier this month we had icicles hanging from the porch eaves."

"Will this coming winter be harsh?"

"Almost certainly. It's just a matter of degree. The last one was exceptionally brutal. I am told that back in '76 they had over three feet of snow fall in one day. It is not unusual for there to be weeks or months of snow piled up to the second story windows, which are then used for entrance. This last winter men had to regularly climb on top of the Miners' Union building to shovel off the snow so the roof would not cave in. And there are often a number of cases of pneumonia that are fatal."

Amanda looked at him with raised brows. "Well, I guess that means I should pile up as much wood as we can afford, and food supplies as well."

"Yes, I'd start canning and drying vegetables, and make fruit leather and jerky. In August you should begin storing bags of potatoes, onions and carrots, too. It's not always possible to get into town for supplies."

Amanda swallowed the last of her coffee and thought to add coffee beans to her shopping list. She listened to Joseph talk about his plans for the brick yard and how he was trying to convince more people to use brick for homes. "Now," he said, "it is mostly used for the mills on the hill and out-buildings there, and only a few businesses such as the new post office."

By the time they had finished cake and coffee, they had spent an hour together. Joseph had encouraged Amanda to talk about her life in Placerville, her relationship with her father, her opinions of Bodie, and her hopes for the future. It didn't occur to her until later that he had shared nothing about himself, other than the fact that he came from Quebec in Canada and had spent a few years in Illinois. He had also shared a funny story about a brick yard employee and another about the local Indians, but nothing at all that was personally revealing.

As they left the restaurant, Joseph walked north on Main while Amanda turned south, intent on getting home so she could gather the dirty clothes and deliver them to Ah Ching's Laundry on Main Street. She had noticed it just south of the Occidental Saloon and Restaurant, conveniently near the southern portion of town so the good women would not have to expose themselves to the rowdiness of the north end.

Focused on her eagerness to get home, Amanda was brought back to awareness by a man clearing his throat nearby. Roger Murphy was standing on the sidewalk just outside Wagner's Saloon, leaning on a post in a pose that made her think he had been waiting for her but was trying not to be obvious about it.

He straightened up and addressed her. "May I have a word with you, Miss Blake?"

"Of course." She was surprised to find her heart beating so hard.

But now that he had her attention, Roger seemed hesitant to continue. After licking his lips, he told her, "I realize it isn't any of my business, but I feel I must warn you about DeRoche."

"Yes?"

"Well, it's just that DeRoche doesn't exactly have the best reputation regarding his treatment of women."

Embarrassed to be discussing something so personal, and acutely aware of her lack of experience with the male of the specie, she was immediately defensive. She also felt that she owed Joseph some degree of loyalty after he had chopped wood for her and bought her a meal. "He's been nothing less than a perfect gentleman to me."

Roger's jaw tightened. "I'm sure he has. But it isn't his manners that I'm referring to."

"Maybe you've been listening to gossip." She boldly met his eyes. "Possibly it was gossip started by some jealous man or one who resents another's success."

Roger shoved his hands in his pockets and told her, "I'm sorry if I've offended you, Miss Blake. I only meant to give you something to consider, seeing that you're new in town." With that, he turned and stepped into the saloon's vestibule, slapping open the wooden batwing doors so hard that they flapped several times before once again shutting out the interior.

Chiding herself for her sharp tongue, and wondering if she should have used the moment as an opportunity to learn more about Joseph, she continued walking. By the time she reached home, she realized that her response to Roger Murphy had been partly due to her disappointment that he hadn't stopped her simply on his own account. But no, he only wanted to criticize another man, as though he had set himself up as an uncle rather than...what?

Did she want him to be something more? He was after all a gambler, even if faro dealers were considered the most respectable of the sports. For that matter, what did she want Joseph to be? "Silly girl," she chided herself, "I expect nothing from either man. I'm not looking for a husband like the girls back home." It was, she had to admit, flattering to have these men interested in her, but she told herself firmly that it was only because she was new to the town.

Her pragmatic nature took over and she shut out all thoughts of Roger and Joseph as she gathered together the pile of laundry. She put the men's dirty clothes and her spare petticoat into four sheets and set off for town with her cumbersome bundle. By the time she had reached Ah Ching's Laundry a block north of Green, she was out of breath and glad that she had only a loose shawl over her shoulders.

The moist and warm interior of the shop didn't help her discomfort. Several folding screens separated the front counter from the back of the open building where two small barrel-shaped stoves with tall stovepipes reached up through the roof, kept hot by piles of wood and charcoal in bins nearby. Sitting on top of the stoves were shallow tin boxes with handles, and the boxes filled with hot coals. Some of the Orientals used these in place of the more usual heavy black flat irons, although there were several of those sitting on a narrow shelf encircling the stove with their flat bottoms against the side of the hot stove.

Small oriental men stood at a number of ironing boards and solid tables over which clothing and bed linens were stretched. One man picked up a large glass of water and filled his mouth to the point where his cheeks bulged. He then released the pressure of the water by spewing it out in a fine spray over a sheet. A slow pass of the hot-box over the fabric and it reflected a crisp starched sheen, as everything white had some degree of starch in it. Amanda blinked a few times in surprise and looked beyond the busy ironing area to another room that was full of drying racks and clotheslines that extended into an outdoor fenced yard.

As she stood in line with her bundle of clothes, she chatted a few moments with a friendly woman standing in front of her. The generously proportioned woman, one side or the other of forty, had an upright corseted posture, dark hair parted in the middle and slicked back into a bun, and deep-set eyes that seemed to look out at the world from an internal protection of hidden thoughts and memories. As the customer at the front left the shop, the woman flashed a smile at Amanda before she moved up in line.

Amanda looked out the window and began to let her thoughts wander to the stories of robbery, murder and general mayhem that had recently filled the pages of the newspapers. Possibly because her thoughts were so occupied, when she heard gunfire popping and echoing in the distance, she jumped and let out a small squeal.

The woman in front of her turned around and said, "Don't worry about that. You can hear its regular rhythm. That means it's simply target practice." She laughed before adding, "And likely attended by wagering as is most everything where two or more men are gathered."

Amanda smiled and nodded, relaxing the clench in her mid-section and laughing at herself for assuming that it had been the sound of violence. Her father had assured her that for all the violence for which Bodie was so renown, the businessmen were an honest lot who needed nothing more than a handshake to bond them to an agreement. This was reassuring, and she realized that maybe Bodie was after all a normal town whose life blood just happened to flow from the mines.

She commented on this to the woman in front of her and found agreement with the premise. The two women were experiencing the temporary camaraderie that so quickly and easily develops between people sharing a mutually trying situation.

"I wish this line would move more quickly," the woman lamented. "I need to get to the telegraph office to send a message."

"It's nice to know we're connected to the rest of the world, being in such a remote location."

"Oh, yes." The woman's wide mouth turned up in a proud smile. "We've had a telegraph office for two years now. Mr. Pratt came here and made an agreement with the business owners and mining companies that if he got it built by June of '78, they'd join together to pay for it."

"And if he had gone beyond that date?"

"Then they wouldn't have to pay." She smiled broadly. "But he did it a month early and they paid happily. It allows the mine owners, and the stockholders and brokers, to stay in touch regarding the progress of the mines. And the shops can place orders and have items shipped right away. Oh, yes, it's been a wonderful *modernity* for the town." Her eyes twinkled with humor. "I learned that word from a traveling salesman."

"I understand that the post office on south Main is new."

"That's right. It's been there about eight months now. We were growing so fast that we really needed it moved from inside a shop at the north end. Why, it's got 560 mail boxes and they're all rented now, with a waiting list."

Thinking the woman had an amazing knowledge of the town, Amanda asked, "Do you mind if I ask how long you have lived here?"

"Seventeen years." She looked at Amanda as though waiting for a reaction.

She got one. Amanda was completely taken aback. "But the boom only started three years ago."

The woman laughed, a warm throaty sound that exuded not only mirth but delight at Amanda's reaction. "Yes, but some of us were here as early as '63. I came here with my first husband, Robert Kernohan, and my two year old daughter from Placerville. I had three brothers who were also here with me and for a while after the war even my father was here. My youngest brother died in '68 trying to return to Bodie from Big Meadows during a snow storm. My sister Marietta moved here a year after I did and married a few years later. In fact, her son Daniel was the first child ever born here. That was on April 3, 1869."

"I was in Placerville at the same time you were then."

"Really?"

"Yes, I was about your daughter's age, but I lived there my whole life until I came here last week."

After they had each turned in their bundles of clothes to be cleaned, the woman declared she could send her telegram later and asked Amanda if she would care to join her for coffee. As they sat at a small round table in a corner of the U. S. Bakery, the woman held out her hand and said, "By the way, I'm Elizabeth Butler Huntoon."

Grasping her hand briefly, Amanda identified herself.

"So you're newly arrived?" Elizabeth asked.

"Yes, my mother passed away this past winter and I've come to join my father. He's a miner at the Noonday."

Elizabeth shook her head. "Such hard work. My husband Almond and I own the Booker Flat Hotel south of town across from the Noonday Mill. Almond isn't the healthiest of men sometimes, so I often have more to do than I can almost handle. We have a bar the mine workers find handy for a quick drink before heading home. We also have a stable so those men with horses have a place to put them during their shift." Amanda noticed the tiny lines of fatigue and stress around Elizabeth's eyes as she sighed and added, "I'm really enjoying this little respite today."

"What do women in this town do for entertainment? It seems such a masculine place."

"Well, it is. I mean, considering that it exists only to support the mines. But we women haven't let that keep us from finding ways to enjoy ourselves or be useful."

"Really?"

"Oh, yes." Elizabeth smiled at Amanda's surprise. "There's the occasional acting troop that comes to town, and musicians and singers too. And some of us put on little skits or plays, and song-fests. The children have recitals at the school, and the women hold bake sales to support them. During the summer we have the baseball club that plays out on Booker Flat, and everyone enjoys the horse races there."

"At the tier of benches you can see from the incoming road to the south?"

"That's right. And the men have a rifle club near the Red Cloud Mine. Some women enjoy the boxing matches and the younger women go to the gymnasium to watch the men work with the weights and punching bags. The older women have put together benevolent societies like The Ladies Relief Society and the Ladies Benevolent Society to provide for the poor and disabled. We have too many of both. The men have their societies of course, including the Veterans of the Union and Confederacy group, and the Society of Pacific Coast Pioneers. Oh, and the Bodie Guards."

"A militia here in Bodie?"

"Well, of a type." She chuckled and shook her head. "It's mainly just a uniformed unit of the state militia where the men get together to play at pageantry in parades and train at marching."

"Like the fire departments. I've seen them west of town mustering and marching."

"We do love a good parade here. Oh, and we women sew for the poor too. There are also a surprising number of dances given to raise money for things. Some women advocate for the elimination of the King Street opium dens, and others even for women's suffrage. Not that they make any progress on either front."

Amanda laughed with delight. "I can tell I won't be bored here."

Elizabeth's smile was rueful. "No, people are seldom bored in Bodie. Of course, some of the men think life is boring if there isn't a ruckus going on around them. So they start a fight with someone to *liven things up*, as they call it. But that's less often than the newspapers in Nevada would have you believe." She waved a hand, dismissing these out of state scribblers. "The Comstock is playing out while Bodie is flourishing, and they're jealous. But one thing that should help you sleep is that what lawlessness there is, isn't tolerated at the south end."

"I suppose all rowdiness ceases during winter too."

Elizabeth shrugged. "During the height of winter, the main activity is just staying alive."

Combined with the other half-joking comments she had heard about Bodie winters, the reality of what Elizabeth was conveying hit Amanda with a jolt. She wondered how she would handle such extreme weather.

As they left the bakery, two men passed them walking south. All of a sudden, the one nearest them turned to the man walking by the edge of the road and shoved him into the path of a large freight wagon going a little too fast. The man rolled as he fell and the wagon's wheels closely passed on either side of him. Elizabeth immediately pushed Amanda against the nearest building, out of the way of whatever might happen next. Waiting for the man in the street to get up or lay broken and dying, both women clamped their hands over their mouths in horror.

When the man stood up, he was obviously shaken, but he managed to reach into his pocket for his gun. However, by that time the other man had merged into the crowd on the sidewalk and disappeared down the street. Amanda, Elizabeth and the others who watched as the victim set off after his tormentor figured the result of this incident would probably be in the papers later in the week, possibly even in the obituary section.

Elizabeth hustled a shocked Amanda north to Mill Street where she had her black rig tied to a post next to the Mono House. They climbed in and Elizabeth hurried the horse forward to Mono Street and then south to Green. There Amanda climbed out across from her father's house.

Still shaken from what she had witnessed outside the restaurant, Amanda thanked Elizabeth for her company and her kindness, assuring her that next time she would prepare them a nice tea at her house. Elizabeth gave her a wave of the hand and pulled away from the edge of the road. A man in a wagon, traveling faster than was prudent, came close to careening into her rig.

Elizabeth leaned out over the side and yelled, "Slow it down, you clod." She turned back to Amanda with a shrug and a grin. "I haven't lived here all these years without learning how to stand up for myself."

Amanda watched Elizabeth continue toward Main. "No," she thought, "there's not much boredom in Bodie."

CHAPTER 3
JULY, 1880

    Out for a walk at the beginning of the month with her shopping basket just in case she found something interesting for that night's supper, Amanda coughed as a passing wagon raised the powdery dust of Mono Street. As she always did now when she passed the Wilson house, she glanced at the tall window beneath its peaked roof edged in decorative cutouts.

    According to her father, who worked with the exceedingly thin Lars Wilson at the Noonday, the Wilsons had no children. This made it all the more puzzling why the backyard was fully enclosed in an eight foot high plank fence, without even one knot hole for a curious passerby to peek through. She knew that such clear wood must have cost them dearly, and wondered why the Wilsons would have found it so important.

    But there was no child looking down at her this day and she wondered if it had only been a trick of the light coupled with her imagination. Or maybe the day she had seen the little girl the Wilsons had been caring for her while the mother was busy elsewhere. Knowing it was none of her business either way, Amanda determined to say nothing to Cherry Wilson, who was at that moment feeding a dozen chickens scratching around in the dirt at the side of the house.

    Amanda paused to wonder why the chickens were not contained in the backyard, but then turned to observe Mrs. Wilson. Cherry was a broad-shouldered woman in her early forties, with a round face, round cheeks and round eyes. This gave the impression of a gentle pliant person, yet she was known as an outspoken woman who somehow managed to speak her mind without giving offense. They had met when both had reached for a large melon at the Central Market, it being the last one in the crate. Amanda had deferred to the older woman as dictated by correct manners, and Cherry had responded by having the clerk split the melon between them.

    "I love your colorful hens," Amanda commented.

Cherry looked down at her scratching and cackling brood with much the same pride as might a mother hen. "They're pretty little things, but they're also good layers. Would you like a few of their eggs?"

"I'd love some. Thank you."

Cherry took four warm eggs from a round wire basket on the ground and placed them in Amanda's shopping basket. She threw a handful of dried corn to the clucking hens, brushed off her hands and said, "We'll enjoy their eggs until winter sets in hard and then we'll have chicken and dumplings, fried chicken, and chicken pot pie." She laughed sharply. "Nothing goes to waste around here."

"Do the chickens stop laying in the cold?"

Cherry looked at her appraisingly. "You haven't been here in winter, have you?"

"No."

"They can't live through the long months of cold and wet snow. Those who've tried to keep their chickens alive just end up making the poor little things suffer. Even the markets run out of chickens after the passes close, and we finish winter with dried beef and salted pork. One winter we were down to jerky and the last of what was in our root cellars before the passes opened to the freighters."

"How deep does the snow get?"

"It varies from year to year. When it gets up to the roofs, you'll see various homes flying squares or triangles of colored calico from the roof corners facing the mines. The miners can find their way home that way."

"The more I hear about winter, the more anxious I become."

"Well, there's some fun in it, too. And of course there's less of the horrid dust inside then." She sighed with the resignation of the put upon housewife. "We skate on the frozen ponds below the mills, and if the snow isn't too deep we can go for a ride in a sleigh. If we can make it to the Miners' Union Hall, there's a party and a dance at Christmas and again at New Years. And the kids have snowman building competitions and skating races on the frozen ponds, and tobogganing down the hills behind the cemetery. It's only when the snow gets over five feet deep that things come to a stop."

Amanda laughed. "You make it sound less awful than the men do."

"That's because I don't have to slog my way to the mines every day." Mrs. Wilson smiled and said, "Why don't you come in and have some tea with me?"

"That's very kind of you. I'd love some."

As Amanda entered the house, she tried to listen for any sound elsewhere in the house, but when she heard nothing, she took in the room around her. Cherry had painted the walls with bright colors in three shades of yellow, as though she was trying to mimic the sun's warm glow indoors. No traditional reds or dark burgundy vertical striped paper on the walls with gaudy flowers for Cherry. Even in winter it would be difficult to believe that cold could be felt here.

The two women settled down on the sofa in front of a low table, Amanda carrying in from the kitchen a large china tea pot and Cherry the cups and the last of a small seed cake.

Only a few minutes later Mr. Wilson arrived home from his shift at the Noonday. He brought with him an accumulation of thick road dust on his shoes, which grime immediately fell off onto Cherry's freshly scrubbed floor, just missing an immaculately clean rag rug.

"Lars Wilson," his wife's sharp tone greeted him, "you take off those dirty shoes this minute. And you can bring me the broom and dust pan after that."

"Sorry, dear." His tone was sheepish but not at all embarrassed. He reached down and untied his heavy work boots, then put his feet into a pair of leather slippers by the door. He then carried his boots to the kitchen and returned with the broom and dust pan as directed. When he handed these to Cherry, they exchanged a smile that illustrated their close affection for one another.

"This here is Amanda Blake," Cherry told him, "John's daughter."

"Hello." His smile was genuine as he said, "John told me he was enjoying having his daughter with him, but I had no idea she'd be so pretty. Nice meeting you." He started to walk away, but then turned back. "You keep an eye on that Mike that's living in the house." With that enigmatic statement, he left the room.

"Funny he should say that," Amanda told Cherry. "Mike makes me a little uncomfortable, but I don't know why."

"Listen to your hunches, honey. They're there for a reason."

As Mr. Wilson disappeared up the narrow stairs, Cherry began sweeping up the dust and small rocks from the soles of her husband's shoes while making clucking noises not dissimilar from her chickens.

Amanda told her, "I can't imagine talking to a man like you did your husband."

Mrs. Wilson laughed. "Honey, men only do what they want and what they respect. Here in Bodie, tough is all they know."

"Maybe, but my father wouldn't take that from me."

"Well, of course not." Cherry carried the dustpan into the kitchen and immediately returned, pouring more tea in Amanda's cup. "He's your pa after all and you have to respect him. But you can start with those lay-abouts that live with him. I've met them." She shook her head in an evident show of disdain. "If you let them act like lazy bums and treat you like a slave, they will. A woman gets treated just as she lets herself be treated. You remember that." Those words would return to Amanda many times during her life, especially over the next year. Cherry smiled as she added, "In fact, last month one man proved that the same is true for men."

"What happened?"

"One of the mining superintendents was at a dance house and started teasing one of the hurdy-gurdy gals. She got angry and called him a name, and the drunken fool challenged her to a fight. Before he knew what had happened, she hauled off and gave him a black eye."

Their laughter over this was more a celebration of a woman getting the upper hand over a man, than based on any real humor in the situation. They had another cup of tea and discussed the big summer sale at one of the shops. Cherry said, "Some of Mr. Boone's yarns were stained when a water jug broke near the stack. He let me have them so I can knit shawls for the poor, as well as the Indian ladies up on the hills to the west. I've already made a few." She looked at Amanda with her head cocked to one side. "Would you like to go with me to deliver them? Or would going into an Indian village make you uncomfortable?"

"Not at all. I'd love to see how they live." Not to sound too unseemly curious, she quickly added, "And of course, help you if I can."

"It's not a fancy place." There was a strong irony in her voice. "Their life is very basic, but satisfactory for their needs." She sighed. "Of course, it's much harder for them now that the mine owners have cut down so many of their pinion nut trees, fouled the streams and destroyed their traditional hunting grounds."

This was a seldom recognized truth, and Amanda admired Cherry for her insight and compassion. "Just let me know when you want me to go with you."

The sound of two doors slamming came to them from upstairs, one at the front and one at the back of the house. This might not have caused comment, except that Mr. Wilson was supposed to be the only person upstairs.

Surprised, Amanda asked, "What was that?"

Cherry grew a little pale and quickly told her, "Why, it's just Lars. He must have dropped something as he closed the bedroom door."

Amanda declined to mention that the sounds had been from opposite ends of the house. She thought to herself that unless Lars was capable of being in two placed at the same time, there must be someone unnamed in the house.

Immediately Cherry got up and began clearing the tea things, talking loudly and rapidly. Amanda carried the large tea pot back into the kitchen and as she placed it on the counter noticed several bottles sitting there of the kind dispensed at the druggist's.

After looking back into the parlor where Cherry was stacking the cups and saucers and folding up the tea cloth, Amanda took a moment to read the labels on the bottles. One was of umbel, which she knew about from when she had cared for her mother. It was a tincture used to tone the nervous system. Next to it was a large brown bottle of bitter tonic, also used to build up a weak system. From a small crock protruded the dried branches of a plant common to the area that was used in the making of a restorative Indian tea. Amanda recognized the little knobs along the thin branches since she herself had some in her own kitchen.

When Cherry returned to shake out the cloth, she found Amanda admiring the tea pot. To distract from the fact that she had been in the kitchen so long, Amanda asked, "Would you like to use the tea leaves while they're still wet?" When Cherry hesitated, her thought obviously on something else, Amanda added, "I always use mine on the dark rugs to gather the dust when I sweep them."

"Oh, of course, so do I. Just leave them in the pot for now."

Amanda took her cue and said, "I'd best be getting on with my chores." Amanda thanked her for the refreshment and then promptly left. Looking back at the house from down the street, she saw the attic curtains just falling back into place.

Amanda walked slowly north, trying to sort out what had just happened. Unable to reach a reasonable conclusion, she turned her thoughts to anticipation of the Fourth of July the following weekend. Although Bodie loved any excuse to celebrate, the Fourth was always something special.

As she reached Standard Avenue, a huge freight wagon rolled past her loaded with a hundred barrels of whiskey. She stopped to listen to the ten little bells raised on a metal frame above the harnesses of the lead horses. The sound was simply pleasant here in town, but out on a mountain trail with its curves and blind corners, they would alert wagons and riders coming from the opposite direction and therefore avoid a possible collision. Her father had once said that to the attuned ear, every team's bells were different and could identify the teamster when hearing a team approaching.

She turned left toward Main with the Standard Mill's waste ponds to her right, remembering that Cherry had said people skated on them in the winter. She wondered at the wisdom of this considering the amount of poisonous mercury that might be in the water, it being used in the processing of the ore at the mill.

A sudden gust of wind grabbed at her light skirt, and she was glad that she had taken the time to sew small lead weights into the hem, a trick of fashion that western women grew up knowing. The weights were only nine cents for a dozen at any mercantile store and well worth the expense. It had been a gust of wind like this that had curtailed the town's unusual and unexpected merrymaking two days before.

On June 29th, almost everyone in town not working a shift at a mine had gathered as one excited mass on the edge of town opposite the Bluff. A small group of men had set up a large hot air balloon and were preparing to launch it skyward. Amanda remembered the morning with a smile.

It had taken them some time to ready the contraption, which of course had only contributed to the growing excitement as well as the size of the crowd. Finally the dark canvas balloon had shot up into the air with a jerk and a whoosh amid jubilant cheers from the crowd, and whoops of joy from the three excited men in the basket. The balloon had slipped upward against the bright blue sky as a collective and long drawn out "Oh" had been exhaled in unison by the crowd. Then, when the basket had been about fifty feet above the ground, the cheering had stopped and the jubilation had changed to gasps and frightened screams.

The top of the balloon had caught fire and the whole thing had begun plummeting to earth in a shower of sparks that had sent people running back into town. The basket had hit the ground with a thud and the men inside it had tumbled out onto the ground shaken, but miraculously unhurt. Dozens of men had rushed forward to stomp out the flames before they caught the dry brush.

The ruination of this experiment was of course discussed in every saloon and parlor for days. It gave many a man the satisfaction of criticizing what the builders of the balloon had done, accompanied by the ever-popular pastime of offering opinions about what the builders *should* have done.

In the days that followed, the air warmed and the winds picked up to a degree that caused problems for everyone. Flags cracked and snapped and ripped, dust devils twirled down the dry streets, and women's skirts were blown up above their knees if they had not put weights in the hem. Horses danced nervously as the wind goosed their tails, the Piutes retreated to their shacks, and people generally avoided being outside as much as possible. If they didn't, they risked being hit by a flying tin can, clothes off a drying line, bits of sagebrush loosed from a Piute shelter, or peppered by blowing sand.

The Fourth of July was breezy but manageable, at least in the morning. It was expected to be a rowdy celebration, as was the tradition in mining camps throughout the Sierra. However, in 1880 the fourth fell on a Sunday, so the festivities would not be allowed until Monday. Even so, on the stroke of midnight on the fourth, thirty shrill steam whistles cut through the air as a welcome to the country's 104th Independence Day.

After the whistles stopped, Amanda fell back on her pillow and sleep finally came again, but only briefly. At 4:30 in the morning the Hoskins Brass Band, from the top of the Belvedere Iron Works played *Hail Columbia, The Star Spangled Banner, America,* and *Red, White and Blue.* After the band had exhausted their patriotic repertory, Amanda again dozed off, the notes of the peppy band music playing through her dreams. At sunrise the Standard cannon put in a noisy note, at which point Amanda woke up with a gasp.

The normal Sunday routine commenced, albeit with the town more gaily decorated than usual, and some degree of sleep deprivation common among the citizens. Throughout the town there were flags flying from every building while red, white and blue bunting hung from upstairs balconies. Men had cut saplings in the far hills and had placed the small trees in buckets of water before roping them to porch posts all along Main. It was a European tradition brought to mining camps years before, and it was the only time people saw trees in Bodie. Services were attended at the Miners' Union Hall in the morning by the Methodists and in the early afternoon by the Catholics, after which the Hall became the gathering place for a miner's meeting.

The Miners' Union members assembled to *"rescind a resolution adopted at a previous meeting which opposed a parade of the members of the Union in the coming Independence Day celebration."* This action had been put in place in the first place because some of the men in the Union had for some reason been hostile to an officer of the day who was to be in charge of the celebrations. Since then tempers had cooled, and no one wanted to miss the opportunity to march in a parade, so it was assumed there would be no problem getting everyone to agree to the rescinding of the motion.

Amanda was out taking a stroll down Green early that evening with a woman she had met the day before while shopping. Charlotte Perry was the wife of Vincent Perry, the owner of a warehouse on the southern outskirts of town. She was a petite, trim woman in her mid-twenties, with thick dark brown hair falling in a cascade of curls entwined this day with a long white ribbon. Her smile, which could easily melt the heart of the most miserly shopkeeper, belied a practical nature that kept her unimpressed with Bodie's daily dramas.

Charlotte had that rare ability to be truly happy for another's good fortune, devoid of envy or the desire that it should have befallen her instead. Her graciousness showed forth in an open countenance and the look of sincere interest while talking to people, convincing them that she felt her day would have been incomplete if she had not spent those few minutes with them.

The evening was mild and the traffic on the streets was lighter than usual, and once again Amanda was struck by the provocative spirit exuded by the town's elements: the smell of sage underlying the occasional whiff of unburied restaurant garbage and the ever-present horse droppings from the streets; the thump of the stamps on the hill and the prosperity this conveyed; the shouts of men and the murmurs of women; the music and laugher and clink of glasses from saloons; and the abundance of fish, beef and poultry displayed in shop windows. The people she met were friendly men with guns bulging in jacket pockets, and smiling women with fancy parasols and hidden judgments. In Bodie the prosperous and the seedy lived next to each other and no one thought this strange. And of course there was always the possibility that something dangerous might occur at any moment.

Amanda and Charlotte were just approaching the Windsor Hotel across from the post office and the Miners' Union Hall when Amanda saw

Joseph approaching from the opposite direction. When he stopped before them and tipped his hat, Amanda quickly introduced him to Charlotte.

Charlotte nodded her head and said, "Good evening, Mr. DeRoche. How is business at the brick yard?"

Realizing that Charlotte already knew Joseph, Amanda was puzzled by her new friend's stiffly formal demeanor.

Joseph tripped his hat to her. "Good evening, Mrs. Perry. Business has dropped off a little, but all businesses fluctuate from time to time."

"Yes, that's very true." Charlotte lightly rested her hand on Amanda's arm and looked him in the eyes. "I would ask you to join us on our stroll, but I have some things to discuss with Amanda and this is my only opportunity to do so."

"I understand." And indeed he did, realizing that Mrs. Perry had obviously heard the rumors of some of his escapades, possibly those with women, and was showing her disapproval. He couldn't help but wonder if she would try to poison Amanda against him, whose puzzled frown told him that at least for now she was in ignorance of the reason for Mrs. Perry's cool tone. He hoped Mrs. Perry would continue to keep her mouth shut, otherwise...

As he tipped his hat again and moved to pass by the women, these musings were abruptly interrupted by loud angry shouts. Looking across the street to the Miners' Union Hall, they saw a man who Amanda later learned was miner Paddy Carroll gesturing wildly as he approached the Union Hall. When he was close enough that he no longer needed to shout to be heard, he drew his British Bulldog pistol from his pocket and pointed it at the men guarding the door.

The lack of wisdom in this was immediately apparent when the six guards pulled their own weapons just as Paddy began firing. The guards seemed to be using their guns with keen accuracy, considering the red beginning to appear on Paddy's torso. But just as Amanda saw this, she felt herself thrust aside by Joseph as he leaped into the entryway of the Windsor Hotel. Almost immediately he grabbed Amanda and Charlotte by their arms and pulled them in after him, which had the unfortunate effect of putting the women between him and the street.

By the time they got themselves sorted out, Paddy was sprawled on the ground with several more holes in his torso than it was supposed to have, each one oozing blood. Two of the guards who had shot him got on either end of Paddy's limp body and picked it up with a grunt of effort, discovering as they did so that he was still alive. Nevertheless, they tossed him in the back of a passing wagon and delivered him to Boiset and Stewart's Drug Store, where he died only a few minutes later.

A man walked past shaking his head and was heard to say, "And another man abruptly changes his address and joins his friends on the hill."

Realizing that he was referring to the cemetery south of town, Amanda was shocked at the man's cavalier attitude. Joseph, however, laughed in response as he ushered the women back onto the sidewalk.

Amanda said to Charlotte, "Maybe we should return home now."

Joseph laughed again, his voice taking on a slightly mocking tone. "Don't worry ladies. I doubt there will soon be a repeat of gunfire, at least not in this part of town."

Charlotte turned to Amanda. "I think you're right about going home. Good afternoon, Mr. DeRoche." Not waiting for him to reply, she took Amanda's arm and immediately turned her toward Green.

After a moment, Amanda spoke up. "You don't like him, do you?"

Charlotte took a deep breath. "No. He has a less than savory reputation when it comes to women, and some of his business dealings as well."

"He's only been a gentleman with me." Amanda heard her timid tone and cleared her throat before adding, "I mean he's given me no reason to object to his behavior."

Charlotte smiled. "Well, every man has some good in him. Maybe he has decided to settle down."

Alarmed, Amanda hurried to explain. "I'm not saying that I'm serious about him. I just enjoy his company."

Charlotte turned to her with a gentle smile. "He is very charming, isn't he?"

Amanda looked up at her father's tiny house as they stood on the corner of Green and Mono. "I guess I'm a little lonely. My father hasn't exactly been the warm parent I had fantasized he would be. And it isn't easy sharing the house with the other men who expect me to be their cook and housekeeper, and act like conversation is beyond their ability. So when I'm out with Joseph, it feels as though it's my turn." She shook her head and laughed. "Oh, goodness, that seems so dramatic."

"I do know what you mean, though." Charlotte put a hand on Amanda's arm. "Every woman needs to feel special to someone. But no matter what happens, know that you do have a friend here."

Amanda felt a rush of gratitude and gave Charlotte a spontaneous hug, something usually only relatives might do. "Thank you so much for your kindness. Now you'd better get home to that husband of yours."

"Speak of the devil," Charlotte said as she looked past Amanda. A tall broad-shouldered man in his late twenties was walking up Green toward them while looking down at the ground in a study of concentration.

"Vince!" Charlotte called out. The man looked up in surprise and hurried toward the two women with a bright smile on his clean-shaven face. He was dressed in denim pants and a dark blue shirt with a brown leather vest over it, and his rangy brown hair stuck out from below a hat that shaded soft brown eyes with unusually long lashes.

"Hello, my dear," he greeted his wife. "And who is this lovely young lady?"

"She's John Blake's daughter." She then added with a warm glance at Amanda, "And a good friend of mine."

After a few minutes of polite conversation, Charlotte made reference to getting supper started and the couple turned toward their home a block further up Green. Amanda watched the Perrys walk away, Vince's arm around Charlotte's waist and their laughter drifting back on the warm air. Stifling an urge toward envy, Amanda entered her father's house and began preparing supper.

As they ate later that evening, Amanda related in detail what had happened outside the Miners' Union Hall. She was not prepared for their laughter.

Matt shook his head. "Poor Paddy was always unpredictable when he was drinking. Otherwise, he was a decent enough fellow."

John nodded, but when he spoke it was only to ask for more coffee.

Mike huffed and shrugged. "His going is no great loss." He then immediately changed the subject to a poker game the night before where he had won a good-sized pot.

Amanda, on the other hand, could not let go of what she had seen, and found it difficult to get to sleep that night. The images of Paddy's bloody body lying in the dirt haunted her compassion. Was there a loved one somewhere hoping to someday see Paddy again, and who would wonder for years why he never again contacted them? But she mostly wondered at the nonchalant acceptance by so many men of the sudden and violent death of someone they had known.

Finally, she could no longer deny what was really keeping her from sleep. Everything had happened so rapidly after Paddy and the guards had begun shooting, but not so fast that she hadn't been aware of Joseph's first reaction, which was to protect himself and not the women with him. Of course, she rationalized, it was said that human nature's first instinct was to survive. And after all, having lived several years in Bodie, he must be deeply impressed at how lethal a gun fight can be. But shouldn't that have made him all the more primed to protect the women?

Then she recalled that when he had heard the first shots, he had not looked at Paddy but rather up and down the street. Could it have been the reaction of a man worried that the shooting might be meant for him? If that was true, what could Joseph have done that would make him instantly suspect such a thing? It had to be more than just the womanizing that Charlotte had mentioned. How serous could that be? After a moment's thought, she concluded that it would depend on whether or not the woman was married and who the man was that was being cuckolded. It was after midnight before she finally fell into a fitful sleep.

At dawn on Monday morning, July 5, the noise of the Standard's cannon, along with hundreds of cheering people in the streets, was followed by the brass bands warming up somewhere north of Green. Amanda awoke refreshed and eager for the holiday, with the questions and moody doubts of the night before now seeming foolish and like a silly dream.

She wasted no time getting out of bed and preparing a pot of coffee. Matt came out and joined her, showing how eager he too was to get into town to enjoy a day off. Her father had left at his normal time and wouldn't start enjoying the holiday until his shift ended that afternoon.

She wasn't sure where Mike was and didn't really care. The passing of time had not changed her opinion that there was something about him not quite right, even though she could not define what. When she had told her father of her feelings, he had laughed and said she needed to "loosen her laces". She hadn't asked for clarification of what he meant for fear she would like his explanation even less than she did the original comment.

After dressing carefully in a new frock of white summer lawn, she wrapped a pale blue sash around her waist and looked at her reflection in the small mirror on the wall of her room. She perched a new straw bonnet at a jaunty angle atop her carefully arranged hair, and put some coins and a handkerchief in a small purse on a long ribbon that she tied to the sash.

Anyone walking into town that day was immediately immersed in band music, parades, speeches, contests of athletic prowess, and a procession of the town's four fire companies; Babcock Engine I, Pioneer Hook and Ladder I, Champion Hose I and Neptune Hose II. All were manned by volunteer firemen proudly sporting freshly cleaned and pressed uniforms.

One of Amanda's favorite parade entrants was a miniature brass cannon belonging to the Booker Mine that was mounted on a small wagon. It was drawn by ten boys in fancy uniforms, one in the lead mounted on a pony whose saddle and bridle were richly decorated with flowers from Bridgeport, and flounces of gathered cloth.

In the afternoon, on the north edge of town, Amanda pushed her way to the front of a crowd of people arranged around a series of athletic demonstrations. She wanted to see her friend Duncan McMillan in the hammer throw, and was just in time to see him step up and take hold of the heavy hammer. Before he started his windup he caught sight of Amanda. She was feeling gay and bright on this day of patriotic celebration, and gave him a spontaneous wink. She laughed when he blushed.

A man behind Duncan frowned, slapped him on the shoulder and said something sharp. Duncan became immediately serious and focused, and after taking a deep breath that he expelled slowly, he took another deep breath and began a lumbering twirl until finally releasing the hammer. His throw was measured at 92 feet 9 inches, out-distancing the next furthest throw by seven inches. The crowd cheered, men pumped the young man's hand, and money exchanged even more hands.

When Duncan looked up to find Amanda, she had disappeared into the crowd. He shrugged and turned his thoughts to enjoying the congratulations of his friends. After all, Amanda was a nice young *lady*, but his friends would later take him to Bonanza Street and treat him to time with a nice accommodating *woman*.

A competition between the Cornish miners drew Amanda's attention. The men were shoveling a large pile of ore tailings from one four foot by four foot wooden frame into another, with the one to first transfer all the rocks to be heralded the winner. This turned out to be not the youngest of the five competing men, but rather a muscular middle-aged man of thirty-two years who immediately upon winning downed a glass of lager handed him by friends.

There were a good number of Cornish miners in Bodie, many of them participating in the competitions that day. Amanda wondered how they felt about living somewhere so different from what they were used to, which she pictured vaguely as very green. Indeed, the dry rolling hills that formed the Bodie flats could not have been more different from the southwest corner of England in Cornwall, a land of fisheries, rocky coasts beneath tall cliffs, miles of mysterious moors littered with the rock huts of ancient civilizations, narrow roads edged with low rock walls, and big tin mines.

It was this last where they had learned how to mole underground, and from which they had longed to escape. Now, with the brutality of the tin mines in their past, the loneliness of Bodie's austere dry hills invited into their dreams images of their native land so far away. It was a land that didn't seem so bad now, but which they knew they would never see again.

Amanda merged with those around her who were heading to the area where they could hear the orations by the town leaders and chosen speakers of the day. But Amanda came to a sudden halt when she heard a woman nearby call out, "Mr. DeRoche, here we are."

Hidden from view by other revelers, Amanda spotted Joseph making his way through a crowded area of the street. He was approaching a man who frowned at him and a smiling woman dressed in a low-necked pale yellow dress with a series of swags across the front. The woman's smile displayed obvious delight from beneath a small lace-covered umbrella blocking the sun, but which could not block the rising color in her cheeks as she looked at Joseph. The man with her had not relinquished his frown. This duality of reaction to his approach was not lost on Joseph, who greeted them courteously with a nod without even trying to hide an insouciant smirk. When he held out a hand to the man, after a slight hesitation it was grasped briefly.

Amanda moved closer, still keeping people between the trio and herself as Joseph muttered, "Tom, Joanna. Lovely day for the celebrations, no?"

Tom responded with a surly, "You here with anyone?"

"I am looking for a friend of mine, yes, but I have not yet seen her."

It was now Joanna's turn to frown. With a toss of her light red curls interwoven with a yellow ribbon, she linked her arm through that of her husband and stated loudly, "We must be on our way." Tom could not hide his look of relief as he willingly allowed himself to be led away into the crowd.

As Joseph watched the couple walk away, a man wearing a red vest over his white shirt approached Joseph and clapped him on the back. "Hey, Frenchie, how you doin' today?"

"Fine, Bill. You appear to have already tasted your share of the saloons' offerings."

The man laughed. "You could say that."

At that moment, Joseph spotted Amanda and murmured, "Excuse me."

Looking up at Joseph, Amanda felt her heart beat faster. An aura of mystery and danger hung on him like a second skin and it drew her to him even while she told herself that it would be wiser to walk away.

Joseph looked down at her trim figure dressed all in white as though advertising her untouched innocence, her straw hat cocked at a flirtatious angle, and her large amber eyes glittering with excitement. In that moment he was overwhelmed with the dual urges to protect and to defile. The one thing he wanted more than anything else was to remove her from the crowd and spend even a brief moment alone with her.

He grabbed her hand and hurried her away from the throng of people milling around them, pulling her into a narrow alley not far away. Just past a tall stack of crates they merged into the shadows where Amanda leaned against the wood siding of a shop, laughing as though they had just done something incredibly clever.

They both took a moment to breathe deeply, something most people did in the high altitude after running. Caught up in the rare moment of such complete privacy, and mesmerized by the rise and fall of Amanda's breasts as she fought to catch her breath, Joseph leaned into her and murmured, "I would very much like to kiss you."

And caught up in the excitement of the day, the mysterious but nebulous warnings of Charlotte, and a sense of recklessness foreign to her proper upbringing, Amanda did not immediately resist. Before her hesitation could change to prim objection, Joseph pressed his mouth hard upon hers, forcing her head against the wall and knocking her hat to the ground. She at once felt vulnerable and devoured, and incredibly wanted.

When he did not immediately stand back, however, and the intensity of his ardor increased, Amanda placed her hands on his shoulders to give him a gentle push. He showed no inclination to cease the insistence of his yearning, and she began to taste blood as her lower lip split under the pressure of his teeth trying to force her mouth open. Fear that was close to panic seized her.

She dug the heels of her hands into his shoulders and at the same time placed the heel of her shoe on the toe of his boot with a pressure she found difficult to judge. He not only released her, but took a step back from her, smiling in a manner more triumphant than romantic. He was clearly irritated, and Amanda wondered if it was the first time a woman had tried to end his advances before he was ready.

Not knowing what was expected of her, and feeling incredibly awkward, Amanda began to babble. "I should really be going. I'm supposed to meet father after he gets off his shift. He'll need to eat before coming into town, especially as he'll probably be drinking a lot later."

There was a flash in Joseph's eyes she could not identify. Disappointment or anger, possibly, but he stood aside so she could pick up her hat when he didn't do it for her. She passed out into the afternoon sun and turned back to him just before emerging onto the sidewalk. "Will I see you in town later?"

He shrugged, his face a mask showing no emotion. "I don't know what I'll be doing later. If I can, I'll meet you in front of the Can-Can for the fireworks."

With that, he passed her without further words and strode down the sidewalk as though he had already forgotten her. Rather than stand by the side of the road feeling like a fool, Amanda hurried toward home while dabbing at her swelling lip with her handkerchief.

Further down the alley a tall man in a dark suit moved out from behind a stack of crates where he had earlier exited the side door of the shop. He was frowning and his eyes blazed with impotent fury. He checked a gold time piece attached to his dark blue silk vest, tucked it back into its small pocket, and adjusted the red string tie trailing down onto his white shirtfront. He then walked down Main toward Wagner's Saloon, releasing his anger in oaths and curses at a man whose nose he would happily have bloodied if he had come across him right then.

As John Blake finished his supper, he noted that Amanda was unusually quiet. Of course, he said nothing to her about this, knowing how moody women were known to be. He was eager to get to his favorite saloon to meet up with his friends, and he didn't want to invite discussion that would delay him. He did manage to mumble his thanks before hurrying out the door, and felt virtuous for having done that much.

Amanda stacked the supper dishes in the dry sink and walked back into town. It wasn't the first time she had felt lonely since arriving, but now she also felt adrift of purpose and longed for nothing more than the show of a little kindness. She would even settle for people with whom she could make insignificant small talk. She almost immediately saw Charlotte and Vince with another couple, but hesitated to join them. They were laughing and having an obviously wonderful time, and just as obviously enjoying one another's company. An unattached young woman would most likely not be a welcome addition.

Finally, with darkness descending quickly, Amanda stood by one of the posts holding up the porch roof in front of the Can-Can Restaurant. Soon other people crowded around her, all eager for the fireworks to begin, but there was no sign of Joseph among them. Eventually a weak display of bursting lights filled the night air northeast of town. Amid the complaining and disappointment of the crowd, Amanda again looked around for Joseph. And again he was nowhere to be seen.

As soon as the fireworks ended, people began to disperse and head for their beds or the nearest saloon. Amanda was one of those who hurried toward home, for as well as being tired, she also felt foolish and used. As she walked up Green Street toward the house, she told herself that if Joseph could be so casual in his treatment of her, then she certainly did not want his attentions.

Late that night, with the saloons mostly deserted, and with the colorful and celebratory swags of bunting now torn loose by gusts of wind, the sound of gun fire filled the air. But it was *not* celebratory.

James Kennedy, a wood chopper at the Booker Mine, having consumed too much alcohol throughout the day, spotted his enemy of long standing, Bill Baker, in front of the Mono Brewery. Standing on the sidewalk as Bill passed, James unwisely reached out his hand and tipped Bill's hat forward. He realized too late that Bill was not as drunk as he had thought when Bill pulled a gun from his pocket and shot him in the stomach. Bill was grabbed by a constable and dragged off to jail.

The bullet was removed from James by Dr. Robertson, but two days later he died from loss of blood and infection. When famous Bodie attorney Pat Reddy took Bill's case, no one doubted that Bill would be acquitted after a plea of self-defense. Pat Reddy was known to get his clients freed more often than not.

Some of James's friends began agitating for a 601 to be formed, so Bill was secretly escorted to the Bridgeport jail. Three days later he was indicted for murder. He would be found not guilty the following month.

In the middle of the month, Charlotte and Amanda dressed in their finest summer frocks and headed to the new Odd Fellows Hall on south Main near the post office. Amanda was especially proud of the fact that her father, dressed in an old suit that she had spent an hour pressing, had agreed to escort them on his one day off. They found that the new hall more than lived up to the rumors of its extravagant decorations and rich dark wall coverings. Even John appeared to be impressed.

They entered a room sixty feet long and twenty-five feet wide, with enough upholstered chairs to seat 200 people. The whole of the interior, with its high ceilings and tall windows, was fashioned in the Corinthian style with columns and statues at every angle. Unbeknownst to those present, it was one of the last new buildings that would be built in Bodie.

Most of the town's citizens were taking turns touring the interior and it had become a social occasion as well as an opportunity to satisfy ones curiosity. Upon entering, after the women greeted those standing nearest them, they walked slowly past a row of statues to their right representing the continents of Europe, Asia, Africa and Australia. On the left were statues representing Faith, Hope and Charity.

Amanda looked at the overwrought art surrounding them and said to her father, "Who would think that something so completely and utterly elegant could be found in a town such as this?"

He answered with a shrug, his short-lived interest having been satisfied. Arriving at the conclusion that there was nothing there of further interest to him, John looked longingly toward the door.

Seeing this, Amanda asked him, "Do you want to leave already?"

"Well, we've seen it."

"Can't you just enjoy it for a few minutes more?"

In answer, John crossed his arms over his chest and leaned back on the heels of his boots, not attempting to hide his impatience. "Okay, I'm here."

Charlotte did not miss the awkwardness between father and daughter, and was trying to hide her embarrassment at being a witness to Amanda's rejection.

However, to Amanda, it was only a representational moment in the history of their relationship. Instead of feeling angry or disappointed, the familiarity of his indifference left her feeling merely resigned. A few moments later she watched him join three men by the front door, the laughter of her father's friends in response to something he said carrying to her. She sighed and hoped that she had at least inherited his sense of humor.

Her mother had seldom expressed humor or a sense of fun, and in fact while growing up Amanda had witnessed little joyfulness between her usually bickering parents. Thankfully, she had always had friends whose parents had welcomed her into homes both loving and supportive, allowing her to realize that these qualities did at least exist in some families. This knowledge had kept her from becoming embittered about domestic life, and had kept alive a flicker of hope for her own future.

Her introspection was interrupted by a deep voice behind her. "Does all this magnificence surprise you?"

She turned around and looked up at Roger Murphy, frowning with irritation that he should so precisely agree with her earlier opinion. At the same time she felt her chest tighten when she realized she wanted to reach out and gently push the loose strands of hair off his forehead. To cover her confusion, she spoke more sharply than she had intended. "Why shouldn't Bodie have quality to enjoy, especially considering that it will be enjoyed by those with most of the money? I doubt there will be many miners off shift lounging here."

He nodded. "You're right, of course. But it's meant for use by the whole town. And the miners do have their own entertainments."

"In your saloon? Or on Bonanza Street?" Roger looked at her in surprise, aware of some underlying tension in her. Seeing his discomfiture and mistaking it for criticism, she asked, "Do you suppose that I'm so naive that I haven't realized what the jokes and sly comments around me so often are about?"

"Miss Blake," Roger bowed to her, "I am determined to assume nothing about you. I feel it would do you a grave disservice." He tipped his hat and walked swiftly out of the Odd Fellows Hall, obviously perturbed and wondering what he could have done to upset her.

As Amanda watched him pass through the doors, she felt a strong stab of contrition and almost called him back to apologize. But the urge disappeared at the same time he did, and she was left only with an anguished self-questioning of why she had been so rude to him.

Charlotte moved to her side. "Who was that? He looks vaguely familiar."

"He's a faro dealer at Wagner's Saloon."

"He's very good looking," Charlotte teased. "And he obviously admires you."

Amanda felt herself blush. "I don't know about that." To change the subject, she told Charlotte, "You look especially fair today."

The group of men that included John Blake moved noisily as one through the door and out onto the sidewalk. Amanda watched her father leave without saying anything to her.

"Have you been deserted, mademoiselle?"

The women turned around, a stiff smile on Amanda's face at the recognition of Joseph's voice. "It would seem so." She glanced at Charlotte who had quickly turned away to inspect more closely one of the statues.

"If you are now on your own, allow me to escort you wherever you want to go."

After a moment's hesitation, she told him, "I would like to see your Booker Flat brick yard." She ignored Charlotte's gasp from behind her, knowing she had made a bold pronouncement as his place of business was south of town. But her curiosity as to the source of Joseph's situation in the town overcame her usual propriety and its reticence.

Joseph's smile was radiant, and he pointedly ignored Charlotte's presence as he told Amanda, "Continue to enjoy the festivities here and I will get a rig. It is too far for you to walk."

Amanda quickly bid Charlotte good-bye before she could voice an objection and moved to the sidewalk. Joseph met a friend outside who agreed to loan him his rig for half an hour, and consequently he was able to claim Amanda only a few minutes later. They headed south down Main and then turned left onto the Booker Flat Road. It was a fair day with the sheer gauze of windswept white clouds stretched over a bright blue sky, and two mountain bluebirds sitting atop a large sagebrush plant watching them pass.

It was a short trip and Joseph talked about his plans to expand the brick yard. Amanda was enthralled to see him so animated and relaxed as he spoke about something of interest to himself. Neither of them referred to their tryst on the Fourth of July.

"When I was a child in Canada," he told her, "we had a brick house and when only ten years old I built a low brick wall around the front garden."

"When did you leave Canada?"

"In the early '70's."

"Really? You were a pioneer from the wilderness traveling in America then?"

"Oh, I found much wilderness in the States after crossing the border. I felt very American, for to be American is to love wilderness and desire to discover what is in it. Many people from cities long for an unexplored frontier to conquer, but most would rather read about it instead of facing its discomforts and inconveniences."

She laughed and asked, "Where did you go after you arrived in the States?"

"I drifted around and then settled in Chicago for a while before heading to California by train."

"Men have such great adventures," she mused wistfully. "Imagine coming across the country on a train. And Chicago is such a large cosmopolitan city. What was it like?"

"The train was comfortable, I suppose. But it was still a long trip and I grew bored over the scenery after a while."

She forbore to tell him that her question had been in reference to Chicago, but sensing that he had known that, she ceased to ask any more questions.

The tour of the brick yard was fated to be short. Just as Joseph and Amanda approached the large two-story brick building and the small one next to it housing the kiln, several men on horseback approached from the direction of town. As soon as they dismounted, they glanced at Amanda and asked to have a private word with Joseph.

Amanda told them, "Don't worry about me. I'll just wander over to watch the men working at the kiln." She turned her back on them, picked up the skirts of her dress a decorous height above the dirt, and walked toward some men stacking bricks into the back of a wagon not yet hitched to horses.

Immediately, angry murmurings started up behind her. After a few minutes she realized that their anger was not directed at Joseph. But it was also obvious that Joseph was trying to resist involvement in something they thought important. When the name Chatto Encinos was repeated several times, she realized what it must be about.

On the morning of July 9, Sam Chung had been at his cabin on Rough Creek northwest of Bodie when he got into an argument with Chatto

Encinos, a Mexican who regularly packed wood into the town. Chatto's mules had found Sam's vegetable patch irresistible and Sam had objected strongly. When Chatto had suggested that Sam was over-reacting, the escalating shouting match had ended when Sam grabbed a double-barreled shotgun and attempted to blast Chatto into the next realm. And indeed, Chatto died several hours after being brought into town, at which point Sam had been arrested. Deputy Sheriff Kirgan now had him in jail with several guards attending to him.

After the men mounted their horses and started back toward town, Amanda walked to the rig where Joseph stood frowning at the backs of his retreating friends.

"That was about the arrest of Sam Chung, wasn't it?" she asked him.

He looked at her for a moment, his thoughts obviously elsewhere, then blinked and answered her slowly. "Yes. The men are planning to break him out of jail tonight and, well, they're very angry."

"Are they threatening to hang him?"

"You've heard of such a thing?"

"I'm from Placerville, remember? It used to be called Hangtown." She smirked and added, "I know the concept."

He nodded, still distracted by what had just occurred. "Oh, yes, of course you do." With a shake of his head, he told her, "And yes, that's the plan. They want me to join them. It's difficult to turn them down."

"Why?"

"Because if I don't show that I am on their side, they could refuse to purchase from me in the future and my business will fail. And they will not include me in their society, which is much the same thing."

"It seems so calculating."

"My dear girl, it's the way of the world." He smiled in a patronizing manner and even added a mild chuckle. Nothing so irritates youth on the verge of adulthood than to be reminded that they are still young, and Amanda looked at Joseph with this thought obvious in her eyes and the line of her mouth. Seeing that he had somehow irritated her, he was quick to pacify. "I only mean that in places like this, I must look out for my own interests because no one else ultimately cares if I live or die."

Rather than comment on such a cynical opinion of life, she said nothing. But he did not miss her pursed lips and stiffened shoulders as she looked away from him toward the men disappearing onto the main road into Bodie. Consequently, she did not see the look of exasperation that flitted across his face.

She turned back to him and asked, "Will they continue to put pressure on you?"

"They don't have to. They fully expect me to join with them, even though I did not promise to do so."

Joseph immediately brought Amanda to her house where he bid her good-bye. He neither helped her down or walked her to the door, and after a curt nod merely turned the rig around and headed toward the heart of town. She wondered whether or not he was going to give in to the wishes of the men later that night.

The next morning when Amanda went into town, the topic of discussion was the same everywhere she went. Almost every conversation included a version of how a small group of heavily armed men had approached the jail to take Sam Chung away. Unfortunately for them, when they got there John Kirgan had displayed to them an empty jail. He then informed the gathering that Sam had been taken into the mountains by guards to protect him from their rash act.

The town had experienced several murders in the past couple of weeks, as well as untold muggings that for some odd reason in Bodie were called garrotings. Consequently, many citizens felt that Kirgan should allow the desired hanging as an example to other miscreants. Their comments were not so much because they were outraged at the loss of Chatto from their midst, as it was a general desire to show the world that offenders should not think Bodie a place where villainy would go unpunished.

Indeed, the next day the editor of the *Daily News* reported that, *"It is our opinion that a little 'hemp practice' would be beneficial in this town."*

When Amanda saw Joseph on the street and stopped to chat for a moment, she chose not to ask him if he had been part of the group that had approached the jail. However, she noted that he was very careful to avoid the subject that practically everyone else in Bodie was discussing.

CHAPTER 4
JULY, 1880

Early on the morning of July 15, after her father had left for work, Amanda found she was not at all sleepy. Consequently, she sat at the kitchen table drinking coffee and reading a copy of Godey's Ladies Magazine by the light of a coal oil lamp.

Just as the sun was suggesting itself over the divide between Silver Hill and Queen Bee Hill, a small explosion nearby brought her to her feet quivering with fear. Then she realized that it had been the loud report of a gun discharging on Green right next to the house. Instinctively Amanda ducked down and hurried into the parlor just as another blast of the gun came to her from a little further east and not far from the Perry house. The men's bedroom door burst open and Matt rushed out with his pants hastily pulled on over his white one-piece, his feet bare and his hair sticking up all over.

Seeing Amanda by the front window, he hollered, "What the hell's going on?"

"Some man is walking east on Green just firing randomly. He doesn't look to be hitting anything." She raised the sash of the window until it was wide open.

Just then a man following the shooter about thirty feet behind called out, "Okay George, give me your pistols before someone gets hurt."

Matt huffed indignantly. "That's Constable Richard O'Malley."

"Do you know the shooter?"

"Yeah, it's George Center. He's a town rowdy and a blacksmith at one of the mines. He's obviously been drinking. But basically he's harmless."

"This doesn't look harmless," Amanda commented with heat. "A bullet could go through a window and hit someone."

"Maybe. But there's no law against shooting a gun in town."

Amanda looked around. "Where's Mike?"

"Don't know. He didn't come home last night."

Amanda returned her attention to the street as Center stopped at the corner of Wood and Green with his hands in his pockets, obviously gripping his guns hidden there. "No son of a bitch is going to take my pistols from me."

Evidently the constable wasn't afraid of Center, because he walked toward him until they were close enough to touch. Center must have thought it too close, as he brought out his guns and pushed both barrels against O'Malley's chest. O'Malley yelped and jumped back about fifteen feet as he pulled out his gun.

Immediately there was an exchange of gunfire and Constable O'Malley's long coat flicked up on one side just above his knees. Center's second shot ricocheted off O'Malley's Colt. But O'Malley's shots were more effective. One hit Center in the leg above the knee and the other his right gun hand, which had the immediate effect of bringing the incident to an end. Center was marched off to jail after O'Malley kindly wrapped his leg wound in a large handkerchief. As he limped along, Center held his hand up, one of his fingers broken and dripping blood down his arm.

Not long after they left the area, the bell in the cupola atop the schoolhouse on Green began clanging. As Amanda carried in wood from the shed out back, she observed only about a dozen children showing up and shook her head sadly. There were at least 500 children enrolled, but no more than 200 attended on any regular basis.

The school house was an interesting building shaped like a shortened cross seventy-two feet long and with the vestibule at the top facing Green. The side wings were classrooms that held fifty students, with the kindergarten children taught in the room furthest from the street. Where these rooms converged in the middle was a gathering room where coats were hung from a row of hooks and dirty boots were placed beneath in winter. Lunch pails were placed directly above on a shelf. Since there were times when the rooms were full to over-flowing and it was hoped that more children would be willing to attend, a new schoolhouse was being planned. But everyone knew it would never see the presence of even half of those enrolled.

Instead of attending school, some of the older boys congregated along Green and harassed the girls as they left school, stopping just short of doing them any serious physical harm. It was an issue of contention between some of the parents, and it was assumed that in a few years some of these boys would end up as a guest at the jail that many jokingly referred to as Hotel de Kirgan.

Besides the more obvious criminal atrocities on the minds of the community, the owners of the Standard and the Bodie mines had begun to complain about thefts of gold. High-grading had always been part of mining camps. Workers with dubious ethics or in great want of funds sometimes carried out a few tiny chunks of gold hidden in pockets, cut seams of clothing, the bowls of pipes under the tobacco, false bottoms of lunch pails, and boot soles. One man had been discovered packing gold dust into the middle of his cigar. But now it was felt that a whole gang of men were doing this, and taking more than just a little dust.

Eventually an assayer was caught hanging around on one of the levels of the Bodie Mine where considerable quantities of rich quartz had recently been worked. There was no good reason for him to be there, so the foreman grabbed him and trussed him up with a gag in his mouth before calling co-workers to join him. They then hid nearby to wait for what was assumed would be the man's cohorts. They had to wait over twenty-four hours, but eventually others showed up who also didn't belong in that location. The fact that they were calling out for the assayer clinched the deal. Unfortunately, the last two of these realized what was happening further down the tunnel and were able to escape unseen. These arrests caused quite a stir in the town.

The incident also caused quite a stir in the household of John Blake. Mike came home late the morning after the arrests in an obvious state of anxiety that he refused to explain. After declining to go into town with Matt for a drink, and refusing even to leave the house, Matt left him on the sofa with a stack of recent newspapers. Amanda set to work preparing bread to rise, and then began paring apples she planned to stew with cinnamon, brown sugar and raisins.

Her thoughts were occupied with the events of the last few days, and she didn't at first realize that Mike had entered the kitchen. Then she heard his raspy breathing close behind and whirled around to face him. "Mike! What do you want?"

"I thought we might get to know each other better." His lips were smiling, but his eyes were hard and bright.

"If you want to talk, do it from the table." She tried to divert his attention. "Do you want a cup of coffee?"

"Naw." He looked her up and down and grinned as he said, "I want you."

Amanda had no delusion as to what he meant. "Are you out of your mind? My father will horsewhip you if you're too familiar with me."

His laugh was brutal. "I've seen how he is. He treats you like a servant. No matter what you tell him, if I say you're over-reacting he'll believe me just so he doesn't have to deal with something awkward."

She had to admit that Mike wasn't far off the mark. But whether or not this was true of her father, right then no one was around to rescue her and she was only too aware of her vulnerability.

"That may be as you say." She looked into his eyes and hardened her resolve. "However, there *are* men in this town who consider me a nice woman, and who are interested in me as more than a friend. They would not take kindly to your pushing yourself on me."

That caught him off guard long enough that Amanda could press her advantage. Raising her voice to a loud, angry shout, she said, "Now back off and get out of my kitchen." She grabbed a long butcher knife from the counter and held it in front of her with the blade only an inch from his stomach. "Now!"

Confronted with such implacable self-assurance, Mike realized Amanda might not after all be the sweet timid female he had assumed her to be, so he backed off. As soon as he retreated to the men's bedroom, Amanda grabbed her shawl and left the house. Walking quickly across Green she stopped at the corner of the schoolhouse where she could meld into the building's shadow.

What had she done to bring on such disrespectful treatment? She was filled with blame and guilt, yet searching her actions, she could find nothing that might have encouraged him. Her confusion was overwhelming, and mixed with dread at having to return home. Even the thought of walking up the street past the house to Charlotte's home brought on a wave of fear as she realized how close to being assaulted she had been. She began trembling as hot tears collected on her cheeks.

"Miss Blake?" Through the blur of her tears she saw Roger Murphy standing next to her with a look of intense concern on his face. "Are you ill? Can I help you to the doctor's?"

"No," she murmured, unable to look him in the eyes. "I'm quite well, thank you."

"Has something happened to your father?" His face expressed his anxiety without reservation or artifice. "Please allow me to help you."

She took a deep shuddery breath and fumbled in the pocket of her dress for a handkerchief. Roger removed his own and held it out to her. She dabbed at her eyes, then blew her nose. Her smile was crooked as she said, "I'll return the handkerchief to you later."

"No need. Now, come with me and we'll have a brandy at the Bodie House." He took her arm and led her down Green. "You can then unburden yourself of what's happened."

Amanda let herself be led down the street, over the foot bridge spanning Bodie Creek and into the hotel on the corner of Green and Main. The hotel had been built by W. A. Johnson in '77 with fifteen well-furnished rooms upstairs, all from the wood of his dismantled hotel in Markleeville when he had heard of the rush to Bodie. Thus having been built with this seasoned lumber and with double walls, it was better insulated against the cold and noises than most hotels in town.

They entered the dining room immediately at the front and across from the bar to the right, and found a table in a shadowed corner. Roger ordered them both a small brandy along with a pitcher of water for Amanda.

After she added water to her brandy and had taken a sip, he asked, "Can you tell me now what happened?"

She looked up and met concerned blue eyes shaded by a beige Stetson, and decided to hold nothing back about Mike's behavior that afternoon. She also told him of her uneasiness around Mike from the time she had first met him. When she described how she had threatened the young man with her kitchen knife, Roger's smile was radiant.

Amanda felt somewhat better after this reaction and told him, "I can't imagine what I did to make him think I'd welcome his advances."

Roger made a sharp noise in his throat. "He wasn't expecting you to welcome his advances. He didn't want to romance you; he wanted to dominate you. You shouldn't blame yourself for what that disrespectful clod did."

"But he's right about my father." She felt the prick of tears back of her eyes. "He'll choose to believe Mike."

After a moment's thought, Roger told her, "I'll return with you. When John comes home, I'll be the one to tell him what happened. He'll believe me." He said this last with such certainty that Amanda wondered what was back of it. But Roger changed the subject and as he talked, she began to relax. And even though she knew he was trying to get her mind diverted, she found herself drawn into his stories.

She especially enjoyed hearing him describe his youth in Jamestown on the other side of the Sierra. Like Amanda, he too had been an only child. "It's a charming little town that started up during the rush in '49. My parents had a small house and a large garden. We also had a dozen chickens so we could have eggs for our own use and enough to give to a poor family down the road. Over the years we had a series of hogs, and usually two dairy cows. I guess we were considered well off. I loved taking care of the animals and the garden."

"You did?" She laughed at the thought of him ankle deep in mud throwing feed to chickens or slopping hogs.

"I know, I know," he laughed, his eyes glistening with mirth. "But I did like it. It wasn't until I left the area that I found out that I had a talent for cards."

"What did your father do?"

Roger hesitated a moment before saying, "You're going to think this odd, but I'm not really sure. We never seemed to want for money, but he didn't go out each day to work, either."

"Had he made his fortune before you were born?"

"I think so. It was never talked about. My mother said something once that made me think that maybe he too had been a gambler at one time. Mom was also pretty closed up about her past. All I know is that she was born in California, and she said once that her character was a product of the gold rush. When I asked what that meant, she just smiled and changed the subject." He shrugged and asked her, "So, overall, how do you like living in Bodie?"

"I'm not sure yet. I like being with my father, but he's not as interested in being with me I think."

Roger nodded. "Some men don't know how to be a father to girls. That doesn't mean he isn't very fond of you."

"I suppose." She looked up at a large clock on the wall and gave a slight involuntary shudder. "Speaking of my father, I'd best get home and finish the supper I started. His shift has ended and he'll be home shortly."

Roger signaled to the waiter, who nodded his head but did not approach with a bill, and together Roger and Amanda left the dining room. She started to ask if he ran a tab there, which she thought odd in a hotel so far from his end of town, but decided it was too familiar a question on the strength of their short acquaintance.

When John came home half an hour later, he was surprised to find Roger on the front porch. It was obvious to Amanda as she peeked out through the curtains that the men were acquainted by the way John shook hands with Roger.

Although their conversation started out in mutually low voices, and Amanda couldn't make out the actual words, she could hear the escalating anger in their tone. She raised the window and quickly returned to the kitchen where she set the apple mixture on the fire. She could hear Roger swear several times as John tried to make light of what he was being told. Eventually, however, the two men came into the house and John went into the bedroom to confront Mike.

After ten minutes, Mike came out carrying his packed satchel. He said nothing to anyone, but merely stomped through the parlor and out the front door. When Roger followed him outside, Amanda crept to the door and carefully opened it a crack so she could hear as well as see them.

Roger, slightly taller than Mike, had the boy by the arm and was leaning into him until their faces were only inches apart. Roger's voice was brittle with a rage he was barely capable of keeping in check. "If you ever so much as look at Amanda again, much less approach her for any reason, the coyotes will be feasting on your sorry carcass after you have an *accident*. Tell me you understand so I don't have to break your arm."

"You wouldn't kill me," Mike sassed him belligerently.

"You know nothing about me or my past deeds." Suddenly the rage disappeared and Roger's eyes took on a cold, unremitting hardness as he told the trembling young man, "Trust me. I'd take care of you and then go back to work whistling a lively tune. Now tell me you'll leave her alone, as well as any other woman here in Bodie."

Mike knew better than to talk back this time and only nodded his head while mumbling, "Okay. Yes."

As soon as Roger released him, Mike stepped back and rubbed his upper arm while glaring at Roger, who turned his back to the boy and started toward the porch. Amanda opened the door wider for him and glanced at Mike, who was reaching into his pocket where she knew he always kept a knife.

She called out, "He's got a knife!"

Roger leapt aside as he caught the action from the corner of his eye. The knife flashed past, barely missing Roger's shoulder and thudding into the old wood of the house.

Before Mike could run away, Roger leaped forward and grabbed his collar with his left hand while knocking him down with a smashing blow to the temple with his right fist. With Mike on his back on the ground, Roger landed the heel of his boot on Mike's face, efficiently breaking his nose before stepping back.

Two men, well known and upright citizens passing by on Green, had witnessed Mike throw the knife at Roger. They came up and jerked the young man to his feet, one of them saying, "We'll take him to the jail. Do you want to press charges?"

"No. He's gotten the point. You'd best get him to a doctor, though."

The men nodded and helped the groaning and choking young man into town. It was the last Amanda ever saw of Mike. She later heard that he left the next day on the first stage out of Bodie for Virginia City.

Roger passed through the door that Amanda held open to him, and without a word she led him into the kitchen. Reaching to the back of a cupboard, she removed the bottle of her father's good whiskey and poured him a small glass. He took it gratefully and swallowed half of it before coming up for air.

John came in and Roger told him, "I had to take Mike down a peg. He came after me with a knife. If I were you, John, I'd add a slide catch to the front and back doors so he can't break in when Amanda's here alone." He went to the windows and added, "At least you have a stick between the window and the top frame so it can't be opened."

"Ah, he'll not do anything so rash," John drawled as he sat down on the sofa and picked up a newspaper. He raised the paper before his face, mumbling from behind it, "If he comes after anyone, it'll be you."

Roger walked over to him and brought his hand smashing down on the paper so that John was forced to look up and meet Roger's blazing eyes. His adrenaline had not yet subsided, and he wasn't in the mood to not be taken seriously. "You would have said the same thing about his threatening your daughter if yesterday someone had suggested to you that he'd ever do that. Or that he'd try to stab me in the back with a knife."

"What?" John's eyes bulged.

"Didn't you see what happened out front after Mike left?"

"No. I was changing out of my dirty clothes."

"Oh." Roger stood up straighter. "Well, he did."

John shook his head and then asked, trying to hide a smile, "And what did you do to him?"

"I knocked him down and stomped his nose. I'm not proud of that."

John laughed. "Maybe not, and I know it's not funny. But he can be such a horse's ass. And he evidently under-estimated you."

Roger shrugged, suddenly uncomfortable; whether with how he had reacted to John or how he had treated Mike, Amanda couldn't tell. But he suddenly uttered a sigh and told her, "If Mike bothers you again, you let me know. Okay?"

She nodded, overcome by his solicitude and feeling tears of gratitude well up in her eyes. Before she could say anything, however, he bid her good-night and left.

She turned to her father, only to watch him continue his perusal of the newspapers. He showed no further interest in what had happened or in how his daughter might be feeling. When Matt came home and asked where Mike was, she explained to him what had taken place while John was forced to listen. She was surprised to see that Matt showed little surprise, but definitely expressed satisfaction that Mike was gone.

He told Amanda, "I'm sorry you had to go through this, but I really don't think you need worry about him now. He'll turn his attentions elsewhere quickly. Either that or leave town."

John told them, his tone quarrelsome, "We'll have to make up the money he contributed for food and rent."

Matt looked at him with raised brows. "Yes, and we'll have to chop the wood too. But so what? He's a bum and good riddance."

Watching her father as he got up and went out through the kitchen to the privy, she told Matt, "I'm so very grateful to Roger for being willing to confront father. For some reason he was sure father would listen to him."

"Not surprising." Matt poured himself a drink from the bottle still on the kitchen table. "When John first came here, Roger broke up a fight that wouldn't have turned out well for your daddy if it had continued. I was there, and I hustled John away while Roger took his place in the fight. He got a few cuts and bruises, but Roger has a powerful right and the whole thing ended quickly. That's how I met John."

"Did the man ever come after Roger?"

"They tossed him in jail and after he sobered up he couldn't remember the fight. Then a day later he was shot in a brawl."

After Matt retired to the parlor to read, Amanda sat for a long time at the table sipping the last of the coffee laced with a shot of the whiskey. She began wondering about her future in Bodie, where violence and death was taken for granted in a society that only grudgingly made way for women, who were carefully ordered in a very rigid societal hierarchy.

Starting at the top were married women with children, then respectably married women without children, followed by the single women of marriageable age who were called spinsters if they were past twenty-one. Then came Amanda's strata of young women needing to be "carefully watched". The bottom, of course, was reserved for the "fair but frail" ladies who resided on Bonanza Street.

The next day being fine, Amanda walked all the way to the brickyard, eager to see Joseph and tell him what had happened between her and Mike. He listened while nervously straightening the items on his desk in the vestibule of the brickyard office, although the desk didn't look like it needed the attention.

Before she could tell him about Roger's intercession, he said, "Mike would never have done anything to you. He was only flirting."

"But when I told him to back off," she objected, "he didn't."

Joseph impatiently brushed aside her assertions. "He would have."

Looking out through the open door at the road, his anxiety visibly increased. He therefore didn't see the look on Amanda's face, and was oblivious to her disappointment in his reaction. He turned to her and said without preamble, "You'll have to excuse me now. I've got important work to do."

"Of course." She fought the uncomfortable awareness of hurt feelings, which she readily acknowledged was unreasonable on her part, and began her walk back to town. She was not so deep in thought, however, that she neglected to notice a woman approaching in a black rig with the top up and the side drapes down. Even though she was wearing a hat with a short veil, Amanda was sure it was Johanna Treloar. It took no leap of imagination to realize that Johanna was on her way to the brickyard.

Amanda continued her walk into town, enjoying the sun on her cheeks and the longer days of high summer with its warmth that lingered until the sun was well down. Pushing thoughts of Joseph aside, she stopped at the Bull's Head Market across from Mr. Boone's barn and corral before wandering back into town and stopping to listen to those making speeches on Main.

Bodie was not known to be a particularly political town. During the Civil War, Aurora's boom had brought men to that area who claimed to be a dedicated Republican or Democrat, and consequently debates had been frequent and sometimes had even led to a fight. It had impacted the Aurora mines and the business of making money, and had made for a contentious atmosphere.

Bodie, however, chose to focus on the business of mining and to just get on with life. The war was seldom referred to, being acknowledged as an easy trigger for emotions that were still raw fifteen years after it had ended.

Nevertheless, with 1880 an election year, each evening after most of the freight traffic cleared Main, people with political opinions climbed on top of crates or barrels and expounded their views in their loudest voices. Most people listened, nodded or shook their heads, and then moved on. But of course others had to respond with varying degrees of argumentative ire. In consequence of this, sometimes a scuffle would ensue that had to be broken up by one of the constables.

One individual, trying to get some sleep at a nearby hotel, climbed out onto the balcony and looked down upon the head of one such orator loudly making his point. The disturbed sleeper proceeded to make *his* point by dumping a chamber pot of well-aimed liquid onto the head of the shouter. Of course, the story spread quickly and was for days the source of much raucous enjoyment throughout the town.

When Amanda noted one morning that the wood shed held only half a cord of wood, she went to the wood lot just up Green from the house. There she ordered two cords to be delivered to the back yard by the shed. She tried not to think about how her father and Matt had grumbled at the expense. As Matt had pointed out, "Several days' wages is a hell of a lot for wood."

Remembering Cherry Wilson's advice, Amanda had informed the men, "If you want to eat, you'll have to pay the price. And better to pay that now than even more when it gets really cold." They acknowledged her logic and decided they were enjoying her cooking too much to have it come to an end, so they gave her the money.

Just as she concluded her business at the wood lot, Charlotte Perry approached with a smile on her face. Her luxurious brown hair, this day held back by a pale green ribbon, glowed in the sun. Her simple pale green dress had only a few knife pleats across the bottom of the skirt, while the tight fitting bodice showed off her small waist.

After they enjoyed a few minutes conversation, a woman who lived just south of the wood lot came to join them. Charlotte introduced her as her good friend Emily Eastman and added, "Her husband Frank is an engineer at the Standard." Amanda now knew who the couple had been with the Perrys on the Fourth of July.

Emily was the tallest of the three women, with green eyes and brown hair showing hints of red and pulled back into a cascade of long curls. She was dressed comfortably in a simple rose colored skirt and a white waist with pin-tucks across the front and a brooch at the throat of the high neck. She had dared to step outside without a shawl, and possibly was not even wearing a corset. Amanda was immediately intrigued by this woman.

Charlotte told Amanda, "Emily just returned from the mill town of Lundy west of Mono Lake. She was nursing the sister of a man who runs the forge at the Standard."

"Oh, are you a nurse?" Amanda asked.

"Not really." Emily smiled and humor filled her face. "I just have a little experience of it in a practical way. And I've occasionally had the opportunity to help people."

"I've heard of Lundy," Amanda told her. "Isn't it at the end of a long canyon into the Sierra?"

Emily's eyes danced with fond memories as she nodded. "Yes. It's very attractively situated, and Ida Steele was a nice woman. All along the dark blue lake and up into the canyon there's mining and lumbering activity, with tents and lean-tos and new cabins filling every spot they can be fitted."

"How long were you there?"

"A couple of weeks, and I'm very glad to be back. It's a far more primitive place than Bodie and much smaller too."

Amanda looked confused. "Your husband didn't mind your being gone that long?"

"Yes, but he's very understanding. And he thought it would do me good to get away from here for awhile."

Thinking of her mother's frustration at always having to argue for permission whenever she wanted to leave the house just to go into town, Amanda said, "You're fortunate that he gave his permission."

"Why is that?"

"Well, a woman can't go against her husband's wishes."

Emily and Charlotte looked at each other and burst into gales of laughter.

Looking at Amanda's obvious confusion, Charlotte repented. "We shouldn't have laughed. What you say is very true of most marriages, of course. It just doesn't apply to us."

Emily added, drying her eyes with a hanky pulled from a skirt pocket, "On the other hand, Frank is usually very wise about the things he expects of me. More than once I've regretted not taking his advice."

Again, Charlotte and Emily exchanged looks that brought forth mirthful smiles. Emily told the two women, "Why don't you join me at home for some tea. I made gingersnaps this morning."

Both women accepted eagerly. Since the Eastman home was right behind the wood lot, they were soon settled at a small table in Emily's kitchen with tea cups and cookies distributed among them.

They soon were sharing information about their lives before coming to Bodie, as well as their current experience. Emily spoke of her time in Lone Pine in the Owens Valley along the southern reaches of the Sierra, and in the process alluded to "her mountain" and the view of it from the boarding house where she had lived. Charlotte explained, with a roll of her eyes but a tolerant twitch at the corner of her mouth, that this meant Mt. Whitney, the tallest mountain in the United States.

Soon Amanda was feeling as though Emily and Charlotte were acquaintances of long standing, and she was enjoying these outgoing women immensely. Their stories of what they called their adventures amused and delighted her. But she sat up in surprise when Charlotte and Emily described those exploits that their husbands knew nothing about, which included the time they dressed as men and climbed down into one of the mines shortly before a cave-in occurred.

"I wrote my friend Carrie about it in such detail that she wrote back a very chastising response." Emily laughed at the memory. "Ah, dear Carrie, what a sweet soul she is."

"Where does she live?"

"In the East. I lived with her family after my parents died in the Chicago fire when I was a girl. I came West in '78 to be married, but not to Frank." Instead of clarifying this mysterious comment, Emily returned to the subject of Carrie, and of course Amanda was too polite to ask her to explain more. "I miss Carrie so much. I write her often and she told me that she's saving every letter. Imagine that. She thinks her children will find them interesting when they grow up."

"I wonder if Bodie will still be here then," Charlotte mused.

Amanda was surprised at such a thought. "Oh, surely it will."

Emily shrugged. "Hopefully, because it's so unique, but mining towns are notorious for their boom and bust ways. Look at Aurora. It's now just a shadow of its former glory."

"Although," Charlotte added, "being so much built of brick, it should last for hundreds of years."

As the women continued to share their stories and tales of Bodie's life in the boom years, which actually only covered the last three years, Amanda enjoyed hearing about it from a woman's perspective. She soon realized that she was also getting a different perspective of marriage than anything she had ever heard before, and was now aware of a surprising degree of willfulness in some women.

Still in the process of defining her view of the world around her, much less who she wanted to be as an adult in that world, Amanda was surprised at how in tune she felt with the views of these women. She was even more surprised at how excited she was by what some would think of as their past questionable choices and behavior.

Watching Emily refill the tea pot with hot water from the heavy iron kettle on the stove, Amanda sighed. "I sometimes wonder if I'll ever marry."

Emily laughed. "You're only nineteen."

"Yes, but many of my friends from Placerville have been married for years."

"I know," Charlotte said. "I myself was younger than you when I married."

"Really? How many children do you have?"

Charlotte looked down at her cup and murmured, "We have no children."

Amanda blushed and blurted out, "I'm such a tactless oaf."

Charlotte looked up and smiled. "Not at all. It's a reasonable question."

Emily cut in quickly. "Well, I was twenty-one when I married and some were calling me a spinster. But now here I am happily situated. I assume I'll have a child some day, and as far as that goes, it's possible Charlotte here might yet have one too."

Charlotte smiled wistfully, but said nothing.

Emily laid a hand over one of Charlotte's. Looking at Amanda, her voice lowered as she said, "I lost a baby several months ago. I wasn't very far forward in the pregnancy, but we felt the loss deeply."

"I'm so sorry. I understand such a happening isn't uncommon the first time." It was more question than statement, not having had a mother willing to discuss the topic, much less what one had to do that led to such a state.

"True," Emily told her, "and I was very ill with a sickness that a lot of people in the town had at that time. Frank was torn between work and my needs, so without Charlotte's care, I might not have made it."

Amanda gasped. "Your poor husband must have been frantic." When Emily only nodded, Amanda asked the women, "Is it very difficult living with a man day in and day out?" She thought of Joseph and felt an underlying uneasiness that she could not define. But when she thought of Roger, her heart began racing and an odd warm sensation passed through her body.

Charlotte smiled. "It depends on the man, and the woman. But one thing you should know." Charlotte looked at her intently. "However thoughtful and attentive a man acts during courtship, it won't last long after he says *I do*."

"Really?" Amanda was surprised that Charlotte would say this, knowing how happy she was in her marriage. "Do they lie to deceive?"

"Oh, no." Charlotte shook her head as her smile twisted into resignation. "They're just very careful to put their best foot forward in order to win a woman's hand."

"And after marriage?"

"Not so much."

Emily laughed. "You could say they relax a bit. So forget the romantic literature. Marriage is a matter of finding someone whose sounds and smells you can tolerate. That's why one should marry for love. It acts to mask much of the reality."

They all laughed, but Charlotte sobered as she shook her head. "We're very fortunate women, with husbands who treat us well. But last year a

Cornish miner here in town was arrested for beating his wife. Unfortunately, it's not an uncommon occurrence."

"What happened to him?"

"He was convicted and put on probation. Tom Treloar is known for having a hot temper. Some think it's related to an injury to his head he sustained in a mining accident a couple of years ago in Virginia City. He's a little slow sometimes." Charlotte's tone sharpened as she remembered the women she knew who were not as fortunate in their marriages as herself. "No woman deserves to have her eyes blackened by her husband."

Amanda put in, somewhat tentatively, "A man I know is a friend of Tom Treloar and his wife Johanna."

"Oh?" Emily teased. "You're seeing someone?"

Amanda blushed. Then, noting Charlotte's frown, she cleared her throat and made light of the idea. "Oh, no. I've shared a few meals with him. And, well, he kissed me once during the Fourth of July celebration." She then added quickly, "But I don't think he has serious thoughts about me, and I certainly have none about him."

"A kiss is pretty serious," Emily pointed out. "Who is this boy?"

"He's a little too old to be called a boy," Charlotte put in, unable to hide the asperity in her tone. "It's Joseph DeRoche."

The sudden freeze of movement in Emily, and the pinched lips of Charlotte as she glanced over at Emily, did not go unnoticed by Amanda. "What is it? I know you don't care for him, Charlotte. But I can tell that you don't either, Emily."

The two friends exchanged looks, but it was Charlotte who said, "There's been some gossip that the reason Tom lost his temper with Johanna, and consequently hit her, was because he thought her to be flirting with Joseph."

"That doesn't mean Joseph encouraged her attentions." She still considered him at the least a friend, so she didn't tell them of seeing Johanna's rig approaching the brickyard the day before.

Emily was quick to speak up. "No, of course it doesn't. And Tom may have imagined it. Besides, all this happened a year ago and nothing has happened since." She tactfully did not mention that the gossip about an affair had not ceased, and had even increased of late.

After writing out the recipe for Emily's gingersnaps, Amanda started out for home. She was barely away from the Eastman house before Emily and Charlotte expressed their concern for the gentle and somewhat naïve young woman who had just left them. Reputation was everything to a young woman, and they considered Joseph not a proper companion.

Nor for that matter was a gambler all that acceptable, but few people knew of her friendship with Roger. Amanda wasn't ready to share him. Why, she couldn't explain. However, if she had mentioned him, she would have discovered that Emily and Charlotte already knew how he had interceded with Mike, because they had husbands who drank beer at Wagner's. It was common talk there because one of the men who had taken Mike away sometimes worked the bar. Roger refused to discuss it with anyone.

On the morning of July 14, dawn was once more greeted by the sound of cannon fire followed by a 21-gun salute. At noon the 21 guns went off again. It was Bastille Day, and those in town from France were eager to celebrate, their tricolor flag seen waving from the staff on Bodie Peak. There was a banquet that evening at the Grand Central Hotel on north Main for those who could afford it, whether or not they were French.

Amanda had been pleased how readily her father had agreed to escort her, and she was proud of how nice he looked in his freshly pressed suit and bowler hat. For herself, she had purchased a new gown with the last of her traveling money. Being a pale pink satin with an overskirt of darker rose silk, it made a delicious swishing noise that only quality fabrics seem able to achieve. The neckline was scooped low without being overtly suggestive and the sleeves tapered to just above the elbow.

As they approached the big white hotel, the glow from the warm kerosene lights that filled the interior reached out to greet them. Inside, the tables in the lobby displayed fresh flowers obtained from Bridgeport, with more flowers in the dining room where the chairs and tables had been pushed against the walls so people had room to dance. A large number of dancers were already enjoying the tunes coming from a small band set up in front of the back wall blocking the dining room from the kitchen.

Amanda and John filled their plates from the rich array of foods arranged on tables along the wall and then settled themselves at a smaller one occupied by three couples. They introduced themselves to one another, and polite conversation began that was full of compliments about the event and the good weather of the week. After only a few bites of his food, however, John got up without comment and wandered off to visit with some men standing in a group on the far side of the room.

The men greeted John just as they were adding their own ingredients to the bland punch in their cups from flasks surreptitiously slipped from coat pockets. When she saw one of the men tip his flask over John's cup, and John saying something that made the others laugh, it was clear that he had settled in with them. Amanda fought the urge to go to him and remind him of his promise to spend the evening with her, but instead she just sighed loudly with disgust and poked at the food on her plate.

The women at the table with Amanda, whose husbands had also wandered off, were soon engaged in conversations related to the hardships of marriage, mothering, and Bodie in general. Amanda felt completely left out and brought her plate to the area set aside for cleanup. Wondering how she could make her exit unseen, she turned around and almost bumped into Roger Murphy.

"Good evening, Miss Blake. Did you enjoy the banquet?"

She smiled pleasantly. It seemed a long time ago that she had spoken sharply to him when he had approached her at another gathering. Yet he had still been so kind over the trouble with Mike. Her smile warmed even more. "The food was good but I'm afraid I didn't enjoy it that much." She shot a glance in her father's direction. "I came here with him, hoping we could spend some time together enjoying one another's company."

Roger nodded with understanding. "And now John is with his friends while you fend for yourself."

Amanda shrugged and turned her back on her father. "Not only that, but the men are drinking, which is not supposed to be allowed."

"I know. I saw their flasks. But as long as they behave themselves, it probably won't be commented on."

Amanda looked down at the floor. "I think the lady manager of the hotel is more concerned about any dirt that might have been tracked in on the floor. I saw her scowling at some of the men's boots."

"Yes. Her name is Mrs. Emee Chestnut and she's fairly new to the hotel."

"Yes, I met her the day I arrived. What does her husband do?"

"She's not married." This meant that the *Mrs.* was just the usual title used to show respect for a single business woman, especially if she was over thirty. "And she's not as strict as the men running the Miners' Union Hall."

"Considering how many men are in and out of the Hall all the time, I find it surprising anyone would think they could keep the floors clean there."

Roger laughed and said, "I was once on the receiving end of a tongue lashing because I forgot to wipe my boots on the rug outside the door. I haven't done *that* again."

Enjoying Roger's company as she was, she nevertheless told him, "I suppose I should find father and head home while he can still walk there."

"Uh," Roger began as she looked around the room, "he left a moment ago with the others. I think they were probably headed north to one of the dance houses to work off some energy."

Amanda smiled, her cheeks warming as she said, "My, but you're tactful."

The corner of his mouth twitched upward and he cleared his throat before speaking. "May I walk you home? It's getting late for a woman to be out alone this far north in town."

After only a moment's hesitation, she agreed and they started walking south down Main Street. Typical in high elevations even in summer, as evening approached the air had cooled considerably after the heat of the day. So much so that Amanda was glad of her short cape.

Sensing this, Roger asked, "Would you like my jacket?"

"Oh, no, I'm quite comfortable." But she turned and looked up at him somewhat surprised. "But thank you for asking."

He looked at her with puzzlement, and she realized that to him such chivalrous behavior was nothing unusual. She told him, "I suppose I've become accustomed to the casual if not crude behavior around me most of the time."

"And yet there are by far more decent people here, running their businesses or working their jobs, not to mention raising families, than there are those of the rough element. They just get most of the attention, that's all. Especially in the newspapers."

"You're right, of course. I'll try to remember that."

Arriving at the house, she thanked him for his company, and he assured her that it had been his pleasure. Once inside and standing at the kitchen window, she pulled aside the lace curtain and watched him walk down Green toward town. Her thoughts as she assessed his physique and the forcefulness of his stride made her blush, and she quickly dropped the curtain and retired to her room.

At the end of the month Joseph stopped by the house to ask Amanda if she would care to join him for coffee in town. On their way to the Can-

Can Restaurant, evidently Joseph's favorite place to eat, they approached the Grand Central Hotel and noticed a small crowd gathered in front.

A man called out to them, "Frenchy, hello. Have you come to see the exhibit?"

Joseph introduced Amanda to Dr. Berry before saying, "What exhibit are you talking about?"

"Louis Sammons from Mono Lake has been up to stuff."

"What stuff?"

The doctor smirked. "You'll see."

And indeed they did. Evidently Louis, living as he did on the shores of a lake so saline that it was sometimes called "the dead sea of the West", had become fascinated with the effects of the water on local wildlife. After a time, however, rabbits and coyotes had ceased to serve his increasingly ravenous desire for his form of scientific knowledge. The only thing that would suffice would be that of a human body, and for that he turned to the Piutes.

He explained to all who would listen, and there were many, how he pickled their bodies for two years in a strong solution of carbonate and sulphate of soda, chloride of sodium and anything else he could think of that mirrored the chemical content of the lake water, and of course the lake water itself. He then noted the condition of the bodies.

On display at the hotel this day was a portion of a scalp. He informed an eager reporter that he intended to ship a whole petrified Indian to the Medical Museum in San Francisco. Whether or not he did this, no one ever discovered, for Louis mysteriously disappeared from the Mono Lake region soon after his trip to Bodie.

Joseph was fascinated with the exhibit, but Amanda asked to leave. He laughed and asked her, "Do you still feel like eating?"

"I'd like a glass of water first I think."

He ordered her a sherry along with the water, and she was more grateful than he knew.

At a table near them was Henry Ward, the young English undertaker who was in charge of the funeral parlor in town and the hearse house out by the cemetery. Henry had originally come to Bodie from Reno with the intention of opening a furniture store, although his trade of choice was undertaking. He also built caskets of quality and style that greatly pleased the families of the deceased. His business as a furniture maker had waned, but he had no problem staying busy with his undertaking business and casket sales.

A fire whistle broke out on the far side of town near the Standard Mill and several people in the restaurant rushed onto the sidewalk while looking in that direction. Even more people stayed in their seat, knowing as they did that it was the day the water system was being tested. Notices had been posted around town for several days.

At their table, Amanda asked Joseph, "I imagine fire in a wooden town like this is a constant fear."

"Absolutely. It's been a problem in small sections, but so far we've avoided a huge conflagration." He shrugged. "But it is inevitable."

Amanda looked at him with a puckered brow. "You seem incredibly sanguine about it."

The shrug of his shoulders was eloquent. "There isn't anything we can do about what is inevitable. Since the first of the year we've established four fire companies. The biggest and first company is the Neptune Hose Company with eighty men and a hose cart. Then we added in February the Babcock Engine Company, also called The Bodie. It has 46 volunteers. After that the Hook and Ladder Company organized with twenty men and after that the Champion Hose Company came along with sixty-five men. They have a very nice carriage with 500 feet of hose."

"Okay, okay," Amanda laughed. "I accept that the fire protection in this town is impressive. But how was all this paid for? By the mine owners and business men?"

"In a way. For awhile we had even more balls and social events than usual. People paid handsomely to attend because they knew the money would help pay for the water hydrants."

"When the fire bell goes off, do they all show up?"

Joseph smiled and shook his head. "It's odd you should ask. Just this May there was a fire at the Central Market and they did all show up. And then they fought over who should hook up to the hydrant of the new Bodie Water Company."

"And meanwhile the fire was burning?"

"Oh, yes." He laughed at the memory. "But it was put out before the neighboring buildings were badly damaged. The good part of what happened was that the fire departments agreed to divide up the town into districts."

"How do they know which district is on fire when the bell goes off?"

"They've devised a system of whistles and bells, with a different sound for each district, so the volunteers for that district are the ones who go to their stations. For instance, that portion of the town north of Standard Avenue is District One, and all south of that is District Two. All east of the avenue is the Third District."

At that moment they were approached by Deputy Sheriff John Kirgan, the town's popular law enforcement officer. Amanda thought him a mild looking man until she met his eyes, and then she saw what so many criminals had seen. There was a cold reserve and caution there, and one knew instinctively that he would put justice ahead of even friendship. At the moment he wore no gun in a holster as he usually did, but no one doubted that he was armed.

Although Joseph stiffened at Kirgan's approach, he quickly plastered a gracious smile on his face. "Hello, John. Looking for a foul villain?"

"No," Kirgan smiled, the sun-baked lines around his eyes deepening. "I'm just going around today reminding everyone to donate to old Johnson's fund. We need to get him out of here to the medical care he needs in San Francisco."

"I've already contributed," a suddenly relaxed Joseph told him. "There may have been men who didn't sign the census last month, but they won't hesitate to step forward to help out poor Johnson."

"Why didn't everyone sign up?" Amanda asked.

Kirgan laughed shortly. "There are a lot of men here trying to escape the law somewhere else. Or maybe a wife or a debt. They'd be afraid of being found. As for the rest, the census takers weren't as conscientious as they could have been."

"True," Joseph agreed. "They avoided most of those living in the boarding houses on the hill because they thought them not permanent residents."

"But that's not true," Amanda commented.

Joseph shrugged. "Yes, but they didn't want to hear it."

"Were the Piutes included?"

Kirgan shook his head. "No, and neither were most of the Chinese or many of the Mexicans and other foreigners who live here."

"It won't be very accurate then," Amanda pointed out the obvious. "What a shame that will be for historians in the future."

The two men looked at her in surprise. It was obvious that neither of them had thought of themselves and Bodie as worthy of future historical interest. Kirgan gave a quick shake to his head, as though ridding himself of the concept like he would a pesky fly, then quickly bid them good day. He moved on to another table, thinking the young Amanda a pretty lass, but capable of fancy ideas.

Indeed, it would be shown in the future that of the foreign born in Bodie in 1880, there were 850 Irish, 750 Canadian, 550 English/Welsh, 250 German, 350 Chinese, 100 Mexican, 120 Scottish, 80 French, 60 Norwegian, and 19 African.

On her way home, Amanda stopped at Eggleston's Market for a few items. It was really more for an excuse to remain away from the tiny house and the preparation of yet another meal, but she also liked Ben Eggleston. He always greeted her in such a way that made her feel welcome, and even though he did this with everyone who came through the door, she had the feeling that he was especially glad to see her. Possibly this was because she was an appreciative audience of his stories about the area that he enjoyed regaling her with if the shop was not crowded.

This day, while an elderly miner friend of Mr. Eggleston's sat on a barrel nearby, he was serving a Chinese gentleman with a long braid flowing down the back of his boxy white tunic. Amanda was surprised to note a Chinaman so far from the district at the north end of town, but when the man faced forward, she saw that it was Ah Ching from the laundry.

Mr. Eggleston told him, "You take care of that cold now. Make the beef tea like I told you and sip it hot."

"Thank you, Ben. I will do that." The man's usually soft lilting voice was hoarse. As he turned to leave, he saw Amanda and received a smile from her. He bowed slightly, shot her a weak smile in return, and left the market.

"What a nice man," Amanda commented.

"Yes, he is," Mr. Eggleston agreed.

"You must know him well, since he called you by your first name."

"I met him years ago in Dogtown."

"I've heard that place mentioned before, but I'm not clear where it is."

The old miner stroked his long grizzled beard and shifted his weight on the barrel. Speaking with an odd lazy accent, he spoke up with a correction. "Where it *was*."

Mr. Eggleston declared, "There's still a few men scratching out an existence there. It's west of here, at the end of the Bridgeport-Bodie Road."

"Why did they call it such an unattractive name?"

"It comes from a miner's term for a primitive camp, and it was always that. In the beginning it was just a few caves dug into the low hillsides and some shacks made from piles of scrub and canvas. Eventually a few wooden shacks were knocked together. This was back in the '50's. By the end of that decade, gold had been discovered at Monoville above Mono Lake, and everyone in the town moved there. The Chinese moved into Dogtown and made a pretty good living off finding what little gold there was in the tailings. They were well established there by the end of the '60's."

The miner looked out the front window, probed a back molar with his forefinger, and said, "Monoville. Old Chris from Dogtown brought back samples of gold dust on July 4. Right proud he was of his find. But no one believed him. Thought he was making a bad joke. Almost gave him the rope for it. But he was knowed to give the straight goods so they checked it out. He was right."

"Poor Chris didn't benefit from his own discovery," Mr. Eggleston put in.

"Why not?" Amanda asked as she pointed to the cans of condensed milk on the shelf behind the counter. She added a bag of green coffee to the items accumulating on the counter.

The miner sucked a tooth and answered with the enigmatic statement, "Chris betook himself somewhere else."

Mr. Eggleston climbed the rolling ladder against the wall to fetch a can of Arbuckle's Ariosa Coffee from a shelf and handed it down to Amanda. "I haven't had it long, so it should still be fresh. Try it on me and see what you think of it."

Back in 1869 John and Charles Arbuckle had patented a method of sealing roasted beans with sugar and egg white to preserve flavor, but since vacuum cans were not yet invented it was important to get fresh cans of the pre-roasted beans.

After counting up the cost of the items now gathered together on the counter, Amanda commented, "You said Dogtown is still a viable town."

"Oh, there's still a few Chinese there. You know that Chinese are seldom hired in the mines, but they're allowed to work old placer locations.

In Dogtown, they planted gardens and built stone huts, and had a nice existence. Until Bodie hit big a few years ago, that is. Then some miners thought Dogtown deserved another look and a thousand new claims were patented."

"I suppose the Chinese were pushed out?"

"From mining, yes. Some moved on, but some stayed to run laundries, restaurants and saloons. These were the ones in place when the rough crowd moved on again after satisfying themselves there wasn't that much there after all."

"Is that when Ah Ching came here?"

"We'd met previously and I encouraged him to come with me to Bodie."

Several women came in at that moment, and Amanda took her basket of items from the counter and hurried home. She was suddenly aware of how often she jumped to conclusions about people, or classes of people, while yet knowing nothing of their background. She was ashamed to realize that would apply to those she held in low esteem, as well as those she liked. It was something to be pondered when alone in her bedroom and awaiting sleep that so often took a long time to arrive.

CHAPTER 5
AUGUST, 1880

John and Matt had worked long enough at the Noonday that they had earned Sundays off in the rotation. When Amanda got up late due to this happy event, it was to find the men in the parlor with the latest newspapers and the coffee already made. But it was their high state of excitement that caught her attention.

"Did something important happen," she asked, "or merely sensational?"

Matt turned to John. "Your daughter has gotten the hang of this town."

"She always was smart," John responded without looking up from the Bodie Standard News.

Pleased at such a rare compliment, Amanda asked them for clarification.

Matt told her, "The papers are reporting that the Jupiter is putting out $4,000 to the ton. There's been a new strike at the 600 foot level."

John added, "They're saying it's some of the richest ore ever taken from a mine here."

"Boy, the Standard won't like that." Matt said this with great satisfaction.

"No," John chuckled, "the Standard must always be the best in everything."

Matt turned the page of his paper and in a moment asked, "Did you know the old Sonora Dance Hall on King Street has been made over into a Chinese Joss Temple?"

Amanda broke in. "What's that?"

John looked up. "It means the Chinese now have a temple where they can worship whatever it is they worship."

Matt mumbled, "It's more than the Christians have."

It was an old argument. The Catholics and Protestants were still collecting money for their churches, and slowly at that. But some of the population didn't care. They were superstitious and claimed an old saying to be true: *When the churches and women arrive, it's the beginning of the end for a camp.* Having seen prosperity continue even with women living in the town, some now claimed it must be churches they should keep out.

Deciding to make them all a fried chicken dinner that evening, Amanda walked into town for a few items needed at the market. But once on Main and feeling restless, she continued walking north until she was past the laundry, past Mill Street on her right, and past Standard Avenue until she was across the street from Wagner's Saloon. In front of the Standard Lodging House where the street remained wet even in the summer heat, she found a lone "board boy" and fetched up in front of the Grand Central Hotel.

Continuing north, she lengthened her stride and passed the Can-Can Restaurant where she glanced in through the big windows across the front, half expecting to see Joseph at a table but surprising herself when she wasn't disappointed at *not* seeing him. She stopped briefly at the Tuolumne Stables to look at the horses, checked to see if a pair of her father's boots was ready at Mr. Walheim's shoe repair, and then approached *The Gymnasium*.

Duncan McMillan was standing outside about to enter. Ed Wilson and his partner had leased McAlpine's Hall and fitted it up with weight-lifting and exercise equipment, including parallel bars, and had even erected a ring for boxing and wrestling. Several nights a week this last attracted gamblers bored with cards, roulette and billiards. There were over 125 regular paying monthly subscribers to the gym, and many more used its facilities for occasional workouts.

The men were careful to wear proper attire, of course, working out in tights and long-sleeved gym shirts under what could be considered one-piece bathing attire, if they had been anywhere near an ocean. That meant that young ladies, as long as they were in the company of other women, could sit in a box set aside for spectators. From there they could enjoy the view of the mostly young muscular men who were of a mind to show off.

"Hello, Amanda," Duncan greeted her with a broad smile. His neck was so thick one could barely see his Adams apple, but other than his biceps, his body from the chest down was quite average, except that he was known to be remarkably flexible.

"You coming in to watch?" She didn't miss his look of eagerness.

She hated to disappoint him, and would have liked to go in, but her common sense and strong adherence to proper decorum was even stronger. "I'm not accompanied, so I'd better not. I'm too new in town to start rude rumors about my behavior."

Duncan shrugged and went inside. Once again he thought such good looks were wasted on a young woman so intent on remaining a proper lady. "She could have steady customers on Bonanza Street," he chuckled to himself, "but she'd have to loosen up some."

Unaware of Duncan's rude understatement, Amanda crossed back over the street and proceeded south until she reached the Sacramento Market on the corner of Main and Standard Avenue. The window of the market was filled to entice passing shoppers, today the owner having hung a dressed deer and a beef quarter, and placed a whole pig with a red apple in its mouth on a silver tray. Fresh branches of sagebrush were mounded beneath it all.

Amanda found nothing she wanted at that market, and upon leaving she passed a group of five men standing together on the sidewalk. They were all focused on one patient individual in a slouch hat and a dusty suit who listened to the others talk over each other while in a state of extreme agitation. All were complaining loudly about someone's behavior in a saloon the night before. Amanda used the convenience of the vegetable bins outside the market to linger and listen.

The lanky man to whom they addressed themselves was John Kirgan, the jailer who was also referred to as Deputy Sheriff. Remembering when Joseph had introduced her to him, she now was able to give him a closer look. His face was pleasant but unremarkable, with a high forehead and dark eyes that missed little going on around him. Although he was not that much taller than the average man of his time he was some years older than the excitable youth now before him. At 51, his years of experience together with his implacable attitude and a stare that seemed to penetrate the soul, presented him as an authority figure not to be questioned.

He routinely dressed in a suit and tie, with his badge partially hidden by the lapel of his suit coat. His white shirt was always clean, unlike his old felt hat, while his boots were solid, square-toed and thick soled. He was one of the few men in town, other than visiting rowdies, who regularly carried his gun in a holster to show that he was willing, if not eager, to use it. Other men were willing, but they concealed their weapons in a pocket or tucked in a waistband so as not to advertise the fact.

Since in Bodie all men did carry a gun or knife, many of those intent on causing trouble thought twice about challenging someone unless they were too drunk or too angry to think it through. Because of this, and underscored by the town's reputation for mayhem, Bodie actually saw fewer violent confrontations than it might have.

Kirgan's first career after arriving in Bodie back in '77 had been as a saloon owner, but he had sold his business in '78 and accepted his current job. He was a veteran of the War with Mexico and that gave him the aura of hero, at least to the younger men. They pictured him fighting in "grand campaigns" and responded to the drama instead of picturing the bloody carnage that is the reality of all war.

Some of the respect afforded Kirgan was due to a local reputation gained during the first year he had served in his present capacity. Although he never talked about it, everyone knew he had given up part of his salary in order to hire two deputies. This had enabled the town to be better covered throughout the day *and* night. He had chosen men he knew, and who were known to carry their Colt Lightnings and Peacemakers in a holster behind their backs and under their coats where they could retrieve them quickly. As a consequence of this presence there had been only one homicide that first year.

Kirgan's voice as he reassured the men now talking to him was deep and calm. But it was his attitude of authority, and possibly the fact that he had survived into his 50's and was therefore sometimes referred to as "the old man", that also encouraged the complainers to relax and disperse. Just as he was about to continue on his way, Justice of the Peace Goodson approached him and together they headed in the direction of Standard Avenue.

Mr. Goodson was Kirgan's boss, appointed by the Board of Supervisors of Mono County to preside over the Bodie Justice Court. So while Goodson reigned supreme in his office and courtroom on Standard Avenue, Kirgan reigned over the town proper. For over a year James Showers, once the Treasurer of the Miners' Union back in '77, had been the County Sheriff living in Bridgeport.

Tales of Kirgan's first forays into keeping the peace were told to newcomers with pride, but also as a warning. John Blake had told Amanda, with great enthusiasm, how Kirgan had faced pistol-wielding drunks with his calm reasoning voice, and had usually won them over. Joseph had glowed as he described how Kirgan's fists had broken up brawls when it would have been easier to have used his gun. And Matt had laughed when describing to Amanda how Kirgan had brought down more than one man bragging about how bad he was.

Deputy Constable Farnsworth approached Kirgan and Goodson on the corner of Standard and Main just as the now mollified men crossed the street to the Senate Saloon. Farnsworth gave Kirgan a lazy salute and stopped next to him, watching the retreating group. The Deputy was a middle aged man of thirty-two with a large frame that was wide, thick and solid, and who was known for his vice-like grip. Any man lured into arm wrestling with him, while hoping their arm didn't snap in two, had been forced to listen to his murmured insults in a broad English accent reminiscent of the hard streets of London.

As Amanda moved on to the fruits in the bins, Kirgan and Farnsworth began discussing the bullion thefts at the Standard Mill.

Kirgan said, "You know they hired P. E. Davis, a private detective from San Francisco?"

"No kidding."

"Yeah. So far he thinks its Hank Morton."

"The battery feeder?" Farnsworth asked in surprise.

Both men looked more sad than angry and Amanda wondered at this, assuming that they must be acquainted with Morton. Within a few days they would be forced to arrest Morton for grand larceny along with William Haight and Fred Smith. It would be alleged that they had stolen anywhere from ten to forty thousand dollars. Pat Reddy would represent the Standard and would easily get Haight to turn state's evidence against Morton, in exchange for a reduced sentence and being allowed to post bail.

Amanda left these fascinating men and events behind and continued to the bakery. Inside she greeted Mr. Mora, the manager, and then spotted Charlotte Perry just as she was preparing to leave with her arms full of packages.

"Why don't you stop by my house before you return home?" Charlotte suggested. "I'll have the tea made by the time you get there. And I have a fresh seed cake somewhere in all of these packages."

Tired from her long walk, Amanda could think of nothing more inviting. She hurried through the rest of her shopping, and was soon seated in the comfortable Perry front room overlooking Green. She walked to the side window to see the view of the tramway sloping down to the back of the Standard Mill from the mine higher up toward the top of Silver Hill. There were hundreds of men swarming these now famous hills and she knew there were at least as many men laboring in the depths below, some at the 600 foot level and working to go deeper. The area was like a giant series of ant hills, all industry and production that stopped only when flooded out or buried beneath snow.

Charlotte set a tray down on the low table in front of the settee and Amanda settled herself. The silver tea tray gleamed under white china cups as Charlotte poured out the hot amber liquid from a pot covered in hand painted yellow roses. Amanda looked longingly at the two large pieces of poppy seed cake off to the side while complimenting the tea service.

"It originally belonged to my mother. This service and a dresser set is all I have to remind me of her. Do you have anything to remind you of your mother?"

"Yes. My father."

Charlotte looked at her with surprise and then laughed, after which Amanda joined in. "No, no. I also have a few of her hat pins, two pairs of good leather gloves since we wore the same size, and an ivory-backed hair brush." Amanda sighed and relaxed against the cushions. "I sold everything else. That way, I could arrive here with a small nest egg of my own that my father knows nothing about."

"What would he do if he knew you had a little money of your own? Would he ask for it?"

"I don't know. But I do know he might not be so generous with the household money." Not comfortable with this subject, Amanda picked up a folded newspaper, glanced at it and returned it to the end of the sofa. "I see they're writing again about last month's Mono County Grand Jury decreeing that gambling is a violation of the law."

"Yes, but mainly they just recited what everyone already knows but have been ignoring for years." Charlotte handed Amanda a piece of cake, which she took eagerly.

With the first small bite she resisted the urge to smack her lips, so moist and sweet was the cake. Instead she asked, "Why bring up gambling now? Heaven knows it's popular and out in the open here."

"Because earlier this year many of the saloons were trying to keep the opium addicts out of their places of business, and that started several brawls with the addicts. Some bystanders were hurt. And there were a few back-alley muggings too. So the Grand Jury stepped in and threatened to close down all gambling."

"Oh, dear. Hard to believe they would do that to Bodie."

"Exactly. So the opium den operators and the saloon owners got together and declared a truce. An uneasy one at best, of course, but neither faction wants the saloons to close."

"If they closed the saloons, wouldn't the opium dens be shut down next? Many of the citizens would be happy to see the last of them."

"That's true enough." Charlotte took a bite of her cake. "Of course, ladies here either tune out what they don't want to hear about, or just refuse to admit that they know about such things."

Amanda laughed and said, "And some people think *I'm* too prim and proper."

Charlotte did not laugh. "You're a single woman in a town that is mostly composed of men. You can't be too careful of your reputation. Has someone ridiculed you?"

"Not really, although when I ran into Duncan McMillan just entering the gymnasium earlier today, I felt that was his opinion of me when he invited me to watch."

Charlotte frowned. "You didn't accept his invitation did you?"

"Oh, no." Amanda shook her head with vehemence. "I told him I couldn't since I was alone. I didn't miss the look on his face, though. I think his opinion of me is that I'm a tiresome prude."

Nodding with satisfaction, Charlotte said, "Better that than gaining the reputation of being a flirt or worse. But it is an interesting place, the gym. Maybe Emily and I can accompany you some time."

"Do the men really wear tights?"

"Oh, yes." Charlotte's eyes twinkled, and even though she was well aware that Amanda had never been married, she told her, "Their attire leaves nothing to the imagination."

Amanda choked on her tea, blushed becomingly, and tried unsuccessfully to hold back a giggle.

"The men like the women to be there," Charlotte continued. "They pose for the ladies as they exercise. However, just before you arrived in town, one young man took his need for admiration too far. You'd have to know this fellow to know how impetuous he is. Josh often gets into trouble without meaning any true mischief."

"What did he do?"

"He started seeing quite a lot of a young lady with an exceedingly prim nature. She surprised everyone when she declared that she would like to see her young swain work out at the gym, so his sister and some other ladies accompanied her. While there they applauded the displays of flexed muscles and feats of agility by all the young men. Josh didn't like that his beloved watched all the men and not just him."

"That's silly," Amanda exclaimed. "What woman would look at only one man when there are a dozen before her?"

"Exactly. Anyway, Josh asked his sister to invite Rose to their house. While the women visited, the impetuous Josh went into the backyard where he began sawing rapidly and noisily at a stack of logs. It was, of course, simply a display designed to show her his strength and virility. However, fairly soon his low cut gym shirt, from which he had removed the sleeves, was soaked with sweat. He also had on knee britches that showed his bare bulging calves." With a decided smirk, she added, "And after too many times bending over, a bit of the devil's crack was showing as well. Finally the women went to the window to see what the noise was, and when the fair Rose saw this raw masculinity so obviously exposed, she swooned and crumpled onto the floor in a dead faint."

"What a frail flower!" Amanda scoffed.

Charlotte struggled to keep a straight face as she continued. "Unfortunately, it was just at that moment that Rose's father arrived to escort her home. When he saw what they were looking at, he charged outside with his gun drawn. The poor boy barely managed to scramble over the fence. Even more unfortunate for him, however, was that he fell at the feet of one of the town officers. He was taken to jail and fined $50 for indecent exposure."

Amanda was torn between the humor of the situation and her compassion for the poor young man whose fervor had overcame his common sense. But the humor of the situation won out and they ended up laughing heartily for several minutes.

Amanda dried her eyes. "I'm glad I didn't tighten my corset very much this morning."

Charlotte took a deep breath, something she could do because she wasn't wearing her corset. "Some of the women here don't often wear one unless dressing for a special occasion, especially the older ladies. I must admit that if I'm wearing a jacket or coat, I often don't either. It certainly makes breathing at this altitude easier." Charlotte took a sip of her tea. "By the way, has anyone asked you to the grand ball Miss Perinette is giving?"

"No. I don't know anything about it."

"She's the owner of the Terpsichorean Dance Hall and she's having trouble making the rent. This dance will help her out." She smiled and added, "There'll be good women there, mostly wives of miners. But it'll be attended mainly by single miners and teamsters."

"Will some of them escort women from Bonanza Street?"

Charlotte raised her brows. "You sound excited at the idea. Are you curious about them?"

Amanda blushed. "I must admit that I am."

"Well, if you do go, just be mindful of what's happening around you at all times."

"Oh, I doubt anyone will ask me."

They discussed several other topics before Amanda alluded to an earlier one. "I guess young Josh should be glad he didn't spend time in the cramped jail. Considering the amount of lawlessness in this town, it's a good thing it's being increased in size. Has it always been like this here?"

"Pretty much, at least since the boom," Charlotte told her. "Being so far away from other towns, and so isolated in its setting, it's the perfect place for those wanting to escape their past."

"I hear the new jail will hold 16 men without crowding, and each cell will have its own stove for heat."

"Vince says they're going to put a twelve foot fence around an area in the back so the men can take exercise."

Amanda recalled the news articles she had read of the results of most trials. "Considering that they'll probably be set free after they go to court, such a yard should help them stay in shape for when they return to work." After a moment of chewing, Amanda thought of her father and Matt. "Men work very hard, don't they? So many of them seem much older than they really are."

"Yes." Charlotte looked out the window at the hill. "Not only do they breathe foul air below, but the daily stress of so much danger working underground must be very wearing."

"Even when they work above ground in the forges, mills and hoisting works, from what my father has told me they're still doing dangerous work."

"So I guess we can't begrudge them their entertainments." Charlotte sat forward. "Speaking of entertainments, did you see the notice in the paper the other day? When Vince said some friends wanted him to go with them, I didn't know whether to laugh or get angry."

"What was it?"

Charlotte pulled the top copy of a newspaper off a pile of them on a chair by the window and found the announcement. "Here it is. This Friday at the Union Hall a Madam Albisuers, evidently a model and artist, is presenting what she calls 'living art pictures' in a presentation she calls 'High Life In Paris'."

"Does that mean nude art?" Amanda gasped.

"I think so, especially since the announcement declares 'positively no ladies'. Oh, and here's the best part: 'Opera glasses to rent for near sighted gentlemen on the night of performance'." Charlotte tossed the paper at Amanda, who picked it up.

After a moment, she asked, "Did you see how they're describing the time? 'Doors open at 7 o'clock; trouble commences at 8 o'clock; agony over at 16 o'clock'." She shook her head and breathed out, "I suppose they think that's funny. They're charging a dollar for it, too."

Charlotte looked contrite, "The money will go to help John Holland who was injured in an explosion at the Bodie Mine, so I guess we shouldn't complain."

"Why don't we do something for ourselves? The next night is a play called 'The Lady of Lyons or Love and Pride'."

"It's a deal."

Replete with tea and cake and local gossip, Amanda went home to begin preparations for the men's supper. It was what she did every day, and what she figured she would be doing every day far into the future. But how far into the future, she wondered? Wasn't she supposed to expect matrimony at her age? But who was she to find suitable in Bodie? But truth to tell, the idea of marriage was not a pressing issue for her. However, she did long to be *in love*, and find out just what that felt like.

She may have assumed she would not be attending Miss Perinette's Grand Ball just off Main on King Street, but Joseph came to the house the very evening after her visit with Charlotte and asked to escort her to the event. She came close to declining, but her present state of boredom and her ever-restless nature prompted her to accept.

It turned out to be less Amanda's version of a grand ball than an excuse for raucous revelry. The men demanded mostly foot stomping fiddle tunes, and very few slower dances where the women could show their dresses to best advantage. Unlike the dances at the Miners' Union Hall, Miss Perinette had made available a considerable quantity of beer and whiskey. By the time an hour had passed, there were few men or women who were not well and truly enjoying the effects of their hostess's generosity. Amanda stood off to the side of the large gaily decorated room as one of the few exceptions.

As is always the case when one is the only sober person in a room full of drunks, Amanda was soon bored by the noise, boorish behavior and shocking laughter of the girls as they lifted their skirts higher above their ankles than was seemly. Just as she gave up trying to find a tactful way to withdraw and return home, Joseph dragged her out onto the dance floor for a quadrille.

It was during the loud clownish antics of some men acting silly instead of dancing properly that she made up her mind to tell Joseph outright that she wanted to go home. They came to rest in a chair against the wall where they could talk, but two men near them began shouting at one another. Resolution was reached when one of the men offered to buy the other a drink.

However, before Amanda could frame her request to Joseph, a Syndicate miner stumbled and bumped into a teamster dancing with a popular Bonanza Street beauty who was new to the town. God forbid the teamster would just move out of the way and accept the apology offered by the miner. Oh no, he had to let off a long stream of vile language in which he cast doubt on the miner's legitimacy of birth, declared that he was probably Irish, and maybe even cheated at cards.

For some reason the miner took umbrage at this and decided to punch the teamster on the nose. After a few more accurate hits, he evidently decided that his fists were not sufficiently making the point, so the miner drew a gun from his waistband. He let loose with a shot at the teamster, wounding him in the arm. While a man stepped forward to knock the gun from the miner's hand, another helped the teamster out the door.

It had all happened so fast that few people had changed positions. Amanda had simply pushed herself against the wall several feet away from the miner who was firing his gun. After the miner was disarmed by his more level-headed friends, Amanda looked around for Joseph. She saw him standing up after having been huddling on the floor with his arms around two young ladies with stained lips and extremely low cut gowns.

Without hesitating longer, and mindful that she would have to exit from King Street by herself after dark, Amanda nevertheless stalked out of the dance hall. As she started down the street toward home, she walked slow enough that Joseph had plenty of time to catch up with her. When it became obvious that he was staying behind, probably with the painted ladies, she picked up her skirts and her pace. She arrived home in a fit of temper, mumbling to herself as she dressed for bed. "If Joseph thinks I'm going to forgive him such an act of disrespect, he better think again." Sleep took a long time coming that night.

A few days later it was reported that a guest at the newly improved jail had decided that he didn't want to wait for his trial. Instead, the thief had pulled a board loose from the exercise yard fence while enjoying his freedom outdoors, having decided he wanted even more of it outside of town. He had simply leaned the board against a post and jumped over, losing himself far from Bodie. Nothing more was heard of him.

That evening at supper Matt commented to John, "I'm surprised the guy escaped before breakfast." John grunted his agreement.

"Why?" Amanda asked them.

"The food served by Kirgan is known to be very tasty," Matt told her. "The County gives him $1.00 for each day a prisoner is his guest."

"Even so," John spoke up, "Kirgan always purchases quality supplies. He should pocket more of the money. Silly not to."

Matt shrugged. "Oh, I don't know. I think it's damn bully of him."

John looked up from the apple pie Amanda had made them. "I'll admit he's been good to a lot of the sudden widows. Remember last February's tragedy."

"Hard to forget."

"What was this?" Amanda asked.

Matt reached for a tin pitcher and poured heavy cream over his pie. "Some of the mine owners used to wager among themselves as to who had the fastest men able to place the most shaft sets in a shift. The timber sets are really heavy and hard to manage while being cut and fit into place to shore up the tunnels."

"They're supposed to go in from the bottom up to join with the completed sets above," John added.

"Yeah, but three young Micks working for Colonel Dunn of the Maryland Consolidated Mine thought they could do it the fastest of anyone and they were right too. Fitzpatrick, Brennan and Fitzsimmons were good. But one day they got careless in wedging up. The timbers they were using, the scaffolding they were standing on, and the men too, all collapsed together eighty feet to the bottom of the shaft."

Amanda was horrified. "Was such competition outlawed after that?"

"Naw," her father laughed. "Whatever gets the work done faster is always condoned. If one of us is killed, there's another to take our place. No job goes unfilled here for more than a day."

It was a common situation in a mining town with high unemployment, but Amanda was always amazed at how the men accepted this harsh reality with such resignation.

At the end of August, Amanda noticed that the colorful Piutes were obvious for their absence. Usually a dozen of them could be seen sitting on street corners at the north end of town. She puzzled over this as she completed her day's chores.

Roger, out riding just before sundown, stopped at the house when he saw Amanda returning home. They were soon sitting on the small back porch where he had carried two kitchen chairs so they could watch the sun go down while drinking coffee.

When she asked him about the dearth of Piutes in town, he explained. "They've gone off to join other tribes at a Fandango at the northeast corner of Mono Lake. It's an annual thing. Been done for generations."

"What do they do there?"

"Eat, drink and make merry, basically. And they trade with each other and hunt too. They feast on wild game and gather the pupae of the flies that live on the edge of the lake. They call it koo-chah-bee. They make a mush and bread from it, and it gets them through the winter." He turned to her. "I hope I haven't disgusted you."

She shook her head. "No, I actually think it's very clever. Whatever it takes to survive, I suppose."

"I'll be going to Bridgeport in a couple of weeks," he announced suddenly.

"Oh?" She wondered if this was what he had been wanting to say since he arrived.

"Yes, I have some business to attend to there." He didn't say anything more and Amanda sensed that it would be intrusive to ask for more details.

However, she did ask, "How will you be traveling?"

"I thought about riding, but it'll be more comfortable to take the Nevada Stage Company's coach over the Bridgeport-Bodie Toll Road. And faster too, even with a change of horses at 16 Mile House. It leaves at three in the morning, but I guess I can survive such an early departure." He smiled at her with that twinkle in his eyes that she found so tantalizing.

Later that evening, she listened as Matt read out from the newspaper that the new county courthouse in Bridgeport was almost ready for the shingles to go on the roof. They were expecting it to be in business during the first week in April of the following year.

The paper also mentioned that there was an important trial taking place in a couple of weeks in Bridgeport at the American Hotel, which the men explained had for years been used as the courthouse. Amanda immediately thought of Roger's trip to Bridgeport in 'a couple of weeks'. Was there a connection? Wondering if Roger was to be on trial or only a witness at one kept her from sleep until the early morning. But she was getting used to a fitful sleep pattern.

The month ended with the camp still in a decent state of prosperity. A new office of the Nevada and California Telegraph Company opened across the street from the Occidental Hotel on the site of its old small storefront. The telegraph's operating office was one of seven offices upstairs, while downstairs Frederick the jeweler and the W. H. Ash Stationery store received ladies of good taste and refinement.

Then, after three years of continuous growth and the building of over 1,800 houses, four large mills, 31 steam hoisting works, and many dozens of businesses and shops, all construction came to a stop. The saturation point had finally been reached, and hundreds of carpenters, construction workers and painters were out of work.

It was commented on with wonder, and a growing fear to which no one wanted to admit, that the smaller mines were becoming much less profitable. And suddenly many of the mine owners were no longer paying out dividends. The stage lines ran a little less frequently and began making more money off of departures than they did on arrivals. Men declared they could do better in Montana Territory or Tombstone, Arizona, and some even headed to the southern mines in Inyo County in the Russ, Beveridge or Cerro Gordo Districts.

There were, of course, many people who stubbornly declared that this was a temporary situation and that soon all these people would be returning. After all, people declared, this was Bodie—the richest, most exciting, most notorious and fastest growing mining town in the country. But that statement, so often repeated during the past three boom years with pride, now more often had a hint of desperation underlying it.

CHAPTER 6
SEPTEMBER, 1880

It was during September that the town's newspapers began discussing in earnest what most of the citizens felt but were fearful of expressing openly. Daily editorials decried in colorful and angry rhetoric the recent spate of violence and lawlessness occurring throughout the town. They focused most vociferously upon what they called *"opium fiends who have no visible means of support, dress fine, and have some money. Men robbed nightly, murders committed without hindrance, an officer shot down in the discharge of his duty brings matters to such a crisis that a 601 will be compelled to clean out the mess of crime."* This was always the ultimate threat, borne of frustration and lack of faith in the local legal system.

Matt and John spent much of their time at home talking about what they read in the many Bodie papers, and even the far away *Reno Weekly Gazette* that was brought to town on the stages. Each paper focused their editorials on the lack of arrests, prosecutions and convictions of the perpetrators of stabbings, shootings and pistol whippings. A special target of their complaints was how often a jury set free someone who several witnesses testified seeing do the crime, or how easily a man got off on the basis of self-defense even if the victim had been unarmed, especially if they were represented by Patrick Reddy, Esquire. The worst was to have the coroner's jury call it *natural causes* when the victim had been beaten to death.

John was reading out loud just such an article as the three housemates sat together in the parlor drinking coffee after dinner. Amanda was curious about the writer who, as so many reporters were doing, suggested the forming of a "601" to take care of the crime rate.

"When did they start calling a lynch mob a 601?" Amanda asked her father.

"It's more than a lynch mob," he told her with considerable heat. This evidently was a subject about which he was oddly opinionated. "When crime and violence got out of hand in the early mining towns before organized law, citizen committees formed to take charge. Many a would-be crook thought twice and skedaddled out of town. Just knowing that a committee was in town helped the crime rate."

"But we have a sheriff and constables," she objected.

"Yeah, right," Matt cut in. His tone was filled with disgust as he said, "But some people here don't think they're doing their job. A saloon owner recently hired Bob Whiteacre to keep the opium fiends out of his Comstock Saloon. Bob has nerves of steel and doesn't take sass off anyone. He used to work security for Wells Fargo. Over a year ago Bob and Jack Roberts cleaned up the town of strong-armed robbery thugs and a rash of garroting that was taking place in alleys."

John nodded. "It's no wonder Williams thought of Bob when he wanted to keep the bad element out of his place. He's a good man. But this article was prompted by something that happened in the Comstock Saloon just *yesterday*."

When Amanda looked at him with her brows raised, he explained. "The other day Winnemucca Jack, who hangs out on Bonanza Street most of the time, told Bob that George Watkins was out to get him some time later that evening. George Watkins has always been an ornery cuss, and a regular at the opium dens too. Anyway, as soon as George showed up, before George could try anything, Bob gun-butted him over the head and dumped him in the gutter out front."

"Yeah," Matt added, "but that wasn't the end of it. Later, just after midnight, George Watkins and his friend Sloan snuck back into the saloon behind a group of men. George blasted poor Bob with a double-barreled shotgun."

John shook his head. "Got him in the gut where he knew he'd die slow. With all the confusion that followed, Watkins and Sloan escaped."

"They got 'em though." Matt didn't hide his satisfaction. "They're in jail now." Matt shook his head slowly, remembering the fun times he'd shared with Bob. "Poor Bob." A few minutes later Matt looked up from his paper and laughed. "It says here that the editor of the *Bodie Standard* almost got killed when a stray bullet hit the front door of his house. Thing was, he was leaning his chair against it on the inside."

"Thick door," John grunted.

"Yep."

After another few moments, John commented, "Says here Pat Reddy has opened a new and bigger law office. Considering all the business he's getting here, it's no wonder."

Amanda recalled seeing him in town. "I noticed he has one arm. How did that happen?"

"He got shot."

When John stopped with just that, Matt added, "The bone was shattered and his arm had to be amputated. It was a few years ago in Virginia City."

Recognizing that her father was falling into his habit of withdrawing communication as the evening wore on, Amanda retired to her room.

The next day as she picked through the onions at Eggleston's market, she heard a thin dusty man in miner's garb talking to Ben Eggleston and was soon reminded of the conversation with John and Matt the night before.

"Did you hear what happened at the jail last night?" the man asked Ben.

"No. What now?"

"George Watkins was having withdrawals from all the opium he was used to taking, as well as in pain from injuries he got during the battle in the saloon. His friend Sloan told Kirgan to give him some medicine he had with him that was a mixture of sarsaparilla, port wine and opium. Kirgan had to leave for a while so he told Watkins to take two teaspoons to relieve the spasms. But the idiot took the whole bottle."

"Is he okay?"

"Christ, no. It killed 'em. Turns out the bottle was mostly chloral hydrate. But one of the doctors said he might have died from a brain hemorrhage from his head wounds."

Ben shook his head. "If he died from what he took, do you think it was suicide or accident?"

"We'll never know. But at least it's one less *bad man from Bodie* we have to worry about." He chuckled at the oft uttered phrase in which people seemed to take a degree of pride. Evidently he had no real regret at the sudden death of Watkins. The man told Ben, "My stomach's been upset. Can I have a bottle of sarsa?"

Ben fetched a brown bottle from a shelf and said, "It's on me." The man took the bottle of sarsaparilla, a concoction tasting somewhere between root beer and licorice, and left with a thank you.

Mr. Eggleston realized Amanda had been listening to the conversation and thought she looked a little uneasy. He approached her and commented, "When you've been here awhile, you'll get used to such things."

Unclenching her jaw, she turned to him with irritation biting at her normal reserve. "Really? Is that what it takes to survive here for a woman? She has to forsake all semblance of sensitivity and compassion?"

Ben resisted taking a step back from her mild assault. "Well, maybe it's more a matter of learning to accept that life isn't always rosy. And that such violence does happen in the world, especially mining towns out in the middle of God's last acres created after He ran out of everything but mineralized dirt." Realizing his tone was sharper than he had intended, he quickly added, "Meaning no offense, miss."

"No offense taken," a subdued Amanda murmured. "I understand what you mean." She took a deep breath and managed a smile. "I do know women who have lived here for several years who are refined and gentle. On the other hand, they have uncommon determination and grit." With a wry smile she added, "I'm not so sure I have all that much grit."

"Of course you do. You up-rooted yourself to come here and be with your pa, didn't you? That took some grit."

"Thank you. But it's not the fact of the violence that bothers me so much as its frequency."

He nodded. "As to that, you're not alone. And I'm speaking for some of the men too. Don't think that we're uncaring. We just don't know what to do about it."

Their eyes met and they smiled in acknowledgement of mutual resignation. It was futile to complain about something one didn't know how to change.

That Saturday evening Amanda and Charlotte went to Delmonico's Restaurant for dinner. Charlotte told her Vince was at "some men's meeting", meaning one of the many fraternal organizations in Bodie. She had decided it was a good opportunity for the two friends to get away from the routine of the kitchen. As they approached the restaurant, Amanda noted a long line outside Ward's Undertaking Parlor across the street and asked Charlotte if she knew why.

Charlotte showed her disgust. "They're lined up to see George Watkins laid out on a slab. It's not an uncommon mode of entertainment here."

Even as they watched, several additional men walked up to join the line. Evidently not wanting to wait, and spurred on by liquid courage, two of the new arrivals cut in at the head of the line. Since they had a bottle with them that they were willing to share with those behind them, no one objected. However, the rest of their friends, who included John Hackwell and Ed Worley, stayed in the street.

"I wanna go see Dora Burnell at the Lower Dance House," Hackwell hollered as he rocked uncertainly on his feet. "I think she stole my gun and some of my money the other night."

His friend Ed Worley let his impatience show. "You think?"

"Well, I was pretty sozzled. I woke up in the dust of lower Main, but I know I'd been with her earlier. I remember being a little harsh with her." His laugh was brutal.

"Well, okay," Ed said, "you go retrieve your gun. I'm going to stay here and get in line."

Although Amanda found the exchange an interesting one, Charlotte took her by the arm and pulled her toward the restaurant. Charlotte understood Amanda's fascination with the rawness of life in Bodie, but having lived there for several years she felt that it was best sampled in small doses.

The women turned toward the door of the restaurant and heard Hackwell bid his friend good-bye as he walked south toward the King Street dance house. Then, just as Hackwell passed a nearby alley, two men jumped out and without comment emptied their guns into him. The women dashed into the restaurant only to be met by a moving wall of people rushing to the door and windows to see what new excitement was taking place.

Having no alternative, Charlotte and Amanda turned around and watched through the door as Ed Worley left his place in line and ran up to his fallen comrade. Everyone also saw Marino Castro running away down the alley from which he had emerged to do the shooting. Another man was ahead of him and unrecognizable.

Looking down at his dead friend sprawled at his feet, Ed realized that Hackwell's vest was on fire where the bullet had entered, so close had Castro been when he opened fire. Ed quickly reached down and patted out the flame with his calloused hands as other men quickly joined him.

Among them was Officer Tex Hitchell who quickly had the body removed to Ward's to keep company with George Watkins.

One of the men in the line out front expressed his pleasure at "the two for one viewing". At the same time, a small group of men emerged from the undertaker's building and crossed the street toward the restaurant. One of them commented on the copious amount of blood soaked into the clothing of Hackwell and the marble-like sheen of the embalmed Watkins. The crowd in the restaurant quickly returned to their seats, including Amanda and Charlotte.

Meanwhile, as the women ate their dinner with subdued enthusiasm, a local woodchopper named John Rann, a friend of Hackwell's, arrived at Ward's to pay his respects. He commented loudly to anyone who would listen that he thought Mareno Castro a cowardly cur dog who should be hanged as soon as possible. He found a constable and went with him to the bordello of Dora Burnell, Castro's cousin. She was visiting with Manuel Costello, an elderly Mexican who had lived in the county for many years and was well liked in Bodie. Although he tried to stand up for Dora, in the process exchanging angry words with Rann, she was questioned regarding her cousin's actions.

After a lighter dinner than they had originally planned, Charlotte said they should return directly home. As they passed King Street, they were in time to see an officer escorting a handcuffed woman toward Bonanza Street, presumably to the jail at its end. She was quite beautiful in an exotic Latin manner, with large dark eyes and long black hair. If she was frightened at her current situation, she didn't show it, and her walk could best be described as nothing short of a flouncing stride.

"Oh, my," Charlotte gasped. "That's Dora Burnell, also known as Spanish Dora. She's the cousin of Mareno Castro, the rowdy that shot Hackwell. This can't be good." Charlotte took Amanda by the arm and hurried her along toward home.

John Rann was making his way through several saloons trying to drown his anger. He ended up at Wagner's where he told the crowd that he would give $100 to anyone who could tell him who had killed his friend. Manuel Castillo, Dora's elderly friend, was drinking at the bar and told him he could identify the killer. With a surly look around at those nearby eagerly listening, the old man told Rann to follow him outside. As they approached a nearby alley, Rann saw waiting for him Old Red Roe, James Flannery, and young Dave Bannon who had recently been hanging out with them. Rann immediately backed up into Wagner's Saloon and hid in one of the private rooms.

Castillo rushed into the saloon, yelling that Rann had insulted him, hoping this would bring a few drunks to back him up. Rann peeked out from his room with his gun drawn, saw Castillo and his fellow toughs from the alley, and yelled, "Keep your distance."

Just as Flannery stepped forward, Tex Hitchell leaped forward and tried to grab at Rann's gun. But as soon as he got his hand on it the gun went off, the bullet removing most of one of Flannery's fingers holding his gun. The bullet kept going, however, and stopped only after entering old Castillo's groin.

The newspapers reported that as they ran from the saloon, a couple of Castillo's friends got off a few wild shots, their bullets only breaking a mirror and a little of the plaster off a wall. Not immediately known and therefore not reported in the newspapers, was that one of their shots did hit someone. A tall, well-dressed and popular faro dealer at the rear of the saloon was slumped over his table, now stained with his blood.

Constable Farnsworth arrived and took Rann off to jail, and not long after that Castillo died from loss of blood. Two men came forward to say that Dora had told them that she had given to her cousin Castro the pistol she had stolen from Hackwell, in this way getting Castro to kill Hackwell with his own gun, which evidently Dora thought clever. But no else came forward and no actual evidence of her guilt could be found, so she was released. Neither she nor Castro was ever prosecuted. Rann had been released even before Dora, when it was determined that he had been defending himself against Castillo.

For most people the episode was forgotten, but for Nellie Bannon it was only the beginning of her increased worry about her brother Dave. Now that she knew Dave was hanging out with Flannery and Roe, and once again unemployed, she knew more trouble lay ahead for him. She tried reasoning with Dave, but he told her to mind her own business and stop acting like she was his mother.

At supper the night after the shooting, John read the reports of these events out loud from the paper folded next to his plate, adding, "There's nothing in the papers about it, but I hear that one of the sports in Wagner's was shot by a stray bullet."

Amanda dropped her fork with a rattle onto her plate. "Who?"

"Hell, I don't know," her father shrugged. "Why do you care?"

Amanda looked down at her plate. "I was just curious."

John shrugged. "Someone at work said it was one of the faro dealers."

Matt gave John a look of disgust before turning to Amanda, "Are you worried it might be Roger?"

As a wave of nausea rose within her, she slowly pushed away her plate. "Of course. It could be him as easily as anyone else." At the sharpness of her tone, Matt raised his brows. For the first time, he wondered if she might have feelings for Roger. How would John feel about that? Unaware of the emotions around him, John merely helped himself to more bread and butter.

After piling the dishes in the sink unwashed, Amanda grabbed her short cape and fled into town. She walked rapidly down Mono to Standard, then to Main. Dusk had settled over the town and lamps were being lit in the shops and houses. Only when she reached the saloon did she slow down. She had never been inside a saloon and knew she was not allowed there, but she figured the most they could do to her would be to tell her to leave.

Taking a deep breath, she passed through the outer glass doors that were braced open and then stepped through the short swinging doors. A man immediately rushed to her side.

"Excuse me, miss, but you shouldn't be in here."

Forming a lie more quickly than she would have thought possible of herself, she said, "My father sent me to find out who the faro dealer was that was shot the other night."

"Oh, that. It was Roger Murphy." Noticing the sudden paling of her face and the trembling in her chin, he hurried to say, "He's going to be okay, but he can't work for a while."

Amanda steadied her voice. "Do you know where he lives? I'd like to check on him." She added quickly, "For my father. I know he'd want me to check on him."

"He has a room across the street at the Standard Lodging House."

"Thank you."

She stopped at a news stand and purchased three newspapers before entering the lodging house. After looking around at the small starkly furnished lobby with its dark wood floors and counter to the left, she walked hesitantly to the receptionist and asked for Roger's room number. The woman at the counter, her pile of hair streaked with gray and her skin the texture of fine leather, looked her up and down. One brow raised slightly as she said, "Number ten on the right at the top of the stairs."

Resisting the temptation to explain herself, Amanda instead climbed the steep wooden stairs. When she found herself facing the door, she almost turned away, suddenly at a loss for what she would say to him.

Before she could give in to this, she applied her knuckles to the thin wood of the door.

"Come in," a familiar voice called out.

She opened the door and entered, and found a pale Roger reclining on the edge of a double bed across the room and facing the door. The top two buttons of his white shirt were undone and the sleeves rolled up, while his boots were on the floor next to the bed. A light blanket had been casually thrown over his legs. But it was the swath of gauze around the crown of his head holding a pad of bandages in place just above his temple that held Amanda's attention. Or maybe it was the dried blood that had seeped through the bandage.

"Amanda! How nice to see you." His smile was broad and genuine as he quickly buttoned his shirt. He made movement to stand up, but she told him quickly, "No, don't get up. This isn't a time for good manners."

He smiled his gratitude and relaxed against the three pillows stuffed behind his back. A book lay on the bedspread beside him and she placed the newspapers on top of it. Then, seeing how she was staring at his head, he told her, "Nothing to worry about. The bullet barely grazed me. But I have a hell of a headache, so I decided to stay home for a couple of days."

She pulled a plain straight-backed chair from the small table to her left and took a moment to compose herself. Sitting next to the bed, she reached out to gently touch his cheek just below the bandage. "You could have been killed." Her voice had trembled and she bit her lip.

"We can all say that every day." His smile was crooked as he realized that she cared for him after all, and that he had not misinterpreted her past treatment of him.

Not knowing what to say, she reached out and pushed a long strand of black hair off his forehead, but it only fell stubbornly forward again. As she removed her hand, he reached to take hold of it. But at a loud knocking at the door, Amanda jumped up as though fearful of being caught doing something disreputable.

"Yes?" Roger called out sharply, irritated at the interruption.

The woman who had greeted Amanda downstairs entered the room. In a tone of voice that could only be described as frosty, she asked, "I was wondering if you and your guest would like drinks."

"Oh, thank you, Mrs. Miller." He turned to Amanda. "Would you like coffee or tea?"

"Tea, please."

Mrs. Miller's demeanor underwent an immediate change and she produced a warm smile, as though Amanda's choice of tea was a verification of the young lady's pedigree. While they waited, Roger gave Amanda a first-hand account of what had happened the night he was shot. She listened in rapt awe until the landlady returned and Amanda rose from her chair to take the tray.

She smiled at the woman and murmured, "Thank you. This was very kind of you." As the obviously appeased Mrs. Miller closed the door behind her, Amanda set the tray on the table and poured Roger a cup, adding considerable sugar as a restorative.

Taking it from her, his eyes sparkled. "This is a treat. Are those cookies on the tray?"

"Yes." Placing the plate on the bed next to him, she sat back in the chair and sipped her tea while he chewed on several of the sweets.

Finally he said, "Now, tell me what has been happening in your world since I saw you." He smirked. "You know what's been happening in mine."

"Did you hear about the holdup that took place?"

"Where this time?"

"About forty miles north. It's in the papers I brought you. It was the Carson to Bodie stage, near Sulphur Springs. That's where I was held up."

"You?" He was obviously startled at the thought. "When you were on your way to Bodie this June?"

"Oh, yes." And she proceeded to describe the event. "I was terrified at first. But once I realized I wasn't going to be hurt, I must admit that I was a little excited by the adventure of it."

Roger laughed and shook his head in amazement at her choice to be honest, rather than simper and act coy as so many young women would have done.

"The saddest part of last month's holdup," she continued, "was that one of the horses was killed by a stray bullet. One robber thought Toby, the express messenger, had gotten down to look for him and shot wildly. They shot back and even though hit, the robber shot again, wounding Toby. Then Toby killed the robber. But the other robber got away with the money in the Wells Fargo box."

"Poor Tobey. He loves all his horses."

"Matt bought him a drink and sat with him while he grieved." She looked out the window by the bed and smiled. "I'll always think well of

Matt for that. Jim Hume, a special agent of Wells Fargo in San Francisco, just captured the robber that got away, a Milton Sharp. Hume brought him to Aurora for trial."

"Sharp will probably get ole Pat Reddy to defend him."

She grinned. "Wells Fargo has already hired Mr. Reddy to prosecute the case."

Roger sighed and looked down at the newspapers she had placed on the bed. "I sure miss being out in the thick of things. I did hear from Mrs. Miller that there was a man arrested after blasting a shot gun at a bartender in town."

"But not at Wagner's." She couldn't hide her eagerness to relate the story she had heard from her father. Roger tried valiantly not to smile at this. "The bartender had thrown him out because he was showing the effects of having been in an opium den. When a mob arrived to take him out of jail to a hanging, they found him already dead in his cell. Or at least that's the story being spread around. I notice no one says how he actually died."

"Ah, another mystery for Bodie."

Missing his mocking tone, she continued, "And on the ninth there was a big badger fight on the north end of town."

"There certainly wouldn't be one at the south end."

Amanda nodded. "But I guess this one got out of control. When the badger won the match with the dogs, the men beat it to death with clubs." She looked out the window again, as though addressing those with the clubs. "I call that very unsporting. Hadn't the badger earned the right to be released? And what about the poor dogs maimed and having to be put out of their misery?" There were tears in her eyes and she fought to control her emotions, knowing she might be perceived as foolish to object to such common sport.

Remembering the times he had bet on such events, Roger shied away from a sudden bout of guilt and thought about justifying himself. But he only said, "Such cruelty flourishes not only here, but also in a lot of other mining camps where competitive men gather." He resisted the urge to take her hand and added, "There are some men in this town that would like to outlaw such events. If it ever comes up for a vote, I'll be sure to vote against it with you in mind. How's that?"

"That would be very nice." With sudden spirit, she looked at him and said, "Until women get the right to vote, I guess all we can do is try to influence the men in our lives."

His brows lifted in surprise. Not knowing whether he was reacting to the idea of women voting or what her words had given away about her feelings for him, Amanda looked at a small clock on the wall and said, "Well, I'd best be leaving."

"Worried about what people will say if they find out you spent time alone with me?" he teased her.

"Not as much as you'd think." She made a face and rolled her eyes. "I believe I have much the opposite reputation. That of a prude destined to be a dried up old spinster if I don't 'loosen my laces', as my father once told me."

He smiled. "With all that goes on in this town, you should embrace that reputation. We do have a large number of good women here, and many normal families raising children. Don't become so impressed with all the bad men and women that you lose sight of the fact that this is still a normal functioning town."

She stood up. "You're right." Then, with an impish smirk, she added, "Meanwhile, I'll try my best to maintain my good reputation, and let everyone think I'm a tight-laced prude."

When he laughed, Amanda thought again how attractive he was, especially when he smiled and created a small dimple in his right cheek.

"Thank you for coming to see me." He looked her square in the eyes, challenging her to tell the truth when he asked, "Why did you, by the way?"

She felt herself slowly blushing. "I just wanted to be sure you weren't too badly hurt. You did me a favor with my father over Mike, and I thought I might return the favor by fetching for you anything you might need."

"Oh." With his disappointment obvious, Amanda felt she should add something more personal. Before she could think of what that could be, he continued, "Well, as you can see, I'm being looked after by Mrs. Miller."

When she held out her hand, he grasped it eagerly. That she allowed him to hold it longer than was acceptable made his heart race with renewed hope. "Take care of yourself," she whispered. Before he could say anything in return, she reluctantly pulled her hand loose and hurried from the room.

Halfway down the stairs Amanda passed a pretty woman only a few years her senior. The woman's hair was a pile of blonde ringlets under a small velvet black hat pinned to the side of her head, and her dress was of bright yellow silk with black lace accents at the neck and cuffs. With her tiny cinched waist and generous bosom, Amanda was reminded of a flirtatious wasp swishing up the stairs.

Dismissing this somewhat catty thought, Amanda hesitated long enough to see that the woman knocked on Roger's door. "Roger, it's Dona." When the woman was immediately bidden to enter, Amanda turned and hurried down the rest of the stairs.

From behind her desk Mrs. Miller greeted her with a sly smile. Affronted by the woman's look of disapproval so obviously displayed on her face, Amanda told her, "Mrs. Miller, I assure you that my visit to Mr. Murphy was completely above-board."

Mrs. Miller looked at her in surprise. "I'm sure it was, my dear. I can recognize quality when I see it. But the woman who passed you on the stairs is another matter altogether. Dona works at the Spanish Dance House."

"That doesn't mean she does anything more than dance with the men."

Mrs. Miller chuckled as she patted her pile of hair, her smile plumping her cheeks. "That's true of some, of course. Some of the girls wouldn't lift their skirts above their ankles for anyone but a husband or fiancé, but this one isn't as choosy. She has no connections in town and knows her way around to Bonanza Street."

Wanting to ask why Dona was visiting Roger, Amanda was afraid she already knew the answer. She merely thanked Mrs. Miller for the tea and her kindness, and quickly left the hotel.

Emotions that she found difficult to sort out churned through her mind. People passed her, wondering why she was so severely frowning. She kept reminding herself that Roger was an unmarried man and she assumed that he hadn't been chaste his whole life. But she had chosen to think of him alone in his room when he wasn't at work. At the same time, she acknowledged that part of his attraction was the sense he radiated of being at ease in the world, even when it was as chaotic and dangerous as Bodie. She sighed and chastised herself for her instability of emotions.

The next morning after the men had been gone for several hours there was a knock on the front door. It was not very loud and Amanda at first questioned that she had even heard it. Checking to be sure, she was surprised to find Roger slumped against the post holding up the small porch roof and looking decidedly pale and unwell. She glanced behind him and saw that there was no horse tethered to the post.

"Did you walk here?" she asked with concern.

"Yes. I thought that saddling my horse would be more difficult than walking and being able to sit down a few times."

"For heaven's sake, come in." While Roger practically collapsed into one of the deep chairs, she picked up the tea pot and poured in hot water from the kettle on the stove. When the tea leaves had infused sufficiently, she made him an extra sweet cup of it.

He looked at the cup and mumbled, "God, more sweet tea." But he took it and drank half of it straight away. He almost immediately gained some color in his face.

"You really should be in bed still," she told him.

"I had to see you." He took another swallow of the sweet liquid. "I know you passed Dona on the stairs after you left me yesterday. I can only imagine what Mrs. Miller said to you."

Amanda tried not to smile. "Well, she did make a few comments."

He hurried to explain. "I hadn't asked Dona to come to my room. It was her own idea."

Trying not to sound judgmental, she said, "You didn't deny her access."

"I didn't deny you access either," he pointed out.

"Yes, but..." She stopped before pointing out that her status was different from Dona's, and instead admitted, "That's true. I have no reason to pass judgment on either you or Dona."

"She's not a bad woman really, no matter what some might think. Just someone who needs to make her way in the world and is all alone. She simply came to see if I was okay. I've befriended her a few times and she wanted to show her gratitude."

"Again, like me." She felt her cheeks grow hot.

Not having missed her slight tone of disappointment, he told her, "But not with the same interest or intentions on my part."

Her only response was the deepening of her color. To change the subject, she told him, "Oh, did you hear? The stage robber Sharp escaped from the Aurora jail. His shackles were found on the road to Benton."

"If they don't recapture him soon, he might just get away for good."

After an hour of talk based on town events, Roger declared he felt fit enough to return to his room. When she held out her hand for the second time in two days, he took hold of it in both of his. After a brief moment of looking into her eyes, he kissed the back of her hand and left her standing on the porch watching him cross Green and walk north down Mono. A small sigh escaped her lips.

The next day Amanda arrived at Cherry Wilson's house in response to a note dropped off at the house by Lars Wilson on his way to work. As Amanda came up the short walk to the front porch, a young woman in her early twenties emerged. Cherry patted the woman on the arm in an encouraging manner and was rewarded by a tremulous smile.

When Amanda walked up, Cherry said, "Oh Amanda, how nice. I would like you to meet Miss Nellie Bannon. She lives south of town in a charming little house with her brother Dave." Nellie reminded Amanda of straw; pale, thin and colorless in body, hair and eyes. She was the most nondescript woman she had ever met, and misery lay over her like a drizzling mist.

"How do you do Miss Bannon? It's nice to meet another single young woman."

"Yes, it is. Mrs. Wilson told me you live with your father. It must be nice to have a parent with you here. Dave and I are not so fortunate. We have only each other." She said no more on that and instead bid them good day before walking toward Green.

"Let's sit outside on the porch," Cherry suggested. "It's such a nice day."

Once settled on the small bench by the door with glasses of bottled soda water with slices of lemon, Cherry sighed and looked down the street. Amanda deduced that it was related to Miss Bannon.

"Is it something you can tell me about?" Amanda asked.

"I don't know why not. Everyone in town knows the story."

"Is it about Miss Bannon's brother?"

"Good guess."

"Well, last month I heard about the trouble he and Bob Whitaker caused when they were special officers at the McInnes and Markey wrestling match."

"But that bit of argument and gun play was suggested to them as a diversion. It was done by some tinhorn gamblers who had bet on Markey who was losing. Dave swings between the best of young hardworking men and the worst of the rowdies. Right now he's working at the Standard and showing up on time every day for his twelve-hour shift. And he's a faithful volunteer with the Pioneer Hook and Ladder Company too."

"He must be keeping his boot off the brass rail then."

Cherry nodded. "Yes, as you've guessed, drink is usually at the bottom of most trouble the men get into. Even the toughs seem to keep themselves under control until they start drinking. But Dave is also easily influenced by those he keeps company with."

"Really?"

"When he came here late in '78 he'd been working in Gold Hill, Nevada, just below Virginia City. He was known as a hard worker and quieter than most. His sister worked in a laundry and other respectable jobs. Then they heard of our boom here. He worked in several of the mines and his sister took care of their small cabin south of town. Then a year later he lost his job and found it difficult to find another."

"Why was that? Had he done something that made it difficult to get another?"

"Lars seems to think so." Cherry shook her head sadly. "Last Saturday night he almost got killed. He was hanging out with Old Red Roe, whose real name by the way is Sylvester, as well as Jim Flannery and Manuel Castillo. Manuel was at least forty and should have known better, but he was friends with that wildcat whore Spanish Dora."

Amanda gasped at a woman uttering such a vulgar description of another woman, but only pointed out, "You know so much about what's going on in this town. But I did read in the papers about the shooting."

"Lars brings me tales and like you I pick up the rest from the newspapers. And of course there are other women who like to sit a spell and have a nice gossip on the front porch. Being confined to the house so much, it helps keep boredom at bay."

"Charlotte Perry and I were nearby when Dora was arrested after John Hackwell was shot down by Moreno Castro."

Cherry nodded her head. "Yes, I heard that from Mrs. Cain, who heard it from Mrs. Perry herself."

"Mrs. Cain's husband runs the Bodie Bank, doesn't he?"

"That's right. Now there's a man who will never accept anything less than the success he aims at. He and Lester Bell came here together in 1870. Lester is the manager of the Standard Mill. The men married sisters Delilah and Charity and then settled here."

"Mr. Cain is a good looking man."

Cherry gave her a surprised glance. "I suppose." She then picked up the original story. "Anyway, it was the aftermath of the Spanish Dora incident that almost got Dave in terrible trouble. He was one of those trying to lure Rann into an alley."

"What would Dave, Red and Flannery have done to John Rann if they'd gotten ahold of him then?"

"I suppose they would have beaten him to death. Thankfully Rann retreated into Wagner's for protection. The newspapers drew a pretty good picture of what happened then. I guess Rann's bullet hit a main artery, because I hear Castillo bled to death by morning." There was a hint of satisfaction in her voice.

"I was surprised at how big the funeral was," Amanda commented. "I saw all the people and carriages and wagons following the black hearse pulled by four black horses."

"That's just show." Cherry sniffed and shrugged, her scorn not to be mistaken. "That hearse only needs two horses. Odd how some fellows are more popular in death than they are in life."

"My father says Castillo was a good man, but had a bad temper sometimes. I can see why Miss Bannon would be upset about the whole thing, considering that it could have been Dave struck by the stray bullet."

"Or in jail for murder. I just hope Dave stays away from his old friends."

"Roger says Dave's trouble began in January, again because he was with Flannery."

"Roger?"

"Roger Murphy, a faro dealer at Wagner's. He's a friend of mine."

"Yes, well." This was news almost startling enough to take Cherry away from her story, but she soldiered on. "As I was saying, Nellie says Dave was shocked last January when Flannery knocked out Florentine Herrera and rifled his pockets."

"He may have been shocked, but he got arrested along with Flannery for attempted robbery."

"But the court found him innocent after hearing his story."

"So why did he continue to associate with Flannery?"

"I don't know." Cherry pursed her lips. "In March they were with Mike Noonan and all were arrested for beating up some men. It wasn't the only time they did that. It's odd because Dave is so proud of being a member of the fire company."

Both women shook their heads, sighed, and gave up their speculation. Only future events would tell the status of Dave Bannon's stability of character, or lack of it.

On the way home, it suddenly occurred to Amanda to wonder why Cherry had said she was "confined to the house so much", especially given that Cherry was only a street away from markets and other shops.

The following week brought strong emotions to several people in town besides Amanda, principle among them being Emily Eastman and Charlotte Perry. Being in her sixth month of impending motherhood, Emily had finally agreed with her husband Frank that it was best for her to return to Lone Pine in the southern reaches of Inyo County. Charlotte had announced this news with tears in her eyes, so Amanda knew this was going to be a difficult day for her friend.

The morning of Emily's departure, Amanda stood at the side of the Bodie House in its shadow and watched Emily and her tall dark-haired husband walk down Green toward the stage waiting in front of Mr. Boone's store. Two men stopped them and tipped their hats to Emily while muttering a few words; a woman stopped their progress and pressed Emily's hand; a girl of about fifteen waved as she passed; and Ben Eggleston's wife stopped to say a few words. Amanda had heard much of Emily's good works in the town, but as she watched husband and wife cling to one another, she felt that they were barely aware of these people.

Amanda had already said good-bye to Emily and did not want to intrude on these last moments, as she knew Emily didn't know how long it would be before Frank could leave his job and join her in Lone Pine. So Amanda sat on the bench outside the hotel on the Green Street side, and almost immediately saw Charlotte half walking, half running down Green toward the stage.

Several minutes later, Frank strode up the street toward the Standard Mill with his head down and his jaw clenched, obviously fighting more emotion than he was willing to advertise. His long strides quickly took him up Green toward what had always been a welcome haven for himself and his beloved wife, but now was merely an old house.

From the window of the stage Emily called out good-bye to her friend just as the coach leapt forward, leaving Charlotte behind in a cloud of dust. Charlotte stood in front of Mr. Boone's store like a forlorn child, watching the dust settle back onto the road. As she stepped off the sidewalk to begin her walk home, Amanda called out to her and stood up. Charlotte looked over at the hotel and Amanda standing there, and quickly wiped at her eyes brimming with tears.

Amanda hurried to Charlotte's side, taking her arm and leading her up the street toward their houses. Charlotte acquiesced and accompanied Amanda to the small Blake house. She stood in the parlor blowing her nose and said nothing while Amanda heated the morning's coffee on the stove and poured them each a strong cup.

After Charlotte had taken a swallow and allowed herself a deep sigh, she told Amanda, "Thank you. That helps a little."

Amanda avoided alluding to Emily's departure and instead asked, "Did you hear that a Wells Fargo special agent arrested Sharp, the Sulphur Springs highwayman that escaped?" Without waiting for an answer, she continued, "It was in San Francisco of all far away places. Then Sharp was brought to the Aurora jail. And guess what? He escaped again. Now I hear he gave himself up in Candelaria.

"Oh, and I heard from a friend in Placerville the other day. The fall color in the trees is bright now, and the leaves are beginning to pile up along the creeks, but it's still not as cold at night as here. Oh, Charlotte, if you ever have the opportunity to go to Placerville, you really should. It's so charming, and the trip over the Sierra to get there is a delightful if somewhat scary adventure." And on she prattled until finally she had Charlotte smiling and munching on oatmeal cookies, and there were no more tears in her eyes.

Charlotte jumped as Amanda exclaimed, "Oh, have you heard about Mike McGowan being made to leave town?"

"You mean the man-eater?" Charlotte used his nickname since most people didn't know his real name. "Yes, I heard. Can you imagine a man actually biting off other men's ears and noses?"

"Roger told me that he was asked to leave Virginia City after he ate someone's bull dog."

Both women shuddered at the probably over-exaggerated claim, and then hoping they were right, hurriedly sipped their coffee. ""Well," Charlotte said with a mischievous smile, "the mistake he made here was to take a bite out of Sheriff Taylor's calf."

Amanda nodded and deepening her voice, proclaimed in her most mock-censorious voice, "A bit rash, that."

With a sudden release of tension, the women laughed so hard and for so long that when Charlotte took another sip of coffee, she decreed that their jollity had turned the liquid cold. This only raised their hilarity to a new height, although Amanda was aware there was a bit of desperation beneath it all.

It was in this state that Vince found his wife after knocking on the door of the Blake house and receiving no answer other than the sound of near hysteria. He opened the door cautiously and stuck his head inside. Vince had expected to find his wife in tears over the departure of her best friend. He had also been eager to "commiserate" in man's most favorite manner, and was a little resentful at finding Charlotte at Amanda's. But after a moment, thoroughly ashamed of himself for his selfish desires, he merely told Charlotte he would be home repairing a loose window frame.

Amanda sensed that Vince wanted to be with his wife, although not for the reasons he had in mind, and suggested that Charlotte might want to join him. Charlotte gave her a quick hug, commenting that she needed to start peeling potatoes and carrots for supper that night.

The month ended with civic pride celebrated in Bodie's typically effusive style. The Knights Templar of the Bodie Commandery was to receive a highly decorated banner as a reward for having the largest and fastest growing membership in the country. They had been invited to the triennial conclave in Chicago, and several of the local representatives had accepted the invitation earlier that summer and had made their way east by train.

On the morning of September 26, a telegram was received from Aurora that the three exalted Knights were on a stage headed to Bodie with the sacred banner. Amanda and most of the town watched as six brown horses pulled the stage onto Main Street, where it was met with flags flying, the whistles of the hoist and mill works blasting, and the Standard's cannon booming. Burlinger and Frank's Brass Band played on the corner of Main and King Streets next to a gathering of the Knights Templar standing at attention and dressed in full regalia.

As soon as the stage was on Main, it slowed down so the Knights could march ahead of it all the way to the Masonic Hall at the south end of town. It was enough ceremony and pageantry to impress the most celebratory among the crowd, and at least for a short time everyone forgot rumors about declining mines and the all too frequent bloodletting on the streets.

CHAPTER 7
OCTOBER, 1880

Fall was well established in October and was accompanied by nights of biting cold that penetrated beyond clothing and gave torment to bare skin. So bitter cold was it to Amanda that the chill of it made the nights seem darker and more suppressive than she felt any night had the right to be. She had felt cold before, of course. It had been cold in Placerville, tucked as it was into the mountains, but this was different. There was a brutal quality to it here, a snap and sharpness that allowed no mercy and that ridiculed the futility of complaining.

That October was a good month for those who sold ammunition or owned a saloon, as well as for Mr. Ward and his undertaking business. But it was a bad month for those longing to live in a town free of almost daily gunfire, surly men riding into town with their guns worn where they could be seen, and gory retellings in the newspapers of men found stabbed or clubbed in an alley.

The last day of September had seen Deputy Sheriff Kirgan riding up to Bodie Bluff with a serious and determined look on his face. He had received word that an escaped convict from the Nevada State Prison, John McTeague, was probably hiding out with a friend in his cabin on the side of the Bluff. After kicking in the door and finding the cabin empty, Kirgan had returned to town thinking that someone had pulled his leg and wasted his time. McTeague, however, had indeed been in the cabin earlier. He had simply tired of his hiding place, and eventually his desire for a drink had overcome his better judgment.

Just past midnight deputies Grant and Monahan discovered McTeague in Wagner's Saloon. After relieving McTeague of his two pistols, they began escorting him down Bonanza Street to the jail. Constable Herrington joined the procession as did Tex Hitchell.

Tex's real name was David and he was thirty-eight years old. He was also a formidable "enforcer" for some of the saloons in Chinatown, where he often took advantage of the easy access there to opium and morphine. Although his bad temper was well known, or possibly because of it, Kirgan felt he was one of the few men who could control the worst of the rowdies. Most of them were so terrified of Tex that just knowing he was somewhere in the vicinity put them on the path to redemption.

Constables Herrington and Hitchell dropped back from the other three marching to the jail after exchanging heated words about who should have been in on the arrest. Almost immediately blows were exchanged between the lawmen, and the surprised deputies holding McTeague rushed to separate the two squabbling friends.

"Hey," Monahan called out a minute later, "where's McTeague?"

"Hell!" Herrington spat out, guilt filling his belly like rot-gut whiskey.

The heat of the argument was immediately replaced by the fear of the consequences due them when it got around that they had let a prisoner escape. They scattered in different directions to look for him, but to no avail.

An hour later, however, McTeague arrived at the jail in front of the rifle of Mike Toby, the Wells Fargo messenger. The next day, the first day of October, saw McTeague on his way to Aurora's jail until he could be delivered back to the Nevada State Prison to complete his sentence. Kirgan was glad of the successful resolution of the matter, although he wished he had played a bigger role in it, and that his deputies had not acted so irresponsibly.

Whether it was the extreme cold, the escalating violence, anticipation of the long arduous winter, or the decrease in the number of people using their services, many of the Chinese began to leave town. Vacant wash houses and "for rent" signs appeared overnight on King Street, fewer yellow flags flapped outside opium dens, all but two of the vegetable stands disappeared, and weeds grew along the foundations of buildings that only days before had been filled with exotic smells and chattering talk.

Some people claimed *the Celestials* had grown weary of the sentiments such as those displayed on signs carried in the last Fourth of July parade or during political campaigns. These ranged from the simple statement of "Chinese must go" to the more prevalent sentiment of "American Soil for American Working Men". Those Chinese that remained, and there were still over two-hundred, huddled by their weak fires like everyone else. They even sometimes sat next to members of the Anglo population who joined them in the opium dens where after a time no amount of ridicule, poverty or physical suffering mattered.

Every time Amanda crossed over King Street, she looked down at the district set aside for the most unwanted element in the West, pity and fear mixed in with her curiosity. Of course, no matter how despised most were, when people wanted their clothes washed or their wood hauled into town, they became less critical of the Chinese individual involved and tried to convince themselves that "this one was a good one".

When Amanda purchased vegetables from their stands, she always thanked them and gave them a warm smile, knowing that most people treated them as though they were not quite human. And many of the good women were afraid to even meet their gaze. In every instance of her kindness toward them, they had shown surprise that a white woman would put forth the effort, and she was sometimes rewarded by a shy twitch of their lips. But beyond that, they dared not show familiarity.

Most of the Chinese in town had earlier worked in Virginia City and had gravitated to Bodie in 1878 at the peak of its boom. Since the 1850's, they had been sent on ships to San Francisco from South China by large companies representing various districts in China. Having signed contracts that would last several years, they were paid four to eight dollars a month. As soon as they could get loose from their commitments, they headed to places like Virginia City and Bodie where their services were most valued, and where they could keep all the money they earned.

Colorful streamers of cloth fluttered in the breeze from upstairs windows on King Street, and exotic odors mixed with a mysterious cloying scent that escaped from buildings with their curtains pulled tight over the windows. Here the Chinese associated with men of all nationalities who had discovered that sucking on water pipes of opium was a means to escape from life's harsh reality into gentle fantasies and illusions. Although seldom mentioned, there were also white women who had discovered this vice, and not all of them were those of easy virtue.

On the other hand, the Irish were allowed to work in most of the mines, and were seldom openly prejudiced against in Bodie. Instead, it was left up to individual businesses to make it clear to these Celtic descendants that they were not welcome in that particular eatery, saloon or merchandise store, which owners did by posting signs at the entrance. Knowing that her grandparents on both sides had been born in Ireland, and having always been proud of her heritage, Amanda looked at these "No Irish Allowed" signs and gritted her teeth.

What had once been a humorous description of the wild and untamed criminal element common to Bodie had now evolved into a vaunted title. To be a *Bad Man From Bodie* was a title assumed by criminals in towns throughout the West who had never even seen the mining town. It created for them immediate status and at the same time warned men with likely faster gun hands to stay away. That fall in San Francisco, one tough braggart named Joe Fisher thought enough of the title to flaunt it to the judge who was in the process of sentencing him. Whether or not he impressed his fellow inmates at San Quentin, where the Judge sent him, is unknown.

In Bodie, meanwhile, the commonality of daily lawlessness and brutality was creating an atmosphere that encouraged over-reaction at the slightest provocation. Few men had the opportunity to apologize for some slight, real or imagined, before they were shot, stabbed, or at the least, beaten. The frequency of someone being discovered in an alley in such condition was increasingly alarming to the good citizens of the town. Those people who were not so drunk that common sense had deserted them, never walked alone after dark.

In the past there had been many instances where just the appearance of a gun pulled from a pocket would be enough for the adversaries to mutually agree to end the dispute. But now it seemed that no one was willing to back down and instead wanted only to wreck as much damage upon their chosen targets as was possible. Fist fights that at one time would have ended with the first drawing of blood, now continued until one of the combatants was unconscious or dead. As Amanda read of these incidents in the paper, she wondered what was giving rise to so much anger and frustration in the male population.

Was the undermining of patience due to the lack of jobs and therefore more crowding in the saloons, or maybe the increasingly higher prices of everything needed for daily life? Or was it because of an unacknowledged fear that the mines were beginning to play out, and the consequent gnawing uncertainty? How far into the future could one plan when they didn't know if they would still have a job? Were these the fears and doubts that had to be bluffed by a show of superior force whenever the opportunity arose, even if it meant backing up your swagger with a gun?

Some of the lovely ladies of Bonanza Street contributed their part to this lawlessness by robbing careless clients after slipping a sedative into their whiskey. It was also being reported that the women were fighting more among themselves, while at the same time their habit of consuming various drugs had increased.

Crime even trickled down to corruption at the meat counter where a clerk might rest his thumb on the scale while weighing a housewife's chops, the dressmaker who cut her yardage short, the bartender who added water to the whiskey and compensated with a large pinch of tobacco for a kick, and even the druggist's clerk who sometimes sold flour pills instead of the real thing.

The reality, however, was that it was *not* a town without laws and peace keepers. There was County Sheriff Summers, jailer and Deputy Sheriff Kirgan, and several lesser officers at work. They did their best to minimize the worst of the crime, but there was no way they could stop it altogether, since there were so few of them in the large town. The fair-minded among the population acknowledged that as bad as the crime rate was, without the efforts of these men it could have been a lot worse.

It was the newspapers that started making the situation volatile. Those in the town and even those in Sacramento, San Francisco, Carson City, and Reno stepped up their decrying of the frequent taking of life and the robbing of hard-earned pay from poor miners in Bodie. Because of their constant hue and cry over the situation, the honest and principled in town pushed for stronger punishments. But the courts and juries continued to set free the perpetrator on the basis of self-defense or not enough evidence, even if there were several witnesses willing to testify.

By the time the country's election was past and Garfield had won, with Bodie contributing 640 votes to him, the summer census revealed that 5,375 people lived in the town. Of course, the locals knew there should be another thousand added to that count due to the number of men who would not have stepped up to be counted. Only the newspapers that tended to exaggeration in all their claims, and writers of florid western fiction, upped the population in Bodie at this time nearer to 10,000.

This didn't change the fact that Bodie was known throughout the West, as well as the brokerage houses in the East, as the fastest growing mining town in operation anywhere in the country. At least this had been its status since 1878 when the boom was well underway. But while it was trumpeted throughout the West as the most infamous of mining towns, this dubious claim to fame was glossed over in the East so as not to upset potential investors.

As evidence of continued confidence in the town's on-going growth, the Bodie and Mono companies had recently sunk a big three compartment shaft known as the *Lent Shaft*. It enabled the development of deep mining in both mines, and would eventually reach a vertical depth of over 1,200 feet, the deepest in the town.

A freshly washed and dressed Amanda carefully rolled down the wick on the lamp in the middle of the kitchen table until the flame went out. The sun was just coming up and casting a warm light through the front windows, and although its warmth could not be felt, it allowed enough light in the kitchen that she didn't want to waste the coal oil. An hour later, just as she finished sweeping the kitchen floor, and with the breakfast dishes still draining on the counter, a knock at the back door startled her.

"Hello!" Charlotte greeted her.

"Come in," Amanda invited. "What brings you out first thing this morning?"

"I have a wonderful idea for us today."

"What's that?"

"Mrs. L. S. Bowers from Virginia City, also known as *The Famous Washoe Seeress*, has arrived in town for a few days. I think we should pay her a visit."

"You mean to welcome her to Bodie?"

"No silly. She tells the future by using what she calls a peepstone that she carries with her."

Amanda laughed and rolled her eyes in derision. "Do you really think she can tell our futures?"

"Oh, I'm sure it's some kind of parlor trick." Charlotte was filled with enthusiasm and her cheeks were rosy, either from the early morning chill or excitement. She sat at the table and reached out to the bread still sitting on a small board and cut off a slice, slathering it with butter and chewing it thoughtfully. "It should be great fun, don't you think?" She then made a silly face and tossed her hands up in surrender. "And it's something different for us to do."

"I'm all for doing something different."

"I thought you'd feel like that. She's accepting callers at the Mono House and I'll pay her fees. Get your shawl and let's go."

Amanda and Charlotte arrived with pictures in their minds of a tall elegant woman with long flowing hair, sunken cheeks and bright eyes filled with visions. Instead they found a short, plump, square-faced woman in her early sixties with a broad mouth and nose, and eyes partially hidden by weak lids. Hair that had once been dark was now mostly gray and held against her skull by tight pin curls parted down the middle.

However, taken altogether she had a soft, kind and approachable aura. One was sure she would understand any problem one might bring to her because she was someone who had led a long and adventuresome life. Mrs. Bowers somehow made women feel their worth in society and their families, and men remember a time in their lives when they had felt safe, and both recall childhoods less lonely than they actually had been. Her readings of people's futures were generally uplifting and encouraging, and most people left her feeling glad of having spent the money she charged them.

She had been blessed with the experience of a happy youth in Scotland. After coming to America she had married twice, both times to Mormons who had left her childless. She had divorced them and settled not far from Virginia City in tiny Johntown, Nevada. There she had built herself a log cabin and began taking in boarders who she treated like her children while cooking them basic meals, mending their clothes, and listening to their problems. It was in this way that she had learned much about mining. During the winters she had removed herself to a small cabin at Washoe's hot springs with the miner's clothing that needed washing, mending and pressing. No one at that time would have thought that someday this plain little mouse of a woman would for a while be the wealthiest female in the country.

After Charlotte and Amanda entered Mrs. Bower's room at the Mono House on Mill Street, she arose from her chair behind the room's small table and invited them to make themselves comfortable. After seating herself behind the table once again, she smoothed the skirt of her black bombazine dress that she wore to advertise to everyone that she was that most respected echelon of womanhood, a widow.

She ran her hands over an oddly shaped stone on the table before her and asked, "Now, ladies, what can I do for you? Do you have any specific questions that are weighing on your mind?"

Charlotte spoke up first. "I'd like to know if my husband and I will continue to be a success here in Bodie?"

"Has he been so far?"

"You tell me."

Mrs. Bowers let out a bark of laughter. "You're right, of course. Let me see now, what does my peepstone tell me?" She sat quietly for several minutes, her eyes closed and her hands on the stone. Suddenly, her eyes opened and she looked at Charlotte with a frown. "Your husband had an injury recently, didn't he?"

"No."

"That's odd." She frowned, then shrugged. "Oh well, he still might."

"Don't sound so gratified," a nettled Charlotte told her.

"Oh, he'll be quite well again. But he won't want to go back to his old job. I see the three of you in a small town far away having something to do with cattle."

"The three of us? There's just my husband and myself."

Mrs. Bowers looked at her and smiled a very sweet smile. She then turned to Amanda, reached out and laid a hand on her arm while placing her other hand on the stone. After a moment, she frowned and said, "The man you live with must stay working where he is."

"My father or the other man?"

"The one you feel strong affection for."

"My father. I don't think there's a problem with his changing jobs."

She looked at Amanda with a concentration that was startling. "I mean it. He must not change jobs until the winter has passed."

"Okay." She didn't know what else to say.

"You're a very independent young woman, but you're afraid to admit it to yourself. You shouldn't be afraid to be who you are. It won't keep love from coming into your life. But if you deny who you are, you will have great unhappiness and a shorter life." While Amanda stared at her in surprise, Mrs. Bowers sat back and smiled while looking very tired. "I'm sorry. But I don't feel anything else."

"I thought you were supposed to *see* things."

"Yes, sometimes. But only if I feel something too. And I can tell when nothing else will come to me about people. Sometimes nothing specific occurs to me and I have to tell them some lot of general things that would apply to anyone." She smiled at the ladies before her. "I didn't have to do that with you, but I am sorry I didn't see more."

"You look weary," Charlotte told her. She was filled with compassion for such a dignified woman having to resort to telling fortunes to make her way in the world. She leaned forward and placed a hand on Mrs. Bower's wrist. "Why don't you let us buy you a meal?"

Mrs. Bowers hesitated only a moment before accepting. Knowing the deficit in her purse, she was in fact grateful for the invitation. And although she didn't tell them, she could sense in Charlotte someone utterly trustworthy and sincere. Otherwise, she would not have accepted their invitation. "That's very kind of you. I'd love to join you. And you must call me Eilley."

Once settled at a table at Delmonico's Restaurant, and with their order placed, Amanda said, "I understand that you lived in Virginia City for a long time. Was it as wild as Bodie?"

Mrs. Bowers laughed. "Oh, much wilder, I fear. But I was there back in '59. I was a single woman with a boarding house in Gold Canyon. Then James Fennimore, also known as Old Virginny, Jim Rogers and Henry Comstock found a big vein up canyon. Me and Sandy Bowers, with the help of the others, packed my boarding house onto mules and we made our way up Gold Canyon and set up next to Old Nick's Bar. When Jim couldn't pay his board bill, I paid him $100 and took over his claim next to Sandy's." She smiled and colored a bit. "I also wanted Sandy, and if his claim was rich too, all the better."

"Is that when you married him?"

"No, that came later. There was only me and about five other women in the new town. Some of them were *available* women, but I made it clear that I'd have nothing to do with that and I was respected. But we all nursed the men when they were ill, sewed for them, and sometimes cooked for them." Without the least hint of irony, she added, "We were true treasures of the camp."

The food came and they began eating. Mrs. Bowers ate slowly while continuing her story, glad to be with kind women she could tell had no hidden agenda and were simply interested in her story.

"By '63, Sandy was incredibly wealthy. And I no longer wanted to work like a dog. I was 47, after all, and we'd both earned the right to enjoy the money coming in from our mines." Her tone of self-justification turned to a wistful whisper. "Oh, and we did." She sighed and looked out the window of the hotel at the wealthy mines on the hill. "Sandy was offered $400,000 for his claims, but he turned them down. I was so proud of him. But people continued to pressure him and he began to think about selling, so I married him and joined my twenty rich feet with his even larger claim. Our claim generated $100,000 a month for quite some time. After paying out to the miners, the mills, and other expenses, we still had plenty. You see, our claims were close to the surface so we didn't have high overhead to get it out." She took a swallow of water before saying with an unaffected nonchalance, "You might think $20,000 a month clear would be hard to spend on ourselves, but we managed."

Charlotte and Amanda stopped eating and stared at her. Only their strict sense of good manners kept their mouths from falling open in dismay.

Mrs. Bowers continued without noticing their reaction. "My peepstone said it was okay and that I would be the queen of the city, so I acted like it and people treated me like it." Her eyes glittered at the memory. "We had a very decent house in Virginia City, but the townsmen helped us build a much larger one near the shore of Washoe Lake that was designed by the great J. Neely Johnson. It cost almost $400,000 to build and furnish by the time we were done with it. The shadow of the Sierra fell over us every afternoon and cooled our evenings as we sat on the veranda. The house was two stories, square, and it had a wrap-around porch on both floors. There was even a fountain out front lined with Spanish tiles."

When she stopped to take a few bites of food, Amanda managed to say, "It sounds wonderful. What was it like inside?"

"Oh, my dear, it was just lovely." Her eyes misted over as she pictured it. "It had silver door knobs, plate glass windows and skylights, hot water piped in from a nearby thermal spring, a library filled with leather covered books, a pair of mirrors in the foyer that had at one time been in a Venetian palace and cost us $3,000. Oh, and lovely imported lace curtains each costing twelve hundred dollars. In the conservatory I had huge trees in pots and among them canaries sang in their brass cages and a scarlet macaw scolded them from its perch.

"We eventually went to England. I'd hoped to meet the Queen, but she had objections over my two divorces so we didn't. Even so, we gave her a silver tea set made from the silver from our mines." She gave a short laugh. "We also took some cuttings of English ivy from the walls of Windsor Castle so I could have ivy on *my* castle walls. And it grew well, too."

"But you're not living there now?" Charlotte asked tentatively, tactfully avoiding the question of why a woman who could afford such opulence would be giving private readings in mining towns.

"No." Her mouth turned down and the light disappeared from her eyes as she picked up her water glass. "Sandy died in April of '68. Weak lungs from all that he'd inhaled in the mines. He was only thirty-five. Then our mines played out, something we thought would never happen. I was spending more than I was bringing in and soon all I had left was my peepstone and my clothes. I had to sell the house in '76, only getting $10,000 for it. I'd already sold off the furnishings. So I moved back into Virginia City and began telling people's fortunes as *The Famous Washoe Seeress*."

After a few minutes of silence wherein the plates were cleared and coffee poured, Amanda asked, "Is there some reason you skipped from 1859 to '63?"

Eilley looked at the women and hesitated, as though taking their measure before continuing. Evidently still feeling their sincerity, she said, "I lost two children during that time when they were only a few months old; a son in 1860 and a daughter in '61. Right after that is when we began planning for our big house. Maybe it was a way of burying the pain, or maybe it was a way of reaffirming life. Either way, our home became everything for us. Maybe that's why we went a little crazy with it." She neglected to mention an older daughter who had been with them upon returning from England, and who died when only twelve.

Charlotte put a hand on Eilley's arm and gave her a warm smile. Eilley met her eyes and Amanda could tell something of understanding passed between the two childless women.

Eilley took a deep breath and smiled. "Now I travel around offering my talents and people pay me to enlighten them about their future. Some listen to me and are better off. Others do not, and pay the price." She turned to Amanda. "Please, Miss Blake, please make sure your father does not change his job until next year."

"But you haven't said why."

She shook her head. "I don't know why. I just know that his very life depends upon it."

A chill passed over Amanda, but she nodded and said, "Well, he's not planning a change that I know of."

Her concern did not seem assuaged, but Eilley said nothing further. After Charlotte paid the bill, they bid their new friend good-bye, Charlotte pressing into her hand a gold coin as they wished her good luck.

Whether or not her peepstone forewarned her, Eilley Bowers would die alone and destitute in 1903 at a home for elderly women in Oakland, California. Her ashes would be buried next to her beloved Sandy and her English daughter, on the hill behind the Bowers Mansion in Washoe.

On the sixth day of the month John returned home at five in the afternoon, presenting Amanda with a wrapped package from the meat market. She opened it to find inside a steak large enough to feed all three of them. John chuckled at her surprise.

"What has you so chipper this evening?" Amanda asked him as she set a large iron skillet on the stove.

"I'm going to work at the Goodshaw Mine."

She stared at him, the chill of her flesh and the rush of hot blood to her face competing in her shock. But all she said was, "Is it already decided?"

"Of course. I've changed to the Goodshaw."

She told herself that maybe Mrs. Bowers had known that men changed employment often in mining towns, and made up a warning in order to say something dramatic to Amanda. In that case, John's doing so now was a simple coincidence. Amanda asked, "Will you be making more money?"

He shook his head. "No. The four dollars I make is the most any miner makes here." Then he smiled. "But my shift will be much better. I'll be working eight in the evening to eight in the morning."

"You'll be getting more sleep, that's for sure." She thought to herself that this change would make life a little easier for her too, not having to get up at three o'clock to see him off and then trying to get back to sleep. And she could make supper later, so it would allow her more time to herself during the day. But as worried as she was because of the prophecy, she also knew that if she told her father about it, he would only scoff or be irritated with her. Rather than cause a rift in the delicate balance of their relationship, she decided to say nothing.

She put a small scoop of lard into the skillet and waited for it to begin sizzling before putting in the steak rubbed with a clove of garlic and crusted with salt and pepper. Into a smaller skillet where she had melted butter she dumped a bowl of sliced pre-cooked potatoes and raw diced onion. With the hissing of frying goodness as background music, she filled a bowl with two cut up large tomatoes, and after dressing them with flavored vinegar, she set the bowl next to a loaf of bread and a small crock of dashed butter on the table. Noting that the bread was on the verge of being too stale to serve, she cursed the dry high-elevation air that made it so difficult to keep bread fresh. Then she shrugged, thinking that it would be good for bread pudding, which she could make that night while the oven was warm.

In the next second, just as she turned toward the sink, the house and most of the town shook with a sharp jarring sidewise motion. As the boom of an explosion contracted the air around them, Amanda was thrown against the counter while John was shoved against the wall next to the table. Almost immediately the sound of the whistles at the hoisting works screamed from the hill, and before the hot skillet fell from the stove, Amanda pushed it back into place.

Fire engine bells filled the evening air as they moved south down Main, over Green, and onto the Booker Flat Road. The fire engines were followed by shouting people, barking dogs, screaming horses, and rattling wagons. Amanda and John ran out onto the front porch and looked at the hill south of town. The Bodie Foundry was on fire, a plume of smoke rising from it and floating south on the rising breeze.

Rather than join the milling throng, Amanda finished supper and John waited on the porch for people to return with the news of what had happened. By the time Amanda went to announce supper, Matt had arrived home and had joined John at his vigil. The men hesitated when called inside by Amanda, but regardless of whatever had happened she wasn't going to have her food turn into a cold congealed mess. But once they sniffed the smells wafting from the kitchen, they willingly followed her to the table.

As soon as they finished eating they all gathered outside on the porch, and eventually John saw someone he knew walking past on his return to town. "Hey, Bob," he called to a tall man with sooty hands and face, "what's up?"

Bob ran a grubby hand over his face. "Some son of a bitch threw a bucket of cold water on a batch of hot molten iron. Idiot should have known the sudden chill would cause a build-up of gasses and an explosion. The man should be horse whipped."

Amanda retreated into the house and returned with a large glass of water that she handed to Bob. He nodded his thanks before drinking it down.

"Was anyone hurt?" Matt asked. Amanda idly thought that the miners always asked if someone was *hurt*, never if they were *dead*, and she realized that the reality of mining accidents must weigh on their minds all the time.

"Naw," Bob answered, "but the damned boy who did it got some burns. Serves 'em right. The whole side of the building is blown out, but the fire was got out fast and no other buildings were burned." He handed the glass to Amanda, ducked his head in polite acknowledgment and strode down the hill into town.

The next day while Amanda stood in Eggleston's Market, she overheard Ben talking to Mr. Kilgore. "What a night," Ben commented. "Can you believe that explosion?"

Mr. Kilgore nodded and said, "It's real sad about Vincent Perry."

"What's that?" Ben asked.

Amanda's head whipped around and she stepped closer to the men.

"You didn't hear?" Mr. Kilgore asked Ben after glancing at Amanda. "One of his workers had stacked some barrels too high in Perry's warehouse and when the blast happened yesterday evening, they fell down right on top of him. He was trapped for several hours."

"Is he going to be okay?"

"No one knows, ma'am. Doc thinks it'll be a miracle if he survives the next few days."

"Oh, God." She pressed her hand to her mouth as she tried to still her racing heart. "I must go to Charlotte."

"You'll find her at home. That's where she insisted they take Vince. No one trusts the old hospital anymore."

Grabbing her grocery bags from the counter, she hurried up Main and turned right onto the up-slope of Green. By the time she reached the Perry house just past Wood, she could barely catch her breath. After a moment's recuperation, she walked up the three steps to the Perry's raised porch, set her packages down, and knocked lightly on the door. It was quickly opened by Charlotte. Never had Amanda seen a woman so pale.

"I heard about Vince," Amanda whispered. "How is he?"

Charlotte shook her head and stepped out onto the small porch, softly closing the door behind her. Gripping the railing, she looked toward the far Sierra and shook her head again. "He's not doing very well. The doctor doesn't hold out much hope." Her voice caught in her throat.

"You didn't have Dr. Blackwell, I hope."

"Heavens no. He'd want to bleed him and Vince is weak enough already."

"Some doctors still think that's best, even leaching their patients sometimes."

"Well, it makes no sense to me and thankfully Dr. Davidson agrees." She dug into the pocket of her long apron and brought out a delicate handkerchief. She dabbed at her eyes and said, "God, he's so weak. I'm so frightened he's not going to make it."

"Oh, Charlotte, you mustn't give up." Amanda put her arm around her friend's trembling shoulders. "He's a strong man, and with you at his side, I just know he'll make it."

Charlotte turned to her and tried to smile, but only accomplished the quivering of her chin. "You're very kind. I needed to hear that."

"Listen, you keep the groceries I have here. I can get more tomorrow. Before I go into town, I'll stop by to see what else you need."

"I shouldn't take advantage of you like that, but I'm going to."

"Don't be ridiculous. I'm happy to do it."

Over the next week Vince held his own, but Dr. Davidson continued to be pessimistic about continued improvement. Charlotte told him in no uncertain terms that he was not to talk that way around Vince, and that if he did she would find another doctor. Thus chastised, the doctor apologized and began making positive and encouraging statements when in the house. Whatever he might have thought the truth, he kept it to himself. And Vince continued to hold his own.

On Saturday morning, October 16, Amanda noticed that her father was unusually quiet at breakfast.

"Is something the matter?"

"Last night was just a bad one."

"For sleep?"

"No, for dying. I was with some friends at a dance house on King Street. Bill Page was one of them. He's been a teamster for a while, in his mid-thirties and a decent man. We'd been drinking for some time. About two-thirty this morning a man from the Syndicate, Pat Keogh, collided with Bill on the dance floor. It happens," he added plaintively. "For some reason Pat took offense and mumbled something. I didn't hear what it was. It looked like they might come to blows, but Shorty, a mutual friend, stepped in and everything settled down."

"Well then, everything worked out."

"Only for a few minutes. Bill couldn't leave it alone and said loudly that it's a good thing Shorty stepped in because he was about to slap Pat across the face. Pat swore at him, and Bill pulled his gun. Pat drew his gun faster and shot Bill in the head."

"Oh, Dad, that's awful."

Amanda learned later that day that Pat Keogh, after shooting Bill, had just walked out of the dance house and disappeared. Within days, Governor George Perkins offered a $500 reward for his arrest and conviction.

Keogh's easy escape while deputies looked for him, so soon after McTeague had eluded them, drew attention to the organization of the town's officers. Up to then it had been agreed among them that no arrest would be made on another officer's beat. To appease the townspeople, the deputies now agreed to cooperate with one another and just make an arrest whenever it became necessary.

Thankfully, Keogh was captured and taken to trial. However, as so often happened, he was found innocent by reason of self-defense. No one was that surprised, but it became one more bit of explosive powder in an already flammable keg that was the town's resentment.

A week later, as Amanda sat in the parlor darning her father's socks, she listened to him and Matt discussing events in the papers.

"It's about time!" John exclaimed. "The Superior Court jury in Bridgeport handed down a verdict of guilty for William Lee."

"Grand larceny, wasn't it?" Matt asked.

"Damn straight it was. It was for sluice raiding."

Amanda asked, "What does that mean?"

Matt turned to her. "It means he stole amalgam from some sluice boxes on a river claim. It's the first felony conviction in three years in Mono County." Matt gave a short derisive bark. "And only the fourth since the county was formed in '63."

On October 24, Amanda was just leaving the Pioneer Market when she heard men shouting, their words carrying easily during a rare break in the traffic flow on Main. They were standing on the west side of the street between Joe Kingsley's City Livery, located amid half a dozen saloons, and Stewart's Drug Store. The benches in this area along the sidewalk always seemed to be packed with men smoking and visiting. Today the benches were quickly deserted as the raised voices of Tom Hamilton and Tom Keefe went from merely angry to shouted threats.

Although most such arguments were resolved when the first gun was removed from a pocket or waistband, Keefe felt the need to pull the trigger. Seeing Hamilton stagger back against the building, Amanda turned and fled before the stain of blood could cover the man's shirt front. She slammed the door to the house and cursed the town, men in general, and a society that couldn't control itself.

However, the cartridges in Keefe's gun evidently had little powder in them, a not uncommon occurrence, because the bullet stopped after passing through the fabric of Hamilton's wool coat and vest, and cotton shirt. Men came forward to take Hamilton to the doctor and there it was discovered that the bullet had barely nicked the skin.

Unaware of this, and assuming that Mr. Hamilton had been seriously injured if not killed, Amanda found it impossible to fall asleep that night. Not only was she worrying about Vince, and trying to forget the shock of the shooting she had witnessed that day, but at midnight her father still had not returned. Amanda finally went in and woke up Matt.

"I'm sorry, but father isn't home yet. He told me after dinner that he was going into town and would be back early."

Matt stared at her with bleary eyes not quite focused. "Yeah?" He belched loudly. "I left him at the dance house." He chuckled and burped again. "He was drunker than me. Maybe he passed out somewhere on his way home. I should go look for 'em." With this pronouncement he made an ineffectual grab at the covers over him, but then fell back on his pillow with a snort that turned into mild snoring.

Amanda had visions of her father lying in the mud at the side of Main freezing to death or possibly robbed and beaten. "Matt? Wake up! Which dance house?" But Matt only snored louder.

The one thing Amanda knew for sure was that the dance house would be located at the north end of Main. Although they were not on Bonanza Street, it was important that the dance houses be close to that neighborhood. Dressing quickly in a wool skirt over a flannel petticoat and a wool snug-fitting jacket, she also wrapped herself in her father's long wool coat that fell to her ankles. Meanwhile, her mind was wrapped in a mantle of determination. It didn't escape her that she was probably being foolish, but she nevertheless stopped in the kitchen and put a short sharp knife into the pocket of the coat before stepping out into the frosty night.

As she headed up Main, she passed the mellow golden glow of candles and coal oil lanterns lighting windows and throwing shadows onto the sidewalks that were only slightly less crowded than during the day. The closer to the north end of town she came, the nature of the crowd changed as well. Once past most of the restaurants, the good women escorted by men in suits disappeared. They were replaced by men whose pockets bulged and whose waist bands were tightened by the gun stuffed into it at the back. She passed miners on the way to their night shifts, dusty freighters in baggy clothes and large-brimmed hats who smelled not much different than their teams, and men in suits who smelled of Mr. Howard's barber shop and who were on their way toward Bonanza Street.

Mr. Howard was one of the most well liked and popular Bodie citizens. His shop was on Mill Street on the triangle and it was heard every day that men were waiting to get in to see "the colored barber of Mill Street". His storied past was a constant source of fascination to the younger men, as he talked about his early years picking cotton in Mississippi, fighting with Sam Houston in Texas, and his trek west on the 1846 wagon train that had brought supplies to Captain Fremont and his men. He especially enjoyed talking about his wounding by Indians where now the Mammoth Mines had started up south of Bodie.

There were hundreds of such interesting men in the town who now wielded a razor, swept the floors of a store, wiped glasses in a saloon, clerked at a bank, pounded nails into new construction, or painted numbers on buildings. It was a perspective Amanda had never considered before and after hearing Mr. Howard's story from her father, she never again assumed anything about the men she passed on the streets.

Across from King Street, the aroma of spices mixed with opium drifted on the breeze out of the west that occasionally gusted and carried smatterings of sand across Main, hitting anything in its path with a ping. With these blasts also came the sound of laughter and cigar smoke from "virgin alley" running right behind the dance houses and saloons, and conveniently close to the Chinese opium dens.

Leaving the area where men were trying to turn boredom and despair into excitement and hope, Amanda stood across from the Grand Central Hotel. Only a few steps further would take her to the dance houses, and she was suddenly unsure of herself.

There were only about six of these dance houses left of the fifteen that had been active during the town's peak years. The most popular were the Miners Exchange, the Central Dance House, the Opera House Dance Hall that was also referred to as the Concert Hall, and the Spanish Dance House. Having heard her father mention this last one several times, she determined to visit it first.

Hesitating across the street from the noisy and brightly lit building, she watched laughing half-drunk men enter and leave by the dozens, and began to think better of her plan. But concern for her father overcame her reluctance. Stepping into the muddy street where puddles had iced over, she carefully picked her way across.

Entering the smoky room, she looked at the boisterous scene before her and wondered why men so often exchanged winks and nods whenever the place was mentioned. It was merely a large room with a bar down the left side and a table near the door where dance tickets could be purchased. There were, however, four dark wooden doors leading into small rooms at the back that lent an air of mystery and intrigue. A small lively band was set up in the far corner and the musicians were producing music that had dozens of couples bouncing around the scuffed pine floor.

The women wore colorful sleeveless and low cut dresses and had their hair adorned with ribbons and clips. Most of the men wore rumpled suits, probably the best clothes they had, while a few had on clean shirts with only a vest over it. There was a buzz of voices among those watching the dancers, but none were raised in anger or drunken slurs as was so often heard in the saloons. Everyone seemed to be enjoying themselves, with laughter generously scattered throughout the room.

When the congestion of dancers cleared a space, Amanda noticed that a short hallway at the rear of the room led to a door at the back of the building. This she realized must open almost directly onto Bonanza Street, and she suddenly understood the winks and nods.

She also realized that some of the fancier dressed women dancing with the men were obviously prostitutes, while other girls were better dressed and only there to dance. The men had purchased tickets for dances with both, and it was up to the girls to declare themselves if their attire and the quantity of makeup they wore did not already do it for them.

The drinks were not included in the price of the dance ticket, and therefore these sales were the main source of income for the hall. Nothing out of the ordinary seemed to be taking place, although when Amanda spotted a number of bullet holes in the walls she realized that there must have been considerable excitement here at some time.

She watched the men stomping across the floor with enthusiasm and smiled at their obvious enjoyment. Some of the women were flinging their skirts so that not only their ankles were visible, but also most of their lower limbs (the socially polite term for a woman's legs). The men were grinning and laughing, and grasping the women to them when they were not twirling them away so they could look at exposed stocking-covered limbs.

A woman moved away from the end of the bar and sauntered toward Amanda. It was the friendly woman called Lou who had stopped her on the street the day she had arrived in town.

"Well, hello," Lou drawled. "I never thought I'd see you here." She was dressed more conservatively than the other women, wearing a dark red silk dress with a low neck and long sleeves. Her hair was a pile of ringlets, some artfully pinned on top of her head and others cascading down her neck. Most of this luxuriance was probably false hair, but it looked fine against the dark silk of her dress. Her face was generously painted and her lips stained brightly red, all in an effort to hide the fact that she was getting on in years and was just the other side of thirty-five.

"Oh, hello." Amanda swallowed with difficulty as she became suddenly self-conscious of her drab and heavily clothed appearance. "Lou, isn't it?"

"That's right, honey." Lou put her hands on her hips and looked from Amanda's face down to her toes and up again. "You looking for work?"

"Oh, no." Realizing that she might have sounded too eager in her denial, and maybe even a little condescending, she hurried on. "I'm looking for my father. A man with him earlier said that he was very intoxicated when they parted. He should have returned home by now and I'm concerned that something has happened to him."

Lou smiled slowly, her eyes dancing with humor. "There are all kinds of things that could happen to him here, honey, but not dangerous ones and certainly none that he wouldn't enjoy."

Amanda realized the woman was trying to shock her, and responded with spirit. "I'm sure that's true. I'm more concerned about what might happen to him after leaving here."

Lou nodded. "Who's your father?"

"John Blake."

"Yeah, I know John." She started to say something more, but changed her mind and added, "He was here earlier, but he left. He wasn't drunk when I was with him. Maybe the man you talked to meant they parted at another dance house."

"Yes, maybe." Now what was she supposed to do? She couldn't spend the night visiting them all and searching the streets in between.

Lou gave Amanda another appraising glance before saying, "If you ever do need a job, I'd be happy to consider you."

Amanda suddenly found the situation ridiculous and laughed. "Thank you, Lou. You're very kind." And feeling a little naughty because she was flattered, she turned on her heel and walked out onto Main Street.

She kept walking south, not knowing what else to do but go home, especially considering the late hour. She was beginning to realize that her rush to help her father had been useless. Taking an honest look at her motivations, she had to admit that maybe her actions had been fueled more by her need to rescue than his need to be rescued. It was just that having found him back in her life, she didn't want to lose him before achieving the degree of closeness to which she still clung with hope.

When she arrived home, she went to see if Matt was awake. Opening the door to the men's bedroom, she found Matt still snoring. She also found her father sprawled on his bed where he had collapsed in his clothes, and also snoring loudly. She fought the urge to become angry while pulling a blanket from under him and throwing it over his rumpled form. She left him to face his hangover in the morning.

Undressing and falling exhausted into bed, sleep came only when she was finally able to turn her pique into resigned acceptance of men's habits. Nevertheless, when morning came and she heard Matt and John moving around, she stayed right where she was, letting them fend for themselves if they wanted anything to eat. They evidently got the message and left without disturbing her.

CHAPTER 8
NOVEMBER, 1880

Summer had merged into winter with barely a hesitation in autumn, which in sagebrush country meant the yellow bloom of the rabbitbrush and the sneezing of those allergic to it. One day they were sweating in the heat, and the next they were rethinking their supply of fire wood, now selling at $20 a cord. The last of the work horses and other resident stock not absolutely needed were being moved south to the warmer climate of the Owens Valley. The mules needed to pull the ore carts in the mines would be housed in a huge heated barn on the hill.

The thermometer at the Miners' Union read 18 degrees below zero at the beginning of the month, and ice had to be chopped from the top of the troughs at the stables so the few riding horses and mules staying in town could drink. These animals were heavily blanketed and housed inside Mr. Boone's barn or one of the livery stables.

Men also wore multiple layers of clothing and even ear muffs under hats pulled low on the head, and when this wasn't sufficient they swore loudly as though the heat of their words would warm the air around them. Beneath their skirts women wore wool tights and a petticoat of flannel and another heavily quilted, while woolen coats and scarves obscured their heavy-weight wool dresses. The purchase of these petticoats cut into Amanda's reserve funds, but she had no choice.

People told Amanda she would get used to the cold in a couple of months, but she could hardly believe in such an acceptance. She did, however, quickly learn that the sun warmed the middle of the day to a tolerable degree to allow for an hour of shopping and other errands. But the inevitable depressive night followed, and with the darkness came a wind that howled furiously at the corners of the little house and whistled past the front door. Anyone entering felt as though they were being sucked inside. With the wind so loud, when sleep was so badly needed it was intermittent at best. Mornings were met with a mixture of dread and exhaustion.

The dread for the *women* was that no matter their wool under and outer wear, they still felt the draughts up their skirts. The dread for the *men* was for the fact that the mines would not close, no matter how cold it was or how deep the snow. Unless, that is, the weight of it crushed the roofs. But after this had happened in the early years of the camp, the mine owners had learned how to shore up their buildings so that now such an event seldom happened.

On this morning, which was merely icy, there was no hope for the miners that they could linger in bed. Soon the wide-webbed snow shoes would come down off the walls, but for now it was just dry piercing cold to be dealt with.

Amanda put on a pair of woolen stockings, a new flannel petticoat under her cotton one, and over her dress John's long wool coat. He would be sleeping well into the afternoon anyway, now that he got off at eight in the morning after his twelve hour shift, so she figured he wouldn't miss her or the coat. She wrapped a woolen scarf around her head and tucked the long ends around her neck. Heavy ugly gloves were the last thing she reached for, pulling them on with a shake of her head and a mumbled oath held back. She then made her way to Charlotte's house, and although it was only a short block away she was grateful that she had made the effort to dress warmly. But the state of her comfort became of no interest when she found her friend sad and depressed.

"What's the matter?" she asked. "Is Vince worse?"

Charlotte handed her the newspaper and pointed to a small article about a woman who had been found dead near the Goat Ranch Road. She had been living in a rude abode that she had shared with her husband, Jobe Draper. Evidence showed that she had been beaten to death with the leaded end of a heavy bullwhip, which had been discovered washed and coiled in a corner of the tent.

Charlotte told her, "The woman's name is Kitty. Well, that was the name she used when she worked on Bonanza Street. Some knew her as Ellen or Helen."

"How do you know that?" Amanda couldn't hide her surprise.

"Emily befriended her and they became special friends. It was a bone of contention between her and Frank, but he finally chose to accept their friendship as long as he didn't have to be part of it and Emily was discrete. Then Kitty married this awful Jobe Draper and moved to his property, finding it less than she thought it would be. Not only did they only have an old tent to live in, while he occasionally worked on a rude cabin, but he abused her frequently. Emily saw Kitty in town in bad condition and tried to intercede, but Kitty wouldn't leave him. She thought it her only chance to become respectable."

"The poor woman."

Charlotte wiped at her eyes. "Her funeral is tomorrow morning. I'd like to go, and Cherry Wilson said she'd stay with Vince. I know it's an imposition to ask, but will you go with me?"

"Of course." Attending the funeral of a woman who had once been part of the *fair but frail* sorority might be counted as bold for a young single woman, but it did not occur to Amanda to refuse since she would be with Charlotte.

And so the next morning the two women stood next to an open grave waiting for the unadorned coffin to be lowered into the ground. There was no minister present. Only Undertaker Ward stood with them while the grave digger, Pat Brown, leaned on his shovel nearby and contemplated the $5.40 the County would give him for the dig.

Finally several miners arrived and acted as pallbearers, helping Mr. Ward carry the coffin to the gravesite from the hearse parked at the edge of the road. They then stood by with their hats in their hands and their heads lowered in sadness. One of them, a large man the others called Fat Back, blew his nose several times with a large red handkerchief.

Several ladies from Bonanza Street stood behind the men, ignored and looking uneasy, but determined to pay their respects to someone they had cared about. The grave had been dug outside the main portion of the cemetery in the area for those not considered sufficiently upstanding in the way they had lived. This meant they were not qualified to have their remains deteriorate among those that Bodie society declared *were* upstanding, or who at least had gotten away with appearing so.

Four men, each holding an end of the two ropes slung beneath the freshly sawn pine coffin, lowered it into the hole onto several fist-sized rocks. After sliding the ropes out, they walked away and Mr. Brown began shoveling dirt into the hole. At this point most of the mourners turned and walked back to town, leaving the muscular workman to complete his grim but necessary work.

Charlotte and Amanda, however, turned to leave only when the back of the shovel tamped the top of the filled grave. As they did, they passed a man approaching with a small bouquet of yellow rabbitbrush tied with a white ribbon. His dark hat was pulled forward so it would be difficult for anyone to recognize him, but Charlotte and Amanda were not fooled. It was Emily's husband Frank and they nodded to him at the same time as Charlotte took an astonished Amanda by the arm to keep her moving. But Amanda's curiosity had been piqued and would not be denied. She craned her neck around in time to see Frank lay the bright yellow flowers on the fresh grave.

Why on earth, Amanda wondered, would a famously loving husband put flowers on the grave of a woman of dubious reputation? Her curiosity nibbled at the edges of her thoughts for the rest of that day and night.

Early the next morning, before attending church at the Miners' Union Hall, Amanda returned to the cemetery with a small bunch of wild flowers. Her gesture was not wholly altruistic, since she had noticed a note attached to the white ribbon on Frank's offering. She looked around to be sure no one was watching before bending down to turn the slip of paper so she could read, "I'll always remember. Your friend, Emily"

Amanda stood up quickly, her curiosity replaced by a guilty sense of having invaded the privacy of something intimate and deeply personal. But it was also a revelation for her that a man might know his wife's heart so well, and be willing to risk ridicule from the good people of the town on her behalf.

So touched was she, and at the same time reminded of how lonely she was, that tears formed in her eyes. After blowing her nose on a scrap of fabric pulled from a pocket, Amanda walked briskly to the church services at the Union Hall. She went to church as much for the social reassurance to others that she was a proper young lady, as the vague hope of being comforted or uplifted. This Sunday was yet another disappointment.

Her restlessness was so intense that she left the service early. She went straight home and got the fire going in the stove in the hope of feeling her hands and feet again, while also setting the coffee to boil. She welcomed the relative quiet of early morning, although at no time was one free of the distant thud of iron stamps and the rattle of wagons going past the house on Green.

She fried some bacon and the last of the bread that she had allowed to go slightly stale so it would not fall apart in the grease. The morning temperature was still brutal. She took off her suit jacket and wrapped herself in her heavy robe, with her wool shawl over that in such a way that it bunched around her neck and ears. But it was her hands that felt most the burn of the cold, and she held them dangerously close to the stove as she waited for the heat from it to fill the room.

She looked down and wiggled her toes in her new heavy boots to see if she could feel them yet. The boots were so much more serviceable than her dainty calf skin shoes, but they were a little too masculine to please her. Assured that her toes were still attached, she poured herself a cup of coffee and wrapped her hands around the warm crockery mug as she settled at the end of the table closest to the stove.

It was Sunday, November 7. Hearing Matt stomping through the parlor, Amanda jumped up and quickly faced the kitchen counter where she began wiping it down. Matt rushed in wearing only his long underwear and carrying his clothes so he could dress in front of the stove.

The timing and the movement of this had become much like a well-choreographed ballet, but it was neither lovely nor graceful. Amanda endured it only by looking at it as what was necessary for the poor man's survival on such a cold morning, and to get him out of the house as quickly as possible. So she kept her back to him and peeled hard cooked eggs until he was finished. This corresponded to the arrival home of her father from his new night shift at the Goodshaw works.

Conversation at meals had never flowed between the three housemates all that smoothly, but it was even less abundant now that the cold had set in. John cleared his throat in preparation of a comment. "I heard ole Mike the man eater was arrested in Virginia City on vagrancy charges."

"I'm surprised he returned there," Amanda answered him.

"Me too."

The *Weekly Standard News* was evidently also surprised, as the next day they made the editorial comment about ole Mike being arrested for vagrancy: *"This must be a mistake on the part of the authorities, for Mike has a visible means of support. He has an upper and lower row of teeth."*

All remaining energy for the men was focused on eating enough food to fuel whatever efforts were needed for the day's hard work and the night's raucous activities. Consequently, Matt stomped out the front door and an exhausted John shuffled into his bedroom to sleep.

Amanda reserved the energy of saying anything to either man while thinking about what she needed from the shops. She also wondered if her life was ever going to be more than a house drudge for these men who were oblivious to a young woman's needs. It occurred to her to go out to the brickyard and see if Joseph would take her to luncheon.

She was well aware that part of her motivation was a lack of funds necessary to treat herself to a meal in the style that her current mood dictated, knowing that no self-respecting man would ever expect a woman to pay for a meal. She was also aware that she was being a bit mercenary. In her current mood, she didn't care if she was, especially considering that her target was the often inconsiderate Joseph. The extreme cold often had that effect on people, making them feel a little angry at life and therefore justified in some of their less than savory choices.

Before leaving, however, Amanda took the newspapers the men had brought home the day before and rolled the pages into long tight tubes. With the help of an already bent butter knife, she stuffed the long rolls into several cracks between the boards of the outside walls. Her efforts paid off when the paper was well into the cracks and chill air was no longer seeping through. She thought of flattening her pile of empty tin cans on the back porch and nailing them on the outside, as so many people did, but she didn't want to waken her father. She told herself she would do it the next day. Besides, it was Sunday and some people would object to her working so hard. Ah, justification, what a convenient thing it is.

Regardless of her desire to have a day more exciting than those recently past, she decided not to look for Joseph after all. Instead, she spent the day shopping for food, new wool stockings, and a sleek pair of flannel-lined gloves.

That evening, at John's request, Amanda prepared an early dinner for him so he could spend some time at a saloon before going to work at eight o'clock. As he walked toward the door, she felt an odd sense of urgency and called out, "Father?"

"Yes?" He turned back, not bothering to hide his impatience to be on his way.

"I just wanted to say...," but then she left her sentence unfinished.

"What?" he snapped at her.

"I don't know. It's your day off tomorrow and I was thinking that maybe we could go see one of the entertainments in town."

He shrugged. "I guess. We'll talk about it tomorrow."

"Okay." And he was gone. She felt less than assured of his enthusiasm at the idea of spending time with her, but she took solace in the fact that at least he had not outright refused.

Earlier, Matt had informed Amanda that he was going to stay in town with a friend, unspecified by name and therefore making it clear to Amanda that it was probably a Bonanza Street demimonde. It wasn't the first time he had done this, and as it was none of her business, she was just happy to have the house to herself. She swept the floors, wiped down the kitchen, stacked the scattered newspapers on top of the wood pile in the kitchen, and went to bed early.

Shortly after midnight Amanda was awakened by the repeated shrill blasts of whistles coming from High Peak Hill, the signal indicating an emergency. Slipping into her heavy robe and then her father's old wool coat, she pulled on her boots and rushed outside. Looking up at the hill, she could see a bright red glow hovering above the Goodshaw hoisting works.

Thinking only of her father and forgetting that she was not appropriately dressed, Amanda ran forward. Over and over, haunted by the words of Mrs. Bowers, she cried out, "No, no!"

In the distance, lights were flickering around the old hoist works building as men arrived with lanterns. At the foot of the hill some men she vaguely recognized grabbed her and held her back. "No, Amanda, you need to stay here. There's been a fire down below."

To her right a few yards away she saw Joseph and hurried toward him. "Joseph, my father is working in the mine tonight."

"He's probably okay." However, he looked at the burning building and shook his head.

"They won't let me get nearer." She grabbed at his arm. "Can you go up there and see if he got out?"

Even in the dim light of nearby blazing torches and kerosene lanterns, she could see him blanch. "Well, I don't think they'd let me near either." He shifted his weight uneasily. "I'd better stay here where I can comfort you."

"I don't need comforting," she snapped. "I need information."

She was suddenly reminded of how he had darted into the restaurant ahead of her and Charlotte. Nevertheless, being so desperate, she persisted. "I need to know if he's okay. Other men are going up to help. Why can't *you?*"

"They have enough help." Without meeting her eyes, he added, "And I have to be somewhere."

She stood watching him walk away with a welter of emotions, not least of which was disappointment and an overwhelming urge to slap his face until it was a mass of bloody welts.

After half an hour of waiting, and with the fire only just getting under control, a very cold Amanda realized that she was standing amid the gathering crowd in her night clothes under her father's heavy coat. She hurried home and changed into flannel underwear and a heavy dress, then grabbed again her father's long coat that she wore more often than he did. Holding her skirts well above her ankles without thinking about it, she ran back up the hill.

Joining a group of women that included the wives of Hugh Smith, Duncan McRay and Arthur Jackson, she was in time to hear a nervous man who was talking to them. "We've determined that the men working below were Hugh, Arthur, Duncan and John." He looked at Amanda and thought to himself how vulnerable and alone she looked. But it was the wives he addressed when he said, "I'm so sorry. I'll let you know more as soon as I can." Soon a dozen friends had formed around the four terrified women awaiting word of the fate of their men, a scene that had played itself out hundreds of times throughout the mining towns of the west.

All through the next few hours they waited amid the protective society of women and men from town who brought them chairs to sit on, hot coffee and emotional support. But the women knew from having watched others who had at one time been in their position that there was no protection from the grief that would most likely soon be theirs. The chill settled over them, numbing their feet, hands, noses and ears--the pain of it actually a relief, giving them something to focus upon other than their terror and dread.

The pink of dawn turned into a cold bright morning. Just after nine o'clock several men trudged down the hill toward the silent waiting group that had now grown into a small crowd. Their steps were slow but resolute.

"Things might not be as bad as we thought," one of them announced to the four women at the front of the gathering. "Your husbands, and your father Miss Blake, were working in the east crosscut on the 600 foot level. The fire is out now and it only went down the shaft about twenty feet, so they should be okay. Although the hoist burned, we hooked up a donkey engine for power and sent down an ore bucket with a light burning. The bucket came back up with the light still burning, so we know there's oxygen down there." He hesitated a moment before adding, "And there was a rock in the bucket. Mr. Oliver and Mr. Steel are preparing to descend in the big bucket."

The relief Amanda felt almost buckled her knees. It must have been even more overwhelming for the wives next to her, as two of them began to weep silently in relief. Mr. Oliver was the Superintendent of the Champion Mine and Mr. Steel was an employee at the Goodshaw, both good men known to be caring and conscientious at their jobs.

After the women watched the men walk quickly back up the hill, they set themselves to waiting once again. After a half hour, the suspended anxiety of it was more than Mrs. Smith could bear. When she broke down weeping, the other wives gathered around her while patting her on the back and mumbling encouraging but useless phrases. Amanda stood back, assuming that although her fear was great, it could not come close to the agony the wives must be experiencing.

"Amanda."

She heard her name spoken in a masculine whisper and turned around to find Roger standing a few feet away. Regardless of the tenseness of the situation, she was aware of the sudden attention those nearby now focused on her. They were obviously wondering why one of the most popular sports in town was calling John Blake's daughter by her first name.

"Roger," she breathed out as she rushed to his side. Grabbing his arm, she asked, "Did you hear? Father is trapped below. They've gone down to get him and the others."

"Yes, I know." He looked into her eyes and took her hands in his, as though trying to keep them warm. "I just came from the hoisting works." Lowering his voice, he told her, "Amanda, he didn't make it. I'm sorry."

She stepped back as though he had struck her a blow. "No. You're wrong. They said a rock came up in the bucket." Denial filled her completely as she refused to accept what he had said.

"They don't know who put it there, but by the time they got down, they found all four men. None were alive."

Amanda swung around to see two of the men who had previously talked to them standing with the wives, all of whom were now weeping. Finally accepting the fate of the four men, she turned back to Roger. Steeling herself, she asked, "Was he burned?"

"No." Glad he could spare her this grisly picture, he told her, "The fire only went down a few yards, but it must have sucked out the oxygen when it did. It would have been like falling into a deep sleep for them." He didn't explain how they would have been gasping for air, unless something else had killed them first.

Thinking back to that moment as she later sat in Charlotte's parlor, Amanda could barely remember collapsing into Roger's arms while she wept on his coat lapel. She could, however, decidedly remember the feeling of how tightly he had held her. She thought of telling Charlotte about it, but decided she was in no mood for a lecture on proper comportment that might detract from the memory. He had asked her if there was some friend to whom he could bring her, and she had thought only of Charlotte. Regardless of the hollow feeling of sadness over the loss of her father, she had watched Roger leave the Perry home with regret.

Although by now it was clear that Vince was going to live, and was slowly healing from the broken ribs and internal injuries, Amanda didn't want to stay too long at the Perry home. But Charlotte demanded that she sit down and drink most of a pot of tea loaded with sugar to keep her from going into shock, a tried and true remedy no woman would dare doubt. And Amanda had to admit that she was beginning to feel much better.

Soon the exhaustion and shock of the long night's events overcame her, and Charlotte insisted she lie down on the sofa. As soon as she closed her eyes and felt a blanket laid over her, Amanda fell asleep. It was early afternoon before she awoke, and another half hour before she had eaten what was put before her and was allowed to leave. Charlotte was the most nurturing and caring woman Amanda knew, and gratitude washed over her as she walked home.

She approached the house on Mono Street filled with the dread of seeing her father's effects and at the same time wondering what to do with them. This thought was knocked from her consideration when she saw in front of the house a spring wagon tied to the hitching post. Who, she wondered with irritation, would call on Matt or herself so soon after the tragedy? She walked into the house just as Matt came out of his room with his arms filled with clothes and carrying a brimming satchel of men's underwear.

"What are you doing?" she asked in alarm.

"I'll be right back and we'll talk." He went out through the front door, leaving it open as he dumped into the wagon all that he was carrying. Along with Matt's own clothing, Amanda also recognized her father's clothes in the pile. Back inside, he closed the door to keep out the rising chill breeze.

"Amanda, my dear, I'm so sorry about your father. These damn accidents are the bane of every mining town. Unfortunately, it caught up with John."

Cutting through his statement of the obvious, she asked, "Are you moving out?"

"Yes. It wouldn't be seemly for me to stay here with you now." Just as she was about to agree with him, he added, "And besides, I've sold the house."

"What?" This news, on top of the shock of her father's death, knocked the wind out of her and she looked around for the nearest place to sit down. Sinking onto the sofa, she thought a moment before asking, "How long before I have to be out? And where will I go?"

Matt had the grace to acknowledge the awkwardness of the moment. "Um, well, the new owners said you could take until tomorrow afternoon." She stared at him with disbelief. "As to the second question, well, I'd try at one of the hotels. You can stay for about seven dollars a week."

"But I have no money." She wasn't about to tell him of the twenty dollars in the bank that she had saved.

"Oh, yes, you do." His eagerness to give her some good news bordered on the pathetic. "You get John's half of the sale of the house. I sold it for $200, so you get $100. I've got it right here."

"But father said you guys paid $300 for it."

"Yes, that's true. But real estate is depressed right now. You've seen all the *for sale* signs at the north end of town. Fortunately, more people want to live at this end of town. It's newer and most of the businesses are moving in this direction." She said nothing, thinking he might have made a better sale if he'd been willing to wait longer than mere hours after his friend's death. Not unaware of this himself, he hurried on defensively, "I'm damn lucky to have gotten as much as I did."

"But you have a means of earning more money, and I'm not sure what I'll be able to do now. I guess I could return to Placerville."

Matt's color deepened. "Haven't you heard? There was an early heavy snow falling the last two nights and the passes over the Sierra are closed."

"It just keeps getting better, doesn't it?" Amanda demanded sarcastically.

Matt murmured uneasily, "I'm sorry." He then set about loading the wagon with his bedding, the throw rugs and one of the arm chairs.

He informed Amanda, with a reluctance to meet her eyes, that everything else was to stay with the house. What he didn't tell her was that he had gotten an additional fifty dollars for the furniture and kitchen contents, but he thought he deserved to keep it for making the deal. Even so, his conscience bothered him, knowing that he should probably share this money too with the sad girl slumped on the sofa. Instead, Matt hurriedly left Amanda to carry on alone. She looked down at the five twenty-dollar gold pieces in her lap and fought the urge to weep.

Instead, she spent the next half hour with the last of the coffee, and pencil and paper. She tried to figure out how long she could survive on the money from the house, the ten dollars John had left her beside his plate the night before, and what she had in savings. She finally computed that she had enough for room and board at a hotel or boarding house, if what they charged included breakfast and supper, for three months. That is, if she never ate out, did her own laundry and needed little else for her survival; which of course was absurd and she knew it.

Her mind raced through the options afforded a single young woman in Bodie, but this soon had her forcing down a rising sense of panic. At the back of her mind were all the stories she had heard of good women who had been forced into prostitution just to survive.

Since the snows would not be clear from the passes until possibly June, she had somehow to earn money to carry her through to the time she could leave town. But if she wanted to return to Placerville, she would also have to save up the stage fare of thirty-six dollars. Of course, she would have to find a job in Placerville too, but she knew that would be easier than in Bodie, and there were friends with whom she could stay. With this in mind, she planned to get out of the house as early as possible in the morning to find a room somewhere in a town known for its limited housing.

Charlotte knocked on the door that evening. "I heard what Matt did. If you need a place to stay for a few nights, you can sleep on our couch."

"That's very nice of you. But I'm sure to find something somewhere tomorrow."

"Okay, but just remember that at least you will never have to sleep on the street."

Early the next morning Amanda began making the rounds of places she thought she could afford to live. Among them was the Mono Hotel, the Bodie House, the Windsor Hotel, the Occidental Hotel, and several of the most respectable boarding houses. They were either full or too expensive.

Amanda finally admitted to herself her exhaustion after she was forced to consider two of the more regrettable boarding houses on the lower reaches of the hill near Bodie Bluff that smelled of unwashed men and rancid cooking oil.

After visiting Mr. Ward's to make funeral arrangements, she decided to spend two bits at the Can-Can Restaurant next door. She found a table and spent several minutes removing and draping her outer wrappings on one of the chairs, and then she sat down facing the windows. She resisted an overwhelming urge to take off her shoes and rub her sore feet. Instead, she consumed a large pot of tea and a cheese sandwich, and helped herself to a piece of the cake under the glass dome on the table. By the time she had sipped the last of the tea in the pot and was trying not to belch, she felt refreshed physically, but was just as uneasy in her mind.

The one hotel she had not approached was the large Grand Central three doors north of Wagner's Saloon, and three doors south of where she sat. Known at one time as the Magnolia Lodging House, early the previous year George Summers had reopened his hotel with an updated sixteen by forty-four foot dining room and an elegant private saloon, and had renamed it the Grand Central Hotel. Mr. S. N. Pitcher had been the manager then, but it was now run by the redoubtable Mrs. Emee Chestnut, who she remembered fondly.

She told herself that the reason she had not inquired there was because of the high price of the rooms, the published price being six dollars a week for one of the twenty-one rooms without food, and three dollars more with breakfast and supper included. But she vaguely wondered if she was avoiding it because it was so close to Wagner's Saloon.

It was one thing to have Roger on the other side of town and not calling on her. But what if she was living near him and he still didn't show interest in her? She would then have to face the fact that to him she was just a nice girl for whom he held no romantic feelings, and wanted only to be her friend. But did she really care if he was interested in her? She tried to tell herself the answer was no, but it rang uncomfortably insincere even to herself.

At that moment, when a man's shadow fell across the table and Amanda looked up with a ready smile expecting it to be Roger, she knew the truth. For when she saw Joseph smiling down at her, she felt her smile waver and tried to ignore the feeling that she had just been served second best.

A lifetime of practiced good manners immediately came to her rescue and she smiled, forcing herself not to think about his less than helpful support the previous morning. "Joseph! Please join me."

"I'm sorry about your father." She poured out water from the tin pitcher into a glass tumbler for him and he took a long swallow. "I hear the funeral is later this afternoon."

"Yes, at four o'clock."

"I went by the house and saw your things piled up in the front room. Are you moving?"

"Matt sold the house already. I have to be out this afternoon."

His surprise was obvious. "That's very fast."

"I know." She looked out the window at what she now perceived as an unwelcoming and hostile town, and fought the return of her earlier panic. "I thought it would be possible to find a room somewhere, but those hotels that haven't recently closed are full or too expensive. And the boardinghouses take in men that I wouldn't consider talking to, much less living with."

"You've tried all of the hotels?"

"Well, not the Grand Central next door. The rates there are too high. Besides, it's probably full."

"How can you know without checking?" He stood up. "Come, I'll go with you."

She rose somewhat reluctantly, tucked the money for her meal under the edge of her plate, pulled on the heavy coat and followed Joseph out the door. They approached the wide front door of the big white hotel and she looked up at its impressive facade. The day Amanda had arrived in town, benumbed by her long journey in a cramped stage, the hotel had seemed large and even forbidding. It had, in fact, taken 30,000 feet of lumber to construct the two floors.

As Amanda looked at the glass double doors, she put out her hand to steady herself against one of the dozen posts holding up the veranda covering the long porch. What if there was not an affordable room available? Where would she go next? Was she going to end up in a dance house, or worse? Fighting a moment of dizziness, she took herself firmly in hand. "No use thinking about that until I'm sure I've looked into every other option." She summoned her courage, pulled the coat tighter around her body, and passed through the door Joseph held open for her.

Joseph had nothing to hesitate about. Indeed, he was eager to have this pretty and naïve young woman situated in a convenient hotel near the saloons he so often frequented. He therefore grasped Amanda by the arm and pulled her forward while thinking to himself how nice it was going to be not having her father hanging around her. He quickly assumed his respectability face and led the way to a dark wooden counter with a large ledger open and waiting for the next customer.

Amanda meanwhile was taking in the gold and red paper on the walls of the lobby and the frosted glass doors to the right, where she could just make out the dark wood of the bar in a cozy private saloon. The entrance to the dining room was left at the back next to the reading room, and to the right of these were the stairs. In a corner by a large window overlooking the sidewalk was an arrangement of a red velvet sofa, two leather easy chairs, several velvet chairs for the ladies, and tables with globe lamps. It was all set for relaxed conversation among the guests, with a parlor stove sending out warmth and inviting guests to linger. It was very appealing, and Amanda marveled that she had thought otherwise the day of her arrival in town.

Mrs. Chestnut smiled brightly from behind the counter. "Good afternoon. May I help you?" She turned to Amanda and asked, "I remember you from the day you arrived this summer." Her voice lowered and she frowned slightly. "Wasn't your father one of the men killed in the hoist works accident?"

"Yes, he was."

"I'm so sorry, my dear." She sounded sincerely interested and Amanda immediately took a liking to her.

"I'm flattered you remember me."

"It's a knack of mine. Comes in handy in this business."

Realizing Mrs. Chestnut would not know about the funeral, she told her, "You probably can't get away, but the funeral is this afternoon at four."

"Thank you, dear. I'll try to make it. Now, is there anything I can do for you?"

Before Amanda could respond, Joseph stepped forward and said, "She needs a place to live for awhile. Would it be possible for you to reduce your rate, considering that she'll be staying through the winter?"

"Of course," Mrs. Chestnut assured Amanda, more quickly than either she or Joseph expected. "It's already arranged." Mrs. Chestnut stammered a little as she avoided looking at Joseph and added, "I mean, I anticipated the request when I saw you enter. If you don't mind a room at the back, I can give it to you for five dollars a week or $20 for the month. That includes breakfast and supper, of course. This month will be pro-rated starting tomorrow."

Amanda could feel her mouth agape and closed it with a snap. "That's so generous of you," she gushed, gratitude and relief welling up almost to the point of tears. "That will take me to April with what money I have. And if I can find work, I can make it into summer."

Mrs. Chestnut smiled. "If you know how to wait tables, I may be able to put you to work in the dining room. We'll talk about that later."

Amanda assured her that she could do such work, without however mentioning that she never had. But how difficult could it be, she flippantly asked herself.

Joseph broke into her thoughts and asked, "Amanda, what's happening this summer?"

She turned to him with her chin up. "I've decided to return to Placerville this summer." She watched his reaction and hoped for something akin to alarm, or at least disappointment, but he only nodded. She turned back to the desk with her lips pursed, ready to be rid of Joseph just at present. "Mrs. Chestnut, I accept your generous offer. I'll go home and get my things right away so I can be settled before the funeral. It'll be dark by the time it's over."

Mrs. Chestnut glanced at Joseph and waited the beat of several seconds. When he said nothing about helping, she gave him a glare of disgust and turned back to Amanda. "You'll do no such thing, dear. The porter will drive you in my rig." She clapped her hand down hard on a brass bell next to the ledger and the resounding ring filled the lobby.

A Mexican youth hurried forward dressed in black pants, white shirt and black silk vest. Jose stood to attention with almost comical military precision and waited for his orders. Upon receiving them, he hurried away and in ten minutes was waiting out front in a black rig with the roll top up and a folded blanket next to him for Amanda's lap. Amanda bid Joseph a curt good-bye and left the hotel.

At the house, Jose finished loading Amanda's cases into the back of the rig just as the new owner rolled up in his wagon. She didn't want to meet him right then, so she climbed into the rig and told Jose to get going. Just before three o'clock Amanda arrived at the hotel with her few possessions, and being overwhelmingly grateful for Jose's help, she handed him four bits.

Consequently, he willingly struggled under the burden of her and her father's suitcases as he climbed the stairs at the back of the lobby. Amanda followed with her two good dresses thrown over her shoulder, her satchel in one hand and the other clutching her good high top shoes. Her heart beat harder as it began to dawn on her that this was the start of a new life for her.

They emerged upstairs into a small secondary parlor at the front of the hotel with a balcony outside over the street, where a stairwell descended down to the sidewalk. She quickly walked to the sash door that led out onto the veranda where three residents were relaxing in wicker chairs while taking in the view. But only the perspective was new; it was the same old wooden town with congested muddy streets and a dozen saloons in every direction.

"Miss?"

She hurried back to Jose, mumbling her apologies as he smiled tolerantly. He turned down a long whitewashed hallway that led away from the street, a narrow runner of thin fabric down the middle of it. Small glowing globe sconces were mounted along the right wall, and it was Jose's job to light them each morning early. They passed ten rooms on each side of the hall, and finally came to a stop at the very end where Jose opened the door on the right.

The room was not nearly as small as she had expected, continuing beyond the end wall of the hall by some fifteen feet. The bed looked especially inviting as it protruded into the room from the wall opposite the door, with a tall carved headboard and matching footboard. It was dressed with a heavy white chenille bedspread and three red tasseled throw pillows.

The far wall that composed the back of the hotel had a small oil painting of a horse in a meadow hung next to a small window that looked out over the back alley. Light from this window poured in on a red velvet chair with a sagging seat and a floor lamp with a tasseled red shade. Next to those was a small parlor stove vented through the roof. A dressing table with eight small drawers and a large oval mirror took up the wall to the left of the door, while a narrow wardrobe protruded into the room from the wall to the right.

Behind a folding screen of black lacquer in the far corner, a lidded white china chamber pot sat on a shelf below a spindle-backed chamber chair. In the near corner, beyond the wardrobe, a small table draped with a white cloth sat between two straight-backed wooden chairs and in front of another small window. Both windows were of course closed, but the sheer lace curtains over them moved inward a fraction due to the cool air blowing against the poorly fitted frames.

Jose placed her bags on the bed and then motioned her back into the corridor where he opened a door across the hall. It was the bathing room, with a large tin-lined plunge tub and a dumbwaiter used to bring up heated water from the kitchen when the hotel's water pump was out of order in the winter. He informed her that those living at the hotel on a permanent basis were allowed one hot bath a week and that she was to let Mrs. Chestnut know when she would like it to be scheduled.

After he left, she returned to her clean but anonymous room. She immediately determined to inflict her personality on it as quickly as possible, but at the same time she was surprised at the realization that she felt more at home here in this small room than she had in her father's house. This room was all hers, with no men running around in various degrees of dishabille to make her feel in the way, and she determined in that moment to do whatever necessary to keep it.

She hummed happily as she unpacked. In the drawers of the wardrobe closet she placed her light corset, chemise, white muslin drawers, three pairs of cotton stockings and two of wool, and her light cotton petticoat. After she hung her dresses, skirts and waists on cloth-covered wooden hangers and her night clothes on the hooks protruding in from the side walls of the wardrobe, she closed the doors with a satisfied smile. Then with a sigh, she realized that it was time to go to the cemetery.

She removed the pink flower from her small black cloth hat and pinned on a spray of black velvet leaves, then donned her heavy coat, glad that it was black. Hearing the wind whistle down the alley outside the window, she draped a heavy burgundy scarf over her hat and around her neck while hoping it would keep the worst of the chill wind from slithering down her neck.

As she left her room, she pulled on her gloves and tried to shut down all feeling, unwilling to show her grief in public, which anyway was more a vague sadness than a deep sense of loss. The gleaming black hearse with its rear wheels larger than the front ones pulled up in front of the hotel. Through the glass sides she could see the plain wooden coffin inside resting on gleaming brass rails.

Mr. Ward, in a black overcoat and tall black hat, sat high at the front on his precarious perch with the reins in his black-gloved hands. The two gleaming black horses had tall black feathered plumes tied to the tops of their heads, and the kerosene lamps on top of the hearse at each corner had been lit. Amanda had paid extra for this. She moved into the street behind the hearse along with several men that had been waiting on the sidewalk. She missed Charlotte, but understood that she could not leave Vince.

Amanda assumed the men who had joined her had been friends of her father, since they had obviously come straight from one of the nearby saloons where they had no doubt been saluting his memory. They tipped their hats to her and the hearse pulled forward, the horses tossing their heads as their nostrils expelled a burst of steam into the cold air. Their harnesses jangled noisily, creating an eerie hollow reverberation that filled the unusual quiet of Main Street. It would be many years before Amanda would be able to hear the sound of a team's rattling harnesses without a brief memory of that moment returning to her.

As the procession passed Wagner's Saloon, Roger stepped out from the doorway and moved to Amanda's side, silently offering her his arm. Taking it gratefully, they walked together down Main, gathering around them a small group of mourners. Amanda was not surprised at the small size of the gathering, as her father had seemed to her to have had only a few close friends.

Reaching Green Street, they turned right for two blocks, then left onto Fuller and followed it south to its end. The tangy fresh scent of damp sagebrush filled the air. Immediately after it had stopped raining, the temperature had plummeted so that now there were patches of ice they had to step over or walk around. Frozen droplets of rain were scattered over the branches of the brush like tiny crystal pellets.

In the first years, people were buried in Bridgeport or Aurora, but this cemetery had been created in 1877. Amanda looked out over the many grave markers of the 109 graves of the People's Cemetery, and the area of eight graves for the Free Mason's, to the open entrance gate of the Miners' Union Plot, holding forty-three graves.

It stood open in anticipation of the service and they passed through. The hearse and those following walked up the hill on the narrow dirt path, past the *dead house* to the left where bodies were kept in winter until the ground thawed, and stopped near the grave.

The wind died down and the heady pungent smell of damp sagebrush immediately filled the air. Amanda stood by the side of the path watching the coffin carried to the open grave just as more people arrived, surprising her with their number as people filed past while trudging up the hill. One of them was Lou from the Spanish Dance House, and her sadness was undisguised.

Other than the occasional murmured whisper, there was little sound other than the swish of high necked black dresses over crisp petticoats. She admired the array of black jet mourning jewelry the wealthiest women wore on their black mantles or capes, some with fur collars. Most of the less affluent women wore brown or gray print dresses under coats, and no jewelry, but they nevertheless wore a dark mourning shawl over their shoulders. Among these was Mrs. Smith, Mrs. McRay, and Mrs. Jackson, whose husbands had perished along with John. Amanda realized suddenly that she would be expected to attend their husband's funerals as well, probably to be held over the next couple of days.

The wind picked up with a howl that masked the crunch of gravel underfoot and the thud of an occasional boot tripping on an exposed rock. But as the service began, the wind showed its respect by dying down, and starting up again only when it was over. Amanda shook her head over this for days.

That most of the men were wearing freshly pressed suits, even those who were single, touched her heart. As the crowd of these men and women grew, a stab of guilt assailed her that she hadn't realized how widely known he had been or how well-liked.

Everyone made room for Amanda and Roger by the edge of the rectangular hole in the ground next to the coffin. Mr. Ward stood nearby chatting with one of several miners who had been allowed an hour off to attend the funeral.

Ben Eggleston and his wife stood near the grave talking to Matt in a low voice. Captain Buckley and Mr. Hood from the Goodshaw Mine were talking with Mr. Kemp the photographer, along with two businessmen in suits and stiff collars who Amanda didn't recognize. Silently waiting was Reverend Hinkle, who would leave Bodie soon after these funerals, his plans for a church in the town still unfulfilled. Noting that Joseph was nowhere within sight, Amanda was more irritated than hurt, but certainly not surprised.

Amanda approached Matt with her hand out to show there were no hard feelings on her part. "Hello, Matt. Thank you for coming. How are you doing?"

"Oh, okay." He took off his hat and held it in his hands, looking down at the ground. "I miss your daddy a lot. How are you doing?"

"I'm okay. I'll be better."

"Where did you fetch up?"

"At the Grand Central Hotel. How about you?"

"I'm staying at the Noonday Hotel out near the mine. It used to be called Brown's Hotel and Restaurant. It's where John and I stayed when we first met."

"Well, I wish you the best of luck. You were always kind to me, and I appreciate that."

Matt swallowed hard and nodded his head, abundantly glad that she couldn't sense the sudden rush of guilt that rose in his throat like bile after a too spicy meal. As she turned to walk away, he put his hand on her arm, and said, "Amanda." He reached into his pocket and handed her a twenty dollar gold piece. "I sold some of your father's clothes and his boots, so you should have this."

"Oh, Matt, thank you. It will make quite a difference."

He smiled as he felt the release of his guilt, knowing that for a certainty it was going to make a difference in how well he slept that night.

Mr. Ward walked up to Amanda and asked in a whisper if she would like to take a final look at her father. She firmly declined. Reverend Hinkle moved over by the coffin and mumbled a few barely intelligible words through lips that were stiff with cold and that sounded vaguely Biblical, then waved to four burly men in overalls standing off to the side. They took the ends of two long ropes threaded under the coffin and lowered the pine box into the gaping maw of the hole.

Amanda recognized Pat Brown, the gravedigger, off to the side and walked over to him. She tipped him fifty cents for his efforts on behalf of her father, and hoped to never again attend a Bodie funeral after the burial of the other three miners. Not knowing that the most disturbing funeral of her young life still lay in her future, she returned to Roger's side. A moment later, Pat Brown began shoveling in the dirt, each clod hitting the coffin with rhythmic thuds.

Amanda clenched her jaw. Into the ground had gone not only her father's body, but also all hope of developing the kind of relationship with him that she had so desired. The time had come to let go of the dreams of the past and instead embrace the possibilities of the future.

Roger took her hand and slipped it through his arm so he could lead her away. "Are you okay?"

"Yes." She looked up at him and smiled. It was tremulous and a little crooked, but he thought it incredibly endearing.

So benumbed by the last two days of events was she that she didn't notice the raised brows of those watching her walk away on the arm of a faro dealer of some repute. But Roger was aware and glared at anyone so bold as to not look away as they passed. He figured she expected him to stop at Wagner's and send her home alone, but he continued to the door of the Grand Central.

There he laid his hand over hers where it rested on his arm. "I'm so sorry you've lost your father. But I don't want you to think you're alone here."

"Actually, I was just thinking about that. I do have good friends in Charlotte Perry and Cherry Wilson." She looked up at him and this time her smile was firm. Trying to make her tone light, she added, "And I have a couple of other friends as well."

But he refused to treat the subject casually. "You'd best go in and get out of the cold. Oh, by the way, a big party came into the dining room just as Mrs. Chestnut was leaving for the cemetery or she would have been there."

"How do you know that?" She looked at him in surprise and wondered at the sudden pink flush on his cheeks.

"I came by to see if I could walk with you to the cemetery, but you weren't down yet so I went back to the saloon."

Amanda frowned, remembering how he had seemed to be waiting for her when the hearse arrived in front of the hotel. "How did you know I was here at this hotel?"

His words came in a rush. "I happened to see you in the hotel's rig as it took you home to get your things and I asked Mrs. Chestnut about it."

She gave him a sidewise glance, feeling that something was being held back. "Well, thank you for seeing me home, especially as it's almost dark. I think it best that I avoid being on the streets alone after dark now that I'm living at the north end of town." She shivered, but it was less from the cold than what she was afraid might happen to her, although a good woman was rarely approached even on the north end.

"You're cold," he told her. "You'd best go inside."

She hesitated only a moment before boldly telling him, "You could come in and have a brandy with me in the bar."

"I'd like nothing better, but I have to go to work. Men and their money await. May I call on you soon?"

"Yes, of course."

Before going up the stairs, she turned aside to the small but elegantly furnished bar. She was still in the mood for a brandy and decided to take it upstairs with her. Standing at the end of the bar close to the lobby while Jerry the bartender fetched her drink, Amanda heard a man and woman laughing just inside the dining room on the other side of the lobby. Turning in that direction, she wasn't sure at first who the woman in the veiled hat was, but she certainly knew the man. Even with his back to Amanda, she was sure that it was Joseph. Then the woman leaned toward him and Amanda could see that she was the very married Johanna Treloar.

As she stared, Jerry approached with her drink and followed her gaze. "Do you know them?" he asked.

"Yes, but not very well." She was beginning to realize how true that really was.

Jerry, muttering more to himself than Amanda, said, "If her husband sees them, he'll beat the holy hell out of DeRoche and probably her too." Realizing suddenly that Amanda had heard him, he sputtered, "Oh, my goodness, miss, I'm so sorry."

Amanda laughed at the thin young man with the curly hair only a few years her senior. "Don't worry. I've heard swearing before. Anyone on the street when a freighter drives his team through town has heard words worse than that."

"True. But I know a fella who was fined $30 and spent a week in jail for swearing in front of some ladies."

"Here in Bodie?"

"That's right, miss. The good people of this town won't tolerate such laxity."

Amanda shook her head. "They must have been very sensitive ladies indeed."

With a glance at the dining room, Jerry chuckled and nodded, and returned to the original topic. "Joseph and Johanna know each other from long ago. Some say she only married Treloar for a large sum of insurance money he came into because of the accident that's left him kind of, well, short-changed in the head. You may have noticed that he has a limp too."

"So you think she's not in love with her husband, but rather Joseph?"

He shrugged. "It's what some say. I do know that last year Treloar caught her talking to DeRoche outside a restaurant. He thought they'd been inside together and he beat her up bad. The law even stepped in. He's now on probation, and if he hits her again, he can go to jail."

Amanda rolled her eyes in disgust. Jerry nodded, knowing why she was reacting that way. The courts seldom convicted on such an offense, whether the woman was or was not the man's wife.

Before she was spotted by Joseph, Amanda picked up her glass, thanked Jerry and told him to put it on her bill. As soon as she was out of sight, Mrs. Chestnut walked over to him and said, "Anything Miss Blake orders, tell her it's on the house if it's small, like a drink, or tell her you'll add it to her bill. Either way, put the expense on Mr. Murphy's tab." He smiled and nodded, making an assumption about the innocent looking Amanda that wasn't true and that would have gotten him a black eye if Roger had known about it.

The next day saw the other three men buried in the cemetery, one in the morning and the other two in the afternoon. By nightfall there were few in the town who had not attended at least one of the burials. Amanda felt it only right that she be present at all three funerals, barely having time to warm her toes between each oppressive event. She spent the following two days cloistered in her room reading Shakespeare's *Taming of the Shrew* to give her emotions a break from tragedy.

On November 15, the Bodie Standard News printed a letter from Mr. Parker, the hoist engineer on duty the night John and the others had died. The mine owners had found it difficult to understand what had happened to spark the disaster, and Mr. Parker had left town under a cloud of suspicion and prompted by the fear of being accused of dereliction of duty. To explain himself, he wrote a letter to the town.

The letter explained that Captain Buckley had gone into the change room and after he left, Parker had turned down the light next to the shaft, but had not checked inside the change room. He thought possibly a candle had been left burning, or clothing with matches in the pocket had fallen onto the steam pipes and started smoldering.

He said he wasn't aware of a fire until he returned to the engine room after a visit to the privy, but that he immediately sent the tub to the bottom for those down in the shaft. Then the flaming beams of the ceiling began to fall down on him and he claimed no human could then stand by the engine, and *"nearly crazed with the thought of those below, I left the building just as Captain Buckley rushed in. Of 22 years' experience in the shop and engine room, this is my first accident. With conscience free from any criminal intent and strickened with pain and remorse, I remain yours truly, L. Parker"*

Amanda felt a little sorry for Mr. Parker and held no ill will towards him, but she wasn't sure if others were going to be as accepting of his story. Frankly, she couldn't think of anything that he could have done different unless it was to have checked the changing room, but nothing of this sort had ever occurred before. As far as she was concerned, it was a closed topic.

On Tuesday, November 23, Joseph tapped on Amanda's door in the early afternoon. She was surprised at his boldness and quickly suggested to him, "Why don't we go down to the reading room? I'll join you there in a moment."

She shut the door firmly in his face, not missing his look of irritation as she did so. After throwing a loose knit shawl around her shoulders, she walked downstairs to the reading room. Sitting in a low velvet chair and arranging her skirts so they fell gracefully around her legs, Joseph was forced to sit on the opposite side of a small marble-topped mahogany table. The chairs were a little forward of the table and angled toward one another so those visiting could see around the large white oil lamp, but still the placement was benignly innocent if anyone happened to look into the room.

"How have you been, Joseph?" she asked somewhat formally. "I imagine it's been very cold at the brickyard."

"Yes, indeed." He leaned back and stretched out his legs. "The wood lots are running out of wood all over town. But more is being brought in as fast as the Mexicans and Chinese choppers can haul it. At least by living in the hotel, you don't have to worry about that. You have no idea how deep the snow can get here."

Amanda nodded thoughtfully. "If I'd had to pay someone to haul and chop the wood for me, not to mention do other things, it may be that it's actually cheaper for me to rent here."

"Possibly." Abruptly, he asked, "What are you doing for Thanksgiving?"

"I hadn't thought about it. I've been busy asking around for a job. Mrs. Chestnut said in a week or so I may be able to work in the dining room here." She smiled while nervously twisting the corner of her shawl.

"I was offered one job, not for the first time. It was from a colorful woman called Lou."

She was gratified to see the look of alarm on his face. "You can't be serious? You don't know what kind of girls she employs."

With a toss of her head and a bit of acid in her tone, Amanda told him, "Of course I do. You must suppose me very naïve indeed. And if you think that's flattering to me, you're wrong."

"I'm sorry." But he didn't sound as contrite as Amanda wished. Seeming to sense this, he repeated, "I really am sorry. But you are such a lady. A very lovely lady. In fact, that is why I am here."

She laughed, noticing that his accent had gotten thicker along with his confusion. "You're here because of my loveliness?"

"No," he laughed. "Well, yes in a way. I would like you to accompany me to the Grand Thanksgiving Ball at the Music Hall."

"The Music Hall?"

"Yes. It's on the second floor of Silas Smith's store on the east side of Main at the bend." This bend in the road was made necessary by the flow of Bodie Creek through the town and its location was used as a landmark. "Berlinger and Frank's Quadrille Band will be playing, and they really are very good."

"It sounds delightful." Thinking to herself that no one else had bothered to ask her, she spoke a little more defiantly than she meant to. "Yes, I'll go with you."

After they had settled the details, he stood up and said, "I will call for you at seven in the evening."

"I'll be ready."

As she watched him walk away, she began thinking about what she could possibly wear. Acutely aware of how little money there was in her account at the Bodie Bank, she went upstairs to get her coat and walked south to the bank where she withdrew the exorbitant sum of fifteen dollars. She then made her way to the dressmaker at the north end of Main where Mrs. Williams was known to sell ready made dresses that she then tailored to the purchaser. Amanda needed all the help she could get, for she was determined to make a good showing at the ball.

Her last thought before falling asleep that night was to wonder if Roger would also be there, and why *he* had not been the one to ask her to the ball.

CHAPTER 9
DECEMBER, 1880

Late in the afternoon of a windy and snowy December day, Amanda stood by the back window of her room and looked out on the gathering drifts filling the narrow alley below. Snow had fallen to a depth where it now blocked the first floor windows of the buildings throughout the town. Single story businesses and homes fared the worst, with the owners having to dig long sloped tunnels down to their front doors. Each morning men had to clear screens on top of stove pipes of the night's accumulations; unless a low fire had simmered throughout the night. Miners took turns climbing onto the insufficiently pitched roof of the Union Hall to shovel off the snow before the roof caved in.

It was the season of the *pogonip*, when the frigid wind is filled with fine ice chips glittering in the bright sun while blowing horizontally, and hitting skin like little bits of shrapnel. The Piutes declared it the cause of great sickness and stayed in their huts with a low fire burning. People in town did much the same, so although the shops did little business during these storms, the saloons did even better business than usual.

The best part of the snow was that it covered the garbage that regularly filled the alleys and dumps around the town, giving these areas a rare appearance of cleanliness. The snow was, however, also covering the water system and pump behind the Grand Central that forced water into the second floor bathing room. Two porters were trying to clear the snow from this equipment in the area between the wall of the hotel and the tall wooden fence opposite that separated the hotel from a building facing Bonanza Street. Mostly the young men were just slipping and floundering in the deep snow.

Amanda was thankful that she had bathed in the plunge tub the night before. It was the one bath allowed her each week due to the amount of water it took and the effort to heat it. A small stove gave warmth to the small room, but until the pump was repaired, large buckets of hot water had to be hoisted up in the dumbwaiter by one of the porters. Nevertheless, this was considered a luxury by those who hauled their water home from wells or creeks. Knowing this, Amanda never took it for granted and tipped the porters generously.

But Amanda was not thinking about the efforts of Jose the day before or the young men beneath her window, but rather the Grand Ball she had attended with Joseph at Thanksgiving. The Music Hall on the second floor of Silas Smith's store had been smartly decorated with garlands and candles, and the buffet generous. Her face relaxed into a smile as she thought of the sumptuous food that had been on offer. But it had been a strange evening, and her smile faded and was replaced by a frown as she recalled what had taken place.

Amanda had worn a simple black dress that, unlike most of the women present, had featured long sleeves and a moderately low neckline. She was after all still in mourning for her father. Mrs. Williams the dressmaker had assured her the dress could easily be updated later for a less funereal appearance, and she had enjoyed her time at the dressmaker's shop. There were a number of magazines on a table in the waiting room and she had spent over an hour perusing them: *London & Paris Ladies Magazine, Ladies' Gazette of Fashion, Journal des Modes, The Milliner's and Dressmaker's Gazette* and the ever-popular *Godey's Lady's Book*.

With her dress enhanced with flounces across the front, she had looked modern and attractive, although she had worn the mourning jewelry that had belonged to her grandmother. To remind everyone of her youth and the festivities of the occasion, she had woven a dark green ribbon in her hair.

Amanda had known that in some societies it would be deemed much too soon after her father's passing to be attending a ball and that even in Bodie some people would heartily disapprove. However, she had felt that as long as she sat out the polka and maybe even the schottische, and kept to the waltz, the three-step or a quadrille, she would not be seen as disrespectful of her father's recent passing. And she was so terribly bored.

She was now working in the hotel's dining room a few evenings a week, after which she usually returned to her room with a book or magazine. The only variance to this routine was when she sat downstairs in the reading room or in the lobby where she could sit near the small parlor stove. Occasionally Roger would join her, but he was in too great a demand at

Wagner's to take too many long breaks. Until the roads closed, she would also be able to watch people arriving and departing on the stagecoaches. It kept alive the hope of returning to Placerville in the summer.

Every couple of days she tramped her way to Charlotte's house, since her friend hesitated to leave Vince in case the fire went out in the stove and he caught a chill. Charlotte knew he might attempt to lift wood, and the doctor said that for now Vince was not to lift anything heavier than a coffee cup.

With a list of things Charlotte needed from town in her pocket, Amanda would make the rounds of the stores and bring the items to the Perry home. But if the snow didn't let up, she might be unable to do this much longer, even with Jose driving her in Mrs. Chestnut's rig. As a form of repaying Amanda's efforts, Charlotte offered to teach her to knit or crochet. Although Amanda knew these to be talents a woman should develop, she also felt it would be the last resort before her boredom brought her to the edge of insanity.

Because of this, the Thanksgiving Ball had been a bright spot on the horizon of her world, and she had looked forward to it more than she would have admitted to anyone. Nevertheless, after a little over an hour at the dance she had been ready to leave.

Joseph had at first been attentive and charming, and had introduced her to many of the people in the town who owned businesses and were therefore of some special status. The wives of these men had been punctiliously polite to her, but she had nevertheless felt their condescending coolness. And they obviously wanted her to be aware of it.

One of the women especially had been difficult to ignore. Her pinched nose and grimaced mouth gave the appearance of one who smelled something unpleasant that no one else was able to detect. She had seemed to care only for a thin woman with a small beak of a nose over which she looked down at other people, much as might a condescending sparrow that thought it should be consorting only with eagles.

Amanda had wondered if these women's faces were the result of heredity, or a perpetually unfavorable view of most other people. But while these women had darted their eyes about the room in an effort to judge if any of those women whose opinions mattered had taken note of their presence, their husbands had been cheerful and outgoing businessmen simply at the dance to enjoy themselves of an evening.

A few minutes of stilted conversation among the couples was a torture for everyone and soon the men had, as was their habit, moved away to gather in a corner of the room. Immediately, noisy laughter flowed between them as flasks were passed around at what was supposed to be a non-alcoholic event. It was then that Amanda's earlier feelings of exclusion had been confirmed, for without an escort present the women had not felt the need for even a veneer of politeness. They had moved to a table with a number of chairs sufficient only for themselves.

Amanda had retired to a chair against the wall, sitting by herself and feeling conspicuously rejected. It was then that she had spotted Dave Bannon dancing with a pretty girl, and not far away his sister Nellie dancing with a young miner from the Standard. The brother and sister looked the picture of happiness, and Dave was obviously behaving himself. But Amanda had recognized the bulge in the pocket of Dave's coat for what it was and realized that he had come to the dance ready to defend himself if necessary. From what, Amanda had wondered, might that be?

At that moment Joseph had returned to her with a glass of punch and a small piece of cake. He had reclined next to her with his legs extended as though about to take a nap, while reeking of whiskey. They had talked for several minutes about general events in the town, but when Berlinger and Frank's Quadrille Band began playing he had insisted they dance.

Amanda had made sure Joseph held her in a decorous fashion, with an appropriate amount of space between them and with his hands held only where proper. This had precipitated an odd change in the women's behavior toward her, and during the next break in the dancing they had talked with her while conveying actual warmth in their manner, and amazingly their smiles had been sincere.

Amanda had hidden her smile, realizing that at first they must have assumed her to be a less than virtuous acquaintance of Joseph's. This made her wonder how fine a line it was between a woman "in the business" and an ordinary unattached young woman. She had been torn between anger and laughter, but settled for a sense of the absurd.

It took Amanda only two dances to realize that Joseph was more often than not looking beyond her shoulder, his eyes sweeping the room while attempting to look as though he was focusing on Amanda. Only when Joseph spotted Johanna Treloar and her husband Thomas had he ceased this canvassing of the room. Amanda had known the moment by the sudden tenseness in his body.

Johanna had been lovely in a sleeveless dress so dark a red that it almost appeared black at first glance. She had worn the low neckline with an awareness of how becoming her figure presented itself, while the fabric flared back of her neck like a modified fan that accentuated the delicate features of her face carefully made up to look naturally rosy and dark of eye. Her ivory skin had glowed in the light of the candles and lanterns, and her green eyes had been offset by long auburn ringlets of hair swept off her face by side combs inset with sparkling glass. Her sensuous beauty that night had reflected well her Irish roots, and she knew it.

Tom Treloar had worn what was arguably his best suit, although one was immediately struck by the fact that his rumpled appearance was not caused so much by his suit lacking pressing, as from the man sagging inside it. While dancing with Johanna, Tom had shuffled back and forth from one foot to the other a beat off from the music and had made no effort to smile. He had held his wife firmly, as though afraid she might run away if his grip on her back relaxed. Considering the arch manner in which she had several times looked over at Joseph, Amanda concluded that Tom Treloar might be a little wiser and aware than most thought him.

After a decent time had passed, Amanda had pleaded a headache and asked Joseph to walk her back to the hotel. He had not been pleased and had accepted her request with ill-concealed impatience. His walk with her had been a rapid march down the street at a pace that had been difficult for her. At the hotel his manner had been polite but rushed and he had parted from her on the sidewalk after briefly kissing her hand.

Mrs. Chestnut had watched Amanda enter and had been a study of someone biting their tongue to keep from saying something sharp. Indeed, in that moment Mrs. Chestnut had wished she was a man so she could punch Joseph square on the nose. Amanda meanwhile had not been deluded by his quick departure, sure that he had planned to return to the dance where he could watch, if not dance with, his precious Johanna.

Amanda turned her thoughts from the images of that evening. She looked down into the alley and took note of the progress the porters were making. One of them reminded her of Frank Eastman, and that reminded her of his departure from Bodie only a few days before. Charlotte was worried about Vince, as he had become somewhat depressed now that Frank had returned to Lone Pine to be with Emily. Frank was hoping to arrive before the birth of his child, and although Vince understood this, the two men had become as close as brothers. Charlotte felt it had been regular visits from Frank that had helped Vince's recovery as much as her careful nursing of him.

With a sigh that was part regret and part resignation, Amanda forced herself to focus on the present. The porters had given up and left the area to the caprice of mother nature. Amanda couldn't stay by the window any longer anyway, as it was her night to serve in the dining room. Several minutes later she was wearing her long black dress with the sleeves tight to the shoulders that poofed outward like epaulets gone askew. She buttoned on a white, heavily starched collar at the neck and deep white cuffs over the tapered wrists, and tying the long white pinafore apron at the back in a bow, she was ready for work. She hoped that the one inch heels of her black boots would not tire her feet too quickly.

As she crossed the hall next to the reading room, she stopped and looked down its dark length toward the back door, having been told to stay out of this hallway unless serving dinners in one of the five private dining rooms there. Mrs. Chestnut had emphasized that she especially was not ever to go through the door at the end.

Kassy, one of the other waitresses, had told her with conspiratorial glee that it opened onto an alley that could be followed to another narrower alley that cut through to what some called "virgin alley"--and the residences of those ladies who were certainly *not* virgins. She had not had the heart to tell Kassy that she'd already figured that out.

She entered the dining room through the double sash doors and took a moment to admire the grand room before her. It was a narrow but long room with a fifteen foot high ceiling with the only window at the far end of the south wall. Diners at the Grand Central were forced to focus on each other. The long expanse of wall was covered in gold tinted floral paper, while the rear wall was mostly occupied by a very large mirror framed in gold. Behind this wall was the kitchen, which was one of the largest in the town with what some said were the largest cooking ranges in the state.

Two long rows of round and rectangular tables down the length of the room were covered with white cloths surrounded by straight-backed wooden chairs. Two pot-bellied black stoves with a tall stovepipe vented out through the ceiling heated the room in uneven degrees of concentrated warmth.

In the center of each table was a silver-plated castor set containing two pressed glass cruets with small corks holding vinegar and lemon juice (better to hide the taste of those meats a little past their prime), a small shaker for cinnamon, and a small glass jar with a gold-washed spoon for mustard (a powder mixed with water fresh each day). Salt was in a small dish with a tiny spoon, sugar was in a glass shaker and thick cream was available from a crockery jug. A stack of white cloth napkins sat between a cut glass spooner holding flatware and a large tin pitcher of fresh water.

But the most unusual item on the table was a glass pedestal cake plate with a high dome cover. Sometimes this offered a layer cake that was frosted and sometimes not, but whether breakfast, early afternoon dinner or light luncheon, diners could always help themselves to cake.

A row of hooks along the length of the wall accommodated coats and hats, and light was provided by coal oil sconces on the walls and candles on the tables.

After several hours of carrying heavy crockery plates piled with chops, steaks, potatoes and vegetables, followed by endless cups of coffee and sometimes pie or bread pudding, Amanda was exhausted. She also was reminded that her boots were definitely *not* ideal for such work, but as yet she could not afford a better pair. Roomier shoes with thicker soles were number one on her list of things to purchase with her first pay parcel.

It was reported in the *Daily Free Press* that William Haight, out on bail until he could testify against Morton for the stolen bullion thefts from the Standard in August, had disappeared after heading to Aurora. No one was unhappier about this than Pat Reddy, but Private Detective Davis told everyone he would bring him back, one way or the other. Knowing what this meant, people looked forward to the next installment of this little drama.

In the middle of December the town took on the festive dress of Christmas. Shops created elaborate displays in their windows fronting Main to showcase their wares and talents. The meat markets hung dressed halves of beef on either side of their windows, with a whole deer or stuffed pig in between, surrounded by pine branches brought in from the mountains above Bridgeport. Market windows showed stacks of tin cans with red and green labels, and were surrounded by red and green fruits and vegetables. Mrs. Williams, the fashionable dressmaker at the north end of Main, hung three fancy dresses in her window on dressmaker's dummies with a chain of paper draped across the top of the glass.

Some of the largest hotels put small pine trees in their lobbies and decorated them with dried berries, seed pods and strings of popped corn. The bakery frosted a tall layered cake and set it in the middle of its display window, surrounding it with cloth-lined baskets of rolls and cookies sprinkled with coarse sugar.

A series of parties hosted by the mine owners and various fraternal organizations were held at the Miners' Union Hall to celebrate the holiday. On the stage at the end of the room, the good ladies of the town placed a large decorated pine tree. Before each event, gifts were placed under it for distribution by "Santa" at some point in the evening's festivities. It was the town tree, as individual trees were rare except in hotels or large homes of the wealthy, of which Bodie had none.

Across from where Standard Avenue met Main was a small saloon known as The Snug. On the fifteenth of the month Billy Deegan entered this saloon. He was a stocky, powerfully built young man with a bad reputation who had been arrested back in '79 for assault and then released on a writ of habeas corpus. As he stood at the bar looking around at the men present, most of whom he knew as fellow miners, he began professing to anyone who would pay him attention that he had just shot his "goddamn landlady", Adelia O'Neill, with his Colt Lightening.

While everyone stood transfixed, trying to assess the reality or fiction of this statement, Billy grabbed a shot glass of rye from the bar and tossed it down his throat. After slamming the glass down on the counter, he crossed the street and proceeded north to the Bank Exchange Saloon. After a quick drink, he smashed a glass on the floor as a precursor to ridding the bar top of the glasses on it with a sweep of his arm. He then picked up a chair and smashed its legs on a table. When he stopped to catch his breath, he backed up into Officers Farnsworth and Monahan who were standing behind him with their hands on holstered guns.

Before they could say anything, however, Deegan screamed at them, "I'll see you dead before morning." With this, he ran outside and headed to the Comstock Saloon.

His belligerence had only grown with his run-in with the officers, and he promptly and loudly threatened those standing at the Comstock bar. He also yelled at the bartender that he was going to shoot him. Instead, after inspecting the gun in his hand as though he was surprised to find it there, he opened his mouth and shoved in the tip of the barrel, saying, "I have a notion to take a ball myself."

The officers had easily followed him and now grabbed the seriously intoxicated young man from behind. They were not in the mood to put up with any more of his shenanigans, so when he struggled with them, one officer pinned Billy's arms behind his back while the other beat him with his fists until the young man was out cold. He was then taken to jail.

The next day, Billy apologized humbly to the judge and pled guilty to disturbing the peace. After paying his $25 fine, he returned to work and told everyone he planned to drink less as a means of staying out of trouble. Fortunately, Mrs. O'Neill had been only slightly wounded when Billy shot her, and she refused to press charges against someone she thought of as a troubled youth.

Of more importance to most people was the fact that the price of a cord of wood had risen to new heights. From $12 in May, it was now the season of heavy snows and therefore had reached $22 a cord and might go even higher.

Amanda's boredom found relief on the twenty-third of the month. She even wrote to a good friend in Placerville about what she had done.

> *My Dearest Barbara,*
>
> *Today I went to a meeting at the Miners' Union Hall. It was held to form a local chapter of the Land League of Ireland. As you know, my grandparents were all from Ireland and I was curious as to the purpose of this organization.*
>
> *Evidently last year the original was formed in Ireland for the purpose of collecting money to give aid to those fighting to free their country from English rule. It also gives money to feed the starving farm families there. Much has been made here of our ill treatment of the Indian tribes across the United States, but I am now informed that English landlords have treated Irish farming families much the same as far as removing them from their lands. My heart broke upon hearing the stories of the suffering imposed on those left without means to support themselves on land that had been theirs for generations until given over to landed gentry from England.*
>
> *I realize of course that some of these tales may be somewhat exaggerated to garner the sympathy of those with sufficient means to donate, but if the truth is even a third as severe, it is too much. That such an invasion of a country can take place is bad enough, but when it happens that the indigenous people are treated as the interlopers and punished for just being where they have always been, it is beyond*

tolerance by the fair-minded. And I mean that judgment for those invading Ireland as much as I do for our government's treatment of the native people in this country. I only wish my ability to do something about both was as strong as my desire.

It is not the first time that I have become aware of the frustration of being a woman in a society that is ruled by and for men. It is my hope that someday women will have the opportunity to vote for those men who run the country so that we may influence for a more just society. It is of course the realm of fantasy to suppose there will ever be a woman sitting in Congress, but oh how my heart would love to be proved wrong.

Meanwhile, with my mind so full of such rebellious thoughts, and my bank account now reduced by $5 given to the Land League, I must ready myself for work here in this strange town; where generous, caring men contribute money to help the plight of Ireland's suffering poor, and then go to a saloon where they get into a fist fight with a fellow who is suffering right here.

Best regards,

Whether due to the snow or the holidays, the dining room was crowded most of the day. Consequently, Amanda was asked to also work the early afternoon crowd, which seemed to have more miners, freighters and packers in the mix than ever she saw at night. She was always polite and efficient, no matter the customer's behavior, intemperate language or poor grooming habits. But sometimes it was an act of tremendous will power on her part.

On Christmas Eve one such customer tempted her resolve. A miner entered wearing clothes so long overdue a washing that they could have stood straight up on the floor if removed. The man was also emitting an odor that would have offended residents of a barnyard.

She poured coffee from the large pot in the kitchen into a silver serving pot and enjoyed the smell of the roasted brew. Real pure coffee was served at the hotel, unlike some places that mixed crushed dried peas into the ground beans. In winter, after the passes had been closed for several months, they might have to parch barley, wheat or bran, depending on what was on the last freight wagons to get through to the town. But for now, they still had green coffee beans that could be roasted daily. Looking forward to her own enjoyment of the coffee at the end of her shift, she returned to the dining room and her disgusting customer.

He was eating like one in doubt as to the location of his mouth, flinging the food in that general direction but often with little success in getting it between his lips. As she poured coffee into his cup, she watched the transport of liver dripping with long slivers of cooked onion. The half that did not quite make it into his mouth was quickly sucked in with a slurp of energy that made Amanda blink. The drip of grease from the corner of his mouth was caught up by a dart of his tongue and the whole performance was followed by a grunt of what could only be interpreted as satisfaction.

It was at this point that Amanda heard giggling from the direction of the wall in front of the kitchen. As she rounded the end of it she found her fellow servers Kassy, Blanca, and Patsy holding onto one another in a fit of mirth.

Kassy told her, "Welcome to the club."

"What club is that?"

"Those of us who have had to wait on him. You should see what he does to eggs."

Amanda laughed and tried not to picture the image too clearly. Gaining control over their laughter before Mrs. Chestnut caught them slacking in their work, the girls got back to work.

Late that afternoon, between her shifts in the dining room, Amanda was visited by Charlotte in her room just as she sat down to a cup of tea. Charlotte brought with her a large box and a gleaming happy face.

"Sit and have some tea with me," Amanda invited. "I need to get off my feet while I can."

"Emily had her baby!" Charlotte declared, unable to hold back the news any longer. "A telegram arrived from Frank announcing the birth of a daughter, adding that Emily was doing fine."

Amanda let out a squeal of delight and gave Charlotte a big hug. "Do you know the baby's name?"

"Whitney." Together they laughed, understanding completely why Emily would name her daughter after the mountain that to Emily defined her love of the Owens Valley. What they would not find out until later was that it had been Frank who had named the baby. But if ever a man knew his wife, it was Frank.

Charlotte smiled. "I also have some other good news. Besides, I mean, that Vince is doing much better."

"That is indeed good news. But what else?"

"It's your birthday in two days."

"Oh my goodness," Amanda laughed, "so it is. It has always been overshadowed by Christmas. And this year, with everything that has happened, I completely forgot. How did you know?"

"Your father told me early last month. He wanted my help in buying you a gift."

"He really was thinking about my birthday so far in advance of it?"

Charlotte placed a hand on Amanda's arm and smiled gently. "Yes, he was."

Amanda swallowed with an effort and asked, "Did he decide on something?"

"I told him that he needed to think about who you are and the things you might like or need."

Amanda looked down at her hands resting in her lap. "I guess I'll never know what he might have thought I liked."

"Don't be so sure." She got up and handed her the long flat box. "He told me what he had decided, so last week I went into town and got it for you. It's sort of from your father and me too."

"Oh, Charlotte." She sat with the box on her lap for several seconds, just looking down at it. Then, after taking a deep breath, she lifted the lid. Inside the box was a long black cashmere and brocaded satin cloak lined with silk. Around the neck and the edge of the hood was a fringe of soft grey rabbit fur. "Oh," Amanda breathed, "it's beautiful."

"Your father told me he recognized that you were attending many social events and this winter would need something fancy to keep you warm. Or words close to that."

"But it must have cost a fortune. You must let me pay part of it from what I got from the sale of the house."

"Nonsense. Vince and I are far better off than most people would ever guess. We invested in the Standard right at the beginning and were among the first to receive dividends. We sold our shares earlier this year, and let us just say that we can afford this cape. Besides, Vince's warehouse has always made money."

Amanda looked at her friend and felt her eyes mist over. "You're so good and so generous. Your friendship is the best thing about living here."

Charlotte blushed and reached for the tea pot on the table between them, changing the subject to the price of wood going up again.

That night, at the end of her supper shift Amanda was exhausted. There had been a rapid turn-over of diners enjoying the festive mood of the holiday and all had ordered lavish meals and desserts. There had been no time for her to sit down even once. She kept an eye on the old wooden clock on the wall, trying to will its progress. With just ten minutes to go before she could leave, Roger entered with a well-dressed couple. She was relieved when they were seated in Kassy's section.

When finally her shift was over, as she made to leave the room, Roger waved to her and she approached his table.

"Good evening, Amanda. I'd like to introduce you to Mr. and Mrs. John Wagner."

"How do you do?" Mr. Wagner greeted her, his German accent heavy but pleasant. Unlike so many of the men in town, he was clean-shaven. He was also neatly dressed in a suit with a bow tie slightly askew, his fedora pushed back from his forehead, and smoking a long black cigarette. He was shorter than Roger by several inches, but he gave forth an attitude that announced clearly that it would be a mistake to cross him. Mr. Wagner had a way of looking up at people with his head cocked to the side as though challenging the speaker to say something important or witty.

"Please join us," he invited Amanda. "We're about to have pie and coffee." When Kassy approached the table, Mr. Wagner ordered the dessert for everyone, including Amanda who sat down gratefully if not guiltily knowing that Kassy would have one more plate to carry. But when she took a bite of the sweet apples followed by a swallow of the strong coffee, she almost verbally sighed with delight.

"Mrs. Wagner," Amanda asked, "I believe that you're a medical doctor?"

The dark-haired woman had strong features with a determined chin and eyes that looked directly at whomever she was addressing. "Yes, I am. But I don't have an office of my own." She exchanged a quick look with her husband before continuing. "I mostly lend my services to the very poor, the Chinese and the Piutes."

"Is that because the manly men of Bodie would never consider a woman capable of binding their wounds?" The tone of Amanda's voice gave no doubt to her criticism of this.

Mrs. Wagner smiled. "You're quite right, of course. But it makes the work I do all the more gratifying, because I'm very much needed by the patients I do have."

"Is it noisy living behind the saloon?"

Rolling her eyes in exasperation, Mrs. Wagner told her, "At times. But it's important that John be able to be close to the action. It's a business where one never knows what might happen from day to day."

"Yes, so I've gathered. One only needs to read the newspapers to be aware of that."

They all nodded and said nothing more on that subject.

Roger had the idea to take Amanda for a surprise excursion, as he called it. Consequently, as he parted from her in the lobby, he told her to meet him at the Tuolumne Stables north of the hotel the following day at Noon.

After trudging through the snow to get to the stable, she found him out front in a small wooden sleigh that was little more than a buckboard on runners. It was light and fast, and easy for two horses to pull. Amanda clapped her hands with glee and allowed him to help her into it.

The horses, excited at the prospect of exercise, were tossing their heads in eagerness to be off. After Roger tucked a heavy blanket around her lap, glad that she had a long knitted scarf around her neck, he hopped up next to her and told the horses, "Get on".

They slid their way down Main to the lowlands south of town accompanied by the hiss of the forged iron blades beneath them and soon had reached the flats by the race course. The cold wind they created as they moved along watered her eyes and numbed her nose so she snuggled down into her scarf, but it was watching the competent maneuvering of Roger as he guided the horses that warmed her heart.

Stopping to give the horses a rest, they leaned back and smiled at one another.

"That was so much fun," Amanda exclaimed. "I've never been in a sleigh before."

"I wanted you to enjoy something here in Bodie during the winter so you can see that it's not all just suffering and bearing up."

"Well, you have indeed given me a wonderful memory."

He turned the horses around and they headed back to town, but much slower now that they were traveling uphill. After a few minutes Roger said, "I don't know about you, but I'd like a cup of hot chocolate."

"I'd like a hot toddy with lots of brandy."

Roger looked at her and laughed. "So would I actually. But I was trying to be respectful."

"Of what? My age or what you perceive as my lack of sophistication?"

"I guess I'm just not used to spending time with single ladies of genteel breeding, and I don't want to set a foot wrong." He paused to give her a look of frank appraisal. "I guess I need to remember that a woman can be both a lady and know how to have a good time."

"Thank you." She turned to him so she could see directly into his eyes. "I've had it impressed upon me that being a single woman here has a lot of pitfalls, and it's easy to have one's actions misinterpreted. When I lived with my father, it acted as a form of moral protection. But now that I'm on my own and living in a hotel, it's easy for people to jump to the wrong conclusion. Maybe that's why I talk so much about the fact that I'm biding my time until summer when I can return to Placerville."

Roger hoped his voice was calm when he said, "Do you really want to return to Placerville?"

"Not as much as I once did." She looked down at her gloved hands gripping the lap rug, then up at him. "You can blame yourself for that."

Roger smiled and said only, "Good." He picked up the reins and they sailed down a slope and up the other side.

Amanda luxuriated in the exhilaration of the moment with her heart racing: the stinging spray of ice and snow as it was flung up by the sharp rails of the sleigh, the chill air flowing past as it nipped at her nose, the hot breath of the horses condensing in the air while the crunch of their hooves broke through the icy patches, and the warmth of Roger's shoulder pressing against her own.

Roger pulled back on the reins and the horses puffed white steam as they stood quietly resting at the top of a swale in the terrain. He didn't say anything, but simply turned to her and putting a finger under her chin moved her face toward him. Slowly and gently he pressed his lips to hers while sliding his hand to the side of her bare neck beneath the scarf. When he pulled back, she laid her head on his shoulder and said nothing.

So many feelings welled up within her, but the greatest was surprise at how different this kiss had been from the one Joseph had forced upon her. There was an almost palpable passion flowing between them, but Roger had nevertheless been able to convey his ardor with the gentleness of a touch and the light press of his lips. His was the desire to please, not to possess—and Amanda knew she had learned something valuable about men.

"Oh, by the way, I have something for you." She removed a small white box from the pocket of her cape and handed it to him.

"What's this?"

"An early Christmas present."

He opened the box and found inside a silver men's lapel brooch meant to hold a small flower. "This is really nice. I've seen men in Bridgeport wearing them, but I've never had one." He looked at her in surprise. "It must have cost you a fortune."

"Actually, no." She blushed and confessed. "I found it on the sidewalk. I asked around but no one claimed it. Mr. Boone said he thought it might have belonged to a fancy man who was in town for a short time, but since no one knew who he was, Mr. Boone told me to keep it."

"Well, no matter. I'll be proud to wear it when I can find a bit of something to put in it." After a moment, he took her by surprise when he asked, "What did Charlotte say when you told her about us?"

Amanda looked toward the town in the distance and felt her cheeks warming. "I haven't said anything to anyone about our relationship yet."

"Why not?" It was difficult for him not to feel a bit hurt, even while thinking he understood.

Sensing this, she knew her answer was important. "Sometimes she can be a little protective of my reputation and behavior. She thoroughly objected to Joseph and you're, well, a gambler."

"I'm a faro dealer," he responded quickly, and a little defensively. "That's a very respectable profession."

"I know." She shrugged. "Maybe I just don't want to let anyone else into what we share. For a long time I wasn't sure exactly what it would be."

"And now?"

She smiled up at him. "I think it safe to say that we're at least special friends."

"I'd like it to be more than that."

"So would I, but for now..."

His voice low and husky, he told her, "Amanda, I'm in love with you."

She looked up at him and smiled, her heart dancing in her chest. "I love you, too."

This time it was several minutes before they pulled apart, and it took Amanda several more minutes to catch her breath. Roger picked up the reins and they continued towards the town. After a moment's hesitation, she told him, "But for now, that's all I need to know, or want."

Roger was quiet as he thought about what she was indicating. "Okay. But one of these days I may ask you a question you'll need to answer."

"I know."

As they moved smoothly down Main, she looked around her at the dilapidated wooden buildings, the frozen run-off from the mines and restaurants, the mire of horse droppings and mud that the blades of sleighs and large wagons had exposed beneath the snow, and the barren rolling hills dotted with rickety Piute shacks and sagebrush. She realized in that moment that giving Roger the answer he wanted would mean living in Bodie for an undetermined length of time, and she was unaccountably relieved that he hadn't asked her *the question* that day.

CHAPTER 10
JANUARY, 1881

What had been intermittently falling snow for the first part of the month finally slowed to an occasional flake. But even with the unremitting cold, the crush of heavy traffic on Main was able to keep the roads clear of all but the ice along the edges. The cold of it seeped through Amanda's windows and past the weak fire in the small stove in the corner of her room.

The warmest spot was in the bed where Amanda leaned against the headboard in her heavy chenille bathrobe. She had wrapped two shawls over her head and shoulders, and had pulled the quilts up to her chin. She was now caught between the desire to keep her hands beneath the covers and the desire to open the book on her lap. Using a couple of the words no woman would dare utter in public, she cursed Bodie and everything in it. Her sense of isolation was profound.

She knew there were hundreds in the town feeling just as cold, especially those who were outside in the elements. But her discomfort was so acute that she was tempted to think no one could possibly be suffering as much as she was. It occurred to her that she could dress and go downstairs to huddle before the large stove in the parlor, if there was room near it not taken up by others with the same idea. She decided that one of the rare good things about being a woman was that most men in such a circumstance would make room for her. Some women said that if they ever got the vote this might change, even if just so the men could prove they still had the power firmly clenched in their hands. Right then, Amanda didn't know and didn't care.

The courage to get out from under the covers and then to dress failed her, and she stayed where she was until the last moment before she had to dress for work, where she would be in the warmth of the dining room.

Then, in the middle of January, Mother Nature allowed a warm-up for a week and the snow was reduced to only a few feet on the hills and only a few inches along the edges of the rutted roads dividing the areas of the town. Amanda had no idea the condition of the roads winding around the mines and mills on the hill, and was glad of it. Her imagination told her that it had to be a sea of mud, ice patches and mounds of dirty snow, but beyond that she refused to ponder.

Arriving for her shift, Amanda surprised herself when she walked into the warm fragrant dining room and realized that she was looking forward to work that day. She had even adjusted to the sore feet and lower back ache that sometimes accompanied the end of a busy afternoon of serving dinners. Thankfully, she usually worked the dinner shift from noon to five in the afternoon, and seldom served the evening supper when more of the customers were drunk and therefore loud and demanding.

It had recently become her routine to write a letter to one or another of her friends in Placerville about the odd, funny and sometimes outright peculiar customers that she waited on. The customers offered her no end of entertainment, including what she was told by the other waitresses with whom she worked.

Her new friend, Kassy--she of the dancing eyes, dimpled cheeks and frizzy blonde hair--seemed always well-informed as to what local businessman had recently slipped out the back of a dance hall onto Bonanza Street, which lady of good repute had without her husband's knowledge set her lips on an opium pipe in one of the private dens on King Street, and which of the constables might be amenable to a bribe if the offense was not too serious. After only a week of working with Kassy, Amanda was more informed about the blighted side of Bodie society than was proper for an unmarried girl of good breeding. And she loved every gossipy bit of it.

With all that Kassy chattered on about, Amanda still felt there was more her friend was holding back. Several times a suddenly serious Kassy had started to tell Amanda something, then had stopped and changed the subject to something mundane. Amanda didn't miss that each time this had happened it was right after Joseph had come into the dining room to say hello to Amanda before retiring to the bar where he would meet with other men in serious conversation. Kassy told her that men often met there who didn't want to be seen by the general population in larger saloons.

Any complaints Amanda might have about the hard work were balanced by the jingle of coin in her pocketbook as she made her way to the bank the day following a busy afternoon. She always kept out half for laundry, some fruit at a market or Chinese stand, and various feminine sundries. With her growing nest egg in the bank, she was content in the knowledge that come summer, even after having drawn out her monthly rent payments, she would be able to go home to Placerville. But while her friends sent her letters filled with their enthusiasm at the prospect of her return, she still refused to commit herself to a date.

Out for a stroll, Amanda saw a team of men with wagons at the extreme north end of town and wandered over to watch them. The edges of the reservoir that collected water from Rough Creek were frozen, and the men were cutting blocks of ice and loading them into the wagons. It would then be transferred to sheds lined with sawdust and straw to last through the short summer. A wooden flume had been run downhill from Rough Creek Springs about five miles away, and it was this water that then flowed into the reservoir and then through wooden pipes to hydrants throughout the town in an effort toward fire prevention. When finally she could no longer feel her toes, she returned to the hotel's lobby stove to thaw them.

Amanda had seen little of Joseph of late, and even less of Roger. Now that men were spending more time indoors to get out of the cold and wet, Roger was always busy at his stand at Wagner's where the demand was great to "buck the tiger". This phrase came from the fact that the faro cards were decorated with a drawing of a Bengal tiger. Roger was a respected dealer because he was known to shuffle these cards fairly, and not stack up pairs when no one was looking. This was important, as the dealer took half the winning money if he turned up a pair.

Roger also worked with a casekeeper who managed a device similar to an abacus to show how many of each card had so far been dealt during the game, and a lookout who kept an eye on the players' hands. Roger's lookout, seated on a raised platform behind the dealer, was well-heeled with the soft steel glow of his 1878 Colt Peacemaker prominently displayed. Roger's gun was a small Derringer and hidden within the pocket of his coat. On a busy night Roger's team was paid well by him to stay together at the table except for short breaks every couple of hours.

Joseph, when she twice ran into him in town, told her that he was busy at his brick yard with an increase in orders. She found this difficult to believe, considering the rough weather and general decline in the local economy. New construction in the town had completely stopped and enlargements to homes and warehouses had dropped off considerably even before winter had arrived. "For sale" signs were now plentiful at the north end of town, with even a few at the south end. Carpenters were out of work, as were others in the building trades, and most of them had left town.

Amanda had several times heard the rumor that Joseph was seeing "a woman who he had known for many years". Because of this, Amanda was surprised when Joseph stopped by the hotel and asked her to accompany him to a dance at the Miners' Union Hall on Thursday night, January 13, "to take advantage of the lack of heavy snow while we can." It was the first social and ball sponsored by the AOUW (Ancient Order of United Workmen), and while waiting tables that week she had heard people talking about the dance. She had hoped Roger might ask her to accompany him, but since he had not, she decided Joseph would have to do in spite of his ungracious manner of invitation. Such an opportunity to kick up her heels and have a few laughs was not something she was going to pass up.

Knowing what dresses were in her closet and the status of her finances, she realized that one of her current gowns would have to suffice. She laid the black one on the bed and brushed it down, standing back to look at it with a critical eye, and wishing it was sleeveless as was now the current fashion, so she could then wear long gloves with it. But being winter, she left it as it was. She dabbed at a spot on the bodice before repacking the sleeves with newspaper and hanging it in the wardrobe closet.

On Thursday evening Amanda and Joseph, who was dressed cleanly but less formally in tan pants and a calico shirt under his leather coat, entered the gaily decorated Union Hall. American flags flew on either side of the door outside and inside, while red, white and blue bunting was draped along the walls near the ceiling. White cloths covered the old refreshment tables in front of the stage, while wooden chairs were lined up along the walls so the center of the room could be left free for dancing.

Amanda removed the cloak given her by her father and Charlotte, and handed it to the woman manning the coat check table by the front door. She turned to the large room and smiled at the people bouncing around the spring supported floor to a peppy tune produced by a small orchestra arranged up on the stage. As she scanned the room for people she knew, Joseph grabbed her hand and led her onto the floor with a vigor and eagerness that surprised her.

He looked down at her with a merry grin on his face, and soon Amanda was caught up in the heady action of their rapidly twirling bodies moving in unison around the room. Laughter caught in her throat and she was suddenly happy to be with Joseph when he was in such a happy state of mind.

In a chipper mood Joseph might have been, but after a couple of dances he began glancing past Amanda in a distracted manner. Having been through this before with him, she frowned in irritation as she realized she was simply an excuse for his being present at the same function as Johanna.

When the music stopped, instead of thanking her for the dance as a gentleman should, Joseph faced away from her and looked toward the refreshment table. Following his gaze, Amanda realized he was watching Johanna as she helped other women cut slices of cake. Amanda gritted her teeth and felt an anger more directed at herself than Joseph's lack of gallant behavior. She chastised herself for her naivety in not realizing sooner the true reason he had invited her, and told herself that it would be the last time she would accept an invitation from him. However, she was not so distracted that she missed Johanna's black eye.

"Oh, dear," she murmured, "what happened to Johanna?"

Joseph scowled. "The son of a bitch hit her again."

Amanda didn't miss that he spoke as one familiar with the circumstances. To test this, she asked, "What set him off?"

He answered readily. "She talked to him using a tone he did not like, and he hit her." His accent became pronounced. "It is not the first time. Everyone thinks him a mild mannered fellow, and they ignore his ill treatment of his wife. He's touchy because of his limp. Thinks it makes him less of a man, I suppose. He also thinks she married him for the insurance money he receives this year from the accident he was in."

"Did she?"

"Well, yes," he shrugged, "but she also thought him a nice man. Little did she know what a temper he has."

"What kind of an accident was he in?"

"He was working in a mine in Virginia City and fell down a 225 foot shaft. They settled a large policy on him. Johanna had a bit of money set by when she married him that she had saved from the laundry she started here back in '78. He works at the mines in jobs not too challenging."

Goodness, she thought, he's certainly well-informed about Johanna's business. Her next thought was that she could no longer deny that Johanna was "the woman of long acquaintance" so many people were connecting with him.

"You've known her a long time, haven't you?"

He led Amanda back onto the dance floor. "Actually," he told her, his voice a shade overly casual, "we met in Chicago back in '70. We then lost touch with each other for several years, until we ran into each other here. She had moved to San Francisco, then to Virginia City, and in '78 had come here to Bodie. The next year she married Tom."

Amanda was no longer puzzled by Tom Treloar's insecurity in his relationship with his wife. Considering Joseph and Johanna's history, if Tom knew like everyone else that she was seeing more of Joseph than she admitted, no wonder he was jealous. Of course, that was no excuse for blackening her eye, something most men would make light of and some even make jokes about. However, Tom was supposed to be on probation after his conviction the previous year, although Amanda doubted that Johanna would press charges against him. And Bodie's courts might only shake a judicial finger at him and tell him not to do it again.

As she did so often, Amanda wondered if things of this nature might be different if women could serve on a jury or had the right to vote. She would have been surprised to know that it would not be until 1920 and the passage of the 19th Amendment to the Constitution before these events would happen, but maybe she would have been gratified that at least it would take place in her lifetime. On the other hand in 1911 a Judge in Daly City would pick California's first ever jury of twelve women out of a cigar box to try the case of one Mrs. Rudy who would be accused of maliciously breaking Mrs. Pinto's kitchen window. He would explain that only women could relate to her capricious actions. Mrs. Rudy would be acquitted when it was revealed that she had meant her rock to hit Mrs. Pinto's vicious dog and not the window.

When Joseph and Amanda's next dance ended, he announced to her that he would get her a glass of punch. Before finding out if she even wanted it, he made his way through the throng of dancers and headed directly to the refreshment table. Amanda realized it was going to be a long wait when he immediately got into conversation with Johanna.

"Has your escort deserted you?"

Amanda turned around with a smile as she recognized Roger's voice. "It would seem so. I'm surprised he finished the last dance." She laughed lightly to show him how little she cared. "He seems to be more concerned about Johanna's black eye. Or more to the point, how she got it."

Roger frowned and shook his head sadly. "Yes, I heard Tom lost his temper with her again. But DeRoche is the last person who should be talking to her."

"Why?" She wanted to hear his version of the situation. When he hesitated to answer, she rolled her eyes and said, "Let me guess. The argument was about her association with Joseph."

Instead of confirming this, he looked down at his boots, summoned an obvious mustering of his courage, and brought his eyes up to meet hers. "Do you care greatly?"

She started to scoff at the question, then relented as she noted his anxious frown. "No." She almost laughed at his obvious relief. "I've certainly not invited his interest, but he's been kind to me. When I first arrived, he helped me understand how the town functions, and made me feel less of a stranger. But I've always realized that he's selfish and after the main chance, as they say. I'm nothing to him but a legitimate reason for him to be where Johanna may also be. But at least he takes me away from the humdrum of my life to a dance occasionally."

"Where I do not. I apologize for that. I had wanted to ask you to this dance, but didn't think I could get away. When I went to your room, Mrs. Chestnut told me you were here." He chuckled. "From the severe look she gave me, I think she hoped I was upset."

"And were you?"

"Well, let's say I was disappointed. But I came here anyway, you'll notice."

"Maybe next time you won't wait until the last moment."

He sighed. "Yes, yes, I know."

She laughed and slipped her hand through his arm. "I'm only happy that you're here now."

He looked at the refreshment table where Joseph and Johanna were talking. "If Treloar shows up here after he gets off his shift, there may be trouble."

Ignoring this, she reached up to push aside a long strand of black hair from his forehead. He reached for her hand and bent his lips to the pulse point of her wrist in a brief gesture of intimacy that both startled and pleased her.

Before she could say anything, the band began playing a new fashionable waltz. Roger smiled and held out his hand. "Shall we?"

"I'd be delighted." Casting a defiant glare in Joseph's direction, she took Roger's hand and walked with him onto the dance floor.

Almost immediately Amanda was aware of a different sensation in her body as Roger's arm encircled her waist. He held her raised right hand lightly, but his hand at the small of her back brought her body close to his just enough that they almost but not quite touched. Amanda chose to ignore the proper etiquette of the moment and moved into him so that there was the barest of pressure along the length of their bodies. Roger's color deepened and he couldn't hold back the slightest of smiles. As for Amanda, while her heart raced and the heat rose in her body, her most passionate desire of the moment was that the music never end.

But the music did stop, and she forced herself to look away from Roger's bright eyes as he looked down at her. Across the room Joseph had been dancing with Johanna, and even when the music stopped they stood close together at the edge of the dance floor while talking to one another in low voices.

Roger followed her eyes and started to speak, but a loud angry voice cut through the room. A man by the entrance demanded of the doorman, "I want to see my wife."

Quiet descended as everyone looked at the front door. The man was of slight build and dressed in his day's work clothes, making him stand out in a room of clean men in their best clothes. It was Tom Treloar with a sneer on his face and leaning into the miner who was acting as doorman. After they exchanged a few quiet words, Tom stayed where he was while the doorman walked the length of the room to Johanna. All eyes followed them, and Johanna showed her embarrassment as she was led back to the entrance. Treloar immediately took her by the arm and pulled his wife outside onto the sidewalk.

Most people drifted toward the refreshment table while talking in subdued tones, but a few moved onto the dance floor in expectation of music. Johanna came back inside alone and returned to the refreshment table where she tried to act as though nothing untoward had occurred just as the band began to play.

"Oh, damn," Roger mumbled. "This doesn't bode well."

"Poor Tom. He seems such an unhappy man."

"Yes." After a glance at the door to be sure Tom had not returned, Roger told her, "He has a peculiar way of always referring to Johanna as *my wife* instead of by her name. I've often wondered if this is an indicator of his sense of ownership rather than partnership."

Amanda answered thoughtfully, "Maybe it's his way of keeping her at a distance in an effort to be less hurt by her behavior."

Roger looked at her and smiled, thinking to himself how enjoyable it was to converse with an intelligent and insightful woman. He had to admit, however, that her beauty made it even more enjoyable. But he was pleased with himself when he realized that it wouldn't have mattered to him if she had been considerably less attractive. He had learned the importance of character over beauty from a wise and loving mother whose beauty had been marred by a small facial scar that she would never explain.

Everyone seemed to have breathed a collective sigh of relief at Tom's departure, and as the band struck up a lively tune dancers filled the floor. Instead of asking her to dance, however, Roger led Amanda to a chair by the front door where the air was not so close and the music not as loud.

Searching for a conversational starter, he asked, "Are you missing your father?"

Grateful to be off her feet and near cool air, Amanda was feeling happy and carefree in Roger's company. "I don't know how to answer that. I do regret that I've missed the opportunity to know him better. Maybe if we'd had more time we could have finally developed some degree of closeness."

Roger picked up her right hand from where it rested in her lap and held it almost reverently. "People generally only give of themselves what they know how to give," he said gently. "If he had thought he needed to change, don't you think he would have put forth the effort? Your father was who he was always going to be, I'm afraid."

"You're probably right. And I do have a few fond memories I can recall." She smiled and sandwiched his hand between both of hers as she looked up into his face. "I think it's time I begin making good memories of my own."

A flustered Roger broke the intimacy of the moment, which was after all public, by standing up and announcing that he would get them a glass of punch. Their conversation after he returned was easy and relaxed, and after eating some food and enjoying a couple of dances it was well into the first hours of Friday morning before they realized it. They were laughing at this fact when they looked up to see Tom Treloar coming in through the door. Tom looked to where Johanna was dancing a quadrille with Joseph, and his jaw clenched at the same time as his fists.

"I told my wife not to dance with that bastard," Tom mumbled. "She promised me she wouldn't, too. I've got to get her away from here."

The doorman stepped forward. "Now, Tom, don't you go causing any trouble in here. This is a refined gathering of folks."

"I won't cause trouble." He turned to Captain Morgan standing nearby, a man he evidently knew well, and told him, "Johanna has been untrue to me. I intend to kill that DeRoche."

This was a threat always taken seriously in Bodie, and Captain Morgan tried a few reasoning words on Tom. But Treloar was looking around the room, trying to spot his wife with Joseph. Fortunately, the couple had moved out of sight behind the crush of dancers. Captain Morgan slipped off to the right to where he had last seen them and when he found Joseph, told him what Tom had said. Joseph gritted his teeth and told Morgan, "I'll shoot him if he makes an aggressive move at me. It'll be self-defense. Remember that. I'm not putting up with his threats."

Joseph marched past Amanda and Roger without seeing them, took Treloar by the arm and led him out onto the sidewalk. The two men talked for several minutes in a low voice, after which Joseph came back inside alone. He turned to a worried Morgan, who had followed him to the door, and said, "Don't worry. I ran him off. He's going home to start a fire so the house will be warm for Johanna when she gets there."

"How'd you run him off?" Morgan asked him.

"How do you think?" Joseph grinned and patted his pocket that bulged suggestively.

At the refreshment table Johanna was helping three other women put the used plates and glasses into boxes, the band was packing up their instruments, and people were claiming their wraps and leaving in a steady flow. Amanda and Roger, both wanting to stall the moment of leaving, stayed in their chairs by the door. They nodded and said good-bye to people as they passed, but finally they could delay no longer.

Roger was just helping Amanda on with her cloak by the coat table when she exclaimed, "Tom is back."

Roger followed her gaze. "He's probably here to walk Johanna home."

Before this could happen, however, Joseph walked up to Tom and said something to him, after which they left the hall and disappeared into the night.

"Well, that was unexpected," Roger noted.

When Tom did not immediately come back, Johanna walked over to Mr. T. A. Stephens. He was not only a popular local attorney, but also a friend who had been the committee chairman for the ball.

"Would you and your wife have room in your buggy to take me home?" Johanna's voice was tense, and her breathing came in rapid gulps. It was obvious that she was caught in some strong emotional upheaval, a good part of which was fear.

"Of course, my dear," Mrs. Stevens accepted for them. Mr. Stevens stood aside for the women to precede him and the three of them walked past Amanda and Roger on their way out of the building. At the same moment that Johanna and Mrs. Stevens stepped onto the sidewalk, the quiet of the cold moonlit night was shattered by the single pop of a gun not far away to their right.

Being next to the door, Roger leaped forward and stepped out next to Mr. Stevens, who had moved himself in front of the ladies. Amanda grabbed Roger's arm from behind and leaned against him as she sought a view of the street. Nothing further was forthcoming in the way of gunfire, and it was obvious that no one was on the street immediately in front of the Hall, so everyone scanned the area for the source of the gunfire.

People rushed out of the Union Hall and pushed into Mr. and Mrs. Stevens, Johanna, Amanda, and Roger from behind, shoving them to the edge of the sidewalk. Amanda looked south past the post office and saw that near Kilgore's meat market a man was lying face down on a patch of ice, with a copious amount of blood flowing onto a patch of ice from a hole in the left side of his head. A man stood over the outstretched body, his back to the crowd. Not far from this man stood Mr. Alexander, who had been acting as floor manager at the ball, and his friend Mr. Butler.

Johanna screamed as she recognized the fallen man by his clothing, and hollered, "Good God!" Mr. Stevens tried to hold her back, but she broke free and rushed to the fallen man's side. She immediately realized her husband was dead and backed away with her hands over her mouth in horror, ignoring the man in the shadows next to her. Mr. Alexander guided her back to the sidewalk and the ministrations of Mrs. Stevens.

Mr. Butler meanwhile ran up to the man standing over Tom's body and grabbed from his hand a .38 caliber double-action Forehand and Wadsworth, crying out, "What did you do that for?"

The man turned to him, and Amanda gasped as she saw Joseph's face clearly lit by the glow of a bright moon reflecting off the snow and ice.

"He jumped me," Joseph yelled, loud enough that those in the crowd by the Hall could hear. "See where he scratched me?"

"I didn't see him do anything of the sort," Butler said with considerable heat.

Mr. Alexander, who had joined the two men, agreed as he looked closely at Joseph's face and neck. "I don't see any scratches either."

Deputy Sheriff James Monaghan joined the men at that point, but before he could ask any questions, Joseph turned to him. "Treloar drew a gun and I was trying to get it away from him when it went off accidentally."

Mr. Alexander and Mr. Butler exchanged a look accompanied by raised brows, since this was a completely different story from what Joseph had just said to them.

Deputy Monaghan took the gun from Mr. Butler and put it his pocket before turning to Joseph and grunting, "Tell it to the judge." He pulled out his handcuffs and said, "Put your hands out." When the cuffs were snapped onto Joseph's wrists, Monaghan jerked him forward while telling Mr. Alexander and Mr. Butler, "You two stay with the body."

Without waiting for them to agree, he began marching Joseph north down Main. As the pair passed, Joseph spotted Johanna at the edge of the crowd on the sidewalk. His face contorted by an array of anguished emotions, he called out to her, "Johanna, I've killed your husband."

Johanna stiffened but said nothing, simply staring at his back as he was led away. Mrs. Stevens put her arm around Johanna's shoulders, but Amanda noticed that Johanna was remarkably dry-eyed. Mr. Stevens hurried the women forward to his black rig tied up across the street, and wasted no time getting the women out of the area.

Amanda watched Joseph being led away and suddenly cried out, "No!" It was a spontaneous denial of the horror of the moment, and surprisingly not a protest of disbelief that Joseph had shot someone. Roger seemed to realize this and put his arm around her, holding her close as he turned her away from the blood and gore in the street. He brought her back inside the hall with the excuse that she needed to get warm, although it was really so Joseph and the deputy could get out of sight before he and Amanda began walking in the same direction to the hotel.

Deputy Monaghan and Joseph crossed Green and quickly disappeared from the crowd's sight. Most people had by then gathered around Tom's body where it lay on Main just north of Lowe. Soon Undertaker Ward arrived and with help from Mr. Alexander and Mr. Butler, loaded Tom's body into the back of a wagon. Only then did everyone clear the street and the hall, either heading home or hurrying to a nearby saloon.

Bodie's Constable and Jailer, John Kirgan, along with Deputy Constable Sam Williamson, met Monaghan and the prisoner at the jail. Immediately Joseph's handcuffs were removed and he was ensconced in his tiny new room with its heavy iron door. John Kirgan gave him a drink of water, an extra blanket when he saw Joseph shaking, and then left him alone to absorb the impact of what he had done.

At 4:00 AM, Deputy Sheriff Joe Farnsworth, who had been on night duty at the north end of town, arrived at the jail. His agitation was obvious. "Men are gathering in the saloons and a mob is forming. They're not going to wait for a trial, or for morning either."

"Damn!" Kirgan's lips formed a tight grimace and he looked toward the flimsy front door of the new jail.

"Look," Farnsworth suggested, "why don't we move DeRoche to my room at the Standard Lodging House? There's certainly not enough time to get him out of town and to Bridgeport, especially with all the snow on the hills."

Knowing that this maneuver had been successful in the past when a crowd had gotten out of control and wanted to give someone a too-tight necktie, Kirgan reluctantly agreed. He always disliked doing this, not knowing how the crowd was going to react when they discovered the ruse.

As Deputy Williamson unlocked the cell door, Joseph shrank back and asked, "What are you going to do with me? Hang me?"

"No," Sam told him. "We're trying to save you from that. Now get a move on."

Kirgan and Farnsworth hurried a handcuffed Joseph through an alley between Bonanza and Main Street. Partially hidden by a passing wagon, they trotted across to the Standard Lodging House and up the stairs to a room at the back. Kirgan ordered Farnsworth to put the prisoner on the bed and handcuff him to the iron bedstead after putting the leg shackles on him they had brought with them. He was then ordered to stay with Joseph until morning.

The last thing Kirgan told the constable was, "Be sure to have him at the jail at seven o'clock."

Immediately after Kirgan left, Farnsworth realized he had left the key to the leg shackles at the jail. After a moment's consternation, he called to his landlady and one of her boarders. "Will you stay here with the prisoner while I run to the jail for the key?"

They hesitated, but reluctantly agreed, not yet having heard what Joseph had done. When Farnsworth returned again to the room, he dismissed Joseph's temporary keepers and shackled his prisoner as Kirgan had ordered.

Tired, and still feeling the effects of a few too many pints from earlier in the evening, Farnsworth lay down on the bed next to Joseph. But Joseph seemed to be inclined to talk, and for the next quarter of an hour he rambled on until Farnsworth eventually fell into a deep sleep.

Meanwhile, Roger had escorted Amanda into the Grand Central just as the grandfather clock in the corner struck the quarter hour past two in the morning. He became concerned when he noted that she was beginning to shake, whether with delayed shock or the cold, he wasn't sure.

Even though her cape was a substantial one, he pushed her down onto the velvet Eastlake sofa in the corner. Taking a quilt folded on one end of the seat, he gently placed it over her lap before fetching a brandy for them both at the bar. She took a large swallow and continued to shiver. It was only after drinking a large mug of hot coffee laced with more brandy that she stopped. A few minutes later she took a deep breath as she felt warmth rise up through her body, and finally her muscles relaxed.

"Why would he do something like that?" Her words were underscored with anger and not a little disgust. "I want to think that it's somehow a mistake, but we saw him with the gun in his hand."

"And didn't you hear what he said to Johanna as he passed by us? Given the earlier arguments and threats, well..."

"We need to get Pat Reddy to take his case." She tilted her face up to him as he sat down next to her and slipped his arm around her shoulders. "He can get anyone off for anything."

Roger hesitated a moment, wanting to ask why "we" had to do anything for the man. But he liked that Amanda had implied that they were a couple, so he relented. "I'll talk to him if you want, but you must prepare yourself. This isn't going to turn out well for Joseph."

She merely nodded her agreement. After a moment, she told him, "I'll be okay now. I'll go up to my room in a minute. Thank you for your kindness tonight." She smiled shyly. "I did have a good time, before, well...you know."

"It was my pleasure. I'd better relieve the guy who took over my table tonight, at least for an hour or two." He stood up and started toward the door, but then turned back. "You come get me if you need me for any reason."

She smiled, but said nothing. Saloons were strictly off limits to women, and even Bonanza Street girls met the men at dance halls or on the street, but seldom in the saloons. Marching all the way to the back of Wagner's to find Roger was just not something she would ever do. Possibly thinking something along those lines, Roger told her, "Tell you what. I'll come check on you in the morning."

She climbed the stairs and dressed for bed, noting that it was just past three-thirty in the morning. While tossing restlessly, she fretted at Joseph's stupidity and mumbled all the strong chastisements that came to mind that she would never have said to his face. The only thing that kept her from severe worry was her knowledge that in Bodie, Pat Reddy could get anyone off on self-defense. Many people had heard Tom threaten Joseph at the dance, which easily set Joseph up for such a plea. On that note of hope, she fell asleep.

A little before five o'clock, with no hint yet of dawn on the horizon, Amanda was wide awake again and her degree of alertness told her she would not be returning to sleep. She dressed quickly in a plain dark skirt and gray waist over flannel underwear before throwing the heavy black cape over her shoulders.

Creeping down the stairs to the lobby, she stood at the front windows looking out at Main Street. It was a slushy morass of snow, mud and horse droppings and she shuddered as a gust of wind seeped through the ill-fitting sash window. It would not be opened again for several months.

Across the road just to the south of the Standard Lodging House a man slipped out the side door into a narrow alley. Thinking that the man looked alarmingly like Joseph, Amanda drew the hood of the cape over her head and quietly closed the hotel door behind her. Lifting her skirts well above her ankles, she crossed the street with her eyes down as she made every effort to find firm footing.

Gaining the sidewalk, Amanda peered into the darkness of the alley and realized that it was indeed Joseph standing at the far end of it. In a loud whisper, she called to him, "Joseph, it's Amanda." He threw himself against the building and tried to merge into the dark. "I know you're there,

Joseph," she persevered. She walked further down the alley toward him. "I thought they'd taken you to jail. Did you prove to them that it was self-defense?"

He uttered a loud frustrated sigh as he stepped away from the building. "Oh, for Christ's sake, Amanda, of course not. Lower your voice."

She continued walking until she was only a few yards from him. "Why did you do it then?"

"He was going to go home and wait for Johanna, and then he was going to beat the hell out of her."

"He actually said that?"

"He didn't have to." He ran a hand over his face. "I knew him, and if it hadn't been tonight, it would have been some other night."

"That sounds like justification to me."

"It's not," he snapped. "You asked why and I told you."

Anger at his seeming stupidity rose up and almost choked her. "Are you so in love with her that you can kill a man over her?"

"Well, I did, didn't I?" His lip curled like that of a cornered dog, and there was a harshness to his voice that was almost a growl.

She drew back in the face of such belligerence, realizing suddenly that she was facing a dangerous man. "What are you going to do now? I thought you'd be in jail."

"They put me in the hotel because they're afraid I'll be lynched. They're probably right." He looked past her toward the street. "That's why I have to get away."

"Oh no, Joseph, you mustn't. They'll think it's an admission of guilt. You've got to let Pat Reddy plead your case. He can turn it into self-defense. After all, Tom threatened you during the dance."

"Look Amanda, this town has few rules and even fewer morals in their code. But one thing they take a dim view of is the *strong* picking on the *weak*. And Treloar was considered not only weak, but pathetic to boot. There are men in this town who respect my business savvy and a few who are willing to take a drink with me, but there's no man I can call a real friend."

"That can't be true." Having herself never been without the support of friends, even when it was not forthcoming from family, Amanda found it difficult to accept such an idea.

"It's true. I've bested some of them too often." He shrugged as he said, "And I admit sometimes I cheated them. So now I'm on my own."

"But running away will just make it worse for you when you're caught."

"I won't be caught." His laugh was couched in the confidence of a deep cynicism. "I got away from that stupid guard they put on me, didn't I? I could tell he'd been drinking when he arrested me. I waited until he fell asleep and I got the keys to the cuffs off him. A guy I know has a cabin a few miles from here, and he'll hide me until I can get further away." He looked past her to the empty street. All respectable people were of course at home, while the drunks were somewhere in their final stupor, and exhausted freighters and travelers were tucked up in a boarding house or hotel. It was the rare quiet time. "Now go back to your room and don't tell anyone that you saw me."

"But, Joseph…"

"Get the hell out of here," he whispered loudly, all patience gone and only wanting to be on his way undetected. "You shouldn't be out here at this time of morning."

"Good women are never interfered with here." She was reciting the standard line that she had heard so many times, and although true, it was something few women were prepared to test. "So you don't have to worry about my safety."

"I'm not," he hissed. "But you're interfering with mine."

Muttering something unladylike under her breath, Amanda turned and hurried back toward the street. When she reached the sidewalk she turned back and saw that the alley was empty.

Back at the hotel Amanda curled up on the sofa in the lobby, the quilt always kept folded on the seat now over her legs and her cape pulled to her chin like a blanket. Overcome by shock and lack of sleep, the next thing of which she was aware was waking with a start at eight o'clock that morning. Mrs. Chestnut was setting a steaming cup of coffee on the table, her lips pursed and her eyes questioning. Amanda gulped the hot liquid, unmindful of it burning her mouth as she heard a commotion out front of the hotel.

The street and sidewalk was filled with men yelling and arguing as word of Joseph's escape from the lodging house across the street passed among them. Amanda walked out onto the sidewalk where she found a startling degree of rage in the comments flying around her. After a few minutes, she realized that the angriest of these comments were aimed at John Kirgan and Joe Farnsworth. Seeing Harvey Boone not far away, she motioned to him and he came over to where she was standing. "Why are they so angry with Mr. Kirgan?"

"Oh, my dear, things are not looking at all good for John." He shook his head sadly as he looked around at the milling throng of angry men. "Kirgan hid Joseph in Farnsworth's room last night out of fear of a 601 taking him. But when Farnsworth didn't show up at the jail at seven o'clock with the prisoner as agreed upon, Kirgan went to Farnsworth's room only to find him still asleep and Joseph gone. Some men think Farnsworth was bought off by Joseph and that John Kirgan has failed abysmally in his job as jailer."

"But he was trying to do the right thing."

"Good intentions don't count." Mr. Boone shook his head and his eyes were deeply troubled. "Some men even think John still has Joseph hidden away somewhere." He turned toward the crowded street where wagons were trying to get through the throng of people that had become so large that the sidewalks could not hold them. "Listen to everyone. They knew Tom Treloar as a peaceable, quiet man who was never known to carry a gun."

"I suppose everyone has forgotten that he was convicted last year of beating his wife." She didn't bother to hide the asperity underlying her words. "Or that she is even now sporting a black eye."

"Oh, they remember." Mr. Boone expressed his resignation with a sigh. "But now that they're convinced that Johanna has been unfaithful to Tom with DeRoche, they don't care."

Amanda thought of poor Constable Kirgan, who she was sure had done what he thought best for all concerned. About Farnsworth, she wasn't as certain.

A Coroner's inquest was called for noon that day after finding a jury made up of those men with the coolest heads--not an easy task. The Rosedale Saloon, one door north of the Bodie Bank on Main, was owned by Henry Mahlstedt. The year before, he had given the large second floor to the town for use as a courtroom because it could be accessed by an outside staircase. There was only one window and iron bars had been placed over this, so it was a secure venue. Because of the dark interior, light was provided by a large overhead chandelier and wall sconces down the sides.

The room was arranged so that the Coroner this day sat at the far end of the room at an elegantly carved desk set off from the room by a wood railing, while another railing surrounded the jury box to his left and the prisoner's dock to his right. Those testifying sat in front of the judge in a plain wooden chair, while the counsels had large leather armchairs provided for their comfort. The small jury room behind the judge, however, only had wooden benches with no cushions and no stove for warmth. This encouraged juries to linger no longer than absolutely necessary. Besides, as soon as the trial was over everyone knew they would be adjourning to the saloon downstairs.

Amanda and Roger attended together, finding seats at the back of the room just as the doors closed on the thwarted hopeful observers who packed the stairs and the alley below.

Mr. Alexander and Mr. Butler told identical stories of having seen the shooting. They claimed there had been no provocation from Tom, and that DeRoche while walking to Tom's left had simply dropped back a step as the two men stepped off the sidewalk preparatory to crossing Main. The witnesses both had voices that were firm and strong as they testified that DeRoche pulled a gun from his pocket, raised it and shot Tom in the head.

Johanna, dressed in a decorous high-collared black silk dress, was questioned about her relationship with Joseph. She insisted that Joseph, although a sometimes contentious friend of her husband, had been a frequent visitor to their home and that she had never spent time alone with him. Not being able to shake her from this declaration without affronting the jury and the courtroom observers, the Coroner asked Johanna about her relationship with her husband. She informed him that she was often afraid of him, and briefly brushing her fingers over the bruises near her eye, declared that he had a bad temper and was often abusive toward her. The Coroner cleared his throat and allowed her to leave the courtroom.

But the Coroner did more than question Kirgan. He grilled him raw, and his tone was far from friendly. When it came to the fact of Kirgan's decision to transfer the prisoner to a lodging house instead of keeping him in the jail, the Coroner asked, "Do you think, Mr. Kirgan, even if there were a Vigilance Committee, prisoners would be safer outside than inside the jail?"

Kirgan, knowing his town and the impetuous nature of angry men, responded simply, "I do."

"Then," the Coroner smirked, "do you not think that it's a great extravagance to build jails at all?"

Kirgan dropped his head and said nothing. It was obvious he knew that no matter what the truth, it was not the time to try and explain his point of view--especially to someone he figured already understood this fact of life.

Mono County Sheriff Peter Taylor was called next. Back in '78, when Kirgan had become the town's Constable, he had chosen thirty-three year old Pete as his first Deputy. Kirgan had wanted Pete as much for his intelligence and talent with firearms as his large muscular frame built up from years of working in mines. Along with the highly respected sixty year old "Teddy" Brodigan, the three men had kept the town quiet. In August of 1878 Pete Taylor had been chosen by the Board of Supervisors of Mono County to replace the former County Sheriff who had died after a long illness. Pete's first official act had been to put Kirgan on the County payroll as a Deputy Sheriff.

After taking the stand, Sheriff Taylor acknowledged that he had always considered Kirgan and Farnsworth competent officers. After a pause, he glanced at those assembled and added that now he was not as sure. Amanda looked over at Kirgan, sitting in the first row of chairs. He was staring straight ahead at nothing in particular, and although the set of his jaw did not change, his already ashy pallor became a sheen of waxy white with a fringe of red around the ears.

Sheriff Taylor, while he avoided looking at his old friend, insisted that he had never given his permission for a prisoner to be removed from jail and placed elsewhere, even in the case of a possible mob forming in the town. Everyone knew that wasn't strictly true. Taylor had known that prisoners were occasionally moved in the past, and even if not "giving permission" he had not objected.

Most of Taylor's criticism, however, was for Farnsworth, who had gone to sleep with the key to the handcuffs in his pocket. It then came out that Farnsworth had left the prisoner with his landlady in order to retrieve the forgotten keys to the leg shackles. With undisguised heat, Taylor said, "I find it incomprehensively absurd for him to leave the prisoner in charge of a landlady even for a few minutes."

Amanda was surprised at this information, as were most of the people in the room who scoffed out loud when they heard of it. The coroner pounded his gavel for order and immediately the room quieted. The Coroner's hearing having started late, it was adjourned so some of those present could go in search of the escaped prisoner. By night fall they still had not found him.

The questioning continued on Saturday morning, and once again Roger and Amanda were present. It had been a long and mostly sleepless night for Amanda. As she waited for the proceedings to get under way, she remembered how she had waited for morning with the expectation that Joseph would have been found and had wondered if those who found him would lynch him before he could again escape.

Now, thinking back over the various times she had spent with Joseph, she was struck by the wide mood swings of his personality; one time thoughtful and considerate, and the next selfish, impatient and devious. She now wondered if even what she had thought to be good actions toward her had been motivated by indecent expectations. And once again she tended to blame the town, as though it was tainted by some septic evil that could not be resisted by those who were moral weaklings.

After the jury retired to their cold and uncomfortable room, the spectators remained in their seats. They sensed that it would not take the jury long to make their decision and they were correct. Within an hour, the jury rendered its verdict, finding that Thomas Treloar had been killed by Joseph DeRoche and that the killing was "a willful and premeditated murder." But the jury also found that Constable Kirgan was "guilty of gross negligence of duty in allowing the prisoner to be removed from jail." Their judgment of Deputy Farnsworth was even harsher, finding him "*criminally careless in allowing the escape of the prisoner.*"

As Roger walked Amanda back to the hotel after the adjournment, he explained that taking men out of jail had been done many times in Bodie. "Certainly more than the two incidences mentioned by Farnsworth when justifying himself during the hearing. In fact, Bridgeport and Bodie have a long tradition of prisoner exchanges. Of course, it's unwritten. But it's kept many a man alive who otherwise would have ended up at the end of a rope."

"Then why didn't Sheriff Taylor stand up for Kirgan?"

"Self-protection, I suppose. I think the worst that Kirgan actually did was to trust Farnsworth, especially if he knew that he'd been drinking at all. It was a lapse of judgment."

"I wonder if Joseph will be recaptured."

"Most prisoners are."

"But not all?"

Roger shook his head. "Men break out of the jails and are never heard of again. But only a couple of times in Bodie."

When the *Daily Free Press* came out on Sunday, they made bold accusations and pronouncements: *"The insufferable stupidity of Kirgan in allowing his prisoner to be taken away should forever bar him from holding an office of trust in the county. . . . The taxpayers and citizens generally have no further use for Farnsworth as an officer. If he did profit by DeRoche's escape, they certainly do not want him, and if he did not, he is altogether too innocent and childlike for the place."*

Some people later said that the Bodie press flamed the fires of revenge among the population, while others said they merely reported what people were already thinking. Whichever it was, the paper called the murder *"cold-blooded and cowardly, and was committed for a purpose seemingly so base and sordid, and under precedent circumstances so revolting to every impulse and sensibility of manhood, that it has stirred the blood of every human being in Bodie to the very springhead of the fountain."*

Whatever Deputy Farnsworth thought when he read these news reports, he decided that he didn't want to test the patience of his fellow citizens. Before another day passed, he had disappeared from the town and had headed to Carson City. Unfortunately for him, Sheriff Taylor had sent a telegram to the local law there and Farnsworth was arrested the minute he stepped off the stage.

Amanda read these editorials alone in her room. Although angry at the editors, it didn't begin to match her bitter resentment of Joseph. How could he have been so stupid? Realizing there was no logical answer, she had to admit that he simply had been.

CHAPTER 11
JANUARY, 1881

While groups of men rode out to search for Joseph between Bodie and locations as far away as Bridgeport and Aurora, a memorial service was held for Tom Treloar. With all the chairs facing toward the stage and allowing only a narrow aisle down the middle of the room, the Miners' Union Hall was packed. Miners, business people, and the curious filled the right side. The men of the Bodie Volunteer Fire Department, of which Treloar had been a member, took up most of the room on the left side. The widow Treloar stood shunned at the back, no one willing to allow Johanna her place of honor at the front of the room.

The Methodist minister, Reverend F. M. Warrington, conducted the service. Amanda assumed the Treloars must have been parishioners of his and waited to hear what the Reverend had to say about Tom. However, any mention of Tom as an individual was brushed over with a brief few comments. What followed was a strong personal rant about the crime itself that shocked Amanda in its unrestrained rancor and volatility.

His voice increasingly thunderous as he progressed through his comments, the Reverend described the murderer DeRoche as "*the babe on its mother's breast, then the boy, the young man almost imperceptibly diverging from the moral path pointed out by his mother, then the hardened man, and next the assassin and the fugitive from justice.*" When the reverend did appeal to God, it was an entreaty for Him to put His "*hand upon sin and strike down the arm of the assassin.*" He concluded, with broad pantomimed hand gestures suiting his words, "*If a man have an irresistible impulse to take another man's life, I say let the law have an irresistible impulse to put a rope about his neck and take the life from his body.*" As though suddenly recalling that he was a man of the cloth, he quickly added, "*But keep cool, and under all circumstances be men.*"

Amanda sat unaccompanied near the aisle in the center of the room amid the crush of people dressed in their funereal best. Listening to the reverend extoll his wrathful and judgmental opinions, she was soon enraged by his lack of impartiality much less spirituality. Finally reaching the point where she could not bear to hear one more inflammatory word, she abruptly stood up.

While making her way past several people to the narrow aisle, she could feel all eyes on her early departure before the congregation had been dismissed by the Reverend's "amen". Once in the aisle, she stopped a moment to glare at the Reverend, then turned her back on him and stalked toward the door.

A man with a long mustache, who had not removed his hat as most men had done, sat on the aisle to Amanda's right. As she approached, he looked up at her with a sneer. Turning to the man next to him, his voice filled the already stunned silence of the room. "She's one of the killer's harlots."

The instant the man turned back, he found Amanda furiously glaring down at him. Quicker than a striking rattler, her gloved hand shot forward and smacked the side of his smirking face. The echo of the slap was almost but not quite covered by the collective gasp from those present. She wasted no time exiting the building.

Instead of heading for home, however, she walked straight to the cemetery where she knew everyone would be going next. She stood far back from the grave so that once everyone arrived she would not have to be among them. Some of the women who passed her smiled openly, one even winked, and still others nodded politely as a way of letting her know they were sympathetic to her. But of course there were a few women who tossed their heads as they passed, or who refused to look at her.

Amanda stayed at the back of the crowd, determined not to let anyone see how rattled she was. But this did not keep her from seeing Johanna approaching slowly up the path. Although pale and gaunt, she was obviously determined to hold her head high no matter what anyone might think of her. By her very bearing, not to mention her status as the deceased's widow, she demanded the right to be present. Amanda admired her for this and decided that by comparison to Johanna, she had little reason to feel uncomfortable, especially when she noted how the good women turned away from the young widow. The rumor was rampant that Johanna had encouraged Joseph to "take out Tom", but Amanda refused to believe it.

When Johanna tripped on an exposed stone, Amanda leaped forward and grabbed her arm before she could fall to the ground, returning Johanna's smile of thanks with one of her own. With tears in her eyes, Johanna decided to stand next to Amanda rather than risk more hostility by pressing her way to the gravesite. The reverend looked out over the small crowd and mumbled a few auxiliary words to his earlier tirade at the Union Hall, after which the coffin was lowered into the ground.

A few people walked past and threw a handful of dirt on the coffin before walking back into town; however, Attorney Pat Reddy stood next to the narrow path. As Johanna passed him, he put up his arm and asked, "Can I have a word with you, Mrs. Treloar?"

"Of course." If it was possible, Johanna became even paler than she already was.

Amanda moved off to look at a cluster of headstones, but not so far away that she could not hear their conversation.

Johanna looked up at the famous lawyer from beneath her small hat's short veil of black netting. It cast a shadow across her face and she clutched a black-edged white handkerchief to her lips.

"Mrs. Treloar, please accept my condolences," Mr. Reddy began. "This must be a troubling time for you."

"Thank you."

He then came right to the point. "Did you know that Joseph was preparing to kill your husband?"

Johanna's eyes widened and her mouth opened in surprise. Taking a deep breath, she breathed out, "No, of course not."

"You never suggested to him that you would be happier if your husband was dead?"

"No!" She looked up at Pat Reddy in what might have been fear, but was definitely a plea for understanding.

He was unaffected and only hardened his tone. "Now that your husband is dead, you'll be the beneficiary of the insurance money he received for his injury as well as a Miners' Union widow's pension, am I correct?"

Johanna shrugged. "I suppose. I hadn't thought about that yet."

With an expression that showed he didn't believe her, he asked, "The Union may not give you his pension, feeling the way they do, but when does the insurance policy come due?"

"Well, this year, but what does that have to do with anything?"

Amanda stepped forward. Taking Johanna by the arm, she looked up at the tall man with the stony features, fighting the urge to shrink back from the detached look in his cold eyes. "Mr. Reddy, don't you think questions of this sort should be asked only during a trial?"

"Yes, I do. But with the fomenting anger in this town, it's helpful if I know all the facts so I can try and suppress rumors before they're treated as fact."

Johanna put a hand on her chest and whispered. "Do you mean some people think I wanted Joseph to kill Tom?"

"I'm afraid so." His eyes softened. "But I'll do what I can to present your side of things."

"Thank you, sir. I assure you that I'm completely innocent of such a thing."

Mr. Reddy didn't say whether or not he was convinced, but just turned and walked away. Amanda returned to town with Johanna, although nothing was said between them, and they parted at Fuller and Lowe. Both of them pointedly kept their gaze from wandering east to where Tom had died.

Amanda walked slowly home, which by now was what she considered the hotel. She passed groups of men searching through the town for Joseph, and later learned that when they went through all the saloons, they didn't even stop for a quick drink, so focused were they on their errand. Men questioned Joseph's partner, the quiet and retiring Mr. Saunders, and spent considerable time searching both the brickyard and Joseph's large house on Fuller for any secret hiding places.

The town's warehouses were searched in every nook and cranny, and even some large crates opened. They rushed the jail in a surprise raid just in case he was being housed there again. The brothels and cribs were invaded amid much complaining and giggling. Every vacant house or building was gone through more than once. As for the mills and mines, no one bothered, as those who worked there would already have grabbed him if they had seen him.

When Joseph was not found, men were organized by Sheriff Taylor into mounted groups. Some were assigned to travel over the Geiger Grade to Bridgeport and a few more were sent to Bridgeport over the toll road, a new group was sent to the old mining town of Aurora as well as the surrounding area just over the border into Nevada. Half a dozen men rode down the Goat Ranch Road to its end overlooking Mono Lake.

At nine o'clock that night, while the posse riders were gone, a small group of men referring to themselves as Vigilantes for Justice held a meeting at the Headquarters Saloon. They decided that there were only a few men in town they knew who had been close to Joseph and who happened to also be French Canadian. These they brought to Webber's Blacksmith on Mill Street not far from the Standard Mill. There they questioned them one by one, and none too gently. But after some time they realized that these men really did *not* know where Joseph had gone, and were as angry at him as they were.

Near midnight a saloonkeeper called DeGerro was brought to the blacksmith shop for questioning after someone wondered if he might not be French-Canadian. He claimed he didn't understand much English and shook his head whenever he heard Joseph's name. After the men received no answers to their questions, but only shrugs of incomprehension, one of the inquisitors threw a rope over a beam.

"Hey Joe," he told the man helping him, "be sure to grease the rope so it doesn't make any noise when it stretches under DeGerro's weight."

This evidently improved DeGerro's memory, as he began begging for mercy in perfectly clear English. He then told all he knew about Joseph's whereabouts while swearing it was just his best guess. In that way he hoped they wouldn't beat him for not speaking up sooner. They didn't buy it as just a guess, and took it as fact.

As a consequence of this, a group of ten men headed to the ranch of DeGerro's brother, eight miles from Bodie on the Goat Ranch Road. As they mounted their horses, one man told DeGerro, "If we find that you're lying, you'll return to Bodie stone cold and belly down over a horse. So if you're lying, better speak up now."

"No, no. I just think that would be where he'd go." Then, to cover himself, he added, "If he hasn't already moved on."

That was good enough for the inquisitors. Early Sunday morning, not long before dawn, the men approached an adobe cabin that was the main building of a small ramshackle ranch surrounded by corrals and sagebrush.

The mounted and heavily armed posse lined up in front of the cabin and one of them hollered, "Send out DeRoche."

Another added, "Or suffer the consequences."

Another threw in, "Mr. DeGerro, we have your brother out here with us. This isn't your fight. Don't be stupid."

The Bodie DeGerro shouted, "Brother, do as they say. Please."

At that point the brother ran out of the cabin with his hair standing on end screaming unintelligible pleas for mercy, among which was, "He made me. He forced me. He threatened me."

"Is there anyone else inside?"

"No. Just him."

The brothers clung to one another by the corrals and were thereafter ignored. Several of the vigilantes went in with their guns drawn and in only a minute brought out the prisoner with his hands cuffed in front of his body so he could mount a horse.

Joseph defiantly told the assembled men, "Go ahead and hang me!" Whether a plea or a challenge, no one cared. They tied his hands to the saddle horn of one of the horses and its owner rode with him back to town.

On the way, Joseph suddenly volunteered, "I'm innocent, you know."

"Oh, yeah?" the man behind him snorted into his ear. "How did Tom get dead then?"

"Treloar grabbed the gun and killed himself out of remorse at knowing he was losing his wife to another man."

"A gun you just happened to have in your hand?"

Joseph said nothing, but after a few miles of silent riding, one of the men asked Joseph, "How did you get away?"

After a moment of calculating thought, Joseph said, "I told Farnsworth that I'd give him $100 if he'd let me escape. He'd already told me that if I didn't escape, I'd be hanged for sure."

Several of the men exchanged a look of scorn and doubt, and they all spurred their horses to travel a little faster.

Although those who had captured Joseph were determined to abide by the law, those men who had returned to town from unsuccessful searches were not feeling so charitable. Nevertheless, Joseph was delivered to the jail at seven o'clock that Sunday morning. A number of men decided to linger around the jail and hold a watch to be sure the prisoner didn't escape again.

Roger knocked on Amanda's door at eight o'clock that Sunday morning. When he walked inside, he told her, "We can keep the door open if you're concerned about the propriety of my visit."

She smiled and pushed the door closed before offering him coffee from the silver pot on the table, brought to her room only minutes before and still hot. After they sat down at the small table in the corner, she sensed he had something of consequence to say, but he merely sipped his coffee and asked how she was doing.

"I'm fine." She waited patiently and finally he spoke.

"Amanda, men around town are demanding that Joseph be hanged immediately. In fact, a crowd started toward the jail, but Pat Reddy stopped them. Then Attorney John Kittrell and William Irwin, President of the Bank of Bodie, joined him."

"Oh, Roger, this is getting so out of hand." Amanda stood up and began to pace back and forth, a sick feeling in her stomach.

Roger tried to reassure her. "The crowd did listen to their reasoned pleas. The men disbursed after only a few grumbles."

"Does that mean the committee won't be taking him out of jail?"

"Well, at least not for the present." Roger wanted to reassure her, but refused to give her false hope, knowing as he did the mood of the town. He took a deep breath and added, "The bad news is that Pat Reddy has been retained by the prosecution. Joseph chose John Kittrell to represent him at the hearing that's to be held this afternoon."

"Can we be there?"

"I have to return to work, but you can go." Noting her disappointment, he told her, "That way you can report to me all that happens over supper tonight."

She smiled at this clumsy way of asking to see her again and agreed to meet him at seven o'clock at Delmonico's.

Just before two o'clock Amanda made her way alone to the justice court. All the chairs had been taken, but Harvey Boone spoke to Justice Thomas Newman on her behalf and she was allowed to stand at the back of the room in a corner. Joseph sat in the prisoner's dock, his wrists and ankles chained. He looked down at the floor the entire time, not once looking up at those present. Was he so ashamed of what he had done, or had he simply given up hope of finding anyone present who would not look at him with loathing?

The testimony was pretty much the same as had been given at the Coroner's hearing, and Kittrell couldn't sway any of the witnesses from what they had claimed then. With a look at his pocket watch as he thought of somewhere else he had to be, the Justice of the Peace adjourned the hearing until the following morning at nine o'clock.

Only after everyone vacated the Hall was Joseph walked out to a spring wagon where a deputy on the seat held the reins and another in the back helped him in along with the one escorting him. Standing off to the side of the building, Amanda watched Joseph settle himself between the two armed guards before being taken directly back to the jail. He was immediately locked into one of the tiny cells, and the heavy door of inch wide cross-hatched iron mesh clanged shut behind him.

After Joseph ate a surprisingly good supper that Kirgan prepared for him, he huddled under two wool blankets on a narrow cot. The main theme of his thoughts as he lay there was to wonder how he had managed to end up in such a terrible predicament. In answer, the image of Johanna in her party dress and the smell of her as they had danced close together at the ball filled his mind. He finally settled himself with a sickening dread of the long night before him, and eventually drifted into a restless sleep.

Joseph may have settled down for the night, but most of the citizenry did not. Dozens of men convened at various saloons throughout the town, including Wagner's. The most organized group came together at the big upstairs room of the Mono House on Standard Avenue.

Few men at Wagner's were in the mood for gambling, so Roger closed his stand and sent his crew home. After a subdued dinner with Amanda where she told him the little there was to tell about the trial, Roger walked her to her room and then retired to his own at the Standard Lodging House. However, he didn't go to bed. Instead, he sat by the window that overlooked the street below and waited for what he feared would happen next. Not that he cared so much about Joseph, but he did care about Amanda and what she would have to endure if things got out of control.

The men at the Mono House were agitated and each one had something to say. However, for a change, they were amazingly aligned in their opinions. Someone introduced the topic of how many times murderers in Bodie had been set free due to the jury being unwilling to convict. This was a subject they raised several times over the next half hour. Someone else commented that Frenchy DeRoche was after all not really "one of them". A man commented that Frenchy thought he was better than anyone else; you could tell by the fancy way he dressed and how clean he always was. Another man asked why Frenchy thought he needed such a big house, and everyone pictured the two-story brick on Fuller south of town. Once again someone expressed the idea that Frenchy thought he was better than everyone else. A lot of attitudes might be tolerated, but not that one.

A man remembered a loan Frenchy had reneged on, and that brought forth a comment from someone who knew someone who had said Frenchy was a petty thief. When another claimed that they all knew he cheated at cards, several nodded in agreement. Each comment buoyed the justification of what was in their minds to do.

By this time not one man used any part of Joseph's real name, distancing him from any consideration as a Bodie compatriot or fellow businessman. No one avowed him as ever having been a friend. After a lull in the conversation while everyone thought about all of this, bottles of whiskey were passed around and flasks were removed from pockets.

A man broke into the quiet and reminded everyone that Tom Treloar had been an honest, hard-working Cornish miner. Another said it must have been difficult for him, handicapped as he had been. The consensus was that Tom had been a valiant soul who fought against his infirmities with great dignity. The conversation slowly turned to indignation that the strong so often preyed on the weak, and how this just wasn't right.

As Joseph had tried to explain to Amanda the night he escaped, it was an unspoken rule even among the toughs, that it was okay to pick on someone who could defend themselves, but not someone who could not. Even those who derived their entertainment from harassing those considered cowardly or weak in self-defense, did not force themselves on the handicapped or mentally deficient. To do so was to be immediately ostracized by all of society, and even those who tended to violence needed someone with whom they could drink and brag.

Finally, one of the men at the Mono House declared loudly, "What this town needs is a good old fashioned 601 Committee to make sure justice is done."

Most of those present, waiting for just such a moment, loudly agreed. They were feeling not only the effects of the alcohol, but also a surge of masculine hormone that was fueling an intractability seldom experienced before. There were of course a few who didn't like what was brewing, but they nevertheless mumbled their agreement out of fear of what would happen to them if they expressed a different opinion.

One of the men called out, "Let's take a vote. Raise your hand if you think we should form a 601 Committee."

Everyone in the room, whether with enthusiasm or reluctance, raised their hand. At this point, several of the men ran out to make the rounds of the saloons with the announcement.

One man called out, "Now, what are we going to do about Tom's cheating bitch of a wife? Should we stretch her neck too?" Hands went up, but not all, and a careful count was taken. When the result was not as some wished, it was taken again.

Shortly after that the Committee started its march to the jail to mete out the justice they felt the courts would not. Like metal filings attracted to a magnet, as the crowd walked through the town more and more men attached themselves to the edge of the crowd.

While the committee was meeting and justifying their actions, Amanda made her way to the Treloar house on Mills Street where it ran parallel and just east of Fuller Street. It was the first time she realized just how close the Treloar house was to Joseph's house. She tapped gently on the front door, not wanting to alarm Johanna. If she thought her visitor to be an angry townsman, Amanda figured she would not answer the door.

After a long moment of waiting, the door opened a crack and a woman's red bloodshot eye peeked out and squinted at her. "Oh, hello. Amanda, isn't it?"

"Yes. I've come as a friend."

Johanna opened the door wider while asking, "Are you alone?"

"Yes. We need to talk." Even under obvious stress, Johanna was strikingly pretty. She needed no makeup to enhance her dark lashes and rosy cheeks, although a bit of powder might have helped cover the mottled colors around her eye and the ashen pallor that had displaced her usual healthy glow.

Amanda stood in the middle of the front room near a small parlor stove, a luxury few households could afford, with most people using the heat from their kitchen stoves. There were nice paintings on the wall, colorful rugs on the polished wooden floor, and a dark blue velvet sofa across from two matching chairs. The lamps were of top quality frosted glass, and the silver tea service on the low table in front of the sofa was brightly polished. It was a house where the woman's desires had been generously realized.

After this quick look around the room, Amanda wasted no more time. "Listen Johanna, we need to think of something that you can say when the trial resumes tomorrow. Something that can help Joseph. We can ask Kittrell to put you back on the stand."

Johanna barked a dry laugh. "Anything I'd have to say isn't going to help him. I was more than relieved when they dismissed me at the Coroner's hearing not long after I told them I was afraid of Tom. They've had time to think about it, and if they have the opportunity again, they're bound to ask me whether or not Joseph knew that Tom had hit me recently." Johanna turned her back on Amanda and walked to the window. In a low voice tinged by an oddly coquettish inflection, she said, "I'd have to answer yes."

"But that'll only make it worse for him," Amanda objected. "It gives him a motive." Had that been a twitch of Johanna's lips? "Don't you want to help Joseph?"

Johanna turned to Amanda and opened her beautiful eyes wide in a show of surprised innocence. "Of course I do." She paced up and down the length of the small parlor, her black dress and petticoats swishing almost musically. "I too have been trying to think of something to help."

"Have you come up with anything?" Hearing the desperation in her voice, Amanda swallowed hard.

"No. Please, won't you sit?" Johanna sighed prettily as she lowered herself into a chair, while Amanda sat on the sofa. Johanna's back was rigidly straight, either by means of her corset or a sense of pride, but she told Amanda, "If I testify again, they might ask me about my relationship with Joseph when we first met ten years ago."

"What about it?"

"Well, we were…very close, you know?" Johanna glanced briefly at Amanda and then down at her hands clenched on her lap.

Amanda tried not to pass judgment. She reminded herself that they had been adult people who had every right to enjoy their relationship any way they chose. But she did ask, "Were the two of you engaged?"

This was the most polite way of asking if they had slept together. A formal engagement was seen as such a complete and total commitment, expected to end in marriage, that intimacy after the engagement had been announced publicly was not particularly frowned upon if it was discreetly managed.

Johanna looked at her guest with raised brows and an intentness that made Amanda squirm. Before she could be told to mind her own business, Amanda added, "I only ask because it could affect the way your testimony is perceived."

"Then we have a problem." Johanna made a fluttering gesture with her hands. "Of course I wanted to marry him back then, but that wasn't possible, was it?"

"Why not?"

Johanna looked intently at Amanda with a raised brow, as though wanting to be sure not to miss the reaction to her next words. "Because he was already married. Didn't you know that?" Looking at the shocked expression on Amanda's face, she smiled with satisfaction and added, "No, I guess you didn't."

Amanda groped for a rational thought and a justification for Joseph's callous actions. "He must have been very unhappy in his marriage then. How long had they been married?"

"Long enough to have three kids."

To that Amanda had no response, except that she could feel her jaw tighten as she fought a drowning sense of disappointment in Joseph. And a flash of guilt in herself that she had kissed a married man.

"You didn't think he was that type, did you?" Johanna asked, having difficulty hiding her derision. "A knight in shining armor and all that?"

"No, of course not," Amanda objected, "but I did think he was unmarried."

"As, I assume, you think I should have been if I wanted to *visit* with Joseph here in Bodie. Unlike yourself, who could openly toss your loop over him."

Amanda couldn't ignore the bite in Johanna's words and realized the woman must have been harboring some jealousy of her. At the same time that she found this flattering, she was also outraged to be put in such a common category. Amanda looked the older woman directly in the eyes and told her, "If you're insinuating that I was trying to hog tie Joseph into marriage, you're wrong. But I am single and of age, so at least I could have done so openly."

"Meaning that I had to be secretive when *visiting* with him." There was an involuntary arch of her brow whenever Johanna said the word "visit" and Amanda knew then that there had been a physical aspect to the relationship, no matter how much Joseph or Johanna denied it.

"Isn't Joseph's fate our actual concern, and not his marital status back then, or yours now?"

Johanna shrugged. "I guess I've gotten so used to justifying my actions, that, well..." She sighed and softened her focused on Amanda. "As you say, Joseph wasn't happy in his marriage." After a short pause, she spat out, "And he's still married. She writes to him several times a year still, but he hardly ever answers her letters."

Amanda thought she should respond to this but couldn't find words better than, "He doesn't?"

"Back in Chicago when I first knew him, he made it clear that he didn't like being tied down. When he heard about the Comstock and other mines in the west, nothing could stop him from leaving the East. Once he got here, he decided that the hard work of mining was not for him and he headed to Aurora. He learned how to make and build with brick, since they used so many of them in Aurora. He thought that if Bodie grew, it too would start building with brick. Hoping to get on the ground floor, he built his house as an example and went into business with Mr. Saunders who built the kiln."

"He must have done well for a little while. There is considerable brick on the mills, the post office, a few of the buildings built during the boom, and his house. And of course the blasting powder storage shacks on the hill. But only a few homes and nothing recently."

"So he was wrong." She waved one of her expressive hands, indicating the inconsequence of the subject to her.

"He told me that business was picking up lately," Amanda murmured.

Johanna shook her head. "One of the many lies he probably told you. His house is heavily mortgaged and he's sold any of his furniture worth anything." She saw Amanda's discomfiture and asked more gently, "Still want to help him?"

Amanda looked Johanna square in the eyes. "I want him to have a fair trial. I heard men in the saloon at the hotel where I live talking about forming a 601 to deal with him. That's when I decided to come see you."

Joanna turned white. "Oh, God. Put enough booze in 'em and they could follow through tonight before the trial even continues."

A loud knock on the front door rattled the curtained windows on either side of the front door. Startled, both women jumped up and stood facing the door. As Johanna slowly walked toward it, Amanda retreated to a shadowed far corner and then slipped into the bedroom.

"Who is it?" Johanna hollered.

"It's Brian. I've come to talk to you. Don't worry, I'm alone."

She opened the door to let him in, ignoring Amanda after a quick glance to see where she was. Brian was a miner still dressed in denim overalls fresh from his shift at the Queen Bee. His face sported a drooping black mustache that hid his mouth and matched his thick brows, while protruding eyes gave him a perpetually surprised appearance.

He didn't bother to remove his cap, but started right in with the purpose of his visit. "Listen Jo, I've come as a representative of a committee."

"Not as a friend?"

"Jo, please." Brian removed his cloth cap and ran his fingers through his long dark hair, then began turning his cap in his hands non-stop. "I volunteered to come see you because my wife and I have always been friends with you and Tom."

"So a vigilance committee *has* been formed. Does that mean…"

"What it means for DeRoche doesn't concern you." His voice hardened and he raised his eyes to hers. "What they decided about *you* does?"

"Me?" Her hand flew to her throat and her face went white.

"Some of the men in town think you put Frenchy up to it."

"No, I didn't! I swear!" Little beads of sweat formed on her upper lip.

"I told them I didn't think you had, but they're pretty riled up."

Johanna faced him with fists clenched. "And drunk too, no doubt."

"Yeah, that too." With a rush of words, he said, "We took a vote about whether or not you should hang next to DeRoche." As Johanna collapsed into a chair, he hurried on. "The vote was pretty even, but when they were counted again it was decided by one vote that you won't swing." Johanna made a choked noise. "But you have only twenty-four hours to get out of town. If you don't leave by the end of tomorrow, I can't say what might happen to you."

Johanna nodded rapidly. "I'll go. I was intending to anyway. But let them think it's because of them."

"Will do." He turned and left without a further word.

Amanda stepped into the room and Johanna jumped. "I forgot you were there."

"I'm not surprised, considering what that man said." Amanda returned to the sofa and looked at Johanna leaning back in her chair, as though deflated by the shock of her narrow escape. Nevertheless, Amanda had to ask, "Does this mean they plan to hang Joseph?"

"Probably."

"But the trial might go his way."

Johanna didn't try to hide her exasperation as she sat up. "That's why they want to hang him, you fool. Don't forget that he confessed to me within minutes of the shooting. A number of people heard him."

"Oh, God." Amanda put her face in her hands. After a moment, she looked up. "I was planning on going to the jail tonight to talk to him."

"Kirgan won't let you in. And if the committee is going to do something, you need to be off the streets as soon as possible."

Amanda glared at the elegant woman dabbing at dry eyes with a lace handkerchief while at the same time sounding calmly practical. "How can you be so sanguine about the whole thing?"

"I'm just glad to be leaving this miserable town alive." Johanna stood up. "Well, you'll excuse me but I have packing to do."

Amanda walked slowly north down Main, her head reeling with doubts. She still was not sure if Johanna had wanted her husband dead. By the time she crossed Green, she was asking herself if Johanna might not also want *Joseph* dead. Johanna's attitude, one minute seeming to be sincerely concerned about Joseph and the next casually dismissive, haunted her. Could it be true that the whole turn of events was what Johanna had orchestrated; her husband dead and her lover hanged for it? She would after all be left with enough money to start a new life elsewhere, and be unencumbered by any man with his own ideas of how it should be spent.

Amanda stopped across from the Standard Lodging House and thought about going up to Roger's room to discuss with him her conversation with Johanna. But she changed her mind and entered the Grand Central. Roger saw her on the sidewalk hesitating amid a light swirl of snow flakes and pulled his watch from its small pocket in his vest. When he saw that it was almost midnight, a frown marred his handsome face as he wondered where Amanda could have been.

The clocks had not long past struck midnight when the Committee started its march to the jail. It started as a mob of two-hundred, with those carrying shotguns and rifles walking at the front. Some wore masks, but most did not. By the time the crowd reached the jail, it had grown by at least another three hundred. And not all were men.

When Kirgan looked out the front window of the jail, it was to see this huge crowd of determined people descending upon him. He wasn't sure how many were armed, but it was clear that those in the front were carrying rifles, shotguns and pistols. He had no deputies with him because he had told them all to go home and stay off the streets. He wanted them protected, and if they were seen near the crowd, they would be expected to step in or be in dereliction of duty.

Kirgan could tell how serious the Committee was by the fact that the men gathered before him were unusually quiet. There were no shouts to rally one another, no curses meant to inflame, or taunts necessary to dare each other to action. No, they all had decided on the same course.

Kirgan turned to look at the door separating the front office from the cells in the back and shook his head as sadness overcame him. In only a few strides, he crossed the narrow hall to the prisoner. It was easier to think of him that way than by his name, because he knew what was coming and was already mentally cushioning himself against the shock of it.

"I'm afraid there's a mob out front," he told Joseph.

"They've come for me?" Joseph's voice was resigned in its fatalism, even though he had harbored the barest hope that he might avoid this horror of a punishment, at least for a time. But he had carried no delusion that he would avoid swinging, either legally or by mob violence, so why not get it over?

Kirgan told him, "Either they've come for you or they're posting themselves around the jail to be sure you don't escape again."

Joseph looked at him and smirked. "You don't believe that. They already had men out there for that."

"Right." The least he could give the man was honesty. Kirgan turned away and walked to the front door, opening it wide as a few shouts filled the air. "DeRoche." "We want Frenchy DeRoche." "Bring him out." "Open up."

One of the men shouted, "We just want to give 'em a neck massage." The men around the comedian laughed, but it wasn't without a degree of discomfort. They were determined to carry out their plan, but only a few of them had ever participated in such an activity before. Most were more nervous than they would have wanted the man next to them knowing.

Kirgan stood on the steps of the jail's porch and raised his hands. When they had quieted down, he told them, "All right, boys. Just wait a minute. Give me a little time." Then, when five men stepped forward, he shrugged and nodded in resignation before leading them to the cells.

One of them demanded, "Open it."

Joseph watched all this with a detachment brought on by shock and an absolute acceptance of the inevitable. One of the men put handcuffs on Joseph's wrists, while another grabbed a canvas coat off a hook on the wall opposite the cell and tossed it over Joseph's shoulders. Obscured now were the clothes he had worn since the night of the dance, grimy with sweat and mud, and a light spattering of Tom Treloar's blood on the right sleeve.

Joseph stumbled down the steps into the street. He looked up briefly, the bright moonlight reflecting off the waxy pallor of his face and the terror in his eyes. But he said nothing, and looked again at the ground while allowing himself to be led away. They crossed King Street and avoided Main by walking to Green on a narrow foot path, then headed toward Fuller where they turned left. The moon passed behind a cloud and the night took on a glum oppressiveness.

As they passed Fred Webber's blacksmith just past Boone's corrals, one of the men in the lead threw up a hand and everyone came to a halt in front of the Bull's Head Market. They were standing across from Webber's large wooden structure used for raising wagons off the ground, and the man who had stopped the crowd called out, "A gallows frame. Now this is appropriate as hell, isn't it? I say instead of what we planned, we take this to the place the bastard killed Tom."

A cheer went up and a dozen men began lifting and dragging the heavy wooden frame a block further toward Lowe and Main as the moon again lighted the area. Joseph looked up at the frame, and his fate, only once. After a quick shudder he looked back down at the ground, absorbed in his private thoughts.

The reporter from the *Free Press* noticed this, and for a moment felt a wave of compassion for the prisoner. He also felt a stab of doubt that what they were doing was right. But he knew his single voice would change nothing, and possibly even get himself a beating, so he remained silent.

As they reached Main Street, it began snowing and large flakes stuck to the men's hats and shoulders. Any woman present during the march to the jail had by now disappeared. With a thump that echoed in the icy air, the gallows frame was dropped over Treloar's blood that was still evident beneath a thin coating of ice. Another cloud passed before the moon as Joseph was shoved beneath the frame, and the *Free Press* reporter thought of the lights of a stage play being lowered in preparation of the long-awaited performance.

Joseph clasped his hands to keep them from shaking, then looked up at the sky. He mouthed a silent prayer to a God he wasn't sure was even there to listen, and then dropped his eyes to the ground once more.

One of the two long ropes that had been wrapped around the windlass at the top of the frame was let down and a blacksmith fashioned a noose on the short end. After removing the coat covering Joseph's shoulders, the blacksmith placed the loop of rope over his head with the knot under Joseph's left ear. Someone objected and the blacksmith snapped, "I know what I'm doing. I did five of these in Aurora."

But Joseph immediately realized the placement would result in a torturously slow death. After the blacksmith turned his back and walked to the side of the crowd, Joseph reached up his shackled hands and moved the knot to the rear. A few men in the crowd who were talking among themselves saw this and became silent. A somber pall fell over the crowd as the seriousness of what they were doing settled on them. But it was too late for reflection, and the time for regret was not yet upon them, so they kept quiet. More than one man present pulled a flask or bottle out of a pocket and took a long swallow. When they heard the grating of the second rope swinging in the rising breeze, and realized how close they had come to lynching a woman, they took yet another swallow.

One of the leaders of the Committee uncoiled the length of the long rope now around Joseph's neck and ran it south down Main away from the frame. He was followed by a dozen specially chosen large and strong men from the committee who walked down the icy street and lined up along the rope's length. In military style unison they bent down and picked up the rope, holding it firmly in their hands as they faced away from the gallows frame.

"Better tie his legs," someone suggested.

When this was done, one of the leaders of the Committee asked Joseph, "Do you have anything to say for yourself?"

Joseph's lips barely moved. "No, nothing."

"You sure?"

"No, only..." He swallowed with difficulty and murmured, "Oh, God."

A loud voice called out, "Pull 'em!"

And they did. The dozen men holding the rope ran forward as fast as the patches of ice beneath their feet would allow. Joseph closed his eyes and was quickly lifted three feet from the ground. After only a few seconds and with one twitch of his legs, his life on this plane came to an end. A strong gust of wind blew snow at an angle while a man wound the rope around a side support of the frame. The limp body, no longer expressing the animation of a distinctive personality, began swinging to and fro like a heavy pendulum.

A group of twenty men, all masked and carrying shot guns, faced the crowd and formed a human shield in front of the body. The leader of the

Committee stepped forward and pinned a note to Joseph's shirt: "*All others take warning. Let no one cut him down. Bodie 601.*" The crowd was silent, with none of the usual raucous cheering that seemed to attend every event.

Into this silence broke a loud voice at the back of the crowd. "I'll give $100 if twenty men connected with this affair will publish their names in the paper tomorrow morning."

It was the voice of Pat Reddy. He might have represented the prosecution in the case, but he was known to be a righteous man and he was very angry.

A disgusted voice called out, "Ah, Reddy, shut the hell up."

A man near the body shouted, "Give him the rope, too."

Another in the crowd yelled, "Put him out. We don't need his type here."

Pat Reddy quickly disappeared. Shortly after, the leader of the Committee hollered, "All members return to your areas." The crowd quickly disbursed, with only a few armed men left to guard the body.

After half an hour had passed, Mr. Ward arrived with Dr. Deal who checked the body for signs of life. The doctor announced with formal ceremony, "I hereby declare that Joseph DeRoche is dead." The body was let down by Mr. Ward and the rope cut. After the men placed Joseph's body in a plain wooden coffin, it was loaded into the back of Mr. Ward's spring wagon for transport to his undertaking business. Walking behind were those who had guarded the body with their shotguns, now casually held under their arm and pointed at the ground as though returning from a day of hunting.

Men and women along the route peeked through windows while the bolder among them stood in doorways. The newspapers would report that later that night and into the next day people went to the gallows frame to cut pieces of the rope as a souvenir. The newspapers would also report that after Mr. Ward had left with his burden, the area where Treloar had been shot and Joseph DeRoche had just been hanged, was completely deserted.

Such was the assumption of the reporters. However, a young woman with long auburn hair and amber eyes stood across the street in the shadow of the Windsor Hotel and wept into a large silk handkerchief. She was overwhelmed more by the shock of such organized violence than by any sense of personal loss, but her heart was racing and her knees felt almost too weak to hold her up. With a quick glance at the empty gallows frame, she turned and walked north down Main, stumbling several times on the uneven boards.

Another woman stood not far away on Main just south of Lowe, at the side of a partially constructed building. She was a widow of only three days and her face was buried in her hands. With the gruesomeness of what had happened emblazoned on her mind and burning the edge of her conscience, she wished that she could go back in time and change some of her past choices. This woman did feel the heavy weight of loss, but little shock. She removed her hands from her face and quickly returned to the house on Mills Street that she had shared for two years with her late husband and within sight of the second floor windows of her deceased lover's brick house.

Her head aching, Amanda neared the Grand Central with a longing for the quiet sanctuary of her room. As she walked, she tried to understand how such a primitive reaction could overcome normally rational men and take place in a modern society. She knew that some would argue that they had been brought to this point by a court system that too often handed down judgments not befitting the crime. But was it not anarchy when society set itself above the law?

These thoughts were then followed by questions unbidden and despised. Had Joseph felt any regret after he had pulled the trigger? Had he been terrified at the end? Had he a last cogent thought? Did he suffer as the noose tightened? And would there be retribution for the 601 members?

There were no answers for these questions except the last one. There would be no consequences for those who participated in the lynching. The next day the Coroner's jury would declare that Joseph DeRoche met death *"at the hands of persons unknown."* Justice Newman would then declare that the defendant being dead, the trial was dismissed.

Interestingly, with all the various crimes and the attending notoriety during Bodie's boom years, it would be the only lynching in the town's history.

At the corner of King and Main, Amanda climbed the two steps up to the sidewalk in front of Wagner's Saloon, her feet dragging and the toe of a boot almost catching the top step. There was no loud music filling the area as there so often was, and she wondered if there were fewer or more drinkers inside, considering what had happened. When she looked to the closed frosted outer doors, she saw Roger standing in front of them.

She stood before him, her eyes cast down to her tightly clasped hands knotted in front of her waist, and confessed, "I saw it all."

"I know. I saw you following the crowd."

Her head jerked up and she stared at him in surprise. "Then why didn't you stop me?" There was a quiver of anguish in her voice. "Or at least try to talk me out of it?"

He met her eyes without flinching. "I thought about it. I wanted to. But you're a grown woman and can make your own decisions. And suffer the consequences of them, too. It's not my job to rescue you from yourself."

She tried to feel anger, but he had spoken the truth, and she grudgingly admired him for being so forthright. Later, she would realize that he was also respecting her independent spirit and maturity. At the moment, however, she was so full of disgust over what she had witnessed that she had no room for insight. She only wanted to block out the picture of Joseph hanging there with his legs twitching.

As though reading her thoughts, Roger held out his arms and without hesitation she walked into them. Cocooned by the security of his embrace, she laid her head on the lapel of his jacket and breathed in the scent of him. Half expecting to feel like a comforted child, instead she simply felt like a woman who knew in that moment that she was safe with a man she could trust. She was well aware that she never had, and never would have, felt like this with Joseph.

Roger walked Amanda to her room, glad it was too late for anyone to observe them. At the door he kissed her on the forehead and told her to get some sleep. After she had closed the door, he went directly to his own room across the street. She would never know how badly he had wanted to stop her from following the crowd. Or that he had for a while followed her at a distance with the intent of doing just that.

But it had occurred to him that what she might imagine could be worse than seeing the reality. Or she might think he was treating her like a child and never be able to forgive him for it because she could not realize what he had kept her from seeing. He would not gamble with her good regard of him. So he hadn't stopped her, and had instead made sure he would be available afterwards if she needed him.

The next morning, Johanna stood in the pre-dawn chill and awaited the first stage leaving with an uneasiness her pride wouldn't allow her to show. She was terrified that the Committee might change its mind about her. The stage was scheduled to head north to Carson City, but it was her plan that when it reached Virginia City, she would get off and lose herself in the still bustling mining town. She would in fact do such a thorough job of this that no one would ever hear of her again.

At this point a telegram was sent to Carson City informing the Sheriff that *"Judge Lynch has tried DeRoche and Farnsworth can be released."* It also warned that *"Farnsworth had better not return to Bodie, the prevailing sentiment regarding him being anything but favorable."*

As it so often did, the *Daily Free Press* weighed in with its opinion of Farnsworth's actions, calling him *"an officer who betrayed his official trust and allowed a murderer to escape. According to medical statistics Los Angeles, Santa Barbara, or some other Coast town has more health to the square inch than a place 8,500 feet above the sea."*

As soon as Farnsworth became aware of these comments, he wrote a letter to the newspaper, which was happily published in order to sell papers. Farnsworth claimed, *"I took the man away to save his life, and was as anxious as any man in Bodie to produce him; but deemed it best to leave while there was so much wild excitement over the matter, as no man's life is safe when a mob have become bent on his destruction."* Considering what had happened to Joseph, no one could deny the truth of his statement. In defense of the accusation that he took money from Joseph to let him go free, he also declared, *"I left Bodie without a dollar."*

Over the next few days while Joseph's body lay in Ward's mortuary, the temperature plummeted. Although many men braved the cold to view the body, no one claimed it. As the *Daily Free Press* stated so well, *"It is a rare instance when a man lives in a place for years and at his death no friend volunteers to see that his remains are properly buried."* The County paid for his burial.

Outside the fenced areas reserved for the good people, a grave was hacked out of the frozen earth a foot down to receive Joseph's body. The grave digger was told to make sure Joseph's bones would never mingle with those of decent people, so he wrapped it in a canvas shroud and mounded it over with dirt and brush, with no marker ever to be placed on it. From a distance it looked merely like a pile of debris.

As the temperature continued to drop, people who had to be on the street no longer conversed. They simply reported, complained or posed a question before quickly moving on in order to keep their blood circulating. Stove pipes in every business, house or shack puffed columns of smoke-- and wood piles on the hill were guarded by armed men.

Amanda was devastated when Mrs. Chestnut moved on to manage the Syndicate Boarding House. But the offer was more lucrative for her, so she felt it to be what she had to do. Amanda suspicioned that Mrs. Chestnut was also someone who needed a new challenge from time to time, and maybe the Grand Central had become too settled and refined for her tastes. She was replaced by a Mr. Stewart, whose formal ways Amanda could tell would take some getting used to.

The worst repercussion of the DeRoche aftermath was that Deputy Sheriff Kirgan lost his job as the town Constable and Jailer. He was, however, allowed to continue as the jail cook and as a deputy. Sheriff Taylor appointed Pat Roan as the new Constable and Jailer, since he had once been the Douglas County Sheriff in Nevada.

On Wednesday night of January 19, a group of about ninety men came together at the music hall calling themselves the Law and Order Association. Their purpose was to oppose unlawful proceedings by any future 601, and they pledged to aid and protect "the officers of the law in the discharge of their official duties".

In conflict with this the *Daily Free Press* tried to inject irony into their comments by calling the hanging "the sudden taking off of DeRoche by a mysterious collection of citizens." They also painted the picture of those against what happened as "the toughs, rounders, dead beats, pimps, opium fiends, four-time losers, broken down gamblers, garrotters, prostitutes," and such like. After the other newspapers had printed their editorials on the subject, the topic seemed to have been so well covered that the citizens simply moved on to other things.

It would have been bad enough for the town if the hanging of DeRoche had been the only distressing violence that month, but it wasn't to be. Every school yard and every town has its bully. Often the bully's ammunition is cruel teasing or sarcastic condescension, but in Bodie it was always more than that, because the bullies were drunk, angry and armed.

Dave Bannon had lost his job at the Standard and was once again drinking too much. Nothing Nellie said to him made a difference. He had become a perpetually irritated troublemaker who tried each night to drown his poor opinion of life in a bottle. In the middle of a January afternoon he attempted to do his drowning in the Dividend Saloon.

After a couple of hours, he got into an argument with someone, which in itself was not unusual. But Ed Ryan was an Irish miner simply wanting a drink after a long day at work, and at one time a good friend. For no particular reason, Dave drew his gun on Ed and then decided it would be more humiliating for Ed if he just pistol-whipped him instead of shooting him. Ed, however, saw the gun's handle coming for his head and drew his own gun from a pocket. But as he hesitated to shoot a friend, albeit a drunk and well-armed one, Dave struck him several times with his left fist.

Officer Monahan came from the far side of the room where Dave had not seen him, and tried to separate the two men, thinking it only a scuffle. Before he could affect peace, both men's guns exploded. Those who at one time had been Dave's friends watched him fall upon the barroom floor with blood gushing from his nose and mouth. In a few minutes he was dead.

Some men picked him up and carried him to Ward's while two other men went to tell Nellie. Soon after these men left the saloon, Ed Ryan staggered outside. Unfortunately, it was at that moment that Amanda was on her way to Mr. Boone's store. After a bloody Ed Ryan collapsed onto the sidewalk in front of her, blocking her progress, Amanda stopped and looked down at the heap at her feet.

"Oh for Christ's sake," she muttered in exasperation. Several people turned to her in surprise until they saw what lay at her feet.

For a moment she thought of returning to the hotel, but then realized that during such a violent week as this, she might never complete her errands if she allowed dying men and the shedding of blood to alter her plans. Wondering at the hardening of her nature, she stepped off the sidewalk, avoided a patch of ice on the street, and continued on her way.

Meanwhile, Ed's friends gathered around him wondering why he had fallen onto the sidewalk, thinking that Dave's bullet had missed him. Only when they saw the blood from his side oozing onto the planks did they realize that Dave's bullet had indeed hit its mark. Several men carried Ed to a doctor where the bullet was removed, after which he began a long recovery. A collection was taken up to pay for his medical and other bills until he could return to work, but everyone knew it was more a reward in appreciation for removing Dave from their midst. Ed on the other hand felt terrible about what he had been forced to do. The incident haunted him for the rest of his life.

Nellie Bannon was distraught almost beyond her ability to cope. Over the next week it took the almost constant ministrations of Cherry Wilson, Charlotte and Amanda to keep her focused enough to eat and see to her personal hygiene. Twice a day they gave her a teaspoon of whatever the doctor had given her in a dark brown bottle, a good portion of which was probably laudanum.

On the fifth morning following the shooting, Amanda was stretching out her stiff back after spending the night on a small settee in Nellie's parlor when Nellie called her into the bedroom. She was in bed, propped up on pillows. "I must thank you for all you have done for me." She spoke in a stilted, formal manner while looking down at her hands plucking at the edge of the quilt. "However, it's time that I begin to accept what has happened. For that, I need to grieve in private."

"I understand."

"I thought you would." She glanced up for a moment and then back down. "Please let the other women know that I would appreciate being left alone."

"Yes, I'll do that." With that, Nellie lay down with her back to Amanda.

There was nothing for it but to leave the small house. On her way home, Amanda stopped by Charlotte's house and then that of the Wilsons. It would be spring before any of the women would see a thinner and paler Nellie again, so cloistered a life would she lead for the rest of that winter.

The hanging of DeRoche and the killing of Dave Bannon acted like a purgative for the citizen's long-held frustration over the town's state of criminal chaos. The Bodie bad men took measure of the town's mood and realized that sometimes consequences can be lethal, and that maybe it was not a good time to tempt the 601 group. For the month that followed there was a minimum of even minor offences.

The best news for many people was that Vince Perry was definitely out of danger. He was now walking without assistance up and down the street in front of his house twice a day when the weather allowed. He quickly overcame the residual weakness of having been in bed so long, and Charlotte was finally able to leave him alone in order to run errands. With Amanda's companionship and good humor, she also reminded herself that there really was a world beyond the Perry house. At least to Charlotte, Bodie was looking pretty fine--snow and mud and all.

CHAPTER 12
FEBRUARY/MARCH, 1881

Mr. M. Y. Stewart, the new manager of the Grand Hotel, must have been present at the funeral of Treloar at the Miners' Union Hall. He must also have believed the nasty comment from the miner Amanda had slapped that day, because at the beginning of February, Mr. Stewart stopped Amanda before she could report to work in the dining room.

"Would you care to step into my office?"

"Certainly."

He placed a straight-backed wooden chair in front of his dark, handsomely carved desk and eased himself into a large leather chair behind it. His spine was as rigid and unbending as the look on his face as he folded his hands on the polished wooden surface before him.

Looking at Amanda with his eyes squinted to the size of black raisins, he began, "Miss Blake, I've called you into my office to discuss your living arrangements. I thought you might want to continue your habitation elsewhere. Somewhere more befitting your social status."

Amanda sat in shocked silence trying to understand what he was talking about. Then it came home to her. "Are you saying that you believe what that awful man at the Treloar funeral said about me? That my behavior with Joseph was less than proper?"

The man had the grace to blush. "Well, I saw you at some dances with him."

"I assure you that all I did with him was dance, and little of that because it was so soon after my father's passing." The man saw the fire in her eyes and heard the sharpness of her tone, and began to wish he had held his tongue. "We also disagreed on points of correct behavior and I had him bring me home from one of those social occasions when I saw him ogling Johanna. Did you know that?"

"Well, no..."

"Of course you didn't," she accused him as she leaned forward in her earnestness, "because you know nothing of the facts. I barely knew Mr.

DeRoche." She felt that using his first name might give credence to his opinions, so she kept her references to him formal. "I will admit that Mr. DeRoche approached me several times, but I rebuffed his advances, having heard from Mrs. Perry that he had a questionable reputation."

"So the man at the funeral didn't know you?"

She drew herself up tighter than even he was, and in her most haughty tones told him, "Certainly not. The only gentleman I claim as a friend in Bodie is Mr. Murphy at Mr. Wagner's establishment. And he soundly thrashed a young man who overstepped the bounds of propriety with me."

Mr. Stewart now remembered other comments he had heard about Amanda from some of the men around town, which was that she was a cold and unbending prude. Admitting to himself that maybe he should have paid more attention to *those* comments, he said, "Oh, I see. Yes, I know Roger."

The door of the office opened and that very gentleman stood in the opening. "Oh, sorry Stewart. I didn't know you were busy."

Mr. Stewart stood up and motioned to Roger. "No, no. Come in, please. I was just talking to Miss Blake about her living arrangements and whether she might not be happier elsewhere."

The immediate and fierce frown on Roger's face did not go unnoticed by Mr. Stewart. Roger turned to Amanda. "Do you want to live somewhere else?"

Her reply was straight to the point as she looked up at Roger. "No. But I think Mr. Stewart is of the opinion that I was an intimate friend of Joseph's, and that I have social habits not welcome at such a fine hotel as this."

Roger looked at Mr. Stewart with a raised brow and tight lips before turning back to Amanda. His voice tightly controlled, he told her, "I see you're dressed for work and so you probably want to get started."

Suddenly Mr. Stewart was all gushing kindness. "Yes, my dear, why don't you do that?" Amanda nodded and meekly left the men to talk over her fate. Although she would have preferred to fight her own battles, this was too important and Roger too willing to step in on her behalf, for her to object.

Fifteen minutes later, Mr. Stewart approached Amanda in the kitchen by the coffee urn. "I must apologize for my hasty jump to conclusion, Miss Blake."

She nodded. "This whole business about the murder and trial and the 601 has created a very trying and confusing time for us all."

"You're most gracious." He came close to bowing before catching himself and instead said, "I can see why Roger thinks so highly of you. Please give no further thought to moving."

"Thank you." As the man walked away, she smiled to herself and wondered what Roger had said to make Mr. Stewart change his attitude so fully.

A man called out to her that he would like another order of Mono Lake gull eggs, and she hurried to the kitchen. He often left a small gratuity for his waitresses, unlike some, so the waitresses were eager to please him.

That month the Lent Combination Shaft was being prepared to go deeper in the hope of hitting a rich vein. Two of the pieces of equipment necessary to accomplish this weighed fifteen tons each. Since no wagon was known to be able to carry such weight, a logging truck had been rigged to accommodate the equipment. It took two months for it to travel from Carson, through Bridgeport and into Bodie. The incredibly heavy machinery came through town on the giant logging wagon fitted with steel straps to hold down the equipment, and pulled by 56 horses and mules.

People watched in a state of astonishment as it moved snail-slow through town down Green and up to the Lent shaft. As fascinating as this process and the equipment, it was what it represented that brought people out to witness the procession. What they were witnessing was hope on wheels, showing optimism for a solid future of prosperous operation. And if it was possible at one mine, maybe it would bode well for some of the others. But the "others" were not the famous and wealthy Standard, and in time this reality would have to be faced.

At the end of February it was reported in the papers that detective Davis had fulfilled his promise, even tracking Haight to Connecticut in order to do it. He had returned to Bodie with the escaped man in custody, much to the bail bondsman's relief. The trial was set for March 23 at the Bridgeport Courthouse.

Snow and ice was not enough to cool the perpetually hot temper of Billy Deegan, who whiled away his off hours from the Standard by drinking and gambling. On February 22 it was both of these activities that found him in the back room of The Snug Saloon across the street from where Standard Avenue meets Main.

Billy was playing cards with Dan Weir, the Goodshaw engineer, along with Pat Desmond, Bill Cunningham and Andy Donahue. Of course, he couldn't drink for long without getting into an argument with someone and this night it was Weir. Deegan rose up and smacked Weir across the face with his Colt Lightening when Weir said something that upset him, and the lame Mr. Donahue took Weir's side by clubbing Deegan with his heavy cane.

Although Deegan was stunned by the blow, he was able to pull his gun and shoot Donahue in the groin, dropping him to the floor as blood gushed from the wound. Weir, his cheek dripping blood, fired his gun at Deegan and missed. It was at this point that officers Richard O'Malley and Jack Roberts ran into the room. Seeing Weir standing over Deegan with his gun drawn and Donahue off to the side lying in a pool of his own blood, they unfortunately misinterpreted the scene. O'Malley turned his revolver loose on Weir, although after a couple of shots that only nicked Weir's clothing, he stopped.

When the officers took the time to find out what had actually taken place from Weir, they discovered that Deegan had only a minor wound. They also found that Pat Desmond had lost part of an earlobe when a stray bullet hit him while running for the exit.

Donahue's life was saved by the deft work of Dr. Henry Robertson, and after three days of touch and go, he began a steady recovery.

After all of this shooting and blood-letting, Billy Deegan did not end up in custody of the law. However, recalling his long history of rowdy behavior, the *Daily Free Press* was irate and ran an editorial making their ire abundantly clear. It was this article that Charlotte and Amanda, while Vince went for a walk, discussed over tea as Charlotte read it out loud in her parlor.

"It says here that '*The officers displayed a great deal of stupidity on Tuesday night in allowing those engaged in the shooting in the Snug Saloon to escape from their clutches. They would have exercised some judgment if they had marched them to the lockup. As yet none of them have been taken in. It is said that a warrant has been issued for the arrest of Deegan, but Kirgan has not succeeded in finding him. It is remarkable with what vigilance our officers avoid arresting a man after he has committed a murderous act. There are a great many officers in town, more than can be counted on one hand, yet they are not up to business.*" Charlotte looked up at Amanda. "Oh, dear. The officers won't appreciate this."

"They have a big job of keeping peace in this town, that's for sure. Where is Deegan now do you suppose?" Charlotte shrugged and shook her head.

In fact, he had left Bodie and headed to Tombstone, Arizona. There he would get into a fight with another police officer, formerly of Bodie. In 1883 he would return to Bodie and would twice be arrested for disturbing the peace. In March of 1884 Deegan would face a walk-down with Felix Donnelly on Main Street where nine shots would be exchanged and yet both men would walk away. But in Bodie, as elsewhere, for some people old grudges have a way of festering instead of fading. In July of 1884, while Deegan would be helping extinguish a small fire in the block between Boone's Store and Kingsley's Stable, Donnelly would walk up behind Deegan and shoot him in the back several times. His revenge would be short-lived. One of the deputies, while attempting to disarm him, would have to shoot him. He would die almost immediately.

A railroad coming to a town in the West was always an important and exciting event, portending increased prosperity for businesses and growth to the town. For Bodie it was no different. Work was set to begin soon on the Bodie Railroad and Lumber Company's narrow gauge rail line that promised to bring an abundance of cord wood and lumber into the town from Mono Mills south of Mono Lake. It was being speculated if the rail would travel along the west shore and therefore develop freighting business from the Jordon, Homer and Tioga Mining Districts—or if it would travel on the east side of the lake, and therefore run more easily to the hills where the mines were located. It was not meant to be a passenger line, so the eastern route was favored.

The first Sunday of March offered briskly cold but sunny weather after weeks of snow that had started falling February 3. Many people were on the street enjoying this respite of temperate weather and paths of trammeled snow while bundled in coats and heavy boots. But at least they were able to make their way down sidewalks freshly cleared of the snow, now pushed into a four foot continuous and hard-packed mound along the edges of Main. Occasional slices were cut through to allow crossing to the other side.

While out for a walk, Roger and Amanda enjoyed the markets filled with fresh supplies of goods after several freight wagons had managed to get through from Bridgeport two days before. They had earlier gone ice skating on the frozen Syndicate ponds, laughing at their clumsy efforts to remain upright. Eventually expressing gratitude that there had always been one of them on their feet in order to assist the other, and not wanting to tempt Fate, they decided to return to town and visit a bakery for something sweet and hot.

Their outing to the frozen ponds had been prompted by a poem published in the *Free Press* by General Kittrell. In a society where it was scandalous for a woman to lift her skirts above the laces of her high top boots, even to clear the mud on a street, the poem was viewed as somewhat racy. But since it was also considered clever, it became immediately popular.

To Mary
Mary had some little skates.
he, with them, went out to slide.
She slipped, and therefore had a fall
As also did her pride.
Her heels flew up—her head went down
And struck upon the ice
Displaying both her striped hose
Which surely was not nice.
She jumped up quickly on her feet
And said she did not care.
But on those hose, a card was seen
Marked fifteen cents a pair.

On their return to the hotel, Roger stopped at a Chinese fruit stand selling mostly apples and bought them each a bright red orb for their later consumption. They walked on while resisting the enticing aromas wafting from the chop houses and restaurants, the other bakery, and several houses. They laughed at the puffs of steam that escaped the hot interior of the laundry each time the front door opened, passed the gym where people were cheering a wrestling match, and purchased a newspaper from the Bodie News agent.

A small pack of mongrel dogs ran past them as they crossed the street and Amanda commented with a sly smile, "If there were three other men nearby, might not one of you propose a wager as to which dog will reach the corner first?"

"My dear, I would propose it if there were only one other interested."

It was a relaxed afternoon where they enjoyed the cold fresh air and greeted in passing those they had not seen for weeks. Although a few words were exchanged with Mr. Boone where he was sweeping the sidewalk in front of his store, and with Mr. Kingsley out front of his stable shoveling it clear of horse droppings, neither conversation was for more than a few minutes. Only by moving did one keep warm.

Deputy Sheriff John Kirgan passed them heading south in his light rig that was much like a racing sulky. They exchanged a wave as his spirited gray horse tossed its head and pranced in its exuberance at being out after weeks of confinement.

Kirgan had lately been reappointed to his old Constable position, and most of the citizens acted as though they had forgotten the events of January and Kirgan's part in them. His years of faithful service to the town and his ability to handle confrontations between people with calm restraint and authority was important to a citizenry who so often met with violence. The majority of people in Bodie had learned to live for the moment and turn to the best people available to assure peace and lawfulness, and Kirgan certainly fit the bill.

Amanda and Roger stopped to watch a small group of boys playing at the edge of the road where they had packed down the snow. They were tossing a ball and trying to catch it before it fell to the ground while laughing and shouting and thoroughly enjoying themselves. One of the young lads missed the throw in his direction and the ball rolled into the street, rolling in front of Kirgan's on-coming horse and rig. The already over-wrought animal screamed, reared and lurched forward before continuing south down Main at a reckless speed. Kirgan yelled "Whoa" at the top of his voice but instead of stopping, the horse seemed spurred on by his shouts.

The buggy hit an icy patch and swung to the side, the wheels hitting the edge of a ditch across from the Mono County Bank. It turned over, the horse broke free, and Kirgan was thrown out and down with terrific force onto the frozen water of the ditch near one of the hydrants of the town's fire prevention system.

Roger and a number of other men raced to his aid, only to find him with a deep cut over his right eye and unconscious. They got him to a doctor's office immediately, and for the next three days Doctors Rogers and Walker cared for him through his days of delirium, an infection that set in on the 10th, and a coma that overcame him the next day. The newspapers reported that the doctors held out little hope for his recovery, his head trauma being so severe.

An unexpected storm hit the area hard. Business at the saloons dropped off and were visited mainly only by those who lived within easy walking distance. The shops saw little business except from the hardiest of the miners who stopped on their way home for wives who refused to leave the house. Then the school closed and some of the smaller mines did the same. No wagons or rigs broke the fresh deep snow on Main.

The first night of the storm Roger shut down his stand and joined Amanda in her room where they flaunted propriety and brought dinner up to the room. Amanda carried the food in her shopping basket while Roger carried an armload of wood. After enjoying a bottle of wine with their meal, they decided to snuggle together in the chair next to the stove, the excuse being that it was the only truly warm place in the room.

Roger was both surprised and pleased when Amanda showed no reluctance at returning his kisses, and even allowing the familiarity of his hands beneath her shawl. This happy state lasted until Roger's imagination and desires came near to tempting him toward more forward suggestions. He then stood up, allowing Amanda to slide onto the seat of the chair and looking up at him in surprise.

"I think it best that I make my way home before the street can't be crossed. There's no telling how long this storm will last."

"That would be an excuse for you to stay here then." She blushed when she heard the echo of her words, but it was too late to take them back so she waited to see their effect.

Roger sighed, wanting more than anything to toss his hat on the table and sweep her up in his arms. But instead he said, "I don't think Mr. Stewart would be pleased at that, even if I slept somewhere else in the hotel."

"Why?"

"Because I made it very clear to him what my intentions were toward you, and how honorable they are. If he thinks that has changed, you had better be wearing a ring."

Amanda suddenly stood up and began stacking the dishes from the meal into the basket, keeping her back to him. "You're no doubt correct. You can take these dishes down to the kitchen on your way out."

Roger was puzzled at her sudden willingness for him to leave. "I hope I've not offended you. I would much rather stay."

She turned to him with sincere surprise. "And I'd like you to stay, but I'd completely forgotten the danger of the storm, and almost forgotten myself in the moment." They smiled at each other with understanding, and then he picked up the basket. Planting a quick kiss on Amanda's cheek, he reluctantly went downstairs.

But it had been more than the propriety of the situation that had motivated her encouragement of his departure. She only hoped Roger was not aware of that.

On the 12th of the month one of the most powerful snow storms thus far in the season hit the town. It snowed off and on for several days, and each day fewer and fewer people braved their way into town.

Although Kirgan seemed to rally a little early on the 15th, later in the day he began vomiting up blood and his wounds were giving out a bad odor. Finally, on March 16 the famed 53 year old Bodie lawman passed away.

His funeral, sponsored by the Society of Pacific Coast Pioneers, was attended by almost everyone in the town despite the snow. The streets were congested with wagons and buggies carrying people as close to the cemetery as they could find parking. So many people wanted to eulogize the respected lawman that room inside the cemetery fence was soon filled to capacity. Even a number of miscreants who had spent time as a guest at "Hotel de Kirgan" uttered words in praise of his fair treatment and generous meals. As one such recent guest put it, "He made sure there was plenty of wood for the cell stoves, no matter the cost." Few could think of higher praise to be awarded during a Bodie winter.

Mr. B. B. Jackson, President of the Pacific Coast Pioneers, told those gathered, *"John Kirgan was one who was faithful in the end and died in the harness. Thirty-three years ago the deceased and some of us now present fought side by side for our countries in the battles of Mexico, and often mingled together here in California, from the good old days of '49 up to the present time."* He continued on in his eloquent style until hundreds of feet were numb and people were showing an eagerness to leave and find someplace warm.

When Mr. Jackson finally thanked the Fire Department, various civic societies, and officers of the County for their kind attendance and assistance, everyone perked up and hoped for the end of his oration. A Resolution drawn up by the Society was read out, proclaiming at one point, *"As a soldier, he was brave; as a public official faithful, and as a man, he was all that the hearty sons of '49 and '50 have proven themselves to be."*

Men who knew him well nodded and more than a few dashed a sudden wetness from an eye.

Amanda and Charlotte stood together unescorted since Roger had to work and Dr. Deal wouldn't let Vince out into the cold, even though Vince declared he was feeling fine. So the two women attended the sad occasion unescorted, listened to the speeches, and exchanged greetings with others they knew. After returning to town, Charlotte invited Amanda to join her at the Excelsior Restaurant just south of Green.

Once the tea was in front of them and the waitress had left, Charlotte sighed and said, "Vince has improved so much that he's starting to get on my nerves, always being underfoot."

"That's wonderful," Amanda chirped before adding, "in its way."

"Yes," Charlotte smiled. "But it's becoming clear that he'll have some lingering effects, and this winter has been really hard on him." She looked at Amanda and placed her hand on her wrist. "We've decided it will be our last one here."

Amanda stared. "You're moving away?" She felt a sick sinking in her stomach and tried to hold back the sting of tears.

"Yes." Charlotte patted Amanda's arm. "But not right away. In fact, we probably won't leave until April or May when all the snow is gone along the roads south. Vince has to sell the warehouse first anyway, and the economy isn't the best here now."

"South? Where will you go?"

"The Owens Valley."

"To Lone Pine where Emily and Frank live?"

"Yes, although I'm not telling Emily yet, so no hints if you write to her." After a moment's hesitation, Charlotte continued with her cheeks suddenly rosier than just from the cold. "There's something else. I'm expecting."

Joy flooded through Amanda. "Oh, Charlotte, that's wonderful."

"It's a true miracle, isn't it?" Charlotte's eyes danced with happiness.

Amanda giggled. "I guess Vince has been feeling like his old self for a few weeks now." The two women laughed and blushed, and laughed some more. People nearby in the dining room glanced at them and then away again, unable to resist smiling at such a show of unrestrained joy.

On Wednesday, March 23, the first trial was held among the last bit of construction at the new Mono County Courthouse in Bridgeport, with Honorable R. M. Briggs presiding. Those in Bodie were interested because the trial was of George Morton, with the recently recaptured Haight set to testify against him. George Morton had, according to the Grand Jury in Bridgeport, shown great audacity in stealing bullion from Bodie's Standard Consolidated Mine. Since the prosecution consisted of District Attorney W. O. Parker and Bodie attorney Pat Reddy, the Standard was convinced of its success.

Roger, in Bridgeport to visit a friend, attended the historic first trial at the white two-story Courthouse. It was certainly grand in appearance, with its vaulted ceilings sixteen feet tall, eight offices downstairs, two fireproof vaults, storerooms and a pump room. From the lobby below, the ten foot wide Spanish cedar staircase led up to two superior court rooms, judges' chambers and a jury room. People in town bragged about the 3,000 gallon water tank on the roof for fire hydrants and indoor plumbing.

With all of this modern construction, on the street behind was still the small unimproved stone jail. Both of these buildings would be in evidence well over a hundred years later, although only the Courthouse would still be in use. The old stone jail would serve as a sharp reminder of how harsh consequences can be.

As Roger walked up the path to the Courthouse, he stopped to watch some men pounding into the ground a large post near the front corner of the building. It was obvious that at least one wagon had crossed the open area in front of the building too close to the stonework. The post would force any wagons heading for the street next to the courthouse to keep further away. Eventually, the town would place a fence around the property, and this would keep meandering sheep from grazing the weeds.

Upon returning to Bodie, Roger took Amanda to supper at Delmonico's and shared with her what had occurred. "The chief witness for the prosecution, wily ole Haight, took the stand and almost immediately denied what he'd told the Grand Jury. He declared that he had implicated George Morton simply because he was at the time angry with him. This meant that the charges against Morton had to be dropped."

"Oh, my goodness. Everyone must have been very unhappy about that. It was such a certainty that he was guilty."

"Reddy certainly wasn't happy. The angry diatribe he unleashed at Haight outside the courtroom in the hallway was something to behold. Afterwards, Reddy saw me by the door and came over to say hello. I told him I'd buy him a drink and we left the courthouse. As we walked down the path to the road, we passed Morton as he was telling someone that after spending eight months in jail awaiting trial, he was destitute with no place to live. When we reached the end of the walkway, Reddy hesitated a moment and then told me to wait there. He walked back up the path to Morton and said a few words."

"Was he angry at him too?"

"On the contrary. When he shook Morton's hand, I noticed something pass between them. Just as Reddy reached me, Morton looked down at a $20 gold piece in his hand. Tears ran down his cheeks."

"I've only seen his harder side, but I've heard people say Pat Reddy is a very generous and compassionate man."

"It's true. I've known him to help out several families when the breadwinner was laid up with an injury." Roger chuckled. "He's been quoted several times as having passed judgment on some of his fellow attorneys who he said had come West to, as he put it, sharpen their claws on the rough edges of $20 gold pieces."

"You've been in his offices, haven't you? I hear they're very grand."

"Oh, they are. They take up the entire top floor of the Molinari Building on the triangle." The triangle block also held Moinet's hair salon, Kramer & Harris Tailors, and the Sacramento Market. "The streets around them might be drab and dirty, but it's like walking into another world when you enter his offices. He's got thick rugs scattered over the polished wood floor, leather chairs, dark wood desks, and kerosene lamps with frosted globes. The prints on the walls are framed in carved wood with gold-leafing, and the smell of the place is of beeswax, leather and expensive men's cologne. It's welcoming and complementary to the mine owners and stock executives, and appropriately intimidating to the petty thug being graced with Reddy's representation."

"All that must have cost him a pretty hunk of change."

"He can afford it. He charges well for his services when the client can afford it so he can charge little or nothing to those who can't."

"Doesn't he also have ownership in some mines?"

"Yes, that too." Roger smiled and shook his head. "He's one of the most successful men I've ever known, yet still with a good dose of humanity left."

"And tough too. Look how he stood up to the crowds during Joseph's debacle."

After a moment's hesitation, Roger said, "I wasn't sure you'd ever want to refer to that."

Amanda sighed. "Well, it happened. I can't change that. Hopefully, at least a few people learned something from it."

"Like what?"

"The criminally inclined might learn that very few escape and if they do, then when they're caught the punishment will be terrible. Some on the 601 committee might now regret their actions and be willing to think things through more thoroughly in the future. And I'm pretty sure whoever the jailer is will think twice about hiding a prisoner outside the jail."

Roger looked at her and smiled. "I can tell you've been thinking about this. And here I was afraid to raise the subject. Women are always surprising me with their resilience to life."

When he walked Amanda to her door that night, he did more than kiss her hand. He lifted her chin with his fingertips and kissed her firmly on the lips, holding her close so he could feel every curve of her body. When he pulled back and saw her smile, before she could say anything, he turned and walked down the hallway. Amanda went into her room and began to ponder his intentions, still unsure what she wanted them to be.

A few days later Amanda was walking down the sidewalk toward Green and passed a woman who looked familiar sitting on one of the benches in front of a shop. It was Dona, the young Bonanza Street resident that had visited Roger when he was injured. Amanda stopped in front of her and looked at her with concern, as the woman was doubled over in obvious agony. When Dona looked up her face was ashen white.

"You're Dona, a friend of Roger Murphy's, aren't you?"

"Yes," she managed with a groan.

"I'm Amanda Blake. I'm also a friend of Roger's. You don't look well."

Dona hesitated and then said, "I'm not."

Amanda lowered her voice and asked, "Bad monthlies?"

"No." Dona saw only compassion and kindness in Amanda's face and let her words out with a rush. "I'm bleeding bad. I had an abortion yesterday."

Amanda tried hard not to show how shocked she was, although Cherry had told her of such a thing. "Here in Bodie?"

"Yes. One of the Chinese women does it for the girls on Bonanza Street. They've always recovered well. But I think something has gone wrong with me."

"Then we need to get you to a good doctor. We'll go to Dr. Deal. He's close and supposed to be fair."

Dona was too scared to object and by leaning on Amanda they managed to slowly walk to the doctor's office. Not, however, without a good number of shocked stares watching them pass along.

Amanda waited in the outer office after the doctor met them at the door and helped Donna into his examining room. The doctor was a well-groomed middle-aged man with a kind wife and several well-behaved children. As he dealt with the violent and seamy sides of the town, he every day thanked God for the normalcy of his private life.

After half an hour, the doctor came out and sat next to Amanda in one of the waiting room chairs. "Is she family or a friend of yours?"

"We have a mutual friend. She's a young woman alone and in trouble, so I took it upon myself to help her," she summarized defiantly. "Is she going to be okay?"

He sighed, and in that sigh was the resignation of years living amid the foibles and failings of human nature. "I'm not sure. She's lost a lot of blood. I've packed her and given her some laudanum. But there's something else wrong with her besides a botched abortion."

When he hesitated, she asked firmly, "What?"

"She has an advanced case of a disease that's transferred by people who have…well, lain with one another."

"Which disease?" Kassy had told her about these diseases and had said some were more serious than others, and harder to cure.

"Syphilis." Thinking that he was talking to a woman with knowledge of the world, he relaxed his reticence to discuss such a subject, something he would not have done if he had known Amanda was unmarried. "I'm afraid it happens all too often to these women, and they usually try to cure it with silly homemade remedies. Meanwhile, they're just passing it on to their clients."

"Don't they use the protection of some kind of barrier?"

"Some do, but some just think a thorough scrubbing is enough."

"Then why don't they stop working while they're contagious?"

"The poor ladies can't afford to stop. If they can't make their rent, they're kicked out into the street with no way to make a living." He looked around his waiting room and then back at Amanda. "Sometimes they simply take an overdose of something, or take their life in some other way."

Amanda shook her head sadly. "Well, do what you have to and don't worry about your bill. If she can't afford to pay it, I will when I come to check on her tomorrow."

"That's very generous of you, Mrs. I'm sorry, but I didn't get your last name."

"Blake. And it's Miss Blake."

The doctor reddened and his eyes grew larger. "You've risked your reputation for a strange woman you don't know?"

Amanda smiled. "Yes. I know another woman who once did the same thing, and I learned from her act of kindness that *there for the grace of God go I* is not a hollow thought."

The doctor nodded his head and opened the door for her. She hadn't bothered to tell him that she would get the money from Roger, but she knew he would want to help. She wondered if he had ever been intimate with Dona and might therefore be infected. She also wondered how on earth one asks a man such a thing.

She hurried to the hotel to meet Roger as they had arranged. At the end of their meal, as the waitress poured coffee into their cups, Amanda mustered her courage and told Roger about Dona. He looked at her for a long moment before speaking.

"You're a very unusual woman."

"Why? Most women are compassionate."

"Yes, but not all women would be willing to risk their reputation to help a prostitute."

"She's also a woman. And there are precedents for it in this town." She then told him about Emily Eastman and her friend Kitty. "It's not only that she's a friend of yours. If I hadn't had the money from the sale of the house and people willing to see that I had a place to live and a job, I could easily have ended up on Bonanza Street."

Roger found no words in response. He knew she was right, and the thought of such a thing was so abhorrent to him that it made his stomach lurch.

"You said Dona is at Dr. Deal's?"

"Yes."

"Then I'll go see him in the morning and pay him."

"You'll let me know how Dona is doing?"

"Of course."

Roger came to Amanda's room late the next morning, and she could tell from the look on his face that the news was not good. She led him to the table in the corner and sat across from him.

"What did the doctor say?"

He removed his hat, tossed it onto the table and ran his fingers through his long hair. "She didn't make it."

"But...but that's so fast."

"She was already weak from the disease. And the doctor couldn't stop the hemorrhaging. She bled to death."

Amanda felt an unexplainable sense of loss. Sadness and anger poured through her in alternating waves. She was filled with an impotent rage that such things were part of the world they lived in, and could rob such a pretty young woman of her life. Tears fell down her cheeks.

She hurried to her dressing table and groped in a drawer for a handkerchief. After she had wiped her face and stopped the tears with a shuddered breath, Roger came to her and took her in his arms. He picked her up and carried her to the chair in the corner by the window, sitting down with her on his lap. With her arms around his neck, she laid her head on his shoulder and for the next ten minutes they didn't move.

Finally she told him, "I imagine your leg is numb by now."

"I don't care," he mumbled into her hair.

"You will when you try to get up and walk." She climbed off his lap and sat across from him on the corner of the bed. "Roger, how good a friend were you to Dona?"

He looked at her with a puzzled frown. Then his brow cleared and he smiled with understanding. "Not very good at all. One of the other dealers, a good friend of mine, was a very good friend to her. When he left town, I kept an eye on her." He leaned forward and picked up one of her hands. "That's all."

She colored and told him, "Well, I had to ask."

"Yes, I see that." He stood up, tested his leg, and told her, "I'd best get to work. John Wagner likes me, but his patience only extends so far."

After a long, lingering embrace and kiss, Roger left her. She walked to the window, thought about the unfairness and hardness of life, and shed a few more tears before changing her dress in preparation for work.

By the end of the month Bodie was no longer wondering about the route of the narrow gauge railroad into town. It had been decided that it would run out from the eastern verge of Bodie, travel around the eastern edge of Mono Lake past the Warm Springs stage station, and then run in an almost straight line to the south for about ten miles. It would end at a turnaround at the railroad's 12,000 acre timber forests and the new sawmill, ready to process every tree in the forest if necessary.

The builders of this God-send to the town were Seth and Dan Cook from San Francisco, H. M. Yerington of Carson City, Robert Graves voted President, and William Willis of San Francisco as Secretary. Construction, at a cost of $400,000, was to begin at once with $1,000,000 of capital stock backing the project.

Meanwhile, even with the news of this exciting and dynamic development, people who could not find work continued to pack up their belongings and leave the town.

CHAPTER 13
APRIL, 1881

In a corner of the dining room, after Amanda's shift had ended mid-afternoon, she and Roger sat in companionable silence while drinking coffee. Empty plates with the evidence of coconut cake had been pushed aside and Amanda was wishing she could strip off her shoes and rub her feet. She settled for picking at stray strands of coconut on her plate and feeling replete, while being happy to be with Roger on a fine spring day. The snow was melting fast and now only the nights were bitter cold, with the days ten to twenty degrees above freezing.

Each time she was with Roger, there was a greater degree of comfortable ease between them, with their laughter and conversation no longer constrained or self-conscious. Amanda felt she could ask him anything, and when she had questioned him about his reasons for settling in Bodie, he had responded readily.

"From a purely practical standpoint, the population explosion in '78 offered someone in my profession a steady stream of customers. But beyond that, Bodie appeals to me in ways I find difficult to define. There's an atmosphere here. Maybe it's what hope feels like, because let's face it, every day hundreds of people are hoping for a big strike in one of the mines. Or at least hoping that none of them shut down."

"The violence never bothers you?"

"Of course it does." His shrug was eloquent. "But I've learned to accept what I can't change and focus on the good things here."

With her elbow on the table and her chin braced by her hand, she looked around the room at the rag-tag bunch of teamsters, businessmen, miners, and their families, who were finishing late afternoon meals.

Thinking of the cold barely past and the probability of it recurring at least briefly before the warmth of summer, Amanda asked Roger, "Do you think people living in the tropics have any idea the amount of courage it takes to just get out of bed in the morning when it's below zero?"

"It's something one has to experience, I think. I do know that if ever there's a contest for dressing the quickest in the morning, I think I just might win."

Amanda laughed and, trying to make some kind of positive comment, said, "And they miss the pleasure of holding a hot mug of coffee between hands to warm them."

Roger smiled wistfully. "Ah, that first hot swallow that runs down past the tonsils like molten lava over ice. It's the best part of winter mornings."

"Charlotte once told me that people think she likes to bake, but it's really that she just wants to keep the heat up in the stove in a way that justifies using all that wood."

They laughed together, but mostly at themselves for this indulgence of complaint.

Roger leaned back and stretched, "Then there's summer. It's difficult to believe how hot it can get here in the summer."

"Yes, all four weeks of it," she laughed.

"Unless a freak storm comes in and we don't have even that."

"Someone told me that snow can fall here even in July."

"Not every year, of course. But it has."

Men at an adjoining table were loudly discussing the Carson & Colorado Railroad arriving in a small settlement in Nevada known as Hawthorne. Roger was unashamedly listening, so Amanda also began paying attention. The conversation was part pride and part complaint, since the rails were once again bypassing Bodie. But there was now a major wagon road to the small rail town of Hawthorne, with construction having started the previous September. It would eliminate the necessity of having to travel to Aurora before heading north, but this meant an even faster decline for that town.

"What route exactly does this wagon road take?" Amanda asked Roger, wondering if she had passed over at least part of it on her way to Bodie.

"Let's see." He thought a moment. "It starts about ten miles northeast of here near the old Antelope and Del Monte mills where the Aurora and Bodie Toll Road turns south. It goes north along Bodie Creek through Del Monte Canyon, then joins the Carson-Aurora stage road at Five-Mile House near Fletcher's Station, then turns east onto the stage road to Columbus. About five miles later it branches toward the northeast and heads over a narrow pass. It descends along a creek and out onto the desert and to just south of Walker Lake."

"I guess I passed over it at Five Mile House." After several moments she sighed and poked at the crumbs on her plate. "I thought when I arrived here that it wasn't possible to be bored in Bodie. I was wrong. Most of the excitement happens *around* me. I'm little more than an observer of a stage play called 'Bodie's Mellow Days and Rowdy Nights'." Roger could barely suppress his laughter, but sensing that she was serious, he fought the urge manfully and kept quiet. He couldn't hide the shine to his eyes, however, and seeing this Amanda chuckled. "Am I whining?"

"No, not at all." He gave vent to a smile. "But considering all you've been through over the last eight months, I find it interesting that you're eager for new adventures."

"Do you think me callous because I'm not wearing black for my father or purple for Joseph?"

"God, no." He was obviously startled at the question. "It would be hypocritical in the first instance and presumptuous in the second."

"I did wear black for the month following my father's death," she justified. "And for the next after that I wore a black ribbon in my hair and carried a black-edged hanky."

"That was quite sufficient." A few minutes later, Roger said, "You know, I've just had an idea you might like."

"Really?" Thinking it would be something romantic, she couldn't hide the eagerness in her voice.

"Yes," he continued. "The sister of Charlie Carlton of the Standard has moved to Bodie to keep house for him. Ida's husband, Caleb Steele, died in an accident in a Lundy mine just as winter began, so she came here to live with Charlie. As soon as the snow melts enough she wants to return to Lundy to collect some money due her as his widow. Charlie says she's afraid to travel alone and he can't get time off to go with her."

"I see where you're going with this." She sat up straight and fairly glowed with enthusiasm. "I'd love to accompany her. I've heard about Lundy and the people they call Mill Creekers. I'd love to see the area. Lumber mills and mining, right?"

"Yes. It's on Mill Creek that runs down the side of the Sierra. The activity in Lundy is fairly recent. Anyway, I'll talk to Charlie."

It was only a day later that Amanda responded to a knock on the door of her room and opened it to find standing there a tiny woman maybe five feet tall and in her middle thirties. There was a worn and haggard look to her, but although her face was prematurely aged, one could tell that she must have been pretty once. Now she looked out through dull brown eyes and no smile found its way to her lax mouth. Her thin body was draped in a brown dress a size too large for her while around her shoulders hung a poorly knitted and dingy white shawl.

"Hello," the woman murmured, as though putting forth the effort to speak took all her energy. "I'm Ida Steele and my brother is a friend of Roger Murphy's."

"Good morning." Amanda smiled warmly, hoping it would put the woman at her ease. "Come in and let's talk."

As soon as they were seated at the table in the corner of her room, Amanda poured the remainder of the coffee in the pot into a clean mug she kept in a drawer. After pouring in cream and sugar, she insisted Ida drink it before they talked. That Ida was immediately energized was evident by a sudden flush to her cheeks.

"Thank you so much. I ate nothing this morning, so nervous was I about coming to see you."

Surprised, Amanda told her, "I'm happy you did. I've been looking forward to meeting you." This brought a smile of pleasure to Ida's lips, so Amanda continued, "I understand you need to return to Lundy on business?"

"Yes, that's right. Two men owed my husband money when he died. An attorney there collected it and he's holding it for me. And because Caleb was killed in a mining accident, his friends took up a collection for me, and he's holding onto that money too. I could really use it. My brother purchased a small house on Mono last November and I live with him. But I haven't purchased a new dress in over a year and the two I have are becoming disgraceful. I hate to ask him for money for such things."

Amanda tried hard to avoid looking at the woman's dress and shawl, focusing on what she had said about the house. "It wouldn't be a house on the corner of Green and Mono facing east, would it?"

"Why, yes." Her surprise was obvious.

Amanda laughed. "That house used to belong to my father and another man. Your brother purchased it from him immediately after my father died."

"Oh, I hope that wasn't inconvenient for you."

Amanda hesitated, but then smiled. "I thought so at the time, but then I fetched up here. I have a respectable job and a roof over my head, so I'm very fortunate, considering what might have happened to me."

"Oh, yes." A thought suddenly occurred to Ida. "You must be the young woman my brother was talking about."

"Excuse me?"

"Oh, not in a bad way," she assured quickly. "He told me about a young woman befriended by Roger Murphy. So you must be the one Roger is helping out."

Amanda stared at her in surprise. "Helping out?"

"My brother said Roger talked Mrs. Chestnut into taking you in at a reduced rate, and that he pays for some of your expenses."

Amanda was shocked. "If you mean to imply that Roger is keeping me, I..."

Even more shocked, Ida jumped in, "Oh, no. Certainly not. In fact, my brother said the woman doesn't even know Roger is her benefactor." A hand flew to her mouth with a gasp. "Oh, my goodness, I've given something away, haven't I?"

Amanda took a moment to consider what she had just learned. "Yes, but I know you did it without malice. It's just that I had no idea. But now that I'm working, and Mr. Stewart has replaced Mrs. Chestnut, Roger can't still be doing it."

Ida merely shook her head, whether in agreement or doubt, Amanda didn't query her to find out. Ida told her, "Like you said, you're very fortunate, considering what could have become of you in this town."

Putting aside this uncomfortable subject, Amanda asked Ida, "When did you want to leave for Lundy?"

"I think the sooner the better. Like I said, I need the money." She fingered the skirt of her dress. "And then too something could happen to the man holding the money and I might not be able to get it at all."

Thinking of her father leaving for work with plans for the next day and then within hours being dead at the bottom of a mine shaft, she had to acknowledge the fragility of life for men in a mining town. Amanda assured Ida that she could go with her at any time.

The last week in April saw the roads clear of snow, even though there were still drifts on the hillsides. The air temperature was comfortable during the day if one retained a jacket for the early morning and evening, even if freezing at night. Ida and Amanda decided it was an ideal time for their visit to Lundy, and chose Charlie Hector's Lundy and Bodie Stage Line because it returned to Bodie the day after arriving in Lundy.

Mr. Hector was a young man in his middle twenties who was known as an exceptionally skilled driver, and was therefore trusted to carry the U.S. Mail to those in Lundy. He was prosperous because even in winter he drove through to the town unless the road was blocked by a frequent winter avalanche. He had painted his coach red with bright yellow wheels, and it was pulled by two curly mustangs and two sturdy horses of less grand design.

Anyone hearing the yell, "Here comes Charlie," came rushing to surround him in anticipation of word from a dear one many miles away, with the extreme of exhilaration or disappointment to follow.

As they climbed inside the coach in the chill of the morning, Amanda noticed that Mr. Hector had secured his hat by tying it down with his rolled bandana. Amanda took the hint and placed herself and Ida across from each other by the far window so they could hang onto the leather straps that hung next to the window. They pulled out of town and headed down the Goat Ranch Toll Road toward Mono Lake. Only a year before, the Mill Creek Toll Road Company had completed fourteen miles of wagon road that started at the Goat Ranch and penetrated five miles up into the Sierra Nevada to Lundy.

The coach rocked rhythmically on the support of its leather thoroughbraces, but still bounced hard when the iron-rimmed wheels hit a rut. Thankfully, where the road was most in need of grading, the driver was willing to slow down a little. But nothing could be done about the dust roiling up from the road where it had been free of the compacting snow for a few days. Men's hats could be freed of the dust by giving them a sharp whack on a post or their leg. Women's whole heads, hats and all, could be covered with muslin scarves. But no matter what was done for the passengers, at the end of a journey enough dust would be in evidence to proclaim them as just having arrived by stage.

The trip from Bodie to Lundy was made enjoyable by the quality of the views. Amanda admired those first along the Goat Ranch Road with its rock walls, unusual boulders, and short length to recommend it. At the end of it there was the broad panoramic view of the blue waters of Mono Lake with its strange islands poking through and millions of white sea birds along the shore.

The ladies were welcomed by Mrs. Scanavino at the Goat Ranch where dozens of sheep filled the pens and grazed the brush nearby. Mrs.

Scanavino was a severe, plump woman in a dark calico dress and a long white apron over the skirt who stood with her hands clasped in front of her. She had been in the process of schooling her large brood of children, and the two youngest boys of around six years of age took advantage of the stage's arrival to scamper off. The four older boys went out to help their father.

Mrs. Scanavino chose to ignore the scattering of her children and with the help of her four daughters aged twelve to fifteen, brought a wooden bucket of water to the passengers, one dipper for the men and another for the ladies who were offered the bucket first.

Amanda looked up into Mrs. Scanavino's face and saw a woman who obviously was leading a busy and somewhat hard life. It showed in the scowl of her deep-set eyes, and was mirrored by the way her hair was parted down the middle and slicked back into a tight bun. There were deep tired lines around her eyes and mouth, and she looked like someone who had forgotten how to smile.

Mr. Scanavino on the other hand, other than looking aged beyond his thirty-five years, looked energetic and out-going. His brown felt bowler hat was worn back at a slight angle, and he smiled at everyone on the stage as they alighted.

After changing horses, they left the ranch with its adobe and rock buildings and raced over the road that headed down hill through miles of sweet-smelling sagebrush. Straight ahead was the towering magnificence of the Sierra with its jagged crest spreading north and south as far as they could see, giving the impression that it might go on forever.

The coach slipped from the sagebrush steppe of the foothills into a narrow canyon. Hugging the south wall on a narrow and rocky trail, Amanda looked down from the window to glistening Mill Creek flowing past them on its way to Mono Lake. How different the smell here, she thought, and breathed in deeply the mild sweetness of cut lumber that drifted on the breeze coming from the west before mingling with the pungency of the rich damp soil along the creek. The crisp aromatic air was invigorating and Amanda felt a rush of joy, even as she wished she could be sharing it with Roger.

The jays in the mostly leafless aspens along the creek fluffed their wings and shifted from one foot to the other as they screamed at the passengers passing below, followed by the screech of a hawk that flushed upward after having missed its prey. After that, the only sound was the rhythmic rattling of the horses' equipage and the wheels grinding over the hard rocky road.

After crossing to the north side of Mill Creek, the stage continued uphill to a small cemetery on a low rise that sloped up from the road. Before they had started the trip, Ida had received permission from Charlie Hector for the stage to stop a moment at Caleb's grave. After taking a small bunch of wild flowers from her overnight satchel, she climbed out of the coach. Somewhat awkwardly in her long skirts, Ida climbed the gently sloping hill to his grave where she leaned on the wooden railing around it while catching her breath. She then tossed the small bunch of flowers onto the ground where a marker would have been placed if she could have afforded one.

Meanwhile Amanda looked out the window at the creek rushing below the road. It was this energetic flow of water that gave moisture to soil that watered groves of aspens, willows, and cottonwoods along the trail, and higher up large stands of pine. The fresh new growth of spring leaves sprouted on only a few of the trees and the brush at their base, displaying that singular shade of new green seen only at the beginning of the season. It signaled renewal and hopeful expectation in the souls of those who were fortunate enough to see this fresh display each year, portending an easier time of accomplishing errands. It also meant wagons arriving with fresh vegetables and fruit, and badly needed supplies that had dwindled over the winter.

Ida returned to the stage and they continued upward toward Lundy, although almost immediately they were required to stop at a toll house.

"Hi there Uncle," Charlie Hector called out to Dan Olsen, using the nickname given him by those who knew him well. Dan's face and the old leather vest he wore showed years of exposure to hot days, both being dry and cracked. His long full mustache moved when he talked, hiding lips one had to assume were also moving.

"Mornin' Charlie." Dan Olson walked to the stage and reached up to take the coin from Charlie.

"How you feeling today, Dan?"

Dan sighed and shrugged. He was known for having a series of vague health complaints, but today he answered with, "Not too poorly."

"Good to hear it. You take care now." The stage proceeded up the road edging the dark blue lake. Charlie slowed the coach to allow safer passage past the traffic coming toward them, which was considerable. Most of it was men on horseback, but they also passed two freight wagons empty of supplies. Amanda held her breath until they were clear, so close to each other did the stage and wagon pass.

They rolled through the small town site of Geneva Station where during the winter men cut 200 tons of ice from the lake and stored it in the ice house there. It consisted of a two-story hotel, as well as a saloon since late the year before. It was owned by Bodie merchants Rosenwald & Coblentz, but just the month before had been leased by Harry Blackburn who was trying to develop the hotel as a resort. The *Lundy Index* declared "*...the bilious Bodieite, surfeited with dust, impure water and worse whisky, will come to Lundy to rest and recuperate, fill his lungs with pure air, his stomach with pure water, his limbs with new vigor, and go home again a new man.*" It was, however, the women of Bodie who mostly found the small resort a haven of respectable relaxation. The resort had the previous Christmas Eve hosted a turkey and chicken shooting competition simply to attract sportsmen to the area.

As interesting as the trip had been thus far, when the passengers first saw the dark blue waters of Lake Lundy, all else was forgotten. About a mile long and a quarter mile across, the water was 150 feet deep but so clear that on a calm day the bottom could be seen. Most of the time there was sawdust gathered along its edges, having been washed downstream from the lumber mills up canyon.

This day, a few boats were out on the water, although fields of snow were still reflecting the sun along the shore. The water, having mostly thawed from its frozen state of winter, was exceptionally pure and cold. Over the years many a person had been surprised to find that other than boats, little would float on its surface, even a dead fish, so high was the oxygen content.

Those living in Lundy had discovered that when the roads were buried under deep snow, a wagon or stage could pass over the frozen lake once it had set to a sufficient density. They had to be careful late in the season, because if they hit an area unable to bear the weight of the wagon or stage, the ice would crack. So far, those who had gone through the ice had been rescued without too much damage.

A number of men were fishing from the shore, a not inconsiderable pile of speckled trout lying on canvas nestled in the snow near them. In

1878 the lake had been stocked with these trout, and they had thrived in the deep cold water, averaging four pounds each and being sold not only in Lundy but also in Bodie. Only the month before a man had caught "a twenty-two incher" that he was still bragging about.

The stage entered the main road through the town after crossing First Street. It followed parallel roads called Chicago Avenue to the left along the creek and Clark Street to the right at the foot of a canyon wall. They passed the May Lundy Hotel on their right, a number of saloons, the carpenter shop, Billy Robson's blacksmith and then crossed Second Street.

Ida stuck her head out the window, her excitement increasing by the minute, and her cheeks showing more color than Amanda had so far seen on her. "They've added a pharmacy to the town," Ida commented. "Dr. Guirado must be so pleased."

People who were accustomed to the sprawl of Bodie, upon seeing Lundy for the first time often thought it a miniature version of a town. Only five short blocks long and three blocks wide, it was nevertheless packed with new businesses and cabins. Men had set up rough camps among the trees at the mouth of Mill Creek Canyon, but these were mostly for those who were newly arrived and had not yet had time to build a more permanent abode.

The horses pulling the coach slowed to a walk as they passed more saloons, a hotel, and the Wells Fargo Office. Henry Brown, the fifty-four year old distinguished agent, was standing on the porch and waved to Charlie as the stage passed. The arrival of the stage might mean some new excitement or nothing but a couple of tired miners returning to town from Bodie, but Henry was eager to see what it would be.

After passing the assay office of R. A. Wilcox and the Sierra Telegraph Office where men stood in a group outside the door waiting for the answers to messages sent, they crossed over Third Street. The stage pulled to the right and stopped in front of the stage depot and Hector's corrals filled with horses and mules newly arrived now that the snow was melted on the road.

Once they were on the ground with their cloth satchels next to them, Ida told Amanda, "I need to check with Charles Barry, the lawyer. He's just across from the Wells Fargo Office, so I shouldn't be long." She hurried off without further word.

Amanda waited on the sidewalk while eyeing hungrily the Amador Restaurant just up the street. Looking around at the town as she breathed deeply the remarkably fresh mountain air, she felt herself smiling at the welcome presence of the hundreds of tall green trees soon to fall beneath the chopper's axe. Until that moment she hadn't realized how much she had missed trees and tall mountains, and the sharp piney scent of such places.

The people hurrying past on the planked sidewalk radiated with a vibrant energy and purpose, most of whom nevertheless took a moment to smile or nod at her. Amanda felt a sudden thrill for life that filled her with a sense of possibilities to be fulfilled, however undefined that might be.

Lundy was a busy place overlaid with sounds that were distinctly its own. The rasp of saws could be heard amid the pop and crash of branches falling to the ground, and the crunch and grind at the Lundy Reduction Works reverberated off the canyon's steep rock walls rising on either side of the town. Huge metal-rimmed wheels on freight wagons rattled down Main as freighters whistled at their teams of large mules, and horses in the corrals neighed in response.

Under construction was a steep zigzag trail rising up from the south side of the lake to the high mines in Lake Canyon. The narrow trail would be finished in November of that year with twenty turn-outs so wagons could pass, and would create such a scar on the side of the mountain that well over a hundred years later it would still be visible.

Ida had explained that there were no banks in the town, but the saloons cashed checks and a telegraph line had been connected in January to the Bodie banks. In this way the stock markets were also aware of Lundy's flow of wealth along with that of Bodie.

Amanda looked down at the small timepiece pinned to the bodice of her dress and saw that it was just after noon. There were no standardized time zones in the United States yet, but the Mill Creekers followed what they called May Lundy Mill standard time. This meant that whatever time showed on the clock at the mill was the time it was for everyone in town. A man passing by as Amanda looked again at her timepiece smiled and said, "Excuse me, ma'am. It's a quarter to one here."

Amanda smiled back. "Thank you, sir. I was just admiring your town. Even the clouds in the sky are spectacular."

He laughed and looked up at the large fluffs of white. "Enjoy the sunlight while you can. It comes into town around eleven in the morning and in places disappears beyond the cliffs three hours later. The canyon is that narrow."

"Oh my. Well, I guess it makes Lundy all that more interesting."

As the man walked away, Ida arrived back at her side sporting a big smile. "There was more money than I thought waiting for me." She turned a rosy face to Amanda. "I'm famished. We can go to the Amador Restaurant for a bite. My treat." As they walked down the street, Ida said, "The Amador is owned by two sisters, Rosa and Marie Kelly. They came here last year with their parents and have just opened their establishment."

Feeling her stomach rumble, Amanda was only too happy to approach the frame building with smoke belching from the pipe on the roof and carrying wonderful smells. Before going inside, however, they took turns visiting the privy behind the building. When they entered the restaurant, they were immediately descended upon by Rosa Kelly who exclaimed with delight when she spotted Ida.

"It's so good to see you again Mrs. Steele. Have you returned to us?"

Smiling, Ida told her, "Only for today. My friend and I will be spending the night and then returning to Bodie tomorrow. I'd like you to meet Miss Amanda Blake."

"Hello." She turned back to Ida with a broad smile and her brown eyes dancing. "For now, you eat. Sit over here."

They were made comfortable next to a sunny window where they could look out on the road rising to the west between a scattering of trees not yet cut down. Nearby was a small stove that radiated just enough warmth to keep them comfortable, although Marie still threw another piece of wood into its flaming maw before rushing to the kitchen.

Amanda looked out the window and sighed for what must have been glorious old pines covering the hills, but that were now gone at the hands of wood choppers, leaving only stumps. The logs would be planed at the mill and shipped out as lumber for houses in Bodie, Bridgeport, and the Mono Lake ranches. It occurred to Amanda that all these buildings would in their turn fall to ruin and rot away; the huge boulders she had admired along the lake might someday be blasted into gravel to pave the roads; and more trees and boulders might be used to dam the area's waters. But as she looked up at Mt. Scowden, so high that she could not see the top of it from the window, she pondered the comforting thought that this ancient mountain with its sheer face and broken ridge would forever look down upon the canyon.

Amanda and Ida were still looking at the simple hand written menu when a group of drovers entered and sat down at a long table next to them. It was a mystery to Amanda why drovers would be in Lundy, but she recognized them as such by their appearance and the way they talked.

The men immediately removed their hats and laid them crown down on the floor next to their chairs. Each of the men wore their clothes like a uniform; dusty denim pants, long-sleeved checked or striped shirts, leather vests and square-toed boots. Light from the window glinted off the rowels of the silver spurs protruding from the heels of their boots, and when they walked or shifted their weight they all made the same creaking, rattling and jingling noises.

They had no beards but showed the stubble of being several days away from a razor, and all presented leathered faces as they ran fingers through long hair. The loudest of them was obviously the acknowledged leader of the group, partly because he looked 70 although just 35, so weather-worn was his face. The drovers laughed with a camaraderie that was easy and familiar. Much of their talk was of horses, recent events on the trail, and at first how hungry they were. As they ate, however, several of them commented on how eager they were for a drink. When they left, obviously heading for a saloon, Amanda wondered if they would be leaving town in the same gregarious mood and all of a piece. Maybe, she thought, I've been in Bodie too long and find the peacefulness of a town like this difficult to accept.

Indeed, none of the three murders in Lundy's history had yet occurred. Like all such towns, it would see its degree of petty crime; tools stolen, theft from a till at a store, stolen firewood, and whiskey sold to some Piute fishermen. These things would be dealt with by appropriate fines and promises to not repeat the action, and everyone would move on with their lives. Occasional fist fights or threats of a violent nature would occur, and not surprisingly it would be due to too much time in a saloon. Usually apologies would follow after all involved sobered up and everyone would get back to work. Lundy would never have a reputation for lawlessness like Bodie.

Over coffee and cake Ida talked about Lundy, her obvious pride showing without apology. "We came here this time of year two years ago. There was little here then, but we built a small cabin with a dirt floor in two days with the help of four men who had just finished their own cabin and had lumber left over. They had no wives with them, so it was left to me to cook for all of them." Ida chuckled. "Funny how those four men had managed to cook their own meals until a woman showed up.

"When they were done with our cabin, we all helped another newly arrived couple build a log and canvas cabin. By that time, the snow had melted enough that the mines were hiring and Caleb got on with one up canyon in Wasson. So I was alone much of the time. I didn't mind until I fractured my leg last summer. If my brother Charlie hadn't arranged for Emily Eastman to come take care of me, I don't know what would have happened to me. The doctor set the bone but the cut on my leg got infected after he left town to go to Bodie. Emily knew just what to do. I realize now how close I came to gangrene and losing my leg or my life."

"I met Emily not long after she was here. She left Bodie last September."

"So my brother told me. How is she? Have you heard?"

"Did Charlie tell you that she was expecting when she left?"

"No." Ida smiled broadly. "But she's had the baby by now."

"In December she had a little girl. Her husband Frank joined her not long before and they've decided to put down roots in Lone Pine in the Owens River Valley."

"Oh, how nice for them." She sighed. "I was never blessed with a child. My husband held it against me, as though it was something I chose to deprive him of."

"That doesn't seem fair."

Ida laughed shortly. "Men often aren't fair. But other than that, he was a pretty good husband."

Amanda stared out the window, wondering if she would ever be so cynical to think that a *pretty good* husband was sufficient.

"So what do you think of Lundy?" Ida asked eagerly.

"It's certainly in a beautiful setting. How did it get its name?"

"William Lundy had a sawmill in the canyon back in '78. He was also the Mining Recorder when the Homer Mining District was formed. He named his mine after his daughter May Lundy."

"The *Homer* Mining District?"

"Mr. Homer and his friend Mr. Nye first discovered gold in the area in '79. They filed claims on four large ledges, but it wasn't until summer of last year that the boom was well under way, which brought in those setting up stores. In fact, Charley Kilgore and Fred Dames from Bodie were among the first. They set up as partners with Tom Rickey and began bringing in meat for us.

"From there the town grew fast until by the end of summer it was almost as full of businesses as now. I can see where the canvas buildings have been replaced with log or frame structures, and the small ones have been added onto. It's all typical of these places." She held up a finger as a sudden thought occurred to her. "But you know, unlike in Bodie, there are no fraternal organizations here."

"You mean no Masonic Hall?"

"No. And nothing for the Odd Fellows or Good Templars either."

Amanda and Ida looked out upon the busy and rambunctious town. Pedestrians, wagons, strings of pack mules and horsemen filled the narrow muddy streets. Every spot not taken up by a tree was the site of a business, home or rough camp. Stray dogs ran everywhere, most temporary companions left behind by those who had moved on to other mining districts. But they all looked well fed and friendly, so Amanda assumed they were being cared for by someone. In fact, most had merely learned how to forage from the garbage piles back of hotels, saloons and the bakery.

Bodie was only 20 miles away and when a miner there couldn't find work, they often headed to Lundy just as did miners from Mammoth City as it continued to fail. But like every mining town, there was a limited number of mines that could be filed on, and only a limited number of jobs in other men's mines. If a man didn't have a skill needed in the town, he would be forced to move on.

Jim Condon entered the restaurant and upon seeing Ida, a smile split his face. She immediately invited him to sit down and join them, and he wasted no time pulling up a chair while keeping his eyes on Ida. Amanda sipped her water so as to hide a smile, since it was obvious the man was smitten.

"It's good to see you, Ida." With a quick glance at Amanda, he added, "And to meet your friend." His eyes returned to Ida. "I'm glad to know you've settled into Bodie. But it's not an easy place for a woman."

Amanda noticed that he didn't mention any degree of sorrow over the death of Caleb.

"It's easier to live in Bodie when one has friends," Ida responded, "and I've made several." She smiled shyly at Amanda and then turned back to Jim. "A lot has changed here since I left."

"We built all winter despite the snow. This summer there's sure to be a hell of a boom." In his excitement at the prospect, he wasn't aware that he had sworn in the presence of ladies and they tactfully made no comment.

Ida asked, "Has the Boomershine problem been resolved?"

"Oh, no." He shook his head and smiled. "It drags on."

"What's this about?" Amanda spoke up.

Jim turned to her. "John Boomershine was an early prospector here, and he put in an agricultural land claim for the valley floor. Ridiculous, of course. There's no way anyone could grow crops in this rocky soil and short growing season. People already settled here had the town site surveyed and then contested his claim."

Ida told Amanda. "In July of last year the Register and Receiver of the U.S. Land Office at Bodie gave his decision in favor of Mr. Boomershine. Of course, the people appealed the decision to the Interior Department."

"But John still moved his family here," Jim said, "running the old Lundy saw mill. Then in October, he sold his original mining interest to Pike of the May Lundy Mine and moved away. Last month he received a U.S. patent on the land, but it was attached immediately by Attorney Drake. John owed him $8,000 for legal services in connection with the settling of the dispute."

Amanda laughed. "And the town continues to develop as though there wasn't any of this going on?"

Jim shrugged. "Why not? The mines will probably play out before the lawyers settle everything, and we need a town to support the mines and mills."

Amanda resisted the urge to say how crazy she thought it all was. What she didn't know was that Jim had neglected to say that William Lundy had also been a rancher who shared the land claim with Boomershine. But Mr. Lundy carried the name of the town and was still a presence, and loyalty being a strong trait among these mountain brethren, Jim preferred to save his ridicule for the commonly disliked Boomershine.

"We even have a brand new school house," Jim told Ida proudly. "It's at the upper end of Chicago Street near the reduction works. The Chinese businesses are at both ends of Main now, but at least their houses cluster on Clark Street away from our eyes." This was the least prepossessing area of the town, being a narrow and short street on the north edge. Amanda assumed it must be considered a fitting place for the Chinese who were obviously respected no more in Lundy than they were in any other mining town.

"It's become so civilized," Ida sighed. "I wish I had been able to stay on here."

Jim started to say something, hesitated, then said, "Civilized indeed. On March 24, Mrs. Lundy held a meeting at her home along with her daughters May and Minnie. All to form a dramatic club. Harry Medlicott was there and he's been on the stage before."

Ida looked completely charmed, and even Amanda had to admit it sounded like great fun, saying, "Bodie is so violent by comparison. The jail is filled most of the time."

"We don't have a jail," Jim said. "When we have someone that needs holding, Jim Slack lends us his cabin."

"He's from Bodie," Amanda exclaimed. "He was a good friend of my father. Jim was the first foreman of the Hook and Ladder Company."

"That's right. Good fisherman too. But a bad drunk."

Slack would in fact be dead a year later because of a shooting fracas started by his bad temper while drunk. His body would lie in state in Bodie before being shipped to Oakland so his wife and children, left behind years before, could bury him.

Jim thought a moment about any other information he might impart. "The post office opened in March. It has a general delivery window, but also fifty boxes at $1.50 per quarter. Half of 'em have glass fronts and the others have locks. But they cost $2.00. We're paying Alex Rosenwald of the Rosenwald, Coblentz & Company store next door to be postmaster. He gets $218 a month so he'd better do a good job."

"I notice Main has fewer tree stumps now," Ida commented. "It's even graded pretty well."

Jim glowed with pride. "Yup. A couple of months ago I started removing 'em. After the census last year, I started thinking this could become a nice little town, but we'd need to smarten things up a bit.

"The Lake Canyon trail is almost finished. It was started last November, but of course construction had to stop during the winter." He turned to Amanda. "Your Pat Reddy got the project going."

"Really?"

"Oh yeah. He's interested in the mines up in the canyon. If we want to get up to the mines there with wagons, we have to have the road. The route we've been using is only good enough for a man and a mule."

Amanda cut in. "How did the census go here? It was pretty hit and miss in Bodie."

"Here too. Charles Hilton from Mammoth handled it. The way he went at it was a caution. He claims there were 350 here. Of course, we know that's not right, what with so many men up in the mountains living in their mines. Hilton certainly didn't put forth the effort to go up there.

He mainly let people come to him. I ran into someone the other day who didn't know there even had been a census. And some of those at the newspaper right in town said they got missed. I figure you could double the 350 figure and be about right."

"Who's in charge of the *Index* now?" Ida asked.

"Jim Townsend took it over a couple of months ago but he's complaining already about how little money the newspaper brings in. He's thinking of selling out to John Ginn."

Ida put out a hand and touched Jim's arm, lowering her voice as she nodded toward a man just entering. "There's Lying Jim now."

He wasn't a particularly prepossessing gentleman. The most striking thing about him was his perpetual expression of disdain, his head tilted back as he walked so that he appeared to be looking down his nose and over a drooping mustache that partially hid a mouth that formed a slight smirk. He was of short stature with a small head covered in curly hair cut quite short.

"Do people really call him that to his face?"

Jim Condon laughed. "Sure. If a story isn't impressive enough, he just adds more adjectives and stretches the truth a bit. He started his career in San Francisco back in '59 with his friend Bret Harte and then in '62 he worked for the Virginia City Territorial Enterprise with Sam Clemens before he became Mark Twain. He moved on to Grass Valley on the west side of the Sierra where he started his own paper, lost that, and went to Sacramento. Now he's here."

Ida shook her head. "Yes, but for how long, especially considering..." She stopped and took a sip of her water. "Was the winter bad?"

"The worst." Jim blew out his cheeks at the memory. "All the saloons ran out of whiskey in December. Wagons couldn't get through the snow after an early storm. But we made do."

"What does that mean?" Amanda asked.

Jim grinned as he looked around to be sure no one was listening to the secrets he was about to reveal. "The best whiskey was created by Colonel Kikendale at his place. Hot drops, red pepper and absinthe for a real kick. It went down like someone was branding your throat. He called it *Wake Up Jake*." He laughed at the memory. "Bronson put together something he called *Toe Jam*. Ginger tea, pepper sauce and jalap. Haas made a brew he called *Holy Terror* with sheep wash, vinegar and potash. It was okay if you were used to gargling with crushed glass. Of course, Jim Townsend tried them all. That's what you started to comment on a few minutes ago, wasn't it, Ida?"

"Well, yes. Mr. Townsend is known for the amount of liquid refreshment he regularly consumes."

Jim chuckled. "Whenever he belches, someone hollers 'fire in the hole'." The women laughed freely, enjoying the fact that no Bodie woman was present to judge them harshly. Amanda sighed as she thought of how concerned women had to be about how they were perceived. It was so exhausting always being so correct in comportment and phrasing. But remembering the miner's rude comment at the Treloar funeral service, she had to admit there were consequences for social lapses.

Jim went on. "But eventually ole Charlie Hector got a wagon through from Bodie with a supply of the real thing and everyone's guts began to heal." As the women laughed again, Jim was quick to ask, "When are you going back to Bodie, Ida?"

She told him somewhat sadly, "We're returning tomorrow. There's nothing to keep me here after that." Was there a hint of a question in her last statement? Amanda looked out the window and smiled.

Jim nodded slowly and looked down at the table. "Well, the May Lundy Hotel was just remodeled, so if you're staying the night you might try there first."

Jim stood up, tipped his hat to both the women, gave Ida a lingering if not wistful look and left them to finish their meal. Ida looked as though she wanted to say something, but only smiled and watched Jim walk away.

After they finished, they went to the May Lundy Hotel on the northwest corner of First and Main in silence, Amanda sensing that Ida needed time to think. When they reached the hotel, it was to discover that there were no rooms available, even though there had recently been an extension built onto the west end of the main building. Considering the crowding in the town, they began to fear they would find no place to spend the cold night hours.

Finally, about the time their feet felt like hot lead, they found a room at the Oakland House, the last business at the west end of the town on Main. It was run by a friend of Ida's by the name of Puseller Gable. She had a bright smile and was the wife of Fred Gable, whose voice still showed shades of his German birth. Like Ida's husband had done, Fred spent most of his time prospecting or working his mine in the mountains back of the town, and coming home only after an absence of several weeks.

Ida and Amanda stood before the hotel and looked up at a tall flag pole at the corner of the building.

Surprised, Ida said, "That's new."

Two steps up they entered into a small parlor. It had a wooden floor covered in a large rag rug surrounded by a scattering of various cast-off chairs and tables knocked together from pieces of lumber and then painted white. With crocheted doilies tea-stained a dark brown and draped on the backs of the chairs and on the tables, the overall effect was warm and inviting.

As they sat with Mrs. Gable in the parlor sharing a pot of tea and a plate of buttered bread, Mrs. Gable told them, "My husband is working at his Charley Deal Mine today and won't be back until the weekend."

Amanda commented, "The name Charles is certainly common around here."

Both women looked at her, then at each other, and Ida laughed. "Why, I think you're right."

Amanda asked Mrs. Gable, "Do you like running the hotel?"

"Oh, I do." She fairly glowed with enthusiasm. "In fact, one of these days I'm going to find a way to be sure it's all mine."

"How on earth will you do that?" Ida asked.

"I can file as *sole trader*." This meant that she would not need her husband's approval or signature for business transactions, something that now she had to do. With him gone so much of the time, this was a great inconvenience, as some of the freighters refused to deliver goods to her on her own signature.

Mrs. Puseller asked them, "Did you notice my flag pole? It's sixty feet tall."

"How could we have missed it?" Ida chuckled. "It's really something."

"On March 20, we had the first flag raising in the canyon. We're all really proud of it."

After they had retired to share one of the 18 beds in the hotel, they fell sound asleep until morning. After a quick breakfast, they climbed into Hector's stage, each with their own secret reason for harboring regret at leaving the beautiful little town of Lundy.

If the town wanted to grow, it was beyond Amanda's imagination to picture how it could do so, considering the limited amount of flat ground.

In fact, Lundy was as large as it would ever be. In 1887, most of the business district would burn down due to a fire in the Pioneer Lodging House. The lost businesses would not be rebuilt, as the mining activity at that time would not warrant it.

But the town would remain on the map, shrinking gradually until over a hundred years later it would be a tiny fishing village. And although Mt. Scowdon, the beautiful lake, and its trout would never change, the trees would return as a lush second-growth forest.

CHAPTER 14
MAY, 1881

As Amanda and Ida approached Bodie on their return from Lundy, admiring the purple and white of wild flowers blooming along the road, Amanda marveled at how much the town had declined since her arrival a year earlier. From a population of 7,000 it had dwindled to half that, and she wondered if the town would yet rebound like so many people expected it would. Of course, it would certainly do so if the mines hit another bonanza by drilling deeper, but some thought that would only be possible for the largest mines like the Standard and the Bodie. In the meantime, much of the town was in a state of disrepair that angered and disgusted everyone.

On May 18, the *Daily Free Press* reported, "*There are pools of green, foul, stagnant water that cannot run off, deserted cabins are surmounted with slime and odoriferous mud, and it is only lately that the stages could pass along. Coming south, heaps of manure are encountered, here and there a coal oil can looms up out of the mire, and such common articles as old boots and cast off pantaloons are quite prominent. With all this, a dozen different kinds of odors go up at all hours to remind the passer-by that filth is ever with us. Heaps of oyster shells adorn the front of elegant business houses, and it would take a six-mule team to haul off all the cigar stumps, discarded cards, and decayed fruit and vegetables that choke up the gutters.*"

Such was the state of Bodie that met Amanda as she and Ida traveled down Main from the south. It was this, coupled with the violence, cold, and growing atmosphere of fear and doubt, that brought to Amanda the realization that she did not want to stay in Bodie, no matter the inducement. How could she explain this to Roger and get him to agree to live elsewhere? On the other hand, maybe he felt the same and had just not told her. Hope surged in her heart and suddenly the debris along Main didn't look as disgusting.

Although shootouts and various other forms of blood-letting were often heralded in the Nevada press as Bodie's favorite pastime, this exaggerated reputation was surpassed by the town's avidity for any kind of sporting event. In a world of men whose competitive spirit was active every minute of every day whether working, drinking, recreating, or even completing the painting of a house before a neighbor finished his, this was not surprising.

During the intensity of the various sporting events, everything else of importance was put out of the minds of the spectators. Differences and grudges were forgotten. The clergy sat next to those who they often called Godless; the law sat next to those recently released from jail; the parsimonious mixed with the profligate; laborers cheered along with the shopkeepers and mine owners; and when not cheering for their champion, good ladies chatted with Bonanza Street denizens about fashion and the latest cure for coughs. The few rest intervals allowed the combatants were accompanied by a brass band whose musicians played with a gusto reflective of the boisterous event they had been watching.

The previous year, the agile Rod McInnis had been matched against Con Driscoll, a popular wrestler from San Francisco, with $200 a side. Not only did McInnis win that 1880 match handsomely, but his antics after the match had endeared him to the locals and was the source of much talk even a year later. It seems that Rod had, according to the *Bodie Daily Standard*, "*kicked at a hat suspended on a rope about eight and a half feet above the floor, kicking with the foot from which he sprang.*" The few foolish enough to try this trick afterwards had as their only reward a bruised tailbone after crashing to the ground.

A month after that event, in June of '80, McInnis had been in another match at $250 a side with Eugene Markey, who had been a town constable. This had been called off, however, after a fight broke out between the special officers assigned to keep the peace at the event. Some said from the first that it had been done on purpose as a distraction when it looked like McInnis was going to win, because so many of the sports had bet on his opponent Eugene Markey. Considering that one of the special officers had been Dave Bannon, this rumor gained certainty after the rowdy Dave had been killed.

Now in May of '81, Rod McInnis was engaged to be married in July, and had declared to all who would listen that from now on he would "only wrestle domestic problems."

Since returning from Lundy, Amanda had seen little of Roger. She had been working long hours in the dining room, as Kassy had moved to Bridgeport with a new husband. Considering that no one seemed to have known she was even involved with someone, her marriage had been a complete surprise even to her closest friends. Since a replacement for her shift had not yet been found, Amanda was happy to work extra hours.

Roger had been working long hours at Wagner's since men from the boarding houses on the hill descended to spend more time enjoying themselves in town now that the snow had melted on the roads. Not that men needed an excuse to drink, but the phrase "to make up for lost time" was heard often.

Roger sat in the reading room of the hotel with Amanda, since she had declared that she had too often allowed him to be alone with her in her room. Roger thought this funny, considering the degree of intimacy that she had allowed him, but he also understood that it was actually about how they were perceived by others. He could curse society's rules all he wanted, but fitting in meant not flaunting those rules in some way that could easily get you ostracized. Not only was that bad for business, it could make it difficult to survive in a place like Bodie.

So he accepted her decision and asked her, "What did you think of Lundy?"

"I found the setting beautiful, and the people admirable."

"Admirable?"

"Yes." She cocked her head to the side and recalled her impressions. "It's not like living here. They have to climb steep mountains in a high altitude to reach their mines. And in town they're pressed in on either side by those very mountain walls in a world of shadows throughout most of the day. In winter they either leave or suffer avalanches that could cover the town and kill them. But the townspeople carry on with pride in what they have established and celebrate the holidays throughout the year much as we do."

"It sounds like you enjoyed yourself."

"I enjoyed getting away from here to somewhere very different." She smiled. "The one pastime they have that we never will is fishing for trout. What a beautiful blue lake it is." She looked out the window and sighed.

Roger added casually, "And of course they have trees."

Amanda looked at him with a seriousness that surprised him. "I think it's fitting that we don't have the shade of trees here in Bodie."

"Fitting?"

"Yes. As our stage left Lundy I began thinking about what happens in the shade of trees. People gain calmer souls and find cool refreshment, nourishment from the fruit the tree provides, peace out of the way of constant duress, the quiet to think higher thoughts, and maybe time to appreciate the birds and animals with which they share the earth. It's like a small, perfect little world."

Roger laughed. "And it's definitely not like Bodie."

"That's why I say it's fitting that Bodie has no trees."

"Ah. I see." Looking at her earnest expression, Roger realized that there were depths to this woman that he had up to that moment not appreciated. The thought came to him as a pleasant awakening that building a life with Amanda might not be boring at all.

For Amanda, the most important event of the month was the departure of Charlotte and Vince Perry from Bodie. A small crowd of people gathered in front of the Perry house on Green just as the sun was starting its glow over the hills. Soon it would be shining down on the mines that had been part of Vince and Charlotte's life for the last four years, but which they would never see again.

Vince, his body less robust than it used to be, nevertheless shook hands with his friends who tried not to show how worried they were about him. Charlotte hugged her lady friends good-bye, some hiding well their emotions and others not. Amanda felt she did a good job keeping her tears from falling, but the quiver of her chin she could not control so easily. Charlotte pretended not to notice.

It would take the Perrys a good month on the road to reach Lone Pine, and that only as long as the weather remained fine and Vince's energy endured. Their wagon was large and held their clothes, kitchen items, linens, a few treasures that Charlotte would not leave behind, tools needed to repair the wagon if it broke down, and camping gear. A freighter heading to the Owens Valley the next week was bringing with him more of their things that included the kitchen table and chairs, a bookcase, the small pie safe, and two large paintings.

They had chosen to leave the bed and parlor furniture behind, but had managed to sell it all to friends. Charlotte had given Amanda the delicate china tea set that had held pride of place so often as they visited, claiming it was too delicate to transport. But both of them had known that it was so Amanda might have its comfort now that she would be without her dearest friend. The house had not yet sold, but Mr. Boone was going to oversee its sale and send them the money when it did.

Amanda smiled as Charlotte told her, "Emily and Frank have no idea we're on our way to Lone Pine. I want it to be a surprise."

"Promise me you'll write when you arrive so I know you're safe. Better yet, send me a telegram."

"I will."

"And be sure to give Emily my love." Amanda swallowed hard. "I'll miss you. I don't know how I would have survived this past year without you."

Charlotte's eyes glazed with tears. "I'll miss you too. You were so generous and kind during Vince's illness."

"Are you sure that Vince…"

Charlotte turned her back on Amanda with a suddenness that answered the uncompleted question. Charlotte was indeed worried about Vince's health, but didn't want to discuss it as Vince was determined that they were going to leave.

"Okay, Vince," Charlotte called out in her brightest manner that fooled no one, least of all Vince. "Let's go while there's still enough time to reach Vining's Rancho before dark."

Charlotte joined Vince on the seat of the wagon, Mr. Boone and Mr. Eggleston helping her up. Although Amanda knew Charlotte to be perfectly capable of getting up there by herself, she watched Charlotte generously allow the two dear men to assist her. She rewarded them with the sweet smile they always associated with her. Amanda would never forget Charlotte's grace, kindness, and sense of humor that was never at the expense of another.

Finally, with no one left to bid farewell and no more items they could load on the wagon and expect the horses to pull it, Vince and Charlotte rolled south on Green to Main. There they traveled down its length to the Goat Ranch Road, heading to the west side of Mono Lake. Beyond that lay Frenchman's Station at the beginning of the Mono Lake Toll Road, Kings Station at the beginning of the Mono Lake-Mammoth City Toll Road, then Long Valley, Round Valley, the volcanic tablelands, and finally the Owens River Valley beyond that.

Two days later Amanda stood in the lobby of the hotel early in the morning waiting for Roger to arrive and take her to breakfast. He had arranged to have his day off on the same day as hers, and they were both looking forward to a long buggy ride after they ate.

As she started to seat herself on the settee, Pat Reddy emerged from the dining room and walked toward the front door. Being in a spontaneous mood, Amanda called out to him, "Good morning, Mr. Reddy."

He turned to her, his long white mustache that matched his thick hair moving aside to show a smile.

"I'm Amanda Blake and I would like to ask you a question if you have a moment."

As he approached, he gave her an appraising look that she accepted for what it was. "No," she smiled, "I haven't broken the law. I understand that you once lived in the Owens Valley and I wanted to ask you what that was like."

He laughed. "Yes. My first law practice was in Independence between the towns of Bishop and Lone Pine." She gestured to a chair and they sat down. "Those were good days. I was there in March of 1872 when the big quake leveled Lone Pine and parts of Independence. Half of my office ended up on the floor."

"What's the valley like?"

He thought a moment. "I could say it's beautiful, but that doesn't really tell you anything. And it's not even about what it looks like, although the ever-changing light can be very nice. No, it's the feel of the place. It's surrounded by the tallest of mountains and the sweep of meadows and tall sagebrush. The green swath of the Owens River runs the length of it, and dozens of creeks flow to the river from the Sierra. Then there's the huge expanse of the Owens Lake south of Lone Pine. And the whole valley is dotted with ranches owned by nice, hardworking people. May I ask why you're interested?"

"I have some friends who live there."

"I have to be going, but if you ever have the opportunity to spend some time there, I highly recommend it to you."

"Thank you for taking your time to talk to me." As he turned to walk away, she stopped him. "By the way, I'd like to thank you for your willingness to challenge the crowd when Joseph was being lynched."

He looked at her for a long moment. "I'm afraid it did little good."

"I'm not so sure that it didn't give at least a few people pause for thought. Maybe not right then, but possibly later."

"Thank you." His smile was wistful. "I appreciate your saying that."

As she sat down to wait for Roger, Amanda perused one of the newspapers someone had carelessly tossed aside. Her eyes immediately lighted on an item that had transpired two days earlier on May 28 in the Comstock Saloon, only seven doors north of Green and barely out of the respectable south end of town.

It was unfortunately not a surprising article, the ability to be taken off guard by such things now past for anyone in town for longer than six months, and indeed the incident had warranted barely a mention. Police officer Jack Roberts, known to hate Jock Myers, had passed him in a saloon and put four slugs into him. Myers got off only one shot, but it missed Roberts. The well-liked Roberts was pleading self-defense and would no doubt get off, as few people had liked the volatile and gruff Myers.

When Roger arrived, Amanda tossed the paper aside and almost immediately forgot what she had just read. Roger greeted her enthusiastically and then turned his attention back to the street. He was hoping that being alone outside of town in the shadows of the grove of willows situated above the race track, he could tell Amanda again how much he cared for her and maybe even discuss a future together.

Amanda suspicioned that such a discussion might be on the agenda, and she was not sure how she would respond. It wasn't that she didn't care deeply for Roger, but was it deeply enough to marry him? His being a sport did not prejudice her against a proposal, especially considering that he was a respectable faro dealer, but it did limit where they could live.

Her thoughts were cut short when Roger hollered to her from the doorway, "Hey, Amanda, come here. There's a walk-down happening."

"A what?" She followed him onto the sidewalk.

"Two men facing each other in the street and walking towards each other until one decides to draw and shoot. It's a rare thing outside of romantic fiction. With all the killing in Bodie, have you ever heard of this happening before?"

"I can't say that I have." Although she stood next to him, not for a moment did she worry about her safety with him there beside her.

"Let's face it," he murmured, "usually the rowdies just pull their guns and shoot, or stab someone in the back in a dark alley."

"That doesn't seem very sporting."

Not catching the playful tone she had used, Roger told her, "They're not interested in being sporting. They're only interested in the other guy being dead."

Amanda took careful note of the combatants. One of the men was a tall lanky miner with a full mustache and still wearing his canvas trousers and red work shirt, with his jacket dropped on the ground at the side of the road. The other man was just as tall, but with a bulk to his shoulders befitting someone who regularly hefted heavy items. His black hat was pulled low on his high forehead, shadowing dark watchful eyes accentuating a pleasant face sporting the stubble of a developing new beard. He was dressed for the trail in denim pants, a leather vest over a pale blue shirt closed at the neck with a string tie with silver points, and fancy spurs on his boots. Since he was obviously a stranger to the town, many present assumed that he had invited the miner into the street. However, one of the bystanders who had been in at the beginning of the situation quickly set everyone around him straight.

The cowboy had brought in a small herd of cattle to the slaughterhouse north of town from the depot in Hawthorne. Where his fellow drovers were at that moment, no one knew. Unfortunately for him, he had accidentally bumped the miner in Wagner's Saloon, and heated words had been exchanged when the miner would not accept an apology.

When the miner began ridiculing what he called the drover's "sissy duds", the cowboy had refused to be baited and had moved toward the gaming tables in the back without answering. This had incensed the miner and he had screamed that he wouldn't be ignored, but when he had immediately departed from the saloon, it was thought the confrontation over. Then when the cowboy left Wagner's, he found the miner in the street with his hand on a gun shoved in the waistband of his pants.

As the cowboy had moved to the edge of the sidewalk, he had asked the miner, "You going to shoot me where I stand?"

"No. Get yourself out here in the street where others can't get hit by a stray bullet when you miss me."

It was at this point that Roger and Amanda stepped onto the sidewalk, just in time to hear the cowboy say, "I won't miss."

There was such casual certainty in his voice, and maybe a little sadness as well, that for a moment the miner looked less assured of what he was doing. This was especially true when the drover moved into the street at an angle where the sun was behind his left shoulder and said, "I think I should tell you that out on the trail when we get bored we do a lot of target practice."

Roger frowned and exchanged a quick look with Harvey Boone who had just arrived on the scene.

The cowboy was continuing to talk in a slow measured tone. "That's day after day of practice and in my case winning the competitions. Now, I know I bumped into you, but I swear it was only because I didn't see you behind me. I certainly meant no disrespect."

After a moment's hesitation, the miner took his hand off the gun at his waist and walked forward with his hand extended. "I take that as a mighty fine apology and it would be damn unsporting of me not to accept it. Let no man say I'm that."

The two men shook hands, tipped their hats in salute to each other, and walked away in opposite directions. The miner had a band of sweat on his upper lip, and the drover did not. He did, however, decide that he would leave town after a quick meal at the Capitol Chop stand in Wagner's. Maybe he found Bodie a little too unpredictably dangerous after living a peaceful life out on the trail with stampedes, ravenous wolves, and rattlesnakes in his bedroll.

The crowd disbursed, most happy with the outcome, but a few grumbling about the lack of excitement. Roger and Amanda entered the Can-Can to enjoy a nice breakfast.

What the cowboy did *not* see were the two men who had been drinking to excess at the bar across the room from the chop stand, and who followed him from Wagner's after he had finished eating an hour later. Once outside, they hollered to him just as he reached his horse tied to the hitching rail. One of the men yelled, "You're a damn liar."

"Excuse me?" The cowboy turned to him with his brows elevated in surprise.

Roger and Amanda emerged from the Can-Can Restaurant, having finished their breakfast. A small crowd quickly gathered and they joined it on the sidewalk.

The other drunk loudly denounced the cowboy by saying, "Drovers with herds aren't going to have target practice around all those nervous steers. It could start a stampede."

The drover smiled. "You're right, of course."

The two drunks blinked at this easy admission and immediately calmed down. "What?"

"Was the miner a friend or enemy of yours?" the stranger asked them.

Both men mumbled something about more friend than not.

"So don't you think it was a tactful way of ending the confrontation without shedding his blood?"

One of the men asked, "You sure it would have ended with *his* blood on the ground?"

The cowboy's smile turned Amanda cold as he replied, "Oh, yes." That was all that drunk needed to hear, and he swung around and hurried into Wagner's.

But the other man stayed in the street, swaggering a little as he said, "Or it means you're too much of a coward to confront a challenge."

The cowboy sighed and shook his head in resignation, turning to those gathered on the sidewalk to see what new fireworks this stranger was igniting. The drunk suddenly reached around under his coat to his back and pulled his gun from the waistband of his pants. It was obvious that the cowboy had no time to pull his own gun and successfully defend himself. Instead, he looked around at those gathered and said loudly something that sounded to Amanda like, "Is there no one here who will help the widow's son?"

Roger swore under his breath and, along with four other men that included Harvey Boone, rushed forward. While the drunk was thrown off balance by suddenly being surrounded by these men familiar to him, Roger reached out and simply pulled the weapon from his hand, telling him, "You can retrieve your weapon from the bartender in Wagner's when you've sobered up." With that, Roger went into the popular saloon for a moment before returning to Amanda's side.

He quickly led her north to the Tuolumne Stables where he had rented a light black rig with the roll top down for their date. He drove the team with surprising skill, at least to Amanda's judgment, while chatting about the town's plans for the July Fourth celebrations he had been hearing about.

They had attained the southern reaches of Main past Lowe, neither one looking directly at the spot where Joseph had been hanged. After several minutes of silence, Amanda told Roger, "You know, we could have rented horses. I do know how to ride."

"Good to know. Although I don't know how you women can abide a side saddle."

She smiled. "It's an acquired skill, believe me, and it doesn't come naturally. It's much easier to sit astride."

He gave her a glance with raised brows. "You've done that?"

She laughed at him. "Are you scandalized? My father taught me when I was only ten."

"So you do have some good memories of spending time with him?"

"Yes, a few. I guess I let the fact of his leaving us so suddenly, and then writing to us so seldom, gloss over them."

"Maybe now you can recall even more, and with some pleasure."

"Maybe." She wasn't yet ready to completely let go of her resentment, but she was at least beginning to see that maybe she could.

The wheels of the light rig bounded easily over the narrow track as it left Main and headed down the slope that followed the Booker Flat Road. They continued downhill and soon passed the grandstand of the Booker Flat baseball field and race track. The horses strained up a hill and when it leveled off, they were on the edge of a small grove of willows just showing a few bright green leaves rattling in the gentle breeze.

After leading the horses to the spring that watered the trees, they spread a blanket on the ground and opened the box containing pieces of cake that Roger had stored behind the seat to surprise her. As Roger set out the plates, Amanda poured water from a stoppered jug.

"Why did you do that back there in town?" she asked suddenly.

"It won't hurt that drunk to be without his gun for a while."

"I meant how you went to that man's rescue, you and the others all at the same time. Was it because of what he hollered out to the crowd?"

Roger was silent for so long Amanda began to wonder if he'd gone suddenly deaf. "I'll explain later, after we've had our picnic." But he didn't. It was obvious to Amanda that he didn't want to talk about it, and she had enough wisdom not to push him.

"Someone said Mrs. Bowers the seer was back in town. Didn't you and Charlotte visit with her the last time she was here?"

"Yes."

"Are you going to see her again?"

"No."

When she said nothing more, Roger picked up her hand and asked, "Is something wrong?"

Amanda shook her head. "I just don't want to admit to her that her prediction about my father was accurate." But she was also afraid that Mrs. Bowers might tell her something about her future that she didn't want to hear, especially if it included Roger.

"Did you hear that another of Dr. Blackwood's patients died?" she asked him.

"Nasty fellow. I wouldn't let him touch me."

"He gives me the creeps."

If they thought him strange thus far, the following freezing January his actions would cause people to think him beyond bizarre. Assorted dismembered human remains would be discovered in a house, and it would be clear that they had been used for dissection and experimentation. Not long after that grisly discovery, frozen remains would be found dumped into a shaft of the Ajax mine.

After an intense investigation, it would be discovered that although no one was missing from town, there were two recently disturbed graves on the hill. One of them would belong to a beloved wife recently deceased. All of this would eventually lead to Dr. Blackwood. The Grand Jury would meet to decide his fate, but to no avail as he would flee the town and would never be heard from again.

The rest of their outing followed much the same tone, interspersed with moments of intimacy where not only kisses were lingering but his hand felt the slimness of her legs as far as her knees. When they started back, without Roger having talked about their future, Amanda relaxed completely. Roger saw this and took the hint, remaining silent on the subject.

Later that week Amanda went to visit Cherry Wilson. She not only wanted to see her friend, but thought she would know why Roger had responded to the cowboy's strange appeal.

Cherry waved a hand in disgust. "Oh, it has something to do with those men who are members of the Masons. It sounds like one of their coded appeals for help. Another is some kind of secret handshake that lets them know they're a fellow member. Don't know what it's like, though." Beyond that Cherry had no information. "Take some good advice, Amanda, and leave it alone."

Sensing that the subject approached deep and uncharted waters, Amanda decided to follow Cherry's advice.

Browsing around Harvey Boone's store later that afternoon, Amanda enjoyed seeing the recent shipment of goods now displayed along the shelves, countertops and floor space. But it was not only the abundance of his dry goods that kept her there, but also the snatches of conversation between the other customers.

Amanda sidled closer to the register with several items in her arms so she could hear what Mr. Boone was discussing with Mr. Cain. These were men who had made a difference in the town, adding to its stability and thus its future.

Mr. Cain, born in Quebec, Canada, had arrived in Bodie in 1879 newly married to the former Martha "Lila" Wells who was originally from Genoa, Nevada, the oldest settlement in that state. He was at the forefront of the recently developed Bodie Railway and Lumber Company, which derived from the Bodie Wood and Lumber Company back in 1878. His interest in all things Bodie would become legendary, and in 1888 he would purchase half interest in the Bodie Bank, and the other half in 1892. Decades later he would end up owning most of the town as it slowly declined into the following century.

But in 1881, the town was excited to know that soon low-cost timber would be available to the mines and cordwood would no longer be a problem in the winter to heat homes. With a turntable at the end, the train would turn around at Mono Mills, load up wood and return to Bodie. Altogether the loaded train would travel thirty-one miles on narrow gauge rails from Mono Mills after descending onto the flats of the Mono Basin, heading north along the eastern shore of Mono Lake, and finally coming over the hills toward Bodie.

The route would be full of sharp curves, no tunnels, and grades of nearly four percent that would climb 200 feet per mile and require two switchbacks. Three large trestles would bridge wide ravines. Coming into town, the rails would round Nevada Hill and cross Taylor Gulch, entering Bodie below the Red Cloud Mine and ending at a switch yard in the small valley created by High Peak and Silver Hill. It would be met by wagons from the various mines and mills, and the wood quickly distributed to where it was needed most.

Seth and Dan Cook, along with Robert Graves (a Comstock millionaire) were heavily invested in the Syndicate Mine, and they knew the town needed easier access to the wood upon which it relied. At the meeting where investors discussed the wisdom of the railroad, considering that Bodie seemed to be in a slight decline, Graves pointed out that Virginia City had been in worse condition when the Virginia & Truckee Railroad was built to service it.

What sold the idea of the railroad to many was his attitude of certainty when he reminded them that it was those in Virginia City "who had faith and stuck to the camp when it was down who were the ones who came out right in the long run."

Not only would the new railroad own two engines, but also 40 cars that were mostly flatcars built at the Virginia & Truckee's yard in Carson City. It would offer hope to a town that badly needed it. But even a railroad could not keep the mines from eventually declining in production.

CHAPTER 15
SUMMER, 1881

It had been a bright June day, and Roger and Amanda were out walking in the early evening, enjoying the sunset and the cool air. When he had to be at work in a few minutes, they finished their conversation on the corner of Main and King Streets.

Suddenly loud shouts followed by the sound of glass breaking could be heard from one of the opium dens preferred by the white trade.

"Sounds like a helluva fight," Roger exclaimed. A man ran out of one of the dens and passed them, disappearing down Main. "That was Jim Stockdale. I wonder if he was involved in what we just heard."

"Looks like he's returning for more of the same."

She said this as Stockdale passed them walking rapidly back up King, then busted his way back into the same opium den that he had vacated so quickly. A moment later they could hear the sound of three shots fired in rapid succession. Amid much screaming, the house erupted people into the street. They raced onto Main, further up King, and some down Bonanza. Those most familiar with the area found a nearby alley and disappeared into its darkness.

Stockdale ran out and kept going north down Main on a horse he'd borrowed from a man who chased after him screaming curses and threats of damnation. Several constables were soon on the scene, and after a few minutes they came out of the building with four men carrying between them the limp and bloody body of "Tex" Hitchell. They loaded him into the back of a wagon and headed for the County Hospital south of town; a two-story brick building on Fuller that had once belonged to a now-deceased French Canadian.

The *Standard News* gave the details of the fracas the next day. "*It is not known what passed between the two men in the room. It is stated that Hitchell began abusing Stockdale, knocking him down with a six-shooter, an opium pipe, or some other equally dangerous weapon. There was a commotion of considerable magnitude. At any rate, Stockdale left the den and procured a revolver. When he returned, he found Hitchell in a bunk, considerably under the influence of the deadly narcotic. Immediately upon Stockdale spying him, he began to shoot. The first ball struck Hitchell in the abdomen, another ball struck him in the right groin, and the third ball also entered his body."* There were more details of the same gruesome nature, after which it summarized with, *"The wounded man staggered up and rolled out on the floor. The Chinese and other inmates of the house were terror strickened. Chinamen could be seen running in all directions, yelling and shouting as though the house were about to fall and crush them all. Some drew pistols, others drew knives, and within a few minutes King Street was alive with celestials, white opium fiends, and frequenters of the Chinese quarters. Hitchell was removed to the County Hospital where Doctors Van Zandt and Blackwood were sent for. The wounded man was in great pain, but did not display much concern as to his injuries. He died at one o'clock this morning."*

Stockdale was discovered in Aurora and arrested there by that town's Sheriff.

It was a day for tragedy, but not all of it was on the streets or involved a gun. Canadian miner Norm McSwain was assigned to the 500 foot level of the Bechtel Mine. Into pre-drilled holes he loaded a round of giant powder and began tamping it in, the men on either side of him watched with little interest as they waited to move on to the next location.

Those further down the line and at the top heard the explosion and felt the earth rock beneath their feet. The charge was not meant to go off until the area was safely cleared. When the superintendent got to the area, it was to find McSwain slumped against the opposite wall of the level with the top of his head missing and his shift buddies scattered around him, but with no serious injuries.

Alex Larson, a popular Swede, tried to get up but fell back down next to the dead man. When he turned his head and saw his friend covered in blood and his empty eyes staring into nothing just below a forehead that was missing, his screams filled the small space. The others helped him to the cage where he and the rest of those involved were brought to the surface. Dr. Davidson looked them over, patched up their cuts and told them to take a day to rest because over the next couple of days they would begin to feel the bruising from the blast. It wasn't the good doctor's first experience with a mining accident, nor would it be his last.

"Swede", although not hurt physically, seemed to be the most affected by what had happened to his friend and he kept repeating, "Why him?" It may have gone unspoken by the others, but they were all wondering why it had not been them.

June was the month that Amanda had promised herself that she would leave Bodie and return to Placerville, and she was only too aware that she hadn't begun any real plans. Questions plagued her. If she announced that she was leaving, how would Roger respond? So much depended on that. It could mean staying in Bodie as his wife, returning to Placerville with a husband, or returning there alone. Of one thing she was sure; she would not stay another winter in Bodie unless there was a very good reason.

The restlessness that now accompanied her days brought her outdoors one morning in an effort to expend the built-up energy of indecision. Her room was no longer the comforting refuge it had always been, and seemed more often to feel like it was closing in on her. She adjusted the wide-brimmed straw hat that complimented her pink chintz dress and reached to her neck to tie the strings of the matching short cape. Walking down Standard Avenue to Wood Street, she stopped a moment to reflect on how much she wished Charlotte was still in town so she could drop by for tea and wise advice. With a sigh of resignation, she continued up the steepening hill past several nondescript residences to her right and the two-story 20-stamp Standard Mill on her left.

Thinking of Placerville and how much she still loved the town, Amanda told herself that nevertheless sometimes in life plans just change. With one of those bright flashes of realization that hit us so suddenly, it came to her why she had not yet made plans to return to her old home. It would be going backward, and she wanted to go forward. It was that simple.

However, that did not mean she wanted to stay in Bodie with its barely survivable winters, nerve-stripping noise, violence and traumatic deaths, and constant reminders of events she would like to forget. She wanted to be where the winters were milder, the streets safer, and where she could make new memories. She clutched her hands to her chest and thought, "Oh, and where there are big trees and rushing streams." And although she dared not hope too much, if possible she wanted it all within sight of the glorious Sierra that she missed like an old love who had never disappointed.

She looked up at the cluster of mines on High Peak Hill and Bodie Bluff just beyond over its left shoulder. Down its right shoulder she could see first the Standard Mine just below the peak, then the Bodie, and the Mono. She could only try to imagine their vertical shafts descending down through ledges of gold mixed with silver, and smiled as she wished her father had invested years earlier when they had started paying dividends.

At the lower reaches of the hill was the Bulwer Tunnel that extended horizontally into the hill. Near it was the 30-stamp Bulwer-Standard Mill that complimented the 20-stamp Standard. Each week the Standard Mine delivered twelve-hundred tons of rock to these two mills. The main shaft provided ore that was processed at the Bulwer-Standard mill, while from the older incline ore was provided to the Standard Mill, carried to it by the aerial cable tramway. The Standard's main shaft was passing the 900 foot level, showing the owner's faith in the abundance to be brought forth from the deeper levels.

But to get it out would require equipment of a more powerful nature, and that meant spending the shareholders' money. In spite of this, they would order the equipment from San Francisco that October, and in November a two-story structure would begin construction over the existing site so the hoisting and pumping could continue uninterrupted. Nothing was allowed to stop production, even preparations for more.

Although Amanda couldn't see them from her current vantage point, she knew that the mills of the Syndicate and Bodie mines were north at the base of Bodie Bluff and beyond those was The Miners Mill down the canyon to Aurora. From all these mills tall stove pipes extended high into the sky releasing smoke from the forges melting the bullion so it could be poured into molds in the shape of long bricks. From other stovepipes rose steam, but those were at the hoisting works that operated on steam generated energy.

The aerial cable tramway followed her up the hill from the Standard Mill as it stretched to the Standard Mine, and she watched with a mix of horror and amusement as a miner crouched in one of the heavy iron buckets and rode down the tramway to the mill. It was a dangerous pastime and not approved by the management, but men did it from time to time as a dare or a means to get down the hill quickly.

Over both hills zigzagged a web-like network of dusty roads connecting the mills and mines, and along which were scattered dozens of small buildings. These were the storage sheds, cabins and boarding houses built by the mine owners to house men and materials, including the blasting powder used in the tunnels.

Feeling the ground shake while hearing the rumble of a wagon behind her, Amanda quickly flattened herself against a building to her right. Past her strained a huge wagon full of cordwood that was pulled by eight mules and two wheeler horses straining at their harnesses. The muleskinner rode the left horse directly in front of the wagon with the pile of wood looming ten feet above his head. The wide iron wheels of the heavy wagon ground into the road and drove rocks deep into the soil beneath them, but they held up the wagon as wooden wheels could not have. A few minutes later Amanda was once again able to walk on.

Five months later the railroad from Mono Mills would be able to bring in ten times this amount of wood to the mines, at least until deep snow covered the tracks. Considering the building-size pile of wood stacked now on several of the lower flats around High Peak Hill, Amanda was impressed with the efficient job the wagons were doing in keeping the mills stocked. It was also one of the greatest expenses of running the mines.

The presence of each mine was identified by huge sloping piles of waste rock dumped outside each one; the older the mine, the larger the pile of rock. Outside the nearest mine, a Piute woman rummaged through the lower reaches of a dump while holding onto two fist-sized rocks. She would bring them to an assayer for the value of whatever little gold was still in them, and it would buy her supplies at one of the stores with a shopkeeper whose kindness allowed Piutes to shop there.

As the road crested the hill, Amanda turned to her right to see "the southern mines". The first was the large Noonday Mill dominating the area, the Noonday hoisting works, the Oro Mine, and beyond that the defunct Red Cloud Mine and the wealthy Noonday and North Noonday. This last reminded her of her father.

This time, instead of the old familiar combination of frustration and disappointment she had carried as a reaction to years of being disregarded and treated as inconsequential, she felt a gentle fondness. For all that he had not been as an attentive parent, it had still occurred to him to write and ask her to join him in Bodie. She might never know what motivated him to do this, but she had finally arrived at the point of realizing that it didn't matter. He had asked, and she had arrived. And it had given her five months of memories that she had not had before, and for that she was grateful.

Realizing she had walked further from town than she had intended, she started back down the hill. There were huge piles of cord wood everywhere, ready to be fed into the stoves that boiled the water that created the steam that ran the hoist works and mills. N. B. Hunewill's Buckeye Canyon lumber mill above Bridgeport was the source of much of this wood. It was pinion pine, which was full of pitch that burned hot, making it ideal for the steam engines.

Unfortunately, the Indians needed these same trees for their seeds, an historic source of food over hundreds of years. But such a consideration was beyond the ability of the mine owners, and if the trees were needed for fuel, they were cut down. The availability of wood from Mono Mills would at least spare the last stands of the trees in some of the region.

These thoughts reminded Amanda of Cherry's invitation to visit the Piutes with her in a few days. Looking forward to this made her feel less restless, and she walked faster down the hill and back to the hotel.

As she walked, she began to detail to herself the things that to her would make an ideal place to live. Besides wanting a sense of lushness around her and access to the Sierra, most important of all were people who had an interest in more than fighting with one another. After thinking it through, it occurred to her that there was only one place that fitted such a tall order.

She stopped at the corner across from Wagner's, looked up King Street and watched Sam Chung sitting on the verandah of his house while smoking his favorite Meerschaum pipe. Children played in the street and edges of sidewalks, and she could hear the soft strains of a Chinese guitar coming from an old tumble-down building flying colored flags from the roof. She knew that hidden from her view were the dreaded opium dens, but for the moment all was quaintly peaceful.

Before visiting the Indians with Cherry on Friday, she decided to see a play with Roger at the Union Hall, put on by the Bodie Dramatic Society and called *Ingomar*. It was billed as "one of the grandest characters known to the Thespian Art", with Miss Katie Shaughnessy set to play Parthenia, the star of the piece. Amanda and Roger enjoyed it thoroughly, and then decided to return to the hotel rather than go on to a late supper.

That night as they sipped brandy in her room after a light dinner in the dining room, Amanda summoned her courage, stilled her beating heart, and told Roger, "I've decided that I'm not going to return to Placerville after all."

Roger felt himself smiling, trying to hold in reserve his celebration of her decision to stay in Bodie with him. So all he said was, "Oh?"

She took a deep breath, and although she wanted to look anywhere but at his face, she forced herself to do it out of respect for him. "I'm going to move to the Owens Valley where Charlotte and Emily live."

He didn't try to keep his shock and devastation from showing on his face. "I thought you were planning all this time to return to Placerville and rejoin your friends."

"I thought that was what I wanted, but I now know why I've not started planning."

"I thought maybe it was because, well, because of us."

"What about us?" She cocked her head to the side, seriously wanting an answer. "Although you've alluded to our having a future together, we've never actually discussed it seriously."

He ran his hand over his face before weaving his fingers through his thick black hair. "You know I'm making plans for us."

"No, I don't."

"Well, I am." He looked at her in earnest. "I thought we would leave here next spring. I can get a job in the saloons in Placerville or maybe Sacramento. But there isn't anything for me to do in Lone Pine."

"They have saloons."

"But not the traffic that I need for high stakes faro." After a moment of silence, he said, "I mean, can you see me herding cattle or raising alfalfa?"

"Yes, I can." She looked into his eyes and declared with a certainty that she felt more than he did, "I can see you doing anything you want to. And it's a supply town for mines near and far, so they have a lot of people passing through."

"But they don't have the kind of money that I need to make it worthwhile. And I'm a bust at poker or anything else." His eyes were pleading, and it was obvious that he wanted to say more, but didn't know what it should be.

"Roger, that's all about you." She forced herself to keep her voice soft. "You've made no reference to me or my needs, and I have to think about *my* future. I really don't want to stay in Bodie and I don't now want to go back to Placerville. I'm tired of the deep snow, the blowing dust, forcing my way through the crowds on the sidewalks, and each day reading about the latest person to die in a mine or a saloon. I want to be with people who are living normal and at least somewhat refined lives, and who are building a community together. Ever since the great earthquake in '72 that leveled Lone Pine, that's what they've been doing there."

With his tone surly and tending toward the argumentative, he snapped at her, "I don't think you know what you want." The stinging tone of his words hung in the air and he felt like smacking himself in the face. But he didn't know how to take back what he had said. He stood there hurt and feeling awkward, and wondering why he wasn't enough to make her happy. And he resented her for it. In an effort to release his frustration, he began to pace.

Amanda watched him moving up and down the length of her room, not sure what she could say to get him to see her perspective. "I'm not sure *you* know what you want. I know we've declared that we love each other, but maybe that's not enough. All I know is that I don't want to stay here in this God-forsaken town even with you, and you don't want to leave here to go with me to Lone Pine."

He turned to look down at her, noticing the sun gleaming on her dark auburn hair. Although there was sadness in her eyes, there was also a determined set to her jaw, and he knew he wasn't going to be able to change her mind. "I guess you're right."

She stood up and took a step toward him before stopping just out of his reach. They stood and looked at one another, each fighting tears and the constraint around their hearts, but neither wavering in what they wanted. A few moments of this was more than Roger could stand and he turned, leaving the room without saying a further word.

An hour later, exhausted by weeping into several now soggy handkerchiefs, Amanda went to bed. But it was only to spend a restless night, waking periodically to question herself and her motives. A woman should not want more than marriage, she told herself, repeating what she had so often been told. Security is what is important. Find a man and settle down to raise well-behaved children while keeping a clean house and obeying society's rules, chief of which is not to put yourself above your man's needs. It wasn't that she was unwilling to do this, but at least she wanted to do it in a place of relative civility.

The next morning she wanted nothing more than to languish in bed all day, even being tempted to send word to Mr. Stewart that she was too ill to work that evening. She certainly was not in the mood to visit the Indian village outside of town with Cherry in an hour. But she had promised her friend that she would accompany her, so she threw back the bed covers and began to dress. The last thing she did before leaving was to dab powder over her red nose.

As she walked up the path to the front door of the Wilson home, the unexpected sound of a child laughing echoed from the yard at the back of the house. Hurrying to the tall fence, Amanda tried to see through a weathered crack between the boards. All she saw was a flash of blue going in at the back door. Not wanting to be caught spying, she hurried back to the front door and knocked.

It was several minutes later that Cherry opened the door with a composed smile of greeting, closing the front door and joining Amanda on the porch where they each picked up a bundle of items wrapped in old bed sheets. Following Cherry's lead, Amanda tossed the bundle over her shoulder and felt the muscles in her back react as though surprised and not liking it much.

Cherry had with her a long stick that she used as a staff as she walked. Amanda commented on it. "I can tell you've walked up this road before."

"Oh, this. Yes, it helps in the walking a bit, but mainly I carry it in case one of the dogs gets too aggressive."

And indeed, there were dozens of dogs roaming the town now that so many people had left town. Abandoned cats lived under the buildings scavenging mice and other rodents, but the dogs left behind had formed themselves into packs. They were a problem now, but in a few months when the area was a dozen feet under snow, most of them would die of starvation and exposure. The most compassionate of the men would shoot them and put them out of their misery. It was one more thing Amanda added to her list of what she would not miss in Bodie.

It was a long walk north down Main and out onto the Aurora Road, but neither of them could afford the cost of renting a wagon or light rig. So they trudged slowly up a network of paths into the treeless hills that rolled out above the town.

As they walked, they chatted about a number of things going on in the town that had recently been written up in the newspapers. At one point, as they stopped to catch their breath, Amanda said, "I wish we had rented horses."

"Cheaper than a rig, I admit, but difficult to carry these bundles when riding a lady's saddle."

At this Amanda snorted her contempt. "We could always ride astride with the bundles tied on behind."

Cherry, several years older and of an earlier generation, looked at her in astonishment. "Ride clothespin style? No proper woman spreads her legs that far unless she wants a child."

Amanda almost laughed aloud, but made the attempt to look properly chastised. She was, however, thinking that poor Lars Wilson no doubt was very happy that Bodie had so many dance houses.

Tucked into the low swells of the hills, they entered an area of cleared brush and found huts that constituted one of the local Piute villages. Many of the huts were dug into the earth of a natural low hill so that the dwelling was wrapped by earth on three sides. The interior walls were lined with scrap wood, split and flattened tin cans, sagebrush roots, pieces of cloth and old clothes blown out from town during the high winds. Anything they thought might keep out the cold was used. The roofs were more of the same, with a hole in the middle through which a stovepipe protruded for the emission of smoke from a fire in the winter when it was not possible to be outside for any length of time.

This made Amanda think of how cold and hard their life must be when the snow was deep and ice hung from everything. She fought the urge to shudder. But these people did not want her pity, and she did not want to disrespect them by showing how she felt. She turned away to admire some rabbit skin blankets airing on poles and large bushes, evidence of their main source of warmth. Running a hand over one and feeling the slick softness beneath her hand, she smiled in admiration of how beautifully made it was.

Looking around her at the dozen thrown-together huts, Amanda was struck with a wave of sadness as she realized that this tribe was the last vestige of what at one time were hundreds of proud Indians in the area who thought of themselves as "the people". When the white soldiers had arrived the Piute tribes had fought nobly to defend their homeland, but they had not been trained in battle like some of the plains Indians. So when the settlers and gold seekers came and saw so much open rich land, it was in essence over for the local Piutes. Of course, there were skirmishes and battles, with atrocities on both sides, but soon the Piutes' food sources were compromised and that meant disaster for them. Those tribes that didn't move on were forced to make do, much as those near Bodie had done.

On this day, the Piute women were wearing calico dresses under decorative blankets used as shawls and capes. Scarves covered their hair and were tied firmly under their chins, allowing only straight-cut bangs to fall almost to their eyes. Amanda wondered if it might be a way to keep the glare of the sun from blinding them.

Charlotte had once told Amanda that the Piutes of the past had worn nothing more than short grass skirts in summer and the rabbit blankets in winter. With the arrival of white settlers and calico, the women had happily adapted to wearing colorful dresses, and were quick to make friends with town women who owned a new-fangled hand-cranked sewing machine. They did work for them in trade for a dress "cranked out" on such a machine.

The Piutes above Bodie were considered part of the Mono Lake Kutzadika tribal territory. This territory started north beyond the Bodie Hills and extended south to the Mammoth Mine, east to Walker Lake and west to Tuolumne Meadows near the Yosemite Indians' land.

Amanda smiled and nodded as she passed two women sitting in front of a brush hut while making baskets. Reeds were stacked next to them, a large pitch-lined basket full of water between them. Another was washing clothes in a tin-lined wooden wash stand and hanging the items on a rope stretched between two huts.

Several women were pounding harvested grain or kutzavie gathered from Mono Lake, using grinding stones that had probably been used by dozens of generations of women before them. One young woman was scraping rabbit skins and stacking the hides to one side, most likely in preparation of the next winter's blanket. Some of the older children were keeping an eye on the younger ones as they toddled around, and both were being watched over by the gray-haired grandmothers. These older women were making cradleboards for the babies soon to be delivered by three nearby young women with large tummy bulges. There were no men in camp this day, most likely off hunting; or playing hand games on the sidewalks in town.

Unlike a group of women who might be working outside in town, here there was little talking while they did their daily tasks, and that which was necessary was spoken in a low voice. Amanda wondered if that was typical, or if it was because town women were present. She was impressed when the children were told to help with something and they didn't argue or procrastinate. Even the littlest of them, barely old enough to walk, was assigned the task of carrying something like small pieces of wood or bowls of grain. It was obvious that this was a true community, with everyone pulling together and acting as a whole; unlike the white so-called communities she had lived in, where everyone had their own agenda even while trying to look like it was about others. But for the Piutes, cooperation meant survival.

Cherry introduced Amanda to the woman washing clothes. It was then that Amanda learned the woman was washing for two of the wealthier families in town. The woman offered them a small bowl of fresh water and they drank greedily, neither aware of how thirsty they were until they started to drink. At last they sat down on a blanket and placed their bundles in front of the woman who spoke better English than Amanda had expected. After exchanging views on the weather, they discussed the crop of rabbits the tribe had recently trapped by Mono Lake and the number of baskets recently sold at Mr. Boone's store as well as Mr. Bryant's store in Bridgeport.

Finally, it was time to present the items they had brought with them, and without the aid of an announcement, all the women in the village gathered around. Laughter and giggles followed as they grabbed for the used clothing, cast off shoes, hair brushes, ribbons, bits of cloth, side combs, and knitted goods. In five minutes it was all gone, removed to the various dwellings to be enjoyed and fully utilized.

On their way into town, Amanda and Cherry passed several wagons filled with rock. It was all headed to Main where it would be spread over the mud in an effort to provide a solid bed for the heavy road traffic. Also in the way of improvement, ditches were being dug to drain the swampy conditions south of town. Soon a wooden flume would be built to drain water from the Foundry to Standard Avenue, most of it underground, with a fall of 1 5/8 inches per 16 feet.

After the long walk back, somewhat less arduous because it was downhill into town and without their burdens, they arrived at Cherry's house exhausted, hungry and thirsty. Sitting with steaming mugs of hot tea, they munched on several large oatmeal cookies and felt their energy return. Just as she was about to speak, Amanda stopped and looked up. A door had slammed upstairs.

"What was that?"

Cherry stiffened and said, "I didn't hear anything."

"It almost sounded like a door slammed and for sure someone is walking around upstairs."

The stiffening became a solid block of ice. "Is this why you pretended to be my friend?"

"Excuse me?" Amanda was confused and hurt and it showed clearly.

"Oh, my," Cherry gulped. "You really don't know?"

"Know what?" She looked at Cherry and said in her most determined voice, "Look Cherry, your husband is at work and someone is upstairs walking around. And I'm sure I heard a child laughing in the backyard when I arrived."

For a long time Cherry said nothing, then she stood up with obvious resolution and walked to the foot of the stairs. "Marlena, please come down."

A few minutes later a little girl of ten walked into the room, and Amanda gasped. It was the child she had seen in the window, her long black hair flowing over her shoulders and over a loose-fitting light blue cotton dress that fell to the top of her lace-up flat-heeled boots.

"Say hello to Miss Blake, Marlena."

The girl looked at Amanda with wide eyes filled with wonder and said nothing. Amanda, however, smiled warmly and told her, "My, but you're a pretty young lady."

That made Marlena smile, and she then turned to her mother. "May I have a cookie after I take my medicine, mother?"

"Yes, dear. And some milk if you'd like."

When the pretty child had left the room and gone into the kitchen, Amanda turned to her friend and waited, saying nothing.

Cherry looked at her and hesitated a moment before saying, "Can I trust you to keep what I tell you confidential?"

"Of course you can."

"Even from Roger?"

Amanda laughed shortly. "He's only a friend, not a husband."

Cherry couldn't help but smile. "That may change."

"Most likely not, but I wouldn't tell him anyway. Charlotte and Emily taught me that it's okay to keep some things from one's husband."

"Very true. But thankfully I have Lars to share my secret. You see, Marlena is our daughter."

Amanda only nodded her head. "Why do you hide her away from everyone?"

Cherry sighed. "She has a condition."

"A what?"

"She's as normal as any other child, but then suddenly she'll have a fit. She falls to the floor suddenly, jerks a few times, and then passes into a stupor for a few minutes. And then she awakes and it's as though nothing had happened except she's very tired. And she has no memory of anything having happened. Dr. Deal calls it falling sickness and has given her medicines. They help some, but not completely. He says it can be caused by blows to the head, but she's never had any. He also says it can be caused by water in the brain or tumors, but being so young he has ruled that out. He also claims that sudden frights, fits of passion or great emotions of the mind can bring it on, but she's too young for those I would think. So we keep her as calm as possible, and give her the best food and nervine tinctures to tone the nervous system."

"But why do you hide her away from everyone so they don't even know she exists? Don't you think people would understand?"

"No, I don't." Cherry got up and walked to the window looking out onto the street. "I think a few would, but others would think her possessed or something as stupid, and would shun her. Children would tease her too. I won't have her ridiculed, or us thought of as unfit parents."

Thinking of the level of ignorance in the general populace, Amanda could only say, "You may be right."

Cherry turned back to Amanda, a small tear gathering on the edge of her right eye and threatening to fall on her cheek. "As she gets older, she becomes more curious about the world and she wants to get out into it. It's getting more difficult to keep her hidden."

"But if people realize that her affliction isn't contagious, they would surely be compassionate and not frightened. Even if she doesn't go to school, she could at least play freely in the backyard."

"What about the religious people who'll say it's punishment from God on us as her parents?"

"You've been down that road before, haven't you?"

"Yes. One of the ministers in town described Bodie as a sea of sin, lashed by the tempests of lust and passion. I tried talking to him once, but before I could go into detail he started talking about parents deserving the off-spring they brought forth and if something was wrong with *it*, it must be a visitation of judgment from God." She pursed her lips and declared, "In my experience, no one can act more unchristian-like than someone insisting they're a good Christian, or a sanctimonious clergyman."

"Humanity has no denomination, Cherry. And every town has its hypocrites. It's an unfortunate fact of life. But sometimes people can surprise you with their generosity and kindness."

"I know that." She pursed her lips in a grimace of resolve. "But I won't risk it here. That's why we're moving to Sacramento next month. There's a doctor there who has experience with this type of thing who feels he can help us, since her fits are not that severe."

When Cherry had told Amanda his name, she said, "I know him. He used to live in Placerville and looked after my mother. He was indeed very compassionate and well-trained. He was known to read a lot of the latest medical texts, so maybe he's learned something new."

"That's what we're hoping."

"I'm going to miss your being here."

"But aren't you also going to leave here and return to Placerville? It's not so far from Sacramento, so we can visit occasionally."

"That was my plan, but now I'm not so sure." She looked down at her hands clasped tightly in her lap and bit her lower lip to keep it from quivering. "I feel like my future is all up in the air." She then told Cherry about her unsettling conversation with Roger.

Cherry was sympathetic and caring, which didn't make it any easier to hold back her fragile emotions. And after only a few minutes more, Amanda made a quick retreat back to the hotel.

On the morning of a warm July 2, Amanda was serving breakfast to Dan Cook and his brother Seth, both San Francisco major stockholders of the Standard Consolidated Mining Company. Being the largest producer of bullion on the hill, they could afford the best. They were chewing their way through two large porterhouse steaks, along with several eggs and a pile of potatoes.

They were also two of the largest investors in the Bodie Railroad and Lumber Company's narrow gauge railroad currently under construction. In 1876, Seth and Dan had been two of the group of men who had purchased the mine from Essington and Lockberg for a little over $65,000. After they changed the name to the Standard Mining Company and began operation, they installed steam hoisting machinery. Their partners had been Col. J. F. Boyd, William M. Lent, and Colonel Charles Tozer. In 1877 their 20-stamp mill was completed and they no longer had to use the Syndicate's mill on the north side of Bodie Bluff. For years after purchasing the Bunker Hill, now the Standard, they were paying dividends of $50,000 every month for thirty consecutive months until March of '80 when it went up to $75,000.

As they finished eating and were ordering brandies of a type Amanda would have loved to try, a reporter from the *Free Press* joined them, asking what they thought of the future of Bodie.

Dan Cook leaned back in his chair, slowly lit a cigar and between puffs launched into what sounded like a carefully prepared speech, although he made every effort to appear casual in its delivery. "The best answer that could be made to such a query would be to call attention to the fact that we're building a railroad to supply the mines of Bodie with lumber at the expense of $700,000. We wouldn't make this outlay if we didn't anticipate that the district would enjoy a sufficient length of life to make the investment a profitable one. Bodie today is the best and surest camp on the coast. Its bullion output, in my judgment, will be as large or larger ten years from now as it is at present. In the 1,000-foot level of the Standard, we're not far enough in to strike the ledge, but we expect to find it."

Later, just as Amanda's shift ended, people began running into the hotel yelling that the President of the United States, John Garfield, had been "shot by a Chicago nihilist". Throughout the afternoon, people mobbed the street near the telegraph office waiting for news of the President's condition. At six o'clock, the *Free Press* began receiving telegrams. When their first edition hit the streets at 8 o'clock, it was bought out immediately. The President's condition was considered grave.

On July 3,, preparations for the Fourth of July celebration were put on hold. However, very early the morning of the fourth news was received that the President's condition was improving. Consequently, the parade and celebration was back on, although out of respect there was only one brass band playing and some of the competitions were cancelled.

On the morning after, people admired the red glow of a colorful sunrise turn to a bright yellow melding into a cloudless blue sky. It was difficult to believe that anything wrong in the world would not turn out okay.

The town had reason to be optimistic. Besides the improving health of the President, progress on the railroad from Mono Mills was moving forward quickly, and the Standard Mine was sending out ore found at the 300 to 550 foot levels. And the shaft was now 1,034 feet deep. This was why William Irwin, the superintendent of the company, had been the Grand Marshall of the Fourth of July parade the day before.

Late in the month the Swede, Alex Larson, who had survived the explosion and the death of his friend McSwain, was at work at the Bechtel Mine. In the weeks since the accident, Swede had taken to drinking more heavily than he knew was good for him, but it helped blur the picture of his friend without the top of his head and took away the guilt he felt for surviving with only a few bruises. This day, in the middle of the afternoon, Swede stepped backward to avoid a passing ore cart. In doing so, he lost his footing and plunged two hundred feet down an incline to his death. He was buried on the hill, next to his friend McSwain.

In August, after a visit to the beauty emporium at the triangle to get their hair trimmed, Cherry and Amanda were walking south down Main when Cherry asked, "Did you hear about my neighbor's near miss?"

"No."

"She and her daughter were in the front parlor when a stray bullet hit the outside wall of the house. It was only inches from where they were sitting. And right by an open window."

"It's this habit of men to shoot randomly when they're drunk." Amanda shook her head in disgust.

"Why do they feel the need to do such a thing?"

"I think the kick of the guns gives them a feeling of power. But it isn't real power and it lasts only a few seconds so they do it over and over."

Cherry made a noise in her throat that showed clearly what she thought of such foolishness. But she said nothing.

They were on their way to see a woman on north Wood Street who had just given birth to a little boy. They were taking the mother a new shawl that Cherry had knitted, and Amanda had some candies with her. Both women were looking forward to sharing the joyous occasion with the new parents. However, when they reached the house, they found the woman's husband sitting in the parlor with the front door wide open. He was sobbing into a large handkerchief.

The women rushed to his side. "What's the matter, Bob?" Cherry asked him.

"It's Lorraine. She's dead."

The women were stunned. However, after a moment, Amanda asked, "What about the baby?"

"In there." He motioned to the bedroom, where the women found a small pink baby sleeping next to the empty bed that had belonged to his mother.

Cherry picked up the child and held it close. Returning to the parlor, she asked, "Bob, when was the last time the baby ate?"

The man looked at her with empty eyes. After a moment he blinked and said, "I don't know. This morning, I guess, not long before Lorraine died."

Cherry lost no time telling Amanda what to do. "You go to Eggleston's and get me a can of regular milk. And if they have it also get a can of goat's milk."

While Bob alternatively wept and stared fixedly into the distance, Cherry paced back and forth while cradling the child that had begun to whimper. After a several minutes of watching this, Bob said, "You look natural with him."

"Thank you. What's his name?"

"Don't have one."

"You'll have to name him soon, so you'll have something to call him."

"How can I take care of him? I need to work. And I have no family."

Cherry thought for a moment, then said, "I guess I can care for him while you're at work."

"No."

She looked at him and blushed. "I'm sorry. I thought that might be a solution for you."

"No, I mean not just while I'm at work. You keep him. For good." The man's face was set in a grim but determined stare, and he watched Cherry closely.

"You can't mean that." Her voice was barely above a whisper, and her chest was tight with suppressed excitement.

"I do. I can't hardly believe that my woman's gone. I know I'll start drinking, and that means nothing good for the little one. I can see that you're a good woman. I know Lars, and he's a good man."

Cherry looked toward the door where Amanda stood with a sack in her hand. She could tell from the look on Amanda's face that she had heard the last of their conversation. But Amanda said nothing. Instead, she walked up to Cherry and said, "Why don't we let Bob get on with his grieving?" And with an arm around Cherry's shoulders, she turned to Bob and said, "We'll be in touch."

As they entered Cherry's home, she turned to Amanda. "What am I going to do?"

"You're going to feed this child who is obviously hungry and is looking at you like he expects something. I bought a baby's bottle while at the store."

After they had warmed the milk and fed the baby, Cherry showed Amanda how to change the diapers. They then took the little boy upstairs and put him to bed between pillows nestled on either side of him in the middle of the Wilson's bed.

Looking down at him, Cherry asked, "Do you really think I can keep him?"

"I don't know why not. But if I were you, I'd go see Pat Reddy and make it as legal as possible. People have a tendency to change their minds."

At that moment, Marlena entered the room and joined them. Looking down at the child, she asked, "Who is this?"

Cherry hesitated a moment and then asked, "Would you mind if it was your new baby brother? His mother died this morning."

Marlena at first frowned, then smiled broadly. "I'd love a brother."

When Cherry put her arm around her daughter and hugged her, Amanda felt it was time to leave. Before descending the stairs, she looked back at the cozy tableau and smiled. But at the same time there was a constriction in her chest, and she fought off the temptation to feel a little self-pity. But she reminded herself that it had been her decision to leave the town, and Roger, behind.

News came first by telegraph of President Garfield's death on September 16. It quickly was the headline in all the papers. The town immediately draped itself in black and white bunting from verandas and beneath second story windows, and of course all flags were appropriately lowered.

One of the papers offered a black-trimmed box where in it stated: The president is Dead. *Hung be the heavens in black, let the sun hide its face from the sight of man. And the moon and stars refuse to show their light while a nation grieves over the untimely loss of its chosen head.*

This, however, was not sufficient homage for Bodie's citizens. On September 26 a funeral was hastily organized, replete with a riderless horse carrying a reversed empty boot in a stirrup. The horse was led by its owner behind the plumed hearse. Almost everyone in the town donned their best clothes and headed to the cemetery where a mock grave had been prepared. Speeches were made, tears were shed, and threats against the foul assassin uttered.

Not long after this a committee was formed and it was decided that the granite that had been ordered to mark William Bodie's grave would instead be used for a monument to the fallen President. A wooden marker board was placed on Mr. Bodie's grave, but it would not survive more than a couple dozen harsh winters. It would never be replaced.

CHAPTER 16
FALL, 1881

On the eighth day of a cold fall morning, Amanda stood on the sidewalk next to her meager belongings tucked into a cloth satchel and two old suitcases. So much luggage was allowed her because there were only two others traveling with her. The one thing that she had made sure had been safely nestled among her clothes was the tea pot given her by Charlotte. The stage heading south would be leaving in fifteen minutes and would eventually reach Lone Pine after two changes to other stage lines.

All of a sudden a shrill whistle unlike anything heard before in Bodie filled the air, causing everyone in the town to stop where they were and look east. There was no forward movement on the sidewalks, teamsters reigned in their teams and light rigs sat still beside them, men in saloons suspended their glasses in mid-air, utensils were laid down on plates, and riders pulled their mounts to a stop.

This frozen tableau lasted for a brief moment in time, then the same unfamiliar whistle blew again. But this time it was met with cheers as everyone came to life in a rush of excitement. Shopkeepers, businessmen and bartenders rushed outside with their customers to crowd the sidewalks. Men shook hands and slapped each other on the back while grinning, and women smiled wistfully as they thought of all they could now bake and how they would be warm in their homes this winter. For what they were hearing was the whistle of the first train to bring wood from Mono Mills into Bodie. The Bodie Railway and Lumber Company had fulfilled its promise.

The railroad was not meant to carry passengers, but it hauled something much more valuable to the town. It brought wood, without which the mines could not run the equipment to allow the mines to go deeper where the next rich ledge could be found. So if a housewife or child would be kept warmer that winter, all well and good, but it was not the most important aspect of what the increased supply of wood would allow as far as the men were concerned. It meant the mines could run more efficiently and for longer into the future. And that meant more money in their pockets.

All this excitement was still erupting around Amanda when the stage driver called out for everyone to get inside. She looked around a final time, but there was still no sign of Roger. A wave of deep sadness washed over her, but also something more as she glanced down Main. She felt a pride for the bustling town so determined to prosper and become something more than just a short-lived mining town with no hope of permanency. No matter the weather, the stock reports or the violence, people here carried on. And despite all the reasons she could give for leaving Bodie, she knew she would miss it.

When the driver barked again his order, Amanda climbed inside the coach with two men in dusty suits, and wisely took a seat with her back to the driver where the ride would be easiest. Perched on the edge of her seat by the door, almost immediately the urge to leap from the coach began to overwhelm her. It was so strong that the feeling became near panic at the thought of never seeing Roger again.

Her position in the coach gave her a last look at Main and Lowe, with its horrible images. But now, two men were kicking up dust at the edge of the road as they swung their fists at each other. One was yelling something about the other having stolen the last of his opium. In mid-October the County Sheriff had made it clear he was going to uphold California's new law against opium dens, at which time those establishments in Bodie closed.

The fines of $500 for being caught smoking it, or $1,000 for selling it, were such that Amanda was surprised that these men would be fighting over it in public. Maybe they were fueled by the additional frustration of the new Sunday closing law for saloons and cigar stores. Some men felt that if this was what progress brought with it, they would move on to less refined climes.

Suddenly several whistles screeched at the mills on the hill, and a gust of wind flung a blast of grit in at the window. Amanda sat back in her seat and closed her eyes, unable to abide the violence, the dirt and the noise one minute more. If this was what Roger wanted in his life, then she could not have him in hers. She needed peace and at least some degree of quiet in her days, and evidently he did not.

With a lurch the stage driver turned left down the Goat Ranch Road, and Bodie disappeared from view, all its spoiled potential glory left behind with the excitement and human drama of one of history's wildest mining camps. Most people felt that Bodie would someday meet the same fate as hundreds of other such camps and disappear from the map. But that would not be Bodie's fate. Just like the people who had been its first witnesses in its youth, Bodie would adapt and change when it was required, and therefore survive.

But Roger was not so quick to do this—or willing. While Amanda was on her way to Lone Pine, Roger made it clear to everyone what a foul mood he was in. As he left Wagner's, a drunk on the street bumped into him and Roger had to restrain himself from punching him. So when he passed an alley and someone grabbed him and demanded his money, he shoved the man so hard that the stranger fell to the ground. Before the stranger knew what was happening, Roger had drawn his boot knife and stood over the fallen man trying to control his rage.

At that moment a deputy walked by and saw this odd tableau, and immediately grabbed Roger from behind, knocking the knife to the ground. The man on the ground started yelling, "That man attacked me for no reason."

"You dirty lying son of a bitch!" Roger yelled, trying to shake off the young deputy who had never met the popular sport. While Roger was taken immediately north to the jail, the man who had tried to rob him picked himself up and ran south out of town.

Meanwhile, Amanda's stage paralleled the new railroad's route around the east side of Mono Lake so everyone could see the train. The horses were changed at Mono Mills and the coach then headed south to Old Benton, through Yellow Jacket Spring far east of the Owens River Gorge, and then into Bishop Creek.

Some of the journey after that passed through lush green valleys, ancient lava fields south of Big Pine, and then more green sweeping out from the river. The road swung between large scrub, around boulders and low hills, and through more lava fields that had solidified after flowing from the volcanic cones still in the distance along the Inyo Mountains.

The coach splashed through dozens of creeks and stopped at stage stations along the way where fresh horses were changed for those exhausted at the pace they were keeping and the harshness of the terrain. After passing the remnants of old Fort Independence, Amanda changed to another stage line in the town of Independence, the county seat of Inyo County since 1866. They stayed but a short time and she was soon enjoying the miles of ranches surrounded by large fields of wheat, barley and alfalfa, and the hundreds of cattle grazing in the scrub.

They crossed more creeks cascading down from the Sierra and flowing east to the Owens River, each one edged in lines of trees dressed in their fall colors like trailing bright yellow and orange ribbons tossed down from the crest by the mountain gods to accessorize the desert. But the desert had already thought to dress itself in acres of the yellow blooms of rabbitbrush.

Amanda couldn't take her eyes from the window of the stage. How amazingly different it was in this beautiful Owens River Valley. The jagged gray peaks of the Sierra Nevada looked so close she felt she should be able to take only a short walk to reach them. But here distances were deceptive and it would have been a difficult eight mile hike. The leaves of the trees around the homesteads and along the creeks had fallen and blown into the waters or piled along miles of wire fencing held up by posts of tree branches. Fall was short-lived here, and the air already had a sharp nip to it even in the middle of the day.

The stage driver changed horses at Taboose Station and then again at an old station called Halfway House. After that more ranches filled the desert, each surrounded by cottonwoods and black locusts with their leaves now almost gone and showing the dramatic twisting structure of their limbs. After cresting a rise in the road along low dark hills to their right, Amanda looked to her left to see the Inyo Mountains.

In doing so, her gaze was held by the wide sweep of a long deep meadow that followed their progress and she marveled that it was still green with long grass. It covered the valley floor from the Inyos west to the ranches, and was being grazed by more cattle than she could have counted in a day.

And then Amanda had her first look at the Alabama Hills. They appeared at first like long chocolate brown mounds unlike anything she had ever seen. Later she would discover beyond them acres of huge piles of smooth boulders eroded by nature among hundreds of acres of desert plants and cactus. And in the spring, she would discover the addition of colorful wild flowers that blanketed the dirt between these boulders.

Finally the coach approached Lone Pine, and she found her heart racing. But the unexpected bleakness of the small wooden town brought her up short, although at least there were trees down Main and on all the roads leading from it. Along the edges of the green fields she had seen the white dots of bee hives and now many of the white fences surrounding homes held up the trailing vines of grapes. Amanda would find Lone Pine's production of a very different kind than Bodie's.

No stocks were frantically traded with San Francisco or New York, no clanking stamp mills muted the sound of birds or the breeze ruffling through leaves, sleep at night was not disturbed by the sound of gun fire, and the quiet mornings would rarely bring a report of violence in the night.

Men in Lone Pine gathered in saloons, of course, but more frequently at Mr. Meysan's General Merchandise Store around the stove or at The Square north of town at the blacksmith and stage depot. The women preferred to sit on the front porches of one another's homes, all of which seemed to offer sweeping views of either the Sierra or the Inyos.

Amanda's stage entered town between the Lone Pine Hotel to the left and the Edwards Store on the right. It pulled to the right and stopped in The Square in front of the livery and across from a tall flag pole proudly displaying the American flag. After alighting and being handed her bags, Amanda walked slowly into the town itself. She looked up at the large trees shading the street and buildings, and sighed.

Compared to what she had been used to for the previous year, this could only be called a sleepy little village. The wide main street, however, was full of freight wagons, along with small rigs and spring wagons loaded with supplies, and of course riders on horseback. But the wooden sidewalks were not crowded and when she passed a saloon's door, no loud shouting or raucous music blared forth.

She crossed the street and entered the small hotel, both pleased and somewhat surprised to find that they had a room she could rent for half what she had paid in Bodie. Unable to wait any longer, she left her cases on the bed and went down to the lobby where she asked the woman at the counter, "Do you know where I might find either Emily Eastman or Charlotte Perry?"

"I know both of them. But it'll be easiest to find Emily's house as it's on the south end of town on this side of the street. You can't miss it, my dear," the woman smiled. "It's a big two story yellow house. There isn't anything else like it in town."

The wooden planks of the sidewalk sounded hollow beneath her feet and occasionally a plank rolled a little under foot, but she followed Main for half a mile through town. It gave her the opportunity to view Meysan's Merchandise Store, Spear's Wagon Shop, Zaun's Ice House, Dabeeny's

Saloon, and a few other shops along the way. Passing St. Mary's Restaurant, she stopped as a woman large with child emerged and turned awkwardly to shut the door.

When the woman saw Amanda, she yelped and put a hand to her chest. Amanda laughed and breathed out in relief, "Charlotte!"

They hugged with enthusiasm. Although Amanda noted that Charlotte was now obviously ready to give birth, she would never have dreamed of mentioning it in a public place. Instead, she told her, "I've decided I can't bear the violence and filth in Bodie any longer. I've come to make my home here. I just arrived on the last stage into town."

Charlotte scanned the area past her friend before looking back at her. "Um, you're alone then?"

"If you mean, is Roger with me, the answer is no. He feels he can only make the kind of living he wants there. So we decided to part as friends and go on with our lives separately."

"I'm so sorry." Her disappointment was obvious. "I really thought you two would end up together."

Amanda looked down, fighting a sudden impulse to weep in the presence of such tender commiseration. But she swallowed the urge, stood up straighter and stated simply, "I thought so too, but we don't always get what we want."

Changing the subject so as not to embarrass her friend further, Charlotte asked, "Where are your things?"

"I checked into the hotel."

Charlotte smiled, and taking her arm she moved Amanda in the direction she had been walking. "Come with me. Emily will be thrilled to see you."

And indeed she was. Charlotte didn't even stop to knock on the door of the large Queen Anne home. She just walked up the steps to the porch, opened the front door and pulled Amanda in after her while shouting, "Emily?"

Immediately her friend emerged from the kitchen, wiping her hands on a towel. "Amanda! What a wonderful surprise." After embracing, they all went into the kitchen and sat at a big wooden table with drawers inset beneath the edge.

This piece of furniture, and most other pieces in the house, had been made by Ben Kennedy, who had built the house in the early 1870's. After his death, his wife Anne had turned the large home into a boarding house, and when Emily had arrived in town from the east in 1878, she had become one of her boarders. Mrs. Kennedy had died the previous Christmas, only a couple of weeks after Whitney's birth. At the reading of the will, Emily had discovered that the house had been left to her as sole trader.

Over tea accompanied by bread and butter pieces sprinkled with cinnamon sugar, the women caught each other up on the happenings in their lives. Emily and Charlotte were especially eager to hear what had been happening in Bodie. When they were told that Amanda left amid the excitement of the train's arrival, they found this a sentimental moment that brought forth a piquant silence.

It lasted only a moment, however, and Amanda was brought in to the large master bedroom across the hall just beyond the stairs. There, in a wooden crib in a corner of the room sat a smiling girl child playing with a small rag doll, a wooden horse and a pile of blocks with painted letters on them. When Emily and Amanda walked into the room, she dropped the doll and held out her arms to her mother, who picked her up.

"Amanda, this is Whitney. Whitney, this is mummy's friend from Bodie."

Amanda looked at the happy smiling child with her large green eyes and bright auburn hair like her mother's, and felt an overwhelming mix of emotions wash through her. There was of course admiration of the prettiness of the child, and joy for the fact of her friend's good fortune. But there was also some sadness that she might never know the contentment that Emily so obviously radiated as she hugged her daughter. Sensing this, an astute Emily put Whitney back in her playpen and they left the room, little Whitney not seeming to mind as she returned happily to her toys.

Charlotte soon returned to her home a couple of streets away on the other side of Main. Complaining that the baby was overdue, she declared that she hoped the day's walk would encourage it to come forth.

Shortly after that, Frank Eastman came home from working with his cattle. His dark hair, strong chin and broad shoulders reminded her so much of Roger that she found it difficult to look at him. But this quickly disappeared when she noted the dirty denim pants, scuffed boots and worn red plaid shirt typical of someone who spent most of his waking hours with cattle.

His smile was friendly and welcoming as he told Amanda, "So I finally get to meet the beautiful Amanda that Emily has mentioned so often. I was always at work when you were visiting our home in Bodie."

Amanda smiled back at him. "I hope my arrival doesn't disrupt your life too much."

"Good heavens, no." He wandered to the sideboard where a crystal decanter and glasses awaited him next to a pitcher of water. He poured himself a small whiskey and water. "You're staying here with us, aren't you?"

"No. I've checked into the hotel."

"That's no place for a young woman alone. I'll go get your things and bring them here."

There was no room for argument in his statement. He gulped his drink and left the house.

So while Frank hitched up a horse to their light rig and headed into town to retrieve the luggage, Amanda and Emily fixed supper. Frank soon returned with her things and put them in one of the upstairs rooms, after which he got a fire going in the fireplace. After a substantial meal in the dining room behind the kitchen, the women washed the dishes while chatting. After coffee in front of the fire, Amanda felt as though she had not one ounce of energy left and retired eagerly to her room.

The next morning Amanda rose early and sat on the front porch swing watching dawn pass into daylight. As the sun rose to the east, it cast a golden stripe across the crest of the Sierra that slowly melted down its steep craggy sides. It brought enough light that Amanda could now see the blue shadows in the deep canyons and old patches of snow that dotted the rocks along the crest. And in the midst of it all, the proud peak of Mt. Whitney hovered over the north shoulder of Lone Pine Peak.

Amanda thought to herself, "So that's Emily's mountain." A lump came to her throat as she was overcome by the feeling of being incredibly privileged to be witness to such beauty and sweeping magnificence.

Back in Bodie, one of the newspapers that morning, in their gossipy "Brief Mention" column, wrote: *A flower has been plucked from our midst. This bright flower of womanhood, much admired by many and falsely maligned by a few, has been transplanted to lucky Lone Pine. Miss Blake, your Bodie friends wish you the best of luck.*

The next couple of weeks were a whirlwind of activity for Amanda. She met dozens of friendly and welcoming people, attended a local play performed at the school, helped Emily with chores around the house, ran errands for Charlotte and canned the last of the vegetables from her garden. She rode often, sometimes with Emily and sometimes alone. She enjoyed the huge lake south of town, the ponds near it, and the strange boulders in the Alabama Hills, and almost every afternoon she rested on the front porch where she wrote letters to her friends in Placerville. Each evening Frank lit the fire in the parlor fireplace and they visited with anyone who might stop by.

Then one morning Emily came back from her daily visit to a housebound Charlotte, and she was smiling as she rushed up the walk to the boarding house porch. The minute she reached the first step, she spotted Amanda in the swing. "Charlotte had her baby this morning. Mrs. Meysan was there assisting her when I arrived, and I was in time to help. Vince is with her now and I don't think he'll ever stop smiling."

"How's Charlotte?"

"Oh, fine. Tired and sore, of course, but she's radiantly happy."

"Was it a son or daughter?"

"A son. They're calling him Steven after Vince's grandfather. I need a cup of coffee."

Amanda rushed to get it for her and they then spent the rest of the day preparing for a Thanksgiving dinner party Emily and Frank were planning for their friends.

Over the next few days, whenever Amanda talked of finding work, Emily would tell her that in a few days she would introduce her to some people. But those days went by and Amanda's request was put forth yet again, followed by Emily's promise to help.

A week later, with Thanksgiving approaching, Amanda bundled up in her old long coat and set out on a walk through the town while thinking about how she should go about finding a job and a place of her own. She ended up at The Square just as a stage came to a rattling stop in front of Robinson's Stable, the horses' breath fogging the cold air. As she watched the passengers alight, her mouth dropped open.

"Roger!"

He stood next to the coach with a smile cutting his face in two and tentatively holding out his arms. Without hesitation Amanda ran forward, throwing her arms around his neck. After a moment of being crushed by the pressure of his arms, she pushed back from him. "Welcome to Lone Pine, mister."

A man arriving in town for the first time asked the driver, "Do I get a greeting like that too?"

The driver smiled and said, "Nope. It's a friendly town, but not that friendly."

Amanda ignored them. "What are you doing here?"

Roger took her by the arm and walked her to the side of the big red barn where there was a large cottonwood tree and they could stand in the shade of its few remaining yellow leaves.

He took her hands in his and looked into her eyes. "I don't know what I'll do here, but anything is better than being away from you."

She had never felt such a surge of euphoric happiness before, but she was determined to be practical. "Do you like cattle, because there are a lot of them around here. They also raise bees and grapes and all kinds of crops."

"I guess I can learn to be a rancher." He looked down at her and put his hands on her shoulders, drawing her close. "The one thing I know I can't do is live without you." A light danced in his eyes as he added, "I've decided that I want to live in the shade of trees."

"Then you've come to the right place."

Another long embrace followed before Roger retrieved his suitcases and they began walking south through town.

When they walked together into the Eastman home, Vince and Charlotte with the baby were sitting at the kitchen table drinking coffee with Frank. Both men were happy to see Roger again and shook his hand eagerly.

Emily came out of the bedroom beyond the stairs where she had been feeding baby Whitney, and watched the men greeting one another. She showed no surprise and after exchanging a satisfied look with Charlotte, commented, "It's about time."

Amanda then realized that this was what Emily had been waiting to happen, and wondered at her friend's wisdom. But she was also puzzled. "Frank, how do you know Roger?"

He smiled, glanced at Emily, and with a slight pinking of his cheeks answered with a slight defensive edge to his voice. "I went into Wagner's occasionally."

After chuckling to show she didn't care, and wasn't unaware of the fact already, Emily told Frank, "I thought your game was poker."

At that Roger barked out a laugh before Frank could respond. "Oh, it is," Roger told everyone. "I got into a friendly private game with him once, and he cleaned me out."

Watching the men interact, Amanda glowed with happiness. Maybe Roger would be happy to settle in Lone Pine after all. Especially was this true when Frank reassured him that he could get together an occasional game of faro with the locals in one of the three saloons when the freighters arrived with supplies from the railroad town of Hawthorne. Lone Pine was their last stop, so they had plenty of money, as well as finally the time to relax. After that, Vince explained, they would head back loaded with the valley's grain crops as well as honey and fruit to be dropped off at various towns along the way.

But as the men continued talking, Amanda watched Roger trying very hard to muster enthusiasm, and began to wonder how realistic any of it was. Of one thing she was sure, Roger was going to put forth every effort to fit into the town. And she knew it was just to make her happy. Somewhat reluctantly, but unavoidable to her ingrained honesty, she admitted to herself that this was not only unfair to him but also to any future happiness they might share.

That night as they sat on the front porch swing on the front porch of the Eastman home, he told her, "I almost wasn't able to leave Bodie."

"Bad weather?"

"Bad time in jail."

"You were in jail? Why?"

"Some guy tried to rob me in an alley. After I knocked him down, the law arrived. Some new guy I didn't know, and the guy locked me up. After I explained and they couldn't find the thief, who it turned out had left town, they let me go for lack of evidence."

She stared at him, the possible adverse consequences that could have happened bouncing around in her mind like a nightmare riding in the back of a run-away wagon. Instead of trying to put her feelings into words, she put her arms around his neck and held him close.

With her head on his shoulder and his arm around her, he told her, "It made me realize that I didn't belong in the new Bodie."

"Which is declining beyond what works for you anyway," she smiled.

"Well, yes. But I could have gone to Sacramento or San Francisco."

She sat up and took his hand. "Because of the human traffic and so many saloons, is that right?"

"Well, yes, of course, but..."

She put a finger on his lips to stop him from speaking, then sat back and looked out across the valley at the peak of Mt. Whitney. This highest peak, and the jagged crest trailing out on either side of it, was silhouetted against the darkening blue sky behind it. She swallowed a sudden sense of regret that stabbed at her heart and turned away from him for a moment. Then she spoke. "I think we should move to Sacramento after we're married."

"What's brought this on?" The puckered brow turned into an angry frown. "Do you think I can't find something to do here? Do you think I'm only capable of being a gambler?"

"No, no. It's not that. I'm sure you can find something to do. But you should have more than just something to do. You should be doing what you enjoy, and that's dealing faro."

"Oh." He thought a moment and then shrugged. "Well, if I was to continue doing that, we wouldn't have to move out of the Owens Valley. When the stage stopped in Bishop I ran into a man I used to know who now runs a large saloon there. He asked me to work for him, saying he'd advertise me as fresh from Bodie." Roger laughed and shook his head. "He thinks that's some kind of draw for his place. But I said no because I thought you wanted to be in Lone Pine."

Amanda turned to him. "Well, that's my first choice, of course. But Bishop isn't so far that I couldn't take the stage occasionally to see Emily and Charlotte. And if the train comes through near here like they say it will in a couple of years, it will be even easier then."

"You'd be willing to live in Bishop just for me?"

She looked at him and wondered if she should say yes, but decided she would be honest with him whenever it was possible. "Oh, my love, it would be for us. Life is compromise, and especially married life. If something as simple as this can give us both what we want, then why wouldn't we do it?"

Roger gathered her into his arms, kissing her soundly and in no hurry to let her go. After a few minutes, he murmured into her hair, "I think there's something else in the shade of trees you didn't mention."

"What's that?"

"People getting married." She looked up at him and followed his gaze to the street where Frank had planted a row of sycamores along the edge of the road. "I think we should get Vince and Charlotte, Emily and Frank, a minister, and then come together by the new sycamores right here in front of Frank and Emily's home. That is, if you think you can stand being married to me."

Amanda smiled. "Not wanting to wear out our tree analogy, as long as they're around us, and I can see some part of the Sierra, I can put up with anything." She grinned mischievously and rumpled his long hair, this time not bothering to move it from his forehead as she added, "Even you."

Roger laughed as a sudden thought occurred to him. "Wait until they hear in Bodie that the high-toned gambler married the unrepentant prude."

And so a week later they were married beneath the sycamores in front of Frank and Emily's home amid a small gathering of friends. Charlotte, holding her two week old son in her arms, smiled with delight as she watched Amanda and Roger exchange their vows.

And late that night, much to his delight, Roger found out that Amanda was far from being a prude.

A Brief Time Line of Events After 1881

1882
Although the Bodie 601 continues to have an influence for several years after 1881, they carry out no more violent acts. They don't have to, since a note signed by them and sent to someone to desist whatever they are doing garners an immediate response.

The Law and Order League, after several of its members are shot after a meeting, cease their efforts to try and curtail the actions of the 601. After this, all sentences are carried out only after a lawful trial.

Winter 1882
Fifteen foot drifts are common on the rails coming from Mono Mills, closing down the timber to the town when it is needed most. High, icy winds blow almost continuously for months. Stock in the mines plummets.

January, 1882
The Sunday closing law for the saloons goes into effect. The citizens are not happy and much of the time the law is ignored.

February, 1882
Empty buildings are being stripped by petty thieves, right down to locks and hinges.

March, 1882
With hundreds of miners out of work, in Bodie and the Comstock, Bodie petitions Congress to "insure the practical prohibition of Chinese immigration."

A blizzard drops fifteen feet of snow over the town and the mines, and along the Eastern Sierra. Avalanches kill people in Genoa, Nevada, as well as at Mill Creek and Lundy.

Spring, 1882
A rich strike at the Noonday and North Noonday mines energizes the camp.

November, 1882
The Molinari Building on Main and Mill at the triangle, which originally cost $3,000 to build, sells for $625.

December, 1882
The Noonday, North Noonday and Red Cloud mine complex is attached in San Francisco by Wells Fargo & Co. Bank, as it is in arrears $460,000. There are 175 men put out of work and all operations close down. The sudden collapse of these mines is a great blow to the reputation of the District, from which it does not recover.

1883
Many north end buildings are torn down and the lumber hauled in wagons to Hawthorne, Nevada.

January, 1883
The Grand Central Hotel closes, and in the spring it is torn down.

February, 1883
Bodie Evening Miner: The lower end of Bodie presents a lonesome aspect at present. Many of the buildings are going to ruin; the sidewalks are cranky; unlatched doors swing on rusty hinges; demolished stovepipes sway to and fro and here and there the legends "for rent" and "for sale" stand out with great prominence. Nothing is quite so depressing as a row of deserted houses.

1883
The Methodist Church is built at the western end of Green. A Catholic church, St. John the Baptist, is built at the south end of Wood Street.

Summer, 1883
Elizabeth and Almond Huntoon move the Booker Flat Hotel to Huntoon's Station, ten miles north of Bridgeport.

Winter, 1883
From as many as 50 mines in 1879/80, all but six of the larger mines have closed.

Early 1884
The Standard Consolidated stops its dividend payments, although it continues to function. People leave the town in great numbers.

April 10, 1884
With too much snow on the ground to get through, Charlie Hector abandons his Lundy stage sleigh in the canyon, and leads his horses on foot into Bodie. The mailbags are on the back of the lead horse and a rope attached to its tail to help pull Charlie through the deep snow.

May, 1885
Only 500 people remain in Bodie.

1886
Fire! Irreparable damage is done to the north end businesses.

1887
The Standard and Bodie mines merge.

April, 1888
The Bodie House on the corner of Main and Green burns down.

1888/89
There are almost three times as many vacant buildings in town as there are inhabitants.

September, 1890
Almond Huntoon, 56 years old and painfully ill for many years, commits suicide. Elizabeth marries Jessie McGath of Bodie. McGath, a land owner in the Big Meadows and Walker Lake areas in the 1860's, had built a house in Bodie several years before. It would eventually be the home of the Cain family.

1892
The Standard Consolidated sues the adjoining Bodie Consolidated for $283,000 for trespass onto their ground and removal of their ore, which practice they claim has been going on since 1884.

July 25, 1892
Fire starts in the U. S. Bakery and takes out almost all businesses on the west side of Main, north of the Mono County Bank. Gone are 64 buildings. Spared is the residential district and buildings on South Main. As things pick up over the next few years, most of the downtown section is rebuilt.

1895
Virginia City foundryman McCone finds out about the new cyanide process first used in Australia and New Zealand, and tells Jim Cain. McCone brings in an expert to secretly build a new plant while Cain buys up all the piles of "worthless" tailings dumped for years by the mines. With simple charcoal as the precipitant to extract the gold from the cyanide solution, the two men soon are making a good profit.

1890's
A 13 mile electrical power transmission line is run from Green Creek to the Standard Mill, the longest in the world at the time. Electric motors replace steam-driven pulleys.

1899
The wooden Standard Mill burns down. One of corrugated iron is constructed in its place, with 20 stamps. It is still in the town over a hundred years later.

1900
Attorney Pat Reddy dies in San Francisco.

Early 1900
Ed and Warren Loose drive the 1,400 foot long Whitney Tunnel and are able to keep the 20-stamp red brick Syndicate Mill running for several more years.

December, 1900
The hoisting works of the Goodshaw Mining Co. is destroyed by fire. Four men are suffocated in the mine.

1903
Theodore Hoover, the President's brother, arrives in Bodie and becomes a supervisor at the Standard Consolidated Mining Company.

June 12, 1905
The first motor car is driven into Bodie.

1906
Mining men from Tonopah purchase the Bodie Railroad & Lumber Company and rename it the Mono Lake Railway & Lumber Co., with the plan to extend the line into Nevada. It never happens.

1909
Mining accidents are still a way of life, and this is brought home when nine men die when they drop 500 feet into the Tioga shaft.

1910
The new Hydro Electro Plant at Jordan, 20 miles from Bodie, generates electricity, and lights come on in Bodie businesses and homes for the first time.

1911
An avalanche at Jordan strikes and eight lives are lost. The Pacific Power Plant is ruined, but the equipment is saved. Avalanches also hit hard at Lundy and Masonic.

1912
Wells Fargo & Co. closes its Bodie office.

1915
Jim Cain acquires control of the Standard Mill and Mine after winning a settlement of a trespass claim against the company for moving into his Midnight claim, formerly known as the McClinton Mine. The McClinton had been profitable during the boom and into 1888.

March 31, 1915
The Standard Consolidated Mining Company is formally dissolved. Assets distributed at this time are only 13 ½ cents a share. It has only ever

levied three assessments. Over 38 years, it yielded $18,202,855 in bullion, and its dividends amounted to $5,264,407.

World War I/1915
The Syndicate Mill, the camp's first mill and built during the Civil War, makes its last run.

1917
The Bodie Railroad is abandoned.

1918
The Bodie Railroad rails are sold for scrap iron.

Mid-1920's
A San Francisco entrepreneur tries to get profit out of Bodie's dumps, but after processing 30,000 tons of the Standard dump ore, the operation ends in failure.

June 23, 1932
Fire! The downtown section is lost, and the town is reduced to what it is today.

1938
Jim J. S. Cain dies in San Francisco.

1935
The Roseklip Mines Company is formed, a mill built, and work started to convert low-grade dump ores.

1942
Because of World War II, the government shuts down all gold mining. Only a few people remain in the town.
The Roseklip Mines Company shuts down.

November, 1942
The last Post Office closes in Bodie.

Late 1940's
After the war, new Roseklip management starts up the mill. The plant catches fire and burns to the ground.

1962
Bodie becomes a California State Park.

September 12, 1964
Bodie is dedicated as a California Historic Site. It is also a National Historic Site.

1968
The American Smelting and Refining Company investigates the potential of the mines, but they soon lose interest. Other large operators also continue to show interest from time to time.

1988
Open pit mining is proposed by Galactic Mining, using the cyanide heap-leach process. Much debate ensues over the effect this will have on the area, and how it will impact a State Historic Park.

1994
Congress passes the Bodie Protection Act as part of the Desert Bill.

1997
The American Land Conservancy helps the California State Parks to purchase 520 acres of land next to Bodie State Historic Park for inclusion in the park, including the mineral rights. It is supported by the Mono County Board of Supervisors, the State's governor, California's senators, and the President of the United Sates.

December, 1998
The U. S. Bureau of Land Management acquires the property and mineral rights earlier acquired by the American Land Conservancy. This makes all of Bodie publicly owned. However, open pit mine owners continue to investigate the area for reclaiming operations.

FOR YOUR INFORMATION

If you would like to learn more about Charlotte Perry and Emily Eastman in Bodie and the Owens Valley, and their adventures referred to in this book, you can read Kathleen Haun's other novels: *Dear Carrie, Letters from the Eastern Sierra 1878-1899*; and its sequel *Passing Storms*. The third in this trilogy is *Moving On*, a prequel to *Dear Carrie*. You can order these books from amazon.com or barnesandnoble.com. You can also visit Kathleen's web site at www.kathleenhaun.com.

The Standard Company's cannon can be viewed in Bridgeport on the lawn of the same Bridgeport Courthouse mentioned in this book.

The Bowers Mansion is now the *Bowers Mansion County Park* in Washoe County, Nevada, and is open to the public between Memorial Day and Labor Day. Call (775) 849-0644 for information.

A visit to Virginia City, Nevada through Gold Canyon is an exciting and worthwhile trip for anyone interested in experiencing "the way it was" in the glory days of The Comstock.

The beautiful little town of Lundy is now a small fishing village on the northern edge of the Inyo National Forest and bordering the Humboldt Toiyabe National Forest. There is a general store and cabins available during the summer. It's a great area for fishing and hiking. Contact Lundy Lake Resort at (626) 309-0415 or Mono County Tourism at (800) 845-7922.

Placerville has respected its pioneer heritage over the years, and is a wonderful destination. Give yourself several days to immerse yourself in its intriguing atmosphere.

Lone Pine in the Owens Valley maintains its welcoming nature. The sycamores where the boarding house would have been are huge now, and standing beneath them one can look west to see the magnificence of Mt. Whitney. Across the street one will find The Lone Pine Film History Museum where artifacts of the area's western movie history are on display.

Lightning Source UK Ltd.
Milton Keynes UK
UKHW011821301219
356124UK00001B/31/P